Praise for

## The Library of the Unwritten

"This book is so much fun, and you should be reading it. Trust me. Stories about story are some of my favorite kinds. This book definitely makes the list. I am so glad I read this."

—Seanan McGuire, author of *The Unkindest Tide*

"A muse, an undead librarian, a demon, and a ghost walk into Valhalla.... What follows is a delightful and poignant fantasy adventure that delivers a metric ton of found-family feels and reminds us that the hardest stories to face can be the ones we tell about ourselves."

—*New York Times* bestselling author Kit Rocha

"*The Library of the Unwritten* is a tiered dark chocolate cake of a book. The read is rich and robust, the prose has layers upon layers, and the characters melt like ganache upon the tongue. A saturated, decadent treat. An unforgettable, crave-worthy experience. A baroquely imagined and totally unexpected original take on such well-worn topics as Hell, libraries, and the difference between what never was and what never will be."     —Philip K. Dick Award–winning author Meg Elison

"*The Library of the Unwritten* is a story about stories: ones we tell ourselves, the ones we tell others, and the ones buried so deep we hope no one ever finds them. Hackwith has artfully penned a love letter to books and readers alike and filled it with lush, gorgeous prose; delightfully real characters; a nonstop, twisty, and heart-wrenching plot; and an explosive ending that gave me chills."

—K. A. Doore, author of *The Perfect Assassin*

"A delightful romp through Heaven, Hell, and everything in between, which reveals itself in layers: an exploration of the nuances of belief, a demonstration of the power of the bonds that connect us, and a love letter to everybody who has ever heard the call of their own story."

—Caitlin Starling, author of *The Luminous Dead*

"*The Library of the Unwritten* is like *Good Omens* meets Jim Hines's Ex Libris series, a must-read for any book lover. Hackwith has penned a tale filled with unforgettable characters fighting with the power of creativity against a stunning array of foes from across the multiverse. *The Library of the Unwritten* rocks!"

—Michael R. Underwood, author of the Stabby Award finalist Genrenauts series

"The only book I've ever read that made the writing process look like fun. A delight for readers and writers alike!"

—Hugo Award winner Elsa Sjunneson-Henry

"A wry, high-flying, heartfelt fantasy, told with sublime prose and sheer joy even at its darkest moments (and there are many). I want this entire series on my shelf yesterday."

—Tyler Hayes, author of *The Imaginary Corpse*

"Elaborate world building, poignant and smart characters, and a layered plot make this first in a fantasy series from Hackwith . . . an ode to books, writing, and found families."    —*Library Journal* (starred review)

"Hackwith builds her world and characters with loving detail, creating a delightful addition to the corpus of library-based and heaven-vs.-hell fantasies. This novel and its promised sequels will find a wide audience."

—*Publishers Weekly* (starred review)

# BOOKS BY A. J. HACKWITH

*Novels from Hell's Library*

The Library of the Unwritten

The Archive of the Forgotten

# THE
# ARCHIVE
# OF THE
# FORGOTTEN

A. J. Hackwith

ACE

NEW YORK

ACE
Published by Berkley
An imprint of Penguin Random House LLC
penguinrandomhouse.com

ACE is a registered trademark and the A colophon is a trademark of
Penguin Random House LLC.

Library of Congress Cataloging-in-Publication Data

Names: Hackwith, A. J., author.
Title: The archive of the forgotten / A. J. Hackwith.
Description: First edition. | New York : Ace, 2020. | Series: A novel from hell's library ; 2
Identifiers: LCCN 2020002015 (print) | LCCN 2020002016 (ebook) |
ISBN 9781984806390 (trade paperback) | ISBN 9781984806406 (ebook)
Subjects: GSAFD: Fantasy fiction. | Adventure fiction.
Classification: LCC PS3608.A254 A89 2020 (print) | LCC PS3608.A254 (ebook) |
DDC 813/.6--dc23
LC record available at https://lccn.loc.gov/2020002015
LC ebook record available at https://lccn.loc.gov/2020002016

First Edition: October 2020

Printed in the United States of America
3 5 7 9 10 8 6 4 2

Cover images by Shutterstock
Cover design by Faceout Studio/Jeff Miller
Book design by Alison Cnockaert

To the families we make

# THE
# ARCHIVE
## OF THE
# FORGOTTEN

# 1

# CLAIRE

This is my last entry in the Librarian's Log. I don't know why Brevity insists; I never wrote in here as often as I should have. I did, at first, and I have reviewed the entries from my apprenticeship to confirm how rotten they were. I was. I can't believe this damned book even kept them. There's no rhyme or reason to it. I'll be glad to be rid of this log: the nattering of the dead.

That's not true. I suppose I should aim for the truth, now that there is so very little worth hiding. Let us try again.

I am Claire Juniper Hadley, librarian of the Unwritten Wing. Like any proper storyteller, I have lied. I have plotted and hurt and lied, so many lies I can't even recall. And with those plots, lies, and little hurts, I tried to do right by the Library. However, the performance of my duties has been found wanting, so I hereby resign my post to my highly qualified replacement, Brevity. Who will, no doubt, blot out my troubled service with her brilliant care.

Treat her well, old book. Or I'll come back and burn you too.

*Librarian Claire Juniper Hadley, 2019 CE*

THE ARCANE WING WAS a cabinet of curiosities. Libraries have a tradition of maintaining a curio, a house of mathoms, oddities, trinkets, artifacts of inquiry. As curators of obscure and sometimes undervalued things, librarians attract the unusual and misplaced. Hell's Library was no different.

If one was to be accurate, Hell's Library was *slightly* different. What Hell would find curious, others might classify as weapons of gibbering terror.

Claire, for one, found it a refreshing break from books and authors. The objects of the Arcane Wing each had their own story, in a straightforward way. This dented crown was part of a dictator's deal with a demon, with its spot where his blood rusted through the false gold, stained when his people came for him. These ruby seeds, held under the tongue of a desperate child as she braved the underworld to find her lost brother. One is missing, accidentally swallowed, and turned the child to malachite. A sliver of her pinkie finger is cross-indexed three shelves down.

Each item held a story, but the story was done. The End. The Unwritten Wing hummed with unstarted beginnings, while the Arcane Wing was sepulchral with artifacts of untold ends. It was quiet; terrible and quiet. And it left Claire feeling like one more artifact. Like her story was done and told. Here, the disgraced former librarian of Hell's Unwritten Wing. See her shadowed eyes. And here are the cracks in her soul, flaws in her craftwork where all the purpose has sifted out. See how she moves in endless circles to avoid collecting dust.

Claire could have settled, and accepted her ignoble denouement, if she were not constantly being reminded of her ending.

The newest reminder sat cross-legged in a puddle of lamplight between tables. She was in the back of the Arcane Wing, which had been Andras's prison for Valhalla's ravens. When Andras had been Arcanist, the back wall had been a row of cages. Because libraries reflected their owners, that had all been smudged out of existence when Claire took over. Now, instead, smart hickory drawers lined the wall, each identified with a shiny brass nameplate.

Most bore some variation of tea leaf. Even a dead woman was allowed her vices.

Beneath the tisane collection, a damsel girl sat cross-legged, a mop of dark curls curtaining her face. She was a spry and striking shadow, dark as teak and fragile as blown glass right to the tips of her pointed ears. The romper she wore might have once been a pale gothic dress but had been efficiently stripped and tied above her knobby knees. She was a ghostly creature of bony edges, as if peeled out of a nightmare softened into dream.

"Rosia." It was helpful that the latter half of the damsel's name was mostly composed of a sigh. Claire rubbed her forehead. "This isn't the Unwritten Wing. You shouldn't be here."

"I got lonely." Rosia didn't look up; all of her concentration was focused on prying the edge of her thumbnail along the dark varnish of the floorboards. Thin curlicues of flaking varnish next to her toe were the only sign of progress so far.

"How can you be lonely? You have an entire suite of other damsels. And Brevity. Talk to your friends," Claire said with as much patience as she could muster. She tried to keep her voice soft, a feat it wasn't used to performing. Once, she would have known how to handle a wandering character. A warning, a scalpel flick, and stories would fold back into the books that confined them. Back when they were simply that—books to be shelved—and she was simply the librarian.

Nothing was that simple anymore. Claire had been shocked out of her decades of denial when a runaway book had forced her to divert a demonic coup and face the cruelty she'd inflicted in the past. Books, and the characters that awakened from them, might not be human but were worth a little humanity.

Rosia's twin moon eyes blinked a momentary eclipse before she turned back to toying with the flooring. "I am."

Nothing could *ever* be that simple anymore. "I beg your pardon?"

"I *am* with friends. They're so hard to hear, though," Rosia went on without acknowledging the question. "We play hide-and-seeks. They always win."

Claire glanced behind her, but she was patently alone. Damsels were not typically solitary characters, even ghost girls like Rosia. They were the hearts of stories that had woken up and had been allowed to remain as they were in the Library, instead of being shelved into their books again. It'd been a small mercy that Brevity had persuaded Claire into allowing when she'd been librarian. Now, under Brev's purview, the damsel suite seemed to have grown to an annex. It was a suspicious population growth, even accounting for the number of damsels and books lost during the siege.

Claire couldn't say she approved. There was very good reasoning for keeping unwritten books asleep on the shelves. Woken up, personified, characters risked changing, and change was transformative to their books. They could warp away from the story they were intended to be, or just go a little funny in the head.

Claire suspected Rosia of the latter, but it was hard to be harsh with a girl who was part moonbeam. She crouched down, attempting to be less of a, as Brev put it, "boogeyman for books." "This is the Arcane Wing. Characters don't belong here—"

Rosia's face crumpled, and she rapidly turned from eerie ghost princess to plaintive child. "But you'll still take care of us, right?"

"I—" Claire faltered over the ache that knotted in her chest. Her voice was unsteady when she found it again. "I'm not the librarian of your wing." *Anymore.* It made the pain worse to say that, so she didn't.

Rosia, if possible, fluttered with even greater distress. "But you'll take care of them? You have to."

"Who—" Claire bit off the question as heavy footsteps creaked on the boards behind her. Ramiel came around the corner, clapping the dust off his work-hardened hands.

His rumpled trench coat was a shade grayer than normal, a result of a morning spent moving the heavier of the Arcane Wing's residents around in the archives. He stopped short as he spotted Rosia. The pepper-colored feathers peeking from beneath the collar of his coat bristled into a disgruntled ruff. He had the perpetual look of a toy soldier sent one too many times through the dryer. Rami frowned in a way that sent his stony olive-tan features rumbling to concerned peaks. "Again?"

Claire rose to her feet and ignored the judgmental tone in his voice. "Please help Rosia back to the Unwritten Wing."

"Will you be speaking with Brevity?" Rami asked.

"I don't think so."

Rami was an angel of few words but a whole catalog of looks. The one he sent her now was worth an hour of chiding in itself. His expression softened as he offered a hand to Rosia, crouching down so his broad shadow didn't seem quite so imposing. "Up, on your feet, little soldier."

Rosia took his hand and reached down to pat the floorboards fondly before allowing him to guide her out. Her fingers danced along the shelves as they passed, but it appeared even the Arcane Wing's dangerous artifacts knew better than to harm one of her damsels.

*Brevity's* damsels, Claire amended with sour impatience for her own brain. She followed Rami down the row and tried to amend his judgment. "I am sure Brevity has her own people in hand. It's really not necessary."

"I'm a *people* now? Why does no one tell me when I've been promoted? We could have thrown a party."

The voice was too droll, too full of self-amusement, to mistake. Hero lounged against a table, having shoved a jumble of half-assembled (now utterly unassembled) bone relics out of the way to make room for the tail of his velvet coat. Claire hoped they'd cursed his ass in the process. Out of habit, Claire's attention went to the light scar whorling across his left cheekbone. It was a new blemish that Hero tried to downplay in his vanity, but it was healing nicely into a feature that humanized his otherwise eerie perfection, much to Claire's disgruntlement. Hero's assessing gaze flicked toward her for only a moment before settling on Rami with a light of interest. "Well, look at you. So paternal and domestic."

Rami didn't respond, but Claire could imagine the pained tightening of his stoic face. Hero delighted in having that effect on people. She brushed by Rosia to shoo Hero off the table. "Book."

"Warden." Hero managed to stand and make it look like his idea. He picked imaginary dust from the velour of his jacket. This one was dyed a royal blue that matched the fine seams of his ridiculously tailored fantasy breeches and set the red tones in his bronze hair glowing primly. Hero always looked one breath away from delivering a bon mot or challenging someone to a duel. "Rumor has it you've borrowed a damsel. We're not a lending kind of library, as you would know."

"'Borrow' is not an accurate term." Claire twirled her hand impatiently, but Rosia seemed in no hurry to let go of Rami's hand. "This is the fourth time in two weeks, Hero. Your stunt has obviously set a bad precedent for the damsels."

"I'm certain the women of the Library were fully capable of independent mischief before me, if your example is any to go by," Hero demurred.

"Yes, you just help it along," Rami muttered to the floor.

The smile Hero sent Rami was magnificent, shameless, and wasted, for Rami refused to look at him. "In any case, my many charms are not why I am here." Hero turned no less a devilish look to Claire. "Brevity's asked for you."

"No, she hasn't," Claire said automatically. She'd made a purposeful—painful but purposeful—withdrawal in the weeks following the coup that had led to the Library's shake-up. She'd stopped visiting, stopped answering questions, stopped having a say in the welfare of books. Brevity would never fully accept the mantle of Unwritten Wing librarian if Claire didn't provide the breathing room for her to do so.

Of course, Brevity, the best-natured soul in Hell, had wanted the exact opposite. Claire had been forced to use brusque methods and harsher words before the Unwritten Wing had gradually stopped trying to pull her back in. Brevity got the message eventually.

It hurt, the silence. But then Claire was very skilled at finding the most efficient ways to hurt herself.

"The *Librarian* has requested conference with the *Arcanist*," Hero said in a withering voice that capitalized titles out of spite. He leaned back in order to more properly look down his nose at her. "Is that *formal* enough for you, warden?"

Claire's cheeks heated, but she was well practiced at returning Hero's glare. "You don't have to be an ass about it."

"I was just about to say the same thing! How delightful." Hero easily snaked his arm through the crook of Claire's elbow. "And I couldn't help but overhear you ordering your gloomy feather duster in the same direction—"

"*Feather duster?*" Rami objected, half-confused but certain of insult.

"—so we can all go together! Just like old times. Except he's not trying to kill us," Hero amended. "Yet."

Claire allowed herself to be escorted out of the wing, if only to avoid impending bloodshed.

CLAIRE HAD WALKED THE path between the Unwritten Wing and the Arcane Wing countless numbers of times. She also hadn't walked it once in the last six months. She was almost grateful for the way Hero kept up an irritating patter of snark and asides, ribbing Rami endlessly and giving Claire something to focus on besides the familiar creak of boards beneath her feet.

The doors had changed, too, when Brevity had accepted the librarian mantle. They were cherry-stained now instead of buttery oak. It was a cheerier improvement, Claire thought, so like Brevity. The door was adorned with broad silver handles and a knocker that invited someone to come in, find themselves a book, stay awhile. Not that the Library had many visitors in Hell. Even fewer after the fire.

The Unwritten Wing had been quieter than ever after the coup attempt. Andras, the former demon Arcanist, had attempted the unthinkable—taking control of the Library. He'd failed but burned hundreds of unwritten books on his way down. It was a scandal, even in Hell, and prompted even demons to stay away. Somehow the ghost of Claire's failure had musted the air like mothballs, no matter how much Brevity wiped down the shelves.

"Look alive, you brute. Your favorite is back," Hero said, insults rubbed thin with affection as they passed the giant gargoyle that kept guard outside the wing. It was dozing in a span of false sunbeam in its alcove and barely roused with their passing. Claire caught a flash of flower petals on its brow before the familiar dimensional vertigo set in. Probably one of the damsels had done that, though who knew where they'd have gotten flowers.

"Hello," Claire just remembered to say before the pause became awkward. The gargoyle's arm was gritty and reassuringly solid under her fingertips despite his non-euclidean angles. At least not everything had changed. The gargoyle gave an eldritch hum that made everyone wince, but it was a fond kind of abomination. Not everything had forgotten her.

Hero quickened his step to jump ahead and pull the doors open, keeping up lazy commentary that sounded more artificial than normal.

Claire stepped through the entry and stopped. The doors had merely been a prelude to change. The stacks remained in their same general configuration—branching canyons of tall shelves, spoking out from the lobby space in the middle. There was still the librarian's desk, as large and anchored as ever. The desk was the eternal sun around which the celestial array of the Unwritten Wing turned. But everything felt shifted out of alignment. The woods were stained a cherry color, and the brass workings of Claire's preference were gone. Instead, tiny little faerie lights raced up and down the vertical surfaces of the cavernous wing, lighting everything in a diffuse kind of cheer. Instead of brass rails keeping books from falling off their shelves like jailers, delicate wood carvings hemmed each row, almost like picket fences making a garden of the books rather than a confinement. The Unwritten Wing was still as large and echoing as ever, but Brevity's influence on the Library left it feeling almost soft around the edges.

The emptiness in Claire seemed to have taken up residence in her chest. She had thought the complicated dull ache she felt couldn't be dislodged, but when she focused back on the librarian's desk, her heart did a painful lurch up her throat.

The chair behind the desk was occupied, back to the doors. Perched at the opposite end of the desk was a spritely figure, head bent in conversation. For a moment, it was a specter of the past to Claire. How many countless days had they spent in that arrangement? She worrying away at her busywork, Brevity keeping her company with a steady patter of reports and idle chatter intended to draw Claire into something approaching human conversation.

She blinked hard, twice, and returned to her senses. The figure perched at the end of the desk looked like a muse but was not Brevity. This muse had a pin-straight fall of lavender hair, not a teal explosion. Wore ruffles instead of neon straps and pockets. Hero cleared his throat, and the chair behind the desk turned, disgorging Brevity as she leapt to her feet at the sight of the new arrivals. "Claire! Oh, brilliant, you found them."

This last comment was directed at Hero, who sketched a sardonic bow that Claire would have grumbled at him for. But this was not her Library; Hero was not her assistant. Instead, Claire bit her tongue and drafted a smile onto her face. "Brev."

Brevity approached at her usual speed, and if she paused, hesitating on one foot long enough to flinch uncertainly before squeezing Claire in a hug, neither of them was willing to acknowledge it. It was a one-armed hug, the other stiff at her side. Claire tried not to miss it.

"Thank you for coming," Brevity whispered, and this, at least, seemed heartfelt. Claire smiled around the lump in her throat, and Brevity nudged her back toward the librarian's desk. "There are introductions to make. We have a guest! Probity is visiting the wing as an envoy from the Muses Corps," Brevity said, introducing the lavender-haired woman at the desk.

"And as a *sibling* muse," the other muse corrected with a fond tone. She looked like a porcelain shard. Her hair softened the effect, hanging around her pointed chin in sheets of silk. It contrasted with her too-smooth mint-tinged skin and silver eyes set above precise cheekbones. Muses were the couriers of inspiration and naturally attracted to color. She wore a layer cake of soft knits: white cashmere over blue lace and yellow tatter. The bubblegum pink ribbon in her hair was clasped with a tiny bird skull. The effect was as if a porcelain doll had escaped the tyranny of petticoats and discovered the pastel goth aesthetic as an act of rebellion. She had a detached kind of smile as she nodded to Claire, voice airy with politeness. "You must be the former librarian, then."

Claire had the grace not to flinch. "I am the Arcanist of the Arcane Wing. I expect to be pleased to make your acquaintance." She chose her words precisely, and it was petty, but Claire believed she could be afforded that much, all things considered.

"My mistake, Arcanist." Probity's head tilted as if she were about to add something more, but Brev interrupted with a cleared throat.

"And this is Hero. And Ramiel."

Their guest muse turned. "Master Ramiel, shepherd of souls, it's an honor." Her face reshuffled into a formal kind of respect as she nodded to Rami and spared a little wave for Rosia, who was hiding half in Rami's shadow. Her gaze didn't linger until it got to Hero. Probity's eyes widened. "Oh, this is the book? *The* book?"

"Yes?" Hero hesitated as Probity straightened attentively. "Or no. That depends what I'm accused of."

Probity drew up close, peering into his face for apparent confirmation. She only came up to Hero's chest, so she strained to her tiptoes.

There was a little awe in her voice, and a limpid amount in her wide eyes. "You really are. Hero, the character that broke his own book. The book that's forgotten itself."

"Broken, that's me. Charmed." Hero cleared his throat, red in his cheeks. Evidently Brevity had not warned Probity that behind all the bluster, Hero was wary of strangers. He made to step back, but Probity clapped her hands abruptly around his face.

"Oh," Probity whispered with reverence. "You're amazing."

Hero made a noise of stifled discomfort. Claire was about to intervene when Probity withdrew her hands with a blush. "We heard so much about you, after the burning. The book so damaged to reject its own character. Do you . . ." She stepped into his space again. "Do you have it on you? I'd love to see it."

"A gentleman never tells. Quite forward, aren't you?" Hero didn't jump back, but it was a near thing. He stepped sideways, placing the desk between Probity and himself.

"Probity gets straight to the truth," Brevity explained, and Claire thought there was a graphite streak of protectiveness in her light tone. "You get used to it."

"Will I?" Only once Hero was certain that Probity would not pursue did he straighten his jacket. "I had no idea muses took such interest in lost causes."

"Those are the causes I have the most interest in," Probity said, smiling. "I would very much like to examine your book someday, if you would allow me. Nothing is truly lost. That's just where the brand-new opportunities lie. Brevity taught me that."

"I did? Oh, I did. Probity and I grew up together. Back"—Brevity made a purposefully vague gesture—"when we were younger."

Muses did not age, so much as they came into their innate nature. Young muses, from what Claire understood, often clustered and grew relationships around sympathetic affinities. A muse of Brevity befriending a muse of Probity made a certain kind of sense. Brevity did not like to talk about her past as a muse, and Claire respected that. It didn't keep her from eyeing Probity carefully. At least she'd drawn her attention away from Hero, who looked almost grateful for it. "The muses honor us with a visit."

A small crease appeared between Probity's brows, as if Claire had asked a question that troubled her. "Yes."

"Probity's an amazing muse," Brevity interjected. "Her skill with inspiration gilt is better than anyone's, and the way she can work with even old gilt—"

"You remember that," Probity said with a soft color to her cheeks.

"Why?" Claire asked, too sharp and too quick. Hell, her social skills had gotten rusty. "Why visit now?"

The blush curdled on Probity's cheeks and she frowned. Brevity rushed in. "Of course, I'm thrilled to see you again. But the muses haven't been exactly . . . communicative . . . with the Unwritten Wing in recent years."

"And we regret the breakdown as much as we're sure the Library does." Probity's eyes flicked once to Claire, wary as a cat's, but then were all warmth and kindness for Brevity and the others. "I am here because we thought, with the change of curatorship, we could make amends. Offer support to the Library and the books."

"Support." Hero repeated the word, and for once Claire was grateful for his prickly suspicion. He crossed his arms. "Everyone seems so interested in *supporting* us since the fire."

Rami grunted his agreement, and the sour look on his face said he was thinking of Malphas, the entirely terrifying demon general of Hell who had visited Claire in the aftermath and instigated all the changes in the wake of Andras's downfall. To be precise, the books of the Library had removed Claire as the librarian, but it was Malphas who had delivered the message. Probity's genuine interest was a thin veneer at best, so it was no wonder Rami and Hero looked on any new offers of help the way one would look on a rabid raccoon playing dead.

"Hero," Brevity said softly. "Don't be rude."

Claire opened her mouth with a reply but closed it just as quickly. There was a precise tilt to Brevity's shoulders, and her hands bunched at her sides, as if cradling a small and fragile thing.

Claire forced her jaw to relax, her tension to leak out. Probity seemed fond of Brevity, and if they were childhood friends she could imagine what hopes Brev might harbor about muses and the Library. And here her supposed friends were picking fights like alley cats. It was Claire's doing, and she should be the one to make the effort. She took a deep breath, swallowed her dislike, and held out a hand. "Of course. As the Arcanist, I hope we can build a cooperative relationship with the corps."

Brevity's smile was so grateful it made Claire feel even worse. Probity, for her part, considered Claire's hand with a doubtful hesitation. "That is kind but unnecessary. The muses have no relationship or business with the Arcane Wing."

"Probity!" It was Probity's turn to get scolded by Brevity's big eyes. "I invited Claire and Hero up here to introduce you. We're all members of the Library. Claire taught me everything."

Claire was watching closely, so it was possible that only she noticed the quiet anger that flinched across Probity's face, then was gone. "She did. Even in the corps we heard about the former librarian and her methods."

"Probity," Brevity said, a little bit plaintively, "Claire is a *friend*."

For her part, Claire held still, and all it took was a single finger raised behind her back to get Rami to do the same. She reviewed what she could surmise about a muse named Probity. A muse of probity would be a muse of rightness and moral justice, and, like all muses, would maintain a fluid identity influenced by the human world. Brevity had always been the domain of women, by matter of necessity—less air to breathe, less room to speak. Justice, at the moment, appeared to be a pastel-colored woman with the grit of judgment in her eyes.

When someone decided to hate you, for whatever reason, there was rarely any good in trying to convince them otherwise. Claire couldn't stop the old taste of guilt that rose, however. She hadn't been a good librarian. Not for many of the years of her service. She'd been miserable and cold and downright cruel to Brevity even, at first. Until Brevity had worn down her defenses.

Evidently her temperament had gone uncensored, but not unnoticed, by the muses.

There was no fault in Probity's observations. It was deserved, and defending herself would only make Brevity more miserable, so Claire forced her lips into an accepting grimace. "Yet I believe we can both agree that Brevity makes an excellent librarian."

Probity seemed caught off guard but nodded once. "That goes without saying."

It did *not* go without saying, judging by the way surprise slowly melted into a vibrating kind of happiness as Brevity looked back and forth between them. "I knew you two would hit it off. Brill."

Claire ignored the strain in that pronouncement. She could pretend, quite a lot, for Brevity's sake. She owed her that much at least. "Of course. I did have some Library business to discuss with you, as a matter of fact. . . ."

Claire glanced pointedly at Probity, but judging by their faces it appeared neither of the muses understood common concepts like privacy and discretion. Brevity straightened imperceptibly, putting on her very best serious face. "Right. What's up?"

"We found a damsel wandering in the Arcane Wing," Claire said with as much patience as she could muster. "Again."

"Oh." Brevity's face fell. She craned around Claire. "Rosia?"

The shadow behind Rami was empty. He frowned at it, then nodded. "I told her she could run off to the suite when you two started . . . discussing."

Claire ignored the pirouette Rami had executed around the tension in the room in favor of addressing her concern straight on. "That's the third time this week."

Brevity studied her hands. "I know."

"If the damsels are unhappy—"

"That's a concern for the librarian, is it not?" Probity interrupted quietly. She offered a harmless smile when Claire frowned at her. "I mean, I am only a muse, but surely you have your own charges to worry about, Arcanist."

Claire's title slid off Probity's tongue of polite sympathy. A syrupy quality of kindness that made her stomach roil. Claire pursed her lips. "I did not cede my personal investment in the Library when I stepped down. If the damsels are not kept in hand, it puts the entire wing at risk—"

"Which is the sole responsibility of the librarian," Brevity said in a whisper. She was studying her hands, shoulders curved in like shields. "I appreciate your support, Probity, but Claire is right. If there's a problem, it's my fault."

"That's not *true*. None of this is *your* fault; if she hadn't as librarian—" Probity started when Brevity held up a hand.

"I'll speak to Rosia and the rest of the damsels. Maybe this time they'll tell me what I can do to rectify the situation." She hesitated, glancing at Claire. Her cheeks were flushed lavender. "Thank you for bringing this to my attention . . . and I'm sorry." Brevity abruptly walked past her desk toward the stacks.

Damn. There was no end to Claire making a social muck of things. She started forward. "Brevity."

Brevity stopped short and turned, anxiety ringing in every twitch of movement. Claire chewed on her lip and sought the right approach. "I know this falls entirely under your authority," she said slowly, "but the Arcane Wing would consider it a great favor if we could assist with the Unwritten Wing's investigation of this issue."

Brevity's shoulders sagged, if only a little. "Oh, right. Sure you can." A sliver, a ghost really, of the old Brevity was there, easy and warm for just a moment before skittering from sight. "Would you, um, like to . . . ?" Wiggling fingers gestured toward the depths of the stacks where the damsel suite was located.

Claire kept her nod businesslike. "Please lead the way."

It was a pantomime that kept them going. If Claire and Brevity had been intractable from librarian and apprentice, they had been forced to become someone else—something else—now. Arcane Wing and Unwritten. Duties instead of people. Claire, above all, knew how much easier it was to be a duty rather than a person. She also knew the damage it caused. She had worried at it but ultimately decided it was better than losing Brevity entirely. It was as much Claire's unwillingness to let go of the Library as it was Brevity's reluctance to step up, after all. They just needed time to settle. A quiet truce would eventually see them back to rights, or at least somewhere adjacent to it.

Claire followed Brevity down the canyons of wood and leather that made up the Unwritten Wing. Her mind continued to tick and twitch, impossible to not note all the hundreds of little things that had changed. The Unwritten Wing was supposed to be static, a place of preservation, but nothing overflowing with stories ever stayed the same. Claire could see the ways the wing had softened and shifted to suit Brevity, just as the Arcane Wing had for Claire. The biggest changes were immediately obvious; the blond woods and frosted-glass globes were gone, warmed to a ruddy cherry and curious silver starburst lights that had the impression of orbiting, ever so slightly, out of the corner of her eye. There were more subtle changes too. The ends of the stacks were capped with loud paintings that appeared to shift and vibrate with just as much life as the clutch of stacked books nested against the wood. It made Claire flinch to see books stacked on the floor—messy, loud, potentially damaging. Who knew what bad influence each story was having on others, fraternizing higgledy-piggledy like that? But Brevity never was as afraid of making a mess. Claire admired that, the courage to spill things, fix your mistakes, try again. Claire had never had the stomach for it. But then again, Claire's first mistake in the Library had been impossible to take back. A bit of murder had a tendency to make one gun-shy.

The hodgepodge tower of books seemed content, pages fluttering so lightly as to not even disturb the dust on the covers as they walked by. And content, stable books were all the Library hoped to achieve, Claire was forced to remind herself.

The entrance to the damsel suite, at least, had remained the same. The door was inset with frosted glass, behind which the low murmur of discussion, broken with occasional laughter, percolated. Brevity knocked twice before pulling open the door, leaving Claire to follow behind her. In the past, when Claire had visited the damsels as head librarian, the room fell into a curbed silence at her presence. Not so under Brevity's tenure, it seemed. Claire closed the door behind her on a clatter of buzzing conversation. Several of the women waved; one even whistled. The noise began to creep down by inches only when the damsels nearest the door caught sight of Claire. The energy fizzled out of the room.

"Need your attention for a minute!" Brevity said brightly, not seeming to notice the awkward lull. "I've brought Claire for a visit!"

The silence turned from a pause to a flatline. Claire kept her vague smile in place and thought that perhaps Brevity was a bit vindictive after all.

Brevity briefly scanned the cavernous room before frowning. "Where's Rosia?"

A slender scholar at the nearest table shot her a confused look. "We thought she was still with you. No one's seen her since last night."

"She didn't—but an hour ago . . ." Brevity sucked in a breath and turned, but Claire already had the door thrown open. Brevity sprinted back down the Library stacks, and Claire followed at a brisk pace.

At least, for once, they knew exactly where a runaway book was going.

# 2

# BREVITY

❦

The Arcane Wing is not merely a cabinet of curiosities, though many librarians have treated it as such over the years. It's tempting to treat it simply as a storage room for the oddities of the Library, but that would discount the nature of physical objects in the afterlife. The items of the Arcane Wing do not end up there by chance. They were real objects, originating not in the afterlife, but on Earth. That would always carry a certain amount of weight. Pour enough of yourself into anything, and it will gain a gravity and gravitas.

Like attracts like. And here we are.

*Librarian Gregor Henry, 1986 CE*

RUNNING WITH CLAIRE OUT of the Library, past the gargoyle, and headlong into the next emergency was its own kind of comfort. It was familiar, like wiggling your toes into that threadbare pair of fuzzy slippers that you can't bear to toss out. It might have been easy to pretend nothing had changed, if Probity hadn't been there, a flowing blur of pastel and flutter in the corner of her sight.

There was no visible sign of Rosia as they burst through the Arcane Wing's doors, though the wing's sole remaining raven took flight with a riot of protests before landing on the tall shelves toward the back. The torn edges of Claire's dull tiered skirts fluttered as she strode in that direction, purposefully ignoring the auxiliary shadows. She led them unerringly deep into the wing, precisely to where the raven was squawking.

"I hear you, Bird. I hear you, damn it . . ." Claire's voice clipped off abruptly, and Brevity collided with her shoulder. There was no Rosia at the back of the Arcane Wing, nor was there any floor. For a moment, it looked to Brevity as if an obsidian ice had taken over the floor. From the end of the aisle to the L-shaped far wall of old rookery cages, the entire floor was lost in black. Then Rami, Hero, and Probity clattered up behind them, causing a faint ripple at the nearest edge.

The ripples were too deep to be a simple spill. The wood paneling just suddenly . . . ceased to exist half a meter from Claire's feet.

The space had a rough two-meter radius, jagged at the edges with splintered wood. There were no struts, supports, or cobwebs to give the void beneath perspective. Brevity crept in for a closer look. She slipped past Claire to crouch at the edge of the fissure. It was a black, engulfing, depthless nothing that felt like it extended downward forever, until Brevity caught a flicker of movement. A glossy reflection of aquamarine hair and a pale face stared back at her, and her perception pivoted.

It wasn't an empty hole; it was a pool.

"You been doing renovations?" Brevity asked, inserting a strained levity into her voice as she glanced over her shoulder. Claire had that stiff-shouldered stillness, frost on steel, that she got when she encountered something unknown. Brevity knew that look well. Claire hated nothing more than unknowns—they were messy. Personally, that was why unknowns were Brevity's favorite. Improvisation was better than thinking through and giving time to doubt herself, any day.

"Obviously not." Claire lowered her voice, slightly aghast. "She couldn't be—down there—"

"Nah. I'm sure this is just a . . . whatchamacallit happenstance." Brevity's stomach churned on itself. Books couldn't drown, could they? Not down here, surely. The Library would have told her if that happened. Oh gods, if she lost a book, the Unwritten Wing would reject her. She would let everyone down. Again. A terrifying tension threatened up her throat and Brevity tried to take slow breaths.

"What is it?" Hero asked with a hint of skepticism. "I didn't think Hell flooded."

"If it does, it surely isn't water," Rami said under his breath, and Hero perked up.

"Hellfire? Acid? Oversteeped tea?"

"It's ink." Probity straightened from her inspection, rubbing her fingers on her pants though everyone had sense enough not to touch it. "I'm certain."

"Ink?" Brevity's mind recoiled from the implications of that. There was no large amount of ink in the Arcane Wing, as far as she was aware. Ink was the property of books, of the Library. "That can't be."

"Rosia?" Rami breathed the possibility into the air and Brevity's thoughts derailed. She'd nearly forgotten what had brought them here. Probity began to shake her head before Brevity's panic could spin up, and she was immediately grateful.

"Not that fresh. It's ink, though," Probity insisted, before adding a little softly, "I know a story when I see it."

"Well, that's a hypothesis that is simple enough to test. Rami," Claire said without removing her gaze from the wide well of black. "Please fetch me a dip pen and a spare sheet of vellum."

For a big man, Ramiel moved with a cat's-paw quiet. He returned a few moments later with the items Claire had requested, and a small stool. He was such a different breed of assistant compared to Hero.

She knelt next to the black lake, carefully dipped the glass tip in the surface, then straightened.

Under the light, the liquid on the glass pen nib writhed with colors, like in an oil slick. But to Brevity's eyes the colors slid and dribbled off the surface, like languid vapors. Blue and gray and weak green.

Probity exchanged a quick glance with Brevity and the slightest nod to confirm she saw it too. Colors in muse sight meant one thing: the markers of a human story. Brevity's stomach lurched into gear. Somehow, the pool of liquid—ink, if Probity was correct—was related to the Library's unwritten books. That alone didn't scare her—there were a lot of mysteries the Library didn't share—but the idea that *Claire* didn't know was positively terrifying.

But then Claire, as usual, had taken the situation under her presumed authority. She spread the vellum sheet on the stool and bent her head over it. She touched the nib to the paper, and the ink bloomed black and innocuous at the contact.

There had been a moment, just before, when Brevity saw the disaster in the making. Assured the liquid was some kind of ink, Claire let down her guard. She shifted her three-fingered grip on the pen, dropping her thumb and forefinger nearer to the nib to take a proper writing position. The leading edge of her forefinger had a permanent shadow worn into the creases from years, decades, of ink stains. Normal wear and tear for anyone who worked with fountain pens.

The gesture was second nature to Claire. Brevity might not have even noticed if she hadn't been watching the lazy waft of colors rising off the nib and the way they sharpened to invisible barbs as Claire's fingers drew near.

"Boss—" Brevity warned. Then Claire's finger ran against a smudge of ink on the pen grip and all hell broke loose.

The blot of ink leapt off the page, recoiling back up the feed of the nib and toward the grip. A short gasp escaped Claire and she dropped the dip pen to clatter across the hardwood. Rami rushed to secure it against contamination, but Brevity could have told him not to bother; the glass nib was dry. Because a tiny droplet of ink pooled on Claire's out-held hand and wicked into the creases of her fingerprint. It propagated so fast, a deluge in a dry creek bed. Black raced in rivers and veins up her skin, sliding down her cuticle in a sheet and across her knuckle. More ink than could have possibly been in one drop, one smudge, or even the entire pen.

Claire stumbled backward, and Hero jumped in to keep her from tipping into the pool. Claire's clean hand flew up, halting him. "Don't touch me!" The ink veined up her knuckles and across her palm. Claire dropped to her knees and her wide-eyed gaze sought out Brevity.

For help.

Brevity was used to reading Claire's glances. Understanding in a moment what her intended order or judgment was. But a look of *helplessness* was not in Claire's repertoire. Brevity dashed forward, dropping to her knees and hesitating with her hands hovering over Claire. The unseen colors of the ink were lashing ahead of the march of black, as if anchoring and pulling it forward.

All of it happened in perhaps the half a breath since Claire had touched the ink. Panic constricted Brevity's throat and she resisted the urge to grab Claire's hand. "What do I do?"

"It's cold," Claire said with a clinical kind of horror. The skin of her palm turned black and oil-slicked. The ink swallowed her wrist in a seeping pool, increasing in speed. "It's . . . loud."

"Do *something!*" It appeared to be taking every ounce of restraint for Hero to stay out of range. Brevity glanced around and saw Rami had drawn his sword with a pained, stoic look. As if he was steeling himself to cleave Claire's arm at the elbow. Once he built the resolve, Hero would not succeed in holding him back.

Brevity's gaze landed on Probity. She was a pale shadow against the shelf, watching with wide, wondering eyes. She'd seen the color. She'd guessed it was ink. She was a muse and she was here, and Brevity refused to believe in coincidences. "Probity. Please, *help me.*"

Probity's gaze snapped to hers, blank with confusion. Out of the corner of her eye, she saw Claire's arm turning black in lurching patches. The ink moved like an infection, like mold, like death. Brevity felt the air squeezing in her lungs with panicked gulps. "Please!"

A magic word succeeded in breaking the moment. Probity moved, swift and decisive in a froth of lace. She ducked under Hero's arm and slid to the floor next to Brevity. She gripped Brevity's wrist and hesitated with a pleading look. "This is going to hurt."

Brevity could only see the black licking up the inside of Claire's elbow. She nodded her assent, Probity's grip tightened into a vise, and something set fire to her arm.

The world narrowed to a single glimpse of familiar inspiration gilt, peeling away from Brevity's raw skin like viscera, before everything swam to ink black.

# 3

# HERO

I have confirmed my suspicion that the first skill a librarian must require is complete and utter boredom. Brevity has set me to reading through the Librarian's Log at random, as if reading the whining and philosophical angst of my predecessors will teach me something about book curation.

(Teach me! Me! I am already intimately familiar with books, thank you.)

I had thought, at least, that I would be entertained by learning more about the warden. But the log, according to Brevity, has a sense of requirement to its indexing. There is no simply reading the log. The personal notes and errata are not reliably listed in chronological order; the best approach seems to be flipping open the book with a question in mind. Let the log show you what you need, the librarian says.

No Claire details yet. Plenty of Yoon Ji Han essays on bookbinding, though. I think the log is broken.

*Apprentice Librarian Hero, 2020 CE*

HERO WAS OF THE opinion that once decent folks began pulling things out of one another's bodies, one should take a second look at the decisions that led them to that point. So Hero considered all the (many) errors that had occurred. Questioned his choice of life philosophy that had a raven screaming its curses at all of them from overhead. He wrenched his knee terribly as he half shielded Brevity with his shoulder, putting himself in between her and her supposed friend, who had just ripped her tattoo from her skin. It wasn't just a tattoo—it was shimmering, gilded lines of pure inspiration; even Hero knew that. It was the inspiration she'd been trusted with, as a muse, and tried to keep rather than surrender to a human. It was her reason for exile, her most treasured mistake, and Hero knew plenty about how important those were.

Claire had not made a sound through the entire exchange. The silence was a prick between Hero's ribs. He wanted to see—needed to see—but Probity was in the way. He could only glimpse the scuffed toe of one sneaker, peeking out beneath a mess of skirts that lay still, too still.

Steel licked against steel next to his ear. Ramiel stood over them with his broadsword leveled at Probity. The muse looked flatly unimpressed even as the tip of the blade began to waft blue flames. Rather calm, Hero thought, since Ramiel was absolutely terrifying when he went full Wrath of God.

Well, Wrath of Hell now. Wrath of Books? No, that didn't have quite the right ring to it.

"Step back, muse." Ramiel's voice had gone cold and deadly as black ice.

Probity did not step back, though she had enough sense to hold very, very still. The inspiration gilt writhed violently in her grip, glowing and slick with things Hero preferred not to think about. Her eyes seemed wide and bright as the moon. "If I step back, the human woman dies, and my sister begged me not to let that happen. I can do so because I am very, very good at what I do." The inspiration twined, blood slick, to grasp at the air. "And I will do anything for Brevity."

Brevity slumped against his shoulder, unconscious, though Hero could detect shallow breathing. He risked a glance at what he could see of Claire. Probity had shifted; he could see Claire's arm now. Black licked up her forearm like serpents. He couldn't see if she was breathing. Her fisted hands weakly fell open. They seemed smaller, frailer, but perhaps that was a trick of the ink. It had to be.

"Ramiel," Hero said quietly.

The Watcher reined in some of his holy terror, but indecision froze him. The tip of his blade wavered. (Hero didn't have his sword. Why didn't he have his sword? People were always taking away his sword.) Then Rami dropped his arm into a wary guard.

"Save her." His voice was human again and rough as gravel.

Probity was a blur of movement. She propped Claire's shoulder up—taking caution not to touch the infected parts of her arm. With swift efficiency, she looped the band of inspiration around the leading edge of black. The ink appeared to react, surging under the edge.

"No, you don't." Probity muttered an incomprehensible word and executed a flourish that was too fast to follow, lassoing the ink back behind the line. She cinched it, muttered another incomprehensible word. The scent of cardamom and something else filled the air, making Hero's head go fuzzy for a moment. He blinked, and the inspiration encircled Claire's arm, just below the elbow, as if it had always been there.

No one spoke as the tendrils of ink collided with the band of blue, racing along it as if looking for a weak point. Every inch of skin below the band turned starless black. The neon inspiration shivered and then pulsed once. A skin of frost swept down the stained skin, as if the liquid was drying. Then the frost appeared to evaporate.

Claire's arm stayed black.

And Ramiel's sword was back up, advancing on Probity. "What did you do?"

Probity had reverted from awe-striking competence to innocence and lace. Claire was still a limp weight in her arms, and Probity held her like a sack of grain. Hero distantly thought how she would never, *never* have allowed herself to be manhandled so crudely. The wrongness made his lip curl.

"I stopped the advance of the ink. Rather, the inspiration did," Probity said with a certainty in her smile. She tapped her fingers on top of Claire's blackened wrist. "It's safe and held in stasis for the moment, though I'm not sure how we'll be able to extract it intact."

The violent impulse that bloomed in his head surprised even Hero himself. It was a cold kind of rage, the kind that must have been simmering under pressure for some time, but he hadn't seen it form. His hands were full of an unconscious librarian, or he might have done something worse than snarl, "Who *cares* about the ink?! How is *Claire?*"

"Oh." Probity startled, appearing earnest as she blinked at Hero, then glanced briefly at Claire. "I think the band should slow down any damage the ink was causing?"

The muscles in Ramiel's shoulders bunched, causing the feathers sticking out from beneath the coat epaulets to twitch. With some great effort, he lowered the sword again and sheathed it. Hero saw him glance cautiously at the pool of ink. The surface was deceptively still and patient just a few feet away. "Can we move them?"

Probity shrugged. "Sure. This one will be out for a while. Brevity probably passed out from the shock. She should be fine when she wakes up." She betrayed her concern with the way she chewed on her bottom lip as she studied Brevity. But then she shrugged Claire out of her lap and might have damn well let her fall had Rami not jumped in to take her.

Rami adjusted Claire into a bridal carry with significantly more care and respect. Black fingertips brushed against Ramiel's coat and Hero flinched instinctively, but the ink didn't jump or spread. Probity had been accurate in her clinical assessment, at least that far.

Probity came over to Hero's side and fussed briefly over Brevity. The snarling defensive impulse was still jumping underneath Hero's skin, so he was very glad when Ramiel checked Claire's pulse and met his gaze with a silent nod.

Hero wasted no time rising to his feet with Brevity in his arms and executing a graceful turn that might have *accidentally* whacked Probity in the face with his elbow. The raven was still cussing up a storm over their heads and seemed to follow them down the aisle to the Arcane Wing doors.

Hero led the way, a little relieved to have Probity at his back in order to cool his strange rage. It felt like a silent agreement that they should get Claire and Brevity back to the Unwritten Wing, where they could rest in safety and as far away from the black pool as possible.

The pool wasn't just black. It was a reservoir of unwritten ink, if Probity was right. The strange wonder of that warred with the gnawing fear of what had just happened—had almost happened. Hero navigated the hallways in a daze as he tried to make that align in his head. And it occurred to Hero that not once, throughout the entire ordeal, had Probity referred to Claire by her name.

NEWS TRAVELED FAST AMONG the damsels. It traveled even faster when related by Rosia, who had not drowned but instead burst into the damsel suite sobbing about ghosts. Half the Library—at least, half of the characters that were up and walking around—was assembled in the lobby when they arrived. The damsels took charge immediately, ensconcing Claire and Brevity in the suite itself and kicking Probity, Ramiel, and Hero out with the efficiency of hardened combat medics.

Damsels were really *astonishingly*, aggressively pushy, in Hero's opinion.

Still, it allowed him a moment to reassemble himself. He accepted a cup of tea from a helpful damsel—young boy, monk's robes, probably some failed author's idea of a mystical sidekick, poor kid—and sank back in his chair. Brooding didn't come naturally to him, but thankfully Probity had disappeared into the stacks and left him with only Rami for company, grand king of the brooders. They swam in the relative silence for the length of half a cup of tea.

It was a disappointment but not a surprise when Ramiel's cup landed heavily on the table with a click. "We have a problem." He met Hero's gaze with earnest not-quite-silver eyes.

Hero was distantly aware that there was some technical difference between an angel and a Watcher, but whatever it was, it was lost on him. Ramiel might not have had the Heavenly refinement and light of angels in books, but there was no mistaking what he was. Being near Ramiel was like trying to stand next to the sun. Immortal creatures like angels had their own gravity, and Hero constantly felt the subtle tug around Ramiel. Hero's usual nature was about as biddable as a cat with a migraine, and the feeling of an eternal slow draw irritated and got under his skin. This only served to make Hero even less prone to charity than usual.

"My *word*, is that the stunning conclusion you've come to?" Hero let his voice drip with mockery. It was easier to pick a target—any target—than to try to figure out what the existence of ink and Claire's unknown condition meant to himself or the future of his book. He rolled the teacup in his palms. "Heaven truly lost a *master strategist* when you fell."

"I was a soldier," Ramiel said simply. He didn't rise to the bait; he never did. He had an infuriating habit of looking at Hero, obviously finding him wanting, and gliding past as if he and he alone had some greater purpose. As if an insult from Hero was not even worth his concern.

Hero's insults were worth a king's ransom, damn it. It was perhaps the only value he could rely on these days.

Whatever Ramiel had been, he was an assistant now, just like Hero. That made them vaguely equals, he reminded himself. Allies, even. That moment with Rami backing him up with Probity had been nice. Had potential. Somewhere in the back of Hero's mind was a distant plan starting to shuffle into view, but it veered too close to thinking about things he didn't want to consider right now. He set it aside in favor of prodding the fallen angel.

"And I was a rebellion leader and a *king*, facts that did no one a flick of good when magic ink we don't understand decided to start eating our Arcanist." That sentence had lost steam somewhere in the middle, and rather than feeling like a vicious stab, it just left Hero with a queasy feeling of worry. It was an unnatural and unwelcome sensation. Another thing to blame Claire for, when she woke up.

If there was a sport he had trained for, it was guilt bearing. Rami heaved a sigh, proving he was already the champion. "You're right, for once." He leaned forward, intent. "So, what is it?"

Hero choked on his tea. "What is what?"

"The ink." Rami's brows created great trenches of concern above his silver eyes. It was unnerving when they focused entirely on you. "The muse seemed to think it was ink. Ink is the thing of books. So how does it work . . . ?"

Surely Hero must have the answers. What kind of book didn't know what he was made of, after all? Perhaps it was like other things he knew without knowing: the shape of a story, the wrongness of his book without him, the shiver a book had when it was close to waking up a character. He thought about the ink and reached for that well of intuition that always spouted up, from nowhere, to catch him where he fell short.

Nothing caught this particular free fall. He knew nothing. He knew nothing at all. The idea that a story survived in the ink was no more or less ridiculous than anything else he'd suffered, but it stung somehow. He *should* know. What kind of character was he? Hero covered the dip in his stomach with a scoff and drained the last of his tea in one swig. "It's a ridiculous question. Shall I ask you how your feathers work?"

Rami's mood lightened to something approaching earnest interest. "Celestial dynamics is straightforward to understand, really. If you compare it to the aerodynamics of earth-born birds—"

"Please stop talking." Hero buried his face in his hands. Everyone told him to do the same often enough: stop talking. This was a punishment, wasn't it? Was he being punished? Taunted by an ignorant angelic jock and a pool of black liquid potential that should have shown him a reflection where he only saw a question mark? It was wicked and devious, even for Hell.

Hero considered it a minor miracle, then, when Brevity burst out of the gloom of the stacks like an ambitious sunrise, trailed by a curious gaggle of muses and—the knot in Hero's chest eased a little—a drawn-looking Claire. Ink-stained, hunted-looking, but awake.

"Claire's okay, I'm okay, et cetera and so on—" Brevity impatiently headed off their questions. "We got an idea. A really awful idea, but, well— Rami, Hero, on your feet."

# 4

# CLAIRE

Repaired another cover today. The leather had begun to wear along the rail line. I wonder why the books choose leather. It's not as if there are hell-cows for hide, are there? (Are there?) They could be clapboard- or linen-covered hardbacks or—saints forbid—paperback. But it's leather, tanned leather.

An early method of preparing leather for book covers was to cure it covered in wet tea leaves and bark—tanning comes from the word "tannins." Tea and words have always been steeped together, down to the bones. I preferred coffee when I was alive, but Claire drinks this stuff by the pot: to refresh, to fortify, she says. Maybe the English knew something about the Library after all. We're preserving ourselves from the inside, sip by sip.

*Librarian Gregor Henry, 1987 CE*

REGAINING CONSCIOUSNESS WAS A scandal. Claire did not so much wake up as fling herself from one awareness to another. She jolted upright and was only stopped from falling over again by a pair of gentle hands. Fire thudded from her head and dribbled through every joint. It was as if every ache and pain of normal aging Claire had been spared for the last thirty years had come home to roost. "Oh, hellfire and harpies." She rubbed her wrists tenderly. One was bandaged; that was to be expected. "Someone get me a hot compress and half a bottle of paracetamol."

Claire knew Hell had no such thing. She had honestly expected Brevity and a clatter of teacups, not a weary sigh and a low voice full of amusement.

"If only I could."

Claire abruptly forgot about her joint pain. The hold on her shoulders was the only thing that kept her reclined on the couch. The cushions beneath her had a familiar feel, and Claire's careening mind distantly placed it as a piece of Library furniture. Which did not mesh with the sight of Beatrice perched on the edge looking wary as a feral cat.

"Beatrice." Claire struggled not to reel again. "What— You are in Malta. You can't—"

"I really can't," Beatrice agreed amiably. Claire's unwritten character wore the same rumpled suit vest she'd had on when Claire had seen her last in Malta, sans the dirt and blood. Beatrice appeared perfectly recovered from the adventure that had left her on Earth, hair swept in that careless crop of curls that looked soft enough to make Claire's fingers ache again. There was a smudged look about her, an air Claire couldn't quite place, though she tried. Beatrice tucked the blanket back around Claire's lap while simultaneously giving her the chance to gawk.

"You can't—" Claire repeated, finally taking in her surroundings. They were in the damsel suite, which showed signs of swift evacuation. Open books and half-eaten nibbles were strewn across the tables, and on the end table nearest her, steam still wafted faintly from an over-brewed cup of tea. Claire rescued the strainer on impulse, though the tea had obviously gone bitter. She stuck her finger in her mouth, allowing the acidic bite of the tannins to try to clear her head.

"I was arguing with Brevity, there was a— Oh gods, we fought— and the ink—" Claire jerked her hands up. Her right hand was swaddled in a tea towel. Claire wiggled her fingers free. The entire fingertip, skin, nail, and all, was stained black. It had a shine to it, an oil-slick feel as if it were still wet, though when she wiped her index finger on the tea cloth, nothing was left behind.

"I touched the ink. This stain . . ." Claire said blankly. She peeled back the towel, following the discoloration up, over her knuckles, past her wrist, until it came to an abrupt halt just below the crook of her elbow. It jutted right up to a border of iridescent blue, which appeared to be made of different stuff, shimmering like a propane pilot light.

"She thought quick, to do that," Beatrice said quietly.

Claire resisted the impulse to pick at it, no matter how foreign it was on her skin. "Who did? Brevity?"

"No, the other one. Though I think she wouldn't have acted if she hadn't been prompted to." Beatrice gave her a considering look. "You have a very loyal assistant in that girl. I'm glad."

"She's not my assistant anymore." It was a bitter kind of reflex, and Claire shook her head. "She's Librarian now, and—" Claire stopped, feeling eight kinds of idiotic. "Hell and harpies, we're in the damsel suite. In the *Library*. Why—how are you here? You shouldn't be here. You would *never* return here after all that's happened. You escaped. Did Brev force you to come back? How long have I been out? Did—"

"Calm down, Claire." Beatrice seemed remarkably unflustered by being in the very place she'd fled decades ago. "No one brought me here except you. I think I never fully left."

Claire blinked. "I don't understand."

"And I don't have much time to explain. I convinced the others that you would need time to understand, but they're restless. Naturally." A muffled sound, like a wave of small feet, stirred from somewhere outside the suite door. Beatrice sighed. "I need you to stay calm."

"I am *always* calm!" The ache in Claire's joints was returning, with a building kind of pressure. As if there was suddenly more stuffed into her than before. She rubbed her face. "I forgot how exhausting you were. Forget it. We've got to get you out of here and back to the Silent City. It should be possible, while the others are distracted. There's too much going on."

"More than you think," Beatrice said. She nodded to Claire's banded arm. "That thing is like a magical tourniquet, but it's not going to hold forever. You need to stop wasting time."

Claire's mouth dropped open, but before she could protest, a knock came at the door. It was a light, tentative knock, then slowly repeated. The brass door handle began to jiggle.

Beatrice froze, staring at the door before turning an intent frown on Claire. "Listen to me. You need to *listen*. It's the only way the books will have any rest."

"As I said, I'm not the li—"

"I don't *care* if you're not the goddamned librarian!" Beatrice grabbed Claire's shoulder but pulled back when she flinched. "You're not the librarian, you're not an author, you're not alive. Who bloody cares! You think your characters do? I certainly didn't. Your friend Hero didn't. You don't escape your own story, Claire. It's impossible."

"What kind of nonsense are you talking about?"

The door abruptly ceased its rattling, and Beatrice's shoulders tensed. Across the room, the damsel suite door unlatched and crept slowly open on silent hinges. The darkness on the other side of the door was inky and absolute. An unnatural sigh of air washed through, ruffling the pages of open books and chilling Claire to the core.

Beatrice sat in front of her like a shield, but it was as if she weren't even there. The room felt crowded with breath.

Her lungs were chilled when Claire tried to take a breath and try again. "What—what are you asking me to do?"

Beatrice finally turned back to her, looking solemn and sorry. It felt too much like how she'd looked the last time Claire had seen her, half-swallowed in torchlight as she hesitated at the precipice of a realm gate. Hesitated, to stay behind. When Beatrice brought her hand to her face, Claire flinched.

"Wake up," Beatrice said in a voice that wasn't her own. Claire was falling, and it felt like something new and horrible and cold was blooming in her bones. Beatrice's voice splintered and turned fractal. "Wake up, Claire. Wake up."

"WAKE UP! PLEASE, C'MON, boss." Claire's joints still ached. The settee was still soft beneath her. But the next breath she took gave her a lungful of warm air scented with familiar anise, paper, and tea. She opened her eyes.

"Oh, harpies, you're back. That's good." Brevity's nose was an inch from her own before she withdrew with a sigh. "The boys woulda murdered me if you didn't wake up."

"Was there doubt?" Claire grimaced at the sawdust in her voice. She gestured and Brevity helpfully handed her a glass of water. She was still in the damsel suite, resting on a settee. It was occupied again, with a handful of damsels studiously pursuing their hobbies and not at all scrutinizing Claire with absolute self-righteous judgment out of the corners of their eyes. Ridiculous. Claire could hear the sidelong whispering. "Gods, how long have I been out this time?"

"This time?" A small furrow knit in Brevity's brows. "Not long. You fainted—we both did—when Probity did her thing. It stopped the ink, though. I . . ." Brevity looked down. "How do you feel?"

"Like the inside of a Hellhound's mouth." Claire sipped the water and grimaced.

"So about the same as me." Brevity gave her a wan smile. Now that Claire was sitting up, she could take the time to observe the paper-thin energy of Brevity's smile and the shadows under her eyes. For a moment it was overlaid with the memory of a handsome brown face exhorting her to wake up, to—

Claire yanked her arm out from under the covers and cursed loudly. Black stained her skin, held off by a ribbon of bright blue tied off below her elbow. She set down her water and gently pushed Brevity back by the shoulder until she could see the arm she kept half cradled against her stomach. Structurally, nothing appeared to be wrong. Brevity's arm certainly appeared in better shape than Claire's. But a paler band of periwinkle swirled on her forearm where her inspiration gilt tattoo had been. It looked almost as if it had been scrubbed away. Or stripped.

"It's fine," Brevity said too quickly into the silence. "Hurt like a cuss going off, but we both got a nap out of it and now we're fine, see?"

Claire shook her head. "But how—?"

"Probity explained it to me. Later." Brevity's nervous hands skimmed over her bare forearm before she reverted to studying her fingernails. "We can't get the ink *out* of you but because of what they're made of, the inspiration gilt can hold it back. It works kinda like a—"

"Like a magical tourniquet," Claire finished.

Brevity's brows inched up. "Well, yes. But how—"

"Never mind that." The damsels in the room were studiously ignoring them, but Claire could hear the whispers. The constant whorl of rumor around her was beginning to give her a headache. She tried to focus. "You said what it's *made* of. You have a theory about the . . . the—"

"Ink," Brevity supplied, when Claire couldn't quite assign the word. "We know it's ink now. More importantly, its *unwritten* ink—"

"We can't know that," Claire objected, but Brevity was already shaking her head.

"We do. I do. I can see—it looks the same way books do, to muses. Probity saw it too. It's the ink of an unwritten book. Books. Maybe a lot of them."

Claire was caught off guard by the bitterness that came with answers. Brevity had identified and handled the mystery with *Probity*. An outsider, and a muse who seemed to have even more history with Brevity than Claire did. She'd already felt as if she'd fallen out of sync, and there was nowhere for her to get a handhold. She studied Brevity. She knew her face well enough to see the hope starting to form. *Many books*. Brevity was thinking of the lost damsels. She had to nip that in the bud. "It could be many things."

"No," Brevity said, clipped and firm. "It can't." She gave a surprisingly dismissive gesture to Claire's arm. "You can keep on ignoring the obvious or you can trust me. As a former muse. As . . . librarian."

The whispers that drifted around the room really *were* nonstop. Claire had always been aware that damsels were talkative and—in her opinion—prone to too much gossip, but they could at least have the decency to wait until she'd *left* the room. Claire rubbed her temple. "Of course I trust you," she said, wondering why it sounded like such a weak defense. "But the idea that the ink of a story can exist outside its book is . . ."

"A lot, I know."

Brevity had lowered her voice, to be kind, to be patient. To be sympathetic of Claire, the poor human who just couldn't keep up. The ache in her head ratcheted up along with her temper.

"I am perfectly capable—" The whispers intruded again. *Gods.* Claire's patience snapped. "Could you all just *shut up* for one bloody minute?!"

She hadn't meant to yell. She hadn't meant many things. But Claire's voice thudded into the silence. Every pair of eyes, discreetly turned away, focused on her. A teapot clinked, and someone dropped their crochet hook.

"Claire." Brevity's touch was featherlight to her shoulder, but Claire still startled. Brevity was looking at her with fresh concern and a new brush of caution. "No one's said anything but us."

"Don't be ridiculous. I could hear them whispering perfectly—" Permitted to glare around the room straight on, Claire got a clear look. There were only a handful of damsels in the large lounge, scattered and not numerous enough for the voices she'd heard. There was a woman crocheting what appeared to be a star map by the fire, one sole girl napping in an armchair, and a young boy eating jam tarts by the tea table. No one was huddled, or even appeared engaged in conversation. Let alone clandestine whispers.

A foggy, distant sound she could hear, even now, as everyone stared at her mutely. She'd dreamed of Beatrice and imagined voices that weren't there. Claire had always counted on her perceptions being reliable, and a sticky disgrace settled into her stomach. She tentatively touched her clean fingertips to her stained wrist. They came away dry. "My mistake."

Brevity, of course, was the first to smooth things over. "No prob.

It's been a rough day for all of us," she said simply, then appeared to hesitate. "I know the guys are probably plotting ways to make us rest, but I had an idea, if you're up for an experiment."

"Blood and ink, please." Claire needed something, anything, right now to get her out of this eerie damsel suite and propelled along any path that would start making sense of this.

"I'm going to need a sample of the ink to test—safely this time. If there's anything left of an unwritten story in it, we'll probably have better luck testing it on something native to the Library."

Claire struggled to follow that thought. Brevity would never test on a precious Library book, but that only left one thing. There was only one book inherent to the Library that wasn't an unwritten story.

"The logbook. But it's not like the other books in the Library. No originating author, for one." Claire drew in a sharp breath. "Using the Librarian's Log book as a test subject is . . . unprecedented. Dangerous."

Brevity met her eyes, wary, as if it was a test. Everything felt like a test between them these days, a test of boundaries, a test of respect. It made Claire's chest ache, but Brevity just straightened to her feet cautiously. "Librarian's prerogative." And then, perhaps because she saw the minuscule flinch Claire tried to hide, she attempted to soften it. "I learned from the best, after all."

# 5

# BREVITY

I've had a few weeks to get used to it now: being dead. Dead, and a librarian at that. Not even death stops the world from expecting a woman to take care of things. At least it's not eternity at the cook fire.

There was supposed to be another, here in the Library. I've gleaned that much, from what the demons have said. The Arcanist is a glum living statue. She doesn't like me much, but it appears she has as much say in the matter as I do. She says there was a librarian before—an experienced one who would have trained me, taught me all the secrets of this place. She's gone. Exiled? Doubly dead? Deposed? I'm not certain, only that everyone is terribly mute as to why.

The Arcanist, Revka, says I'll just have to pick up the basics. As much as she doesn't like me, there's a deep sadness in her, stone heart and all. I'd like to say I was kind enough not to ask, but I'm not—I was told off for my troubles.

They say this is supposed to be a library, a salon of learned words. But it doesn't feel like a library. It feels like a tomb.

*Librarian Madiha al-Fihri, 602 CE*

RAMI AND HERO HAD, in fact, objected to their plan.

They'd objected—loudly, in Hero's case—and expressed their concerns—gravely, in Rami's case—and then Claire and Brevity had done, as always, what they thought was best. It was almost like working together again. Almost.

The pond of ink had not moved since they left it. It lapped silently against the broken boards at the same level it had been before. Normal liquid might have evaporated, or sunk into porous wood and whatever the bedrock of Hell was made of. Instead, the surface lay flush with the broken wood floorboards, black against beech. Claire allowed Brevity to handle the gloves, tongs, and vial as a small acquiescence to Rami's demands. The unease in Claire's eyes was enough to convince Brevity this was no time for indulging muse curiosity—she came only close enough to the edge of the liquid as was necessary to stopper a vial full. The rubber cork popped on the top, and that was that.

The trip back to the Unwritten Wing was quick and amiable. Brevity let Claire carry the sample, once the vial had been scrupulously wiped and she was certain every smidge of ink was contained. Perhaps the mystery in the bottle would repair some of the unspoken rift that had divided Claire from her since the coup. Perhaps this was all that was needed—a common mystery, a common task. Brevity entertained that hope with a growing certainty.

The liquid in the vial bobbled. That's how Brevity knew that Claire had hesitated a step—just a fraction of a step—just as they turned the corner and the Unwritten Wing doors came into view.

"Claire?" Brevity asked when she didn't say anything.

"It's nothing. No—sorry." Claire fiddled with the dangerous sample in her hand as she apologized. Both actions being wildly uncharacteristic, enough that Brevity stopped in her tracks. Claire shook her head dismissively. "I saw it before; I just keep forgetting. . . . Thirty years is a lot to unlearn."

Brevity glanced uncertainly to the doors, and her stomach did a flip as pieces fell into place. Understanding doused the warm feeling in her chest. The Unwritten Wing had changed to suit its new librarian, just as the Arcane Wing had accommodated Claire. To Brevity, it'd felt like the Library's small way of welcoming her. The doors were a soft ruddy color that reminded Brevity of sunsets, accented by the crisp silver in the handles. Strings of faerie lights just inside the door washed the entrance in a gentle kind of glow.

But Brevity could see it now through Claire's eyes, and that empathy threw it all into sharp, alien relief. The changes Brevity had made to the Unwritten Wing no longer felt cheery—they felt garish. Cherry-stained wood a shade too red and bright, faerie lights illuminating the aisles cheap instead of cozy. A plastic imitation of the distinguished Library that Claire had known. Brevity's heart tilted and fell between her ribs. She kept her face tilted down as she hurried across the lobby to her desk.

"Just a minute . . ." There was one thing that didn't change along with the Library, and maybe that'd smooth over the knot of awkwardness forming in Brevity's chest. She rifled around in the drawer until she came up with a thick, battered-looking book.

The Librarian's Log had a blotchy leather cover the precise color of mistakes—ink smudges and the shadow of grubby fingerprints—with enough scuffs and scars that left the surface feeling more like bark than cured leather. It wasn't the largest book in the Library, but it still took Brevity both hands to wrestle it out and drop it onto the blotter with a solid *whump* that echoed to the high ceilings.

"Open it up, if you would." Claire carefully found an empty teacup to balance the vial upright in. Brevity wasn't as tidy about her desk as Claire. Clutter was conducive to thinking. At least that's what she told Hero when he got on her about it.

Brevity flipped open the log, not bothering to be precise. The log-book always flopped open to the necessary page. Sometimes, your definition of "necessary" didn't line up with the log's, but Brevity had decided long ago that trusting the book was part of a librarian's job too. Letting books take you where they might—that was one part of the Library's magic. The other part was the centuries of log entries from past Unwritten Wing librarians, all in perfectly readable script, no matter the age or the originating language, never in reliable order, but also never an end to empty pages, no matter how much you wrote. The log contained everything from inventories of books to an index of techniques and research and, of course, the personal log of the librarian and their assistant.

Books were a kind of magic everywhere. Especially here, especially this book.

Claire rummaged in her pocket until she found a fountain pen. Brevity preferred the honest feel of charcoal on paper, but for some reason Claire had always preferred the modern inventions. Not too modern, mind you. Brevity once filched some standard ballpoint pens to bring back to Claire as a surprise. You would have thought she'd deposited a dead snake on her desk instead.

Of course, that'd been back when Claire was the librarian. Stern and unwilling to engage with the world. Getting a smile back then had felt like wresting the sword from the stone. But she'd been kind to Brevity, and she'd softened since then. She'd exhibited kindness, even toward books like Hero. But the smiles she gave Brevity now—only Brevity—were tight-lipped, reined in. It felt like Brevity had become one of her ghosts.

"You've kept up admirably," Claire murmured as she ran a finger down the displayed log entries. It was a consoling, awkward comment, and Brevity tried to remind herself Claire might feel as out of sorts with this moment as she did.

Brevity straightened and smiled. "Never liked log work, but Hero's handwriting is *atrocious*."

"All those flourishes," Claire hissed, and Brevity's smile brightened.

"Everything short of dotting his *i*'s with hearts."

"It's not handwriting; it's *script*." Hero emerged from the stacks near the door, Probity and Ramiel in tow. They'd agreed—reluctantly—to speak with the damsels and make sure there would be no curious on-lookers for a second experiment with the ink. Probity, as usual, kept her thoughts to herself, but there was a disgruntled air between the men, obvious and palpable immediately. Brevity offered a questioning look, but Rami just hunched his shoulders while Hero put all his energy into propping himself against the desk. He had never met a piece of furniture he couldn't lounge against. "I guess I should be grateful you lot even know cursive."

"There's nothing innately better about something just because it's old," Brevity said.

"Precisely," Claire murmured, squinting as she concentrated on touching the pen nib just to the surface of the liquid in the vial. It wicked up the groove, just as ink should. And colors rippled and fluttered across the metal, just as ink should *not*. Hero's eyes lit up, an intense speculation sparking in his eyes as he considered the liquid. It was a relief when Probity gave a low whistle and raised her eyes to meet Brevity's. She reveled in the affirmation, someone else seeing what see saw, for a change. Being the only former muse in the room was so exhausting sometimes.

Claire withdrew the nib and gave Brevity an inquiring glance, pen hovering over the paper. Claire, with a fountain pen in her hand again. Nib loaded with ink, clutched—carefully—in a black-stained hand. It felt wrong. A chill crept up Brevity's neck, and she nodded quicker than she needed to dispel it. Claire took a breath and lowered the pen. The colors whipped over her hand like mist, the tip of the nib touched the logbook's parchment, and several things happened in a breath.

The nib touched the page.

Hero drew in a pinched gasp and stepped back just as Rami stepped forward.

And the logbook began to smoke.

Claire began a downward stroke with the pen, but the liquid moved of its own accord. It wicked deep into the parchment and pulled away from the nib. Black veins crept spiderwebs across the page on their own, tendrils encountering the edge and seeming to pulse once before the entire linework recoiled again. The veins left faint wisps of smoke and the air began to smell of burnt turpentine, as if the ink had been burned both in and out of the parchment hide. The ink coiled lazily, like an indecisive snake, splitting into fractal triskeles, then conjoined.

Then writing began.

"What . . ." Claire was frozen, pen to page as if she was afraid to break contact. Letters—*script*, Hero had called it, and Brevity could see the difference now, not calling this simple cursive—spun out across the page. Not in a continuous line of thought, but fragments, the ink seeming to jump from one thought to the next. Brevity could follow it all, not so much by the words but by the colors that burst, like quick-fading comets, through the smoke. A snippet of dialogue, a soft sunset, a warp of stars, a clang of swords, a shattered planet, a sigh against skin. The script filled the page, the ink seeming to multiply on itself. But it didn't stop there; words crisscrossed, mashed, and fought where they intersected. Epilogue versus eponyms. Protagonist versus peril. Pivot versus plot. It filled up the page, blackening without stopping until the ink sopped through the parchment entirely. Still there were words, dreadful, impossible snatches of story that writhed and crested on the page like a swarm. Breaking, forming, breaking again. Over and over, splinters of stories without end.

Iron and anise weltered in her mouth, searing her tongue. Brevity felt pulled, as if she was falling into the ink. The book had become a gateway, a door of potential, and if she just reached, reached, reached—

She heard a strangled shriek. The ink disappeared. When had she stepped closer to the desk? She didn't remember raising her hand, fingertips drifting toward the page. Claire shoved Brevity back, and the fountain pen went clattering across the floor. The logbook was still open, but its page was a creamy ivory expanse. No ink, no script, just the faint waft of turpentine and a wisp of smoke rising slowly off the page.

Claire dropped heavily onto the edge of the desk. The hand she put up to her face was trembling. It was her left hand. Her right hand was clutched into a protective black fist against her stomach. Brevity herself was trembling, she just realized. She turned away and sought out Probity's face. Her expression was cracked open with a soft wonder. She offered a hand and met Brevity's gaze as if they'd just witnessed the holiest of miracles. Brevity scanned the floor before finding where the pen had rolled underneath an overstuffed chair. She picked it up and held the nib under the light. Whistle clean and shiny as brass, no ink.

Disappointment lurched in her stomach for no reason she could think of. They still had the vial—hell, they had the whole *well* of it back in the Arcane Wing. But something instinctual in Brevity's gut told her this ink was precious, should not be let go. *Loud*, Claire had said just before she fainted. That made sense now, so many *stories*—

"We'll bury it," Claire said. Hero and Rami had been murmuring concern for a while, Brevity distantly recognized, but it was Claire's grim voice that cut through the fog. "We'll seal it up in the Arcane Wing. I'll look into something permanent enough that the damsels won't keep sniffing it out."

"What?" The fog—desperate, longing fog—cleared in her head. Brevity stepped forward, aghast. "We can't do that. You realize what this *is*? It's not just ink. It's—"

"Some kind of residue left over from the unwritten books we lost in the fire, yes." Claire pronounced the words the way you'd describe an unfortunate deathbed that needed cleaning up. But this wasn't unfortunate; it was a *gift*. Brevity could see that even as Claire shook her head and turned away. "After the coup, it probably pooled and drained to the Arcane Wing as the nearest reservoir of magic. It's not books anymore, so it couldn't stay in the Library, but I suppose enough remained to call out to the damsels and attract them."

Hero had taken on a particular shade of white as he came to help Brevity to the desk. They were talking about bits of books as body parts. She would have time to worry about him later. For now, the horror of what Claire was saying took all her attention.

All her thoughts felt knocked into free fall. She missed things being simple: unwritten stories being books, not pools of dead ink; her friends being her friends, not estranged colleagues; Claire being a friend she called boss instead of a former boss she still tried to call friend; the Library being the vast yet total edges of her concern. It still should have been, since she'd been named head librarian. But instead of feeling more focused, she was drowning. The world was a library she could never really read.

"How are these not books?" Brevity asked. "You saw it just like I did. Of course those are books, *stories*—"

"Only in the way a clipped lock of hair is human." Claire's brow knit; then her expression hardened. "That ink is the former lifeblood of those books that died because of us. Formerly pure and full of life, now corrupted and muddled. It couldn't even establish itself on the page, Brevity. Think it through. Obviously, the ink of a hundred books has mixed and commingled until it doesn't even know itself. There's nothing to salvage."

"We can certainly *try*, at least." The memory of all those books destroyed, the stories crumbling into searing ashes between her fingertips, struck at her like a lash. "The *Unwritten* Wing can try."

A flinch, like ice frosting over, occurred on Claire's face. She plucked the pen from Brevity's hands and crossed her arms over her chest. "I can't allow it."

Brevity distantly registered they were slipping into a fight, slashing open old wounds along the way, but she couldn't help the way her brow arched all the same. But it was Probity who broke the pause with a soft, curious: "Allow?"

"The reservoir of ink resides in the Arcane Wing and is therefore under Arcanist care," Claire said.

"That's not fair." Hero had recovered from his shock enough to step up next to Brevity and Probity. It felt nice, having support. "These are obviously the sacred remains of books of the Unwritten Wing; therefore—"

"Sacred?" Ramiel objected. "We're in *Hell*." The stoic angel had remained quiet up till now, but he gave Hero a dismissive look, up and down and then away. He gestured broadly to the shadows of the Library stacks. "Nothing sacred or holy about this place."

"There is *no* place more sacred than stories," Probity said lowly.

"Profane remains, then." Brevity took up Hero's argument and he flashed her a grateful smile. "Doesn't matter either way. Those are what remain of books of the Unwritten Wing. We have a duty to try to repair them."

"There is no *repairing* that." Claire's cheeks had turned sallow and taut. She retrieved the vial from its resting place and cradled it against her chest, clutched in a blackened hand that trembled. "You saw how it behaved. Books are potential, Brev. Potential is power. And demons *crave* power. Whatever remains of those in that ink is lost and is essentially distilled power. That's a heady drug. We can't repair it; we can't *use* it. Just its existence is a risk to the whole Library."

"The whole Library? Or just you?" Hero snipped.

"Uncalled for. Watch your tone," Rami growled under his breath.

Hero smiled. "Make me."

"It's too great a risk," Claire repeated. "If we learned *nothing* else from Andras, we should have learned that."

Brevity shook her head. "It's a book—"

"It's not," Claire snapped. "It's just ink. It's a thing."

"Fond of dismissing anything you find threatening as a nonhuman *thing*, aren't you, warden?" Hero said with a sudden chill.

"Don't," Claire gritted through her teeth. "Don't. Start."

Hero's shoulders stiffened. A wild protectiveness rose in Brevity. Hero was her assistant, just as Brevity had been Claire's. What's more, he was a character, a book of the Library, and he was *hers*. He was hers and the Library was hers and the books—the books were *hers*. "Claire. Don't be mean."

"I'm not!" Claire threw up her hands. "This is just . . . parts! Pieces! Bone and blood! Ink doesn't make a story any more than paper does! This thing—"

*Ink, ink and blood and the flare of a fire that destroyed everything she cherished. Andras's laughter, and the dry slide of wyrm scales against crushed pages as the acrid smoke seized her lungs. Blocks of soot black as the Library burned.* Heat washed up Brevity's face, and the memory choked her. Probity was staring at her, suddenly full of concern. She squeezed her eyes shut, but the anger slipped out from her lips. "You don't get it. You never got it. You don't even see them!"

Them, the colors. The color of a story, the light that slips through the cracks of all stories. The cracks where the lights slipped out and the reader slipped in. She saw the colors in the books and the colors in the ink. Bile crept up her tongue. What they'd let happen to the books, what Claire wanted to *do*—to shut them away like they never existed—

A rumble shivered through her feet. The air splintered and groaned. Brevity's eyes snapped open in time to see the faerie lights detach from the stacks and whizz in a frenzy overhead, stabbing light and shadow down on them. One whipped near enough to Claire's face to graze a cut across her cheek. In a distant row, something toppled off a high shelf and the impact echoed. The pause frothed with the sound of ruffled pages, disquiet books.

Brevity. Brevity had done that. She'd gotten upset and the Library had responded. She gasped. "I'm sorry—"

"No." Claire held perfectly still, a stricken look in her eyes. She waited until the air quieted again to speak, voice thin and controlled as a scalpel. "We can speak more of this when—when you're less . . . emotional. We should go."

Claire glanced at Rami with a brief nod that was stiff enough to shatter, then turned and strode purposefully toward the doors. Ramiel's colorless silver gaze skipped over Probity to trace Brevity and Hero with a mournful look, but, ever the soldier, he followed at Claire's

back. The doors of the Unwritten Wing closed behind them, quiet as
snowfall.

It felt as if the air deflated out of the room with them. Brevity fell
into her chair and looked to see Hero sagging against the desk with a
lost look. They both sat heavily in the silence, clinging to the desk as
perhaps everything else felt unmoored. "What . . . what just *happened?*"

# 6

# RAMI

Characters. Boss says "they're just characters" when I press
her about the damsel suite. As if characters are a "just"-ish
thing to be. They're people! Essential, intense, emotional
lives, scrubbed down and stripped away and honed to a cutting edge. That's how you fascinate a reader. Characters are
more real than real. That's what fiction is. Why else do stories
make them suffer or make them change? They're mirrors and
foils. Every muse is taught that. We fall a little in love with
every character we meet. Maybe the story of humanity is
learning to be brave enough to be the character in their own
story.

*Apprentice Librarian Brevity, 2016 CE*

RAMIEL HAD TAKEN TIME over the last half a year to become familiar with the confounding mortal who had upended his chance at eternal rest, and the only thing he'd ascertained for sure was that Claire
had precisely two forms of walking. One was purposeful, when she had
a destination in mind—and she nearly always did. Back straight, chin
forward, heels clicking, long, swift strides that sent the torn edges of
her skirts frothing like waves.

And then there was this walk. Claire had barely paid attention to the gargoyle as they'd exited, and now she took the stairs in a silent flutter. No less swift, no less decisive, but it was as if the space she'd taken up had narrowed. Shoulders tugged in, feet placed one in front of the other as if walking on an eternal tightrope. Narrowed, focused, but drifting all the same.

· It was her thinking walk. Not when Claire was just thinking—the infernal librarian was always thinking—but when she was thinking without *resolution*.

It's not as if Rami knew the resolution to . . . Hell, he wasn't even sure he was clear about what had happened. They'd discovered an anomaly, Claire had been injured, and in the librarian's infinite illogic, that meant they'd tested that anomaly in the Unwritten Wing and everything had gone . . . askew.

Ramiel wasn't used to disorientation. He'd worked in several dimensions of existence, after all, before the Fall. He liked to think he had a reasonably flexible perception of reality. But when Claire had placed the blackened pen point to the page, all hell (to abuse the term) had broken loose.

"Quarantine," Claire said softly to herself. Rami waited a polite moment to confirm that she was actually addressing him before clearing his throat.

"Ma'am?"

"Yes? Oh yes, Rami. I do not like the idea of leaving a pool of that malicious ink open to the air, but we'll need to section off that area until I can convince the wing to repair itself," said Claire as she dropped her pen case on the worktable near the door. "And I'd feel better if we locked up the more . . . porous . . . curio items until this is all settled. Anything cloth or paper should be moved, at the very least."

"Arcanist."

"As part of the Library it's going to be difficult to keep damsels out, but I think we can whip up a ward that will discourage them at the very least. Of course, it would be much easier if the Unwritten Wing had the *sense* to lock down and turn away visitors, but I don't suppose we should hope for that much wisdom right now. It is our duty to crack on. We should also take care to watch the door—"

"*Claire.*" Rami put just enough sharpness in his voice to finally halt Claire's tightrope pacing. She glanced up at him with an affronted look, which Rami tried to mollify with a raised hand. "What happened, up there? You're rattled."

"I didn't—" Claire bit her lip before speaking further. She very carefully looked anywhere but down at her hand. "I hadn't expected it to work. It *shouldn't* have worked. Unwritten stories aren't supposed to last beyond their books, Rami. That's the point of the Unwritten Wing—maintaining and caring for the books. Take Hero, for example; he's stuck as he is because his book's been damaged. If some part of a story can survive the *destruction* of its book, then what really are stories made of? The repercussions . . ."

Claire trailed off. Rami waited, but she didn't continue, instead stared distantly at the fountain pen on the table as if it were a viper. It was a sentence she wasn't prepared to finish—or couldn't finish—and Rami knew better than to press her. Instead, he placed it in a context that was safe for both of them. "And the responsibility of the Arcane Wing in this scenario?"

Claire snapped back to herself. "Safeguard artifacts of power. You're right—of course you're right," she said, though Rami really hadn't said anything clever. "It doesn't matter. Whatever this is, it's too dangerous to experiment with. Hell has always been obsessed with the

Library, and if they find out about this, they'll turn their eyes on the
Arcane Wing as well. And we're not nearly so well warded as the Unwritten Wing."

"When are we not under threat from demons?" Rami muttered.
"But Brevity and Hero seemed to think—"

"Brevity will come around. In the meantime, we have to protect
them from their incorrect assumptions." Claire diverted her eyes again
and began to fiddle with a stack of papers.

"Your hand?" Rami made a placating gesture as Claire glared at
him. "I only ask because it's my duty as your *assistant* to understand if
you are working under any . . . diminished capabilities."

"Do I look *diminished* to you?" Claire's chin jutted up, and it was
such a clear echo of Hero's pride and mannerisms, as much as she
faulted him for them. A distant fondness in his chest surprised Rami,
but he pressed it down. He almost missed that she'd avoided answering the question.

"You know you look never less than a force of nature to me, ma'am."
He'd discovered quickly that accurate observations, spoken as plainly
and earnestly as possible, toppled Claire's defensive airs fastest. "My
concern wasn't for your ability to keep up appearances."

"I—" Claire stopped herself and seemed to weigh the question. Her
voice was softer when she spoke again. "I will let you know, when I
know myself."

It was subtle, and shocking, but only if you understood Claire well
enough. Rami thought he did. Thought he knew what a free fall it
would be to feel uncertain about your mind, especially for one so certain and capable as Claire. But Rami's nature was to guide, not press
and poke. He waited, giving her the silence to say more if she chose.
But the woman just met his eyes and shook her head, ever so slightly.

"I'll be in the back. Get those artifacts isolated," she said over her shoulder, and Claire made a tactical retreat into the depths of the collection.

"POROUS" WAS A LOOSE attribute when one's collection of curiosities numbered in the tens of thousands. Rami had hit a snag when he'd started cross-indexing with an item's composition material. Paper and cloth were obvious, but now he was into the leathers. A stack of waxed dragon hides mocked him from the worktable, and the furrow in his brow deepened as he considered them. Yes, ink could stain leather, but what about variations? Waxed leather? Scale and aquatic varieties? There were too many variables, and Rami was shit at making these kinds of judgment calls.

On reflection, it should have been no surprise that he was a failure as an angel.

The great doors of the wing creaked on their hinges. Rami glanced up only long enough to frown at Hero's face before focusing back on his work. "Don't you ever have real work to do?"

"Watcher! Look at you, so industrious. Just the man I wanted to find. Odd thing, isn't it?" Hero said as he approached, as if he hadn't heard Rami. As if Rami was the kind of person Hero frequently sought conversation with. "Bits of book existing—surviving—that the librarians knew nothing about?"

"Not really." Rami eyed Hero as the character made a circuitous route of the worktable. "A travesty like Andras's failed coup has never been attempted before."

Hero paused, leaning down to inspect some petrified fingers that lay on a bed of velvet on a side table. "Perhaps not on that *scale*, but surely books have been lost before. Mishandling, accident, all those distinctly *human* errors."

The finger bones had a paralytic curse attached to them, Rami recalled. He should really warn Hero. "Are you trying to make a point, or simply enjoying the sound of your own voice?"

"Better than your endless stoicism. I swear, it's like a dull blade against stone."

He definitely wasn't going to warn Hero. The fingers were only a *little* paralytic, after all. Rami shrugged. "How else do you keep a blade sharp?"

Hero's fingertips paused over the artifact and surprise tugged at the arch of his brow. "Repartee? I didn't think you had it in you, old boy."

"Don't call me boy," Rami grumbled. "I'm older than your maker's maker. You have a point, don't you?"

A clever look bloomed on Hero's face. "Why, yes, I do. Cheeky of you to ask."

Rami stared for a beat until the salacious edge of Hero's smile sank in. "You . . ." He needed to clear his throat. "Save it for the damsels."

"Not when I know it irritates. I'm quite aware how repellent I am to you." Hero hummed. Rami steeled himself for another round of endless nattering, but instead Hero braced his hands on the table between them and leaned forward. "Never mind that. As I was saying . . . it raises the question, what else does the Library not know? What really *are* unwritten books?"

Nonporous; that decided it. The dragon hide was scaly, and coated in enough dark magic that it could fend for itself. Rami sniffed. "You are one. You should be able to tell me."

The lightness dropped from Hero's face in increments. "You would think so, wouldn't you? I could tell you every inkblot and footnote about my story, of course. But my book itself? Contrary to the poetry the librarians spout, the medium *is* different from the message. At least in this case." His face flickered before settling into something uncommonly serious. "I have a right to wonder about what I am, don't I?"

Rami shifted, folding his arms in front of himself for lack of something to do. As much as he liked to discount Hero's behavior for plots and antics, there was something disconcertingly earnest about him just now. And Ramiel always did have trouble ignoring earnest appeals for help. "Then shouldn't you be assisting Brevity with her research?" It's what he was supposed to be doing himself right now. For Claire. Yes, that was something safe to do. Rami abruptly grabbed the inventory log and walked toward the rows of storage.

Hero's footsteps followed behind him. Rami tried not to notice how much less springy and more purposeful they sounded now, soft, solid clicks against the hardwood. "With the Unwritten Wing and Arcane at odds, I don't think an answer is set to be found. Not here."

He was right, but Rami focused on locating the next item to be secured per Claire's orders: ah, a span of gold fleece. He folded it up with intense focus. "Claire and Brevity will sort it out. They always do."

"I'm not sure they will, this time," Hero said softly, and Rami risked a glance. Hero's gaze was unfocused, set somewhere at shelf height and a million miles away.

"What makes you think that?" Heaven curse him, Rami had really intended not to ask. But it was the wrinkle that tugged at the corner of Hero's distant gaze. It softened him a little. Made him look almost . . . sad. Almost human.

Rami had always had a weak spot for humans.

Hero's answer was a ponderous shake of the head. "Claire's always been bullheaded. That's not what I'm worried about. The muse always seems to see clear to soften her up and see sense eventually. But Brevity—" Hero's brow crinkled. "She's been under pressure. Not just with taking over the Unwritten Wing. She took the losses of the Library hard—every single book. You knew she was close to the damsels?"

"I assumed as books—"

"No," Hero snapped, then heaved a sigh. "Not as books, as *people*. We're people, not just dusty paper. The muse has always seen us . . . seen books . . . as individuals. Felt each loss individually too. It took a toll on her. There are times I catch her staring at the card catalog like a graveyard. She hides it well, but—" Hero stopped, gaze flinching sideways as if just realizing the way Rami watched him. He straightened, pulling on attitude like a rumpled vest. He plucked a finger at the gold wool in Rami's hands as if it was a displeasing wardrobe choice. "Well, not that I care, but muses are so *transparent*, and one might worry it might affect her ability to maintain my book."

"Your book. Yes." Rami paused with the golden wool enveloping his hands. He hadn't had great call to spend a lot of time with the broken book. He knew Hero was of the antagonist type of his book; he knew he was a fine swordsman; he knew he never failed to taunt and irritate Claire when presented with the opportunity. Rami knew Hero had escaped the Library once, though he seemed to have stayed content here since the coup, for no reason that Rami could discern.

None of the things he knew made Rami likely to trust him. Not, at least, as he'd begun to trust Claire and Brevity. He'd mostly avoided Hero—found him an irritating distraction whenever they shared the same space—and thought the feeling had been mutual, as Hero had returned the favor.

And yet here he was. Asking . . . for what exactly? "You propose an independent investigation?" Rami guessed.

"An independent investigation," Hero said with a horrible stodgy impression of Rami's voice, a mock frown distorting his face for effect. "Yes, that's an excellent term for it. Let's call it that."

Rami didn't find that reassuring, but he couldn't find fault in gathering more information, at least. "Your wing is the one with the books."

"Not," Hero said cautiously, "the ones we need."

It took Rami more than a couple of moments to follow that thought to the insane place it led. He stepped back and had to resist crumpling the fleece in his fist. "You mean *outside* the Library?"

"Not technically!" Hero said quickly. "Just a different wing! Or two. Three."

"Outside of Hell. You, the runaway book. They'll never allow it." Rami shook his head and stomped down the aisle, cursing himself for humoring Hero for even a moment. "This is just an excuse to you."

"It's not. I swear it's not! Watcher—" He heard Hero's steps scrabble with less grace than usual behind him. Rami picked up his speed and Hero uttered a curse. "You plodding stone of an angel, if you would just—"

Rami would not *just*. He stormed ahead, turned the corner to the vault Claire intended for the artifacts—and nearly ran straight into a narrow wall of velvet and copper.

Hero stood in front of the vault entrance, limbs splayed like some kind of particularly stylish spider. The pose was ridiculous, but Hero still managed to look determined.

"Move," Rami gritted through his teeth.

"Not until you listen, stone man." When Rami didn't rush him, Hero slowly lowered his arms. "I've thought a lot about this—"

"I bet you have."

"I've thought a lot about *books*, you clod," Hero corrected, clicking his tongue. "Claire took over the Library prematurely, right? After her little act of heartsick rebellion and murder?"

"Claire has suffered enough. I won't have you—"

Hero fluttered a hand. "Not my point. I mean her training was . . .

truncated. Cut. Short. What did Gregor not get a chance to pass down? I have read the entries, at least what the log would show me. Training went on for *decades* typically. Claire had three years. That's it. What knowledge was lost in that moment? And what knowledge was lost about the Arcane Wing because Andras had to go and get that damned plot in his head?"

Rami shifted with the disquiet thought. "Claire and Brevity—"

"Do the best they can, I know." Hero's face was somber, and more open than Rami had ever seen it. Hero took a step forward, tentatively, then another, until he could put a placating hand on Rami's knuckles.

He was crushing the gold fleece. Blast it. Rami forced himself to loosen his grip. "But that's why this ink business has them with their hackles up and backed into a corner," Hero said, steady but persistent. "They don't know. And they need to know. But neither of them is free to question it. Claire only sees another threat. Brevity only sees redemption. That means it's up to *us*."

"Up to us to do *what*, exactly?" Rami tried and failed to insert the proper amount of skepticism in that question. Worry had begun to gnaw at him too.

"To find answers. Answers that won't be found here, with too much lost from both the Arcane and Unwritten Wings. But answers that might have been preserved in other wings of the Library. Wings not in Hell. You saw Valhalla—there *are* answers out there, Rami. I know it."

"In the other wings of the Library," Rami repeated. And he couldn't quite believe he was saying it, to be honest. "But you're . . ." He made a vague gesture first at Hero's wrist and then at the . . . well, the rest of him.

"Stamped. Part of the permanent collection of the Unwritten Wing, yes. I remember." Hero took on an indulgent tone. "And I won't be breaking the rules. Books are lent between libraries all the time via the IWL."

"*Librarians* lend books. Last I checked, you were not a librarian."

"I'm an *assistant to* the librarian," Hero said firmly, then shrugged. "I've found clever openings in the Library wards before. It's not hard if you know where to look."

Rami narrowed his eyes. "You never told anyone how you did that."

"Well, then." Hero hummed. "I'd think it your duty to take any opportunity to investigate this security flaw."

Hero's wide-eyed look was impressive. Rami was not impressed. "Or I could just tell Brevity and Claire."

"Yes, tell them I discovered a way to escape the wards of the Library. Which they already know. And that I have been a loyal—"

"Stamped—"

"—*loyal* character and book and assistant ever since. Wounded in the line of duty, even." He tilted his head, allowing the light to hit the dark whirl of scar tissue on his cheek, still discolored with inky shadows even after healing. Hero was a vain creature and had definitely taken to standing to the side, tilting his expression just so to show his "good side." He chose not to do so now, and though his smile was crooked and mocking, Rami didn't miss the twitch of discomfort as he did so.

Rami held little pity for him. Watchers might have long lives, but long lives come with long memory, and so he remembered every pointless struggle, every doomed fight. Even with the ones he won he felt the pieces of what he lost. Every survivor wore scars and weariness. Ramiel was an angel, a first creation of his Creator, but he knew he was not finely or gloriously made.

Not like Hero.

But Rami *was* practical. And even if this plan was entirely non-sense, the reasoning behind it was not. The existence of the ink threatened to drive a wedge between the wings of Hell's Library, and the Library had only just become Rami's new sanctuary. His purpose. It even dared to become a home, given enough time, but Rami wasn't foolish enough to hold out hope for that. Still.

It was something worth protecting. And the people in it. Rami had come to that conclusion six months ago, adrift after saving Leto's human soul—then losing him to Heaven. Rami had watched Uriel, the archangel driven vengeful and mad over her own fear, be unmade right in front of him. She'd been unmade, by a single word from Claire's lips. Even as a fallen Watcher, he should have sought justice, exacted vengeance. Instead, he'd told Claire he'd protect the Library, serve the Library. There might indeed be answers elsewhere. But Claire couldn't leave Hell, not without a ghostlight and *especially* not injured and stained with malicious magic. But Rami had no such challenges placed upon him.

He supposed it was a way to serve.

"Supposing . . . we investigate," Rami said slowly. He abruptly remembered the fleece in his hands. He turned away from Hero's intense gaze to place the artifact on a shelf in the vault. He took his time smoothing down the wool and shooing Hero out to lock the vault behind him. It gave him time to think. Rami needed time to think. He finally faced Hero again. "Supposing we investigate. You will swear to return to the Unwritten Wing, with answers?"

"Villain's honor." Hero held out a hand, grinning as Rami's scowl deepened. "I'll come back, promise. What's the use of running? Brevity can summon my book back anytime. I'll have you to keep an eye on me, and a mystery to unravel. What more could I want?"

"A mystery, you call it. To find out what the other realms know that we don't. To find out what books are."

Hero's smile faltered, but he rallied as Rami reluctantly shook his hand. "To find out what I am."

Hero's hand was surprisingly warm, and as Rami closed his hand around it, the book's long fingers fluttered over the skin of his wrist.

*An investigation.* Just an investigation. Rami rooted the thought in his mind, hoping it would drive away the uncertain turn in his stomach.

# 7

# BREVITY

You'll have constant encounters with the Muses Corps in your tenure as librarian of the Unwritten Wing. Don't be alarmed by their strange habits or their ever-changing, ever-colorful faces. Muses are born of desire. They wear dreams like plumage.

When muses mature, they take aspects, not names. There have been a hundred muses of joy and there will be a hundred more. There will only ever be one Library.

*Librarian Yoon Ji Han, 1803 CE*

THE LIBRARIAN'S LOG WAS a thorough bit of magic. To the plain eye it was a thick book with a battered cover, thick pages inside filled with entries from librarians over the ages of the Unwritten Wing's existence. Brevity could tell the difference in the handwriting. Each script in wildly different yet legible scrawl, no matter the librarian's origin, literacy, or native language. Brevity was glad that whatever magics fueled the logbook didn't smooth away those differences, at least. It gave a delightful bit of insight and personality to the logbook. You could tell a lot about a librarian by their handwriting. There were Yoon Ji Han's utilitarian notes in blocky lines, straight and unforgiving as his instructions. And here were Ibukun's warnings, letters like spears. And Fleur's looping lush scribble, always taking over the lines above and below it. Uncontainable, full of life. Brevity always thought she would have liked Fleur.

She liked sitting there, studying the earliest entries by librarians long gone. Occasionally she got carried away and flipped toward the front. Her fingers skimmed over Claire's entries, each loop and dot carefully placed. Not rigid, but narrower and more precise as the years went on. As if her hands had forgotten how to flow. It made Brevity's heart clench, but not nearly as much as when the official entries abruptly stopped.

*21st of June 2019. Book retrieval has led to a complication. I shall close the Library for safekeeping while we investigate this Codex Gigas with Arcanist Andras's kind assistance.*

The next time the Unwritten Wing was logged as open after that was in Brevity's frazzled, scrawling hand. She didn't read those. She already knew exactly what they said.

*I shouldn't be here. This isn't fair. None of this is fair.*

Hell isn't about being fair. The rebuttal formed in her thoughts in Claire's perfect posh voice. Still, Brevity had felt the Library was different, *should* have been different. The Library was not Hell. Books were supposed to be shelter from the demons of the world. The decision the books of the Library had made to cast Claire out wasn't what a Library should have done.

A shiver brought her attention up, away from the logbook. A familiar breeze drifted through the Library stacks, queer and impossible in the best way, and that drove straight to Brevity's heart. It smelled like the color thirteen; it felt warm as violet; it whispered cardamom binaries.

It had a homey tune to it that Brevity had thought she'd almost forgotten.

Every author hopes, prays, for the muses to visit them. Brevity was probably the first librarian in history to wish she could hide under the table.

Instead, she took a slow, centering breath—in four through nose, out five through mouth—and turned toward the figure that approached, not from the wing's front doors, but from the gloom of the stacks.

Probity carried a small pot of balm in her hands like a peace offering. "Sis, how's the arm?" She didn't wait for an answer but did stop a pace sooner than she usually did. She gestured to the pot she held. "I brought this for you. It's a mixture that helps with inspiration gilt burn."

Probity surely meant it to be kind; the stab of guilt Brevity suffered was all her own. Of course she'd know Brevity was in pain. Muses carried inspiration, from the places they were born—called wells—to humanity. It was supposed to be a temporary transcendent state. Muses, gilded in the glow of possibilities, embracing their chosen artists and leaving something behind. Inspiration—and all the hard work of creation that could only come from humans, of course, but muses tended to gloss over that part.

The inspiration that a muse wore was supposed to be temporary. It wasn't healthy for a muse to wear it for too long. When Brevity had stolen it for herself, she knew there would be repercussions.

She just never thought she'd lose it.

"What's in it?" Brevity asked instead.

Probity rolled her shoulders in a shrug. "Your usual stuff. A little mugwort. Tatterdales. Dried fablesnare. Oil of idlesave. A pinch of ear of glint. And a healthy slap of gin."

Brevity tilted her head. "You were never interested in alchemy before."

"I had . . . questions. After you left. And a lot of feelings." Probity ducked her head, hiding her face behind a fall of lavender hair. "Studying something . . . anything. It seemed the best way to settle them."

"You've grown up so much," Brevity murmured, mostly to herself, but Probity's ears still tipped pink.

"Ideas never die." Probity mumbled it under her breath, suddenly shy. The phrase landed with ripples in Brev's memory. It'd been something they'd told each other often, as awe-addled young muses. Half-drunk at the power of humans and with the vague appetite to change the world that all new souls had. Ideas never die. It wasn't a catchphrase, precisely; it was a promise.

Probity motioned, and Brevity slowly held out her bare arm. There was only a pale line where the gilded tattoo had been, but it felt like the raw furrows of a wound. The balm smelled like limes when she opened the lid, and Brevity did her best not to wince when Probity began to gently slather it on. She couldn't help a sharp intake of air as she began to rub it in, though. "Why does it hurt so much? It never hurt when I pulled it off before."

"Because you never truly *gave it up* before. Not just momentarily releasing it, but actually removing its place on your arm. I made you give it up." Probity's fingers were precise and featherlight. As long as Brevity had been in her acquaintance, Probity's demeanor had been as steady and gentle as her cashmere layers. Her bangs were in her face, but they shifted when Probity gave her a shy, sorrowful look. "I'm sorry. I didn't want to do that to you."

"I asked you to." Brevity couldn't keep the loss out of her own voice. She offered a thin smile. "We saved Claire, so it's worth it."

Probity made a huffing sound at that, lips turning troubled. She pulled clean linen from an inner pocket and began to carefully wrap Probity's arm in white. "You're worth a hundred of that human."

Warmth melted a chip off the hollow feeling in Brevity's chest. She smiled. "C'mon, Prob. I thought you were only supposed to tell the truth."

Probity tied off the bandage and pinned Brevity with a small sulk. "I am. That woman was a horrible librarian. She used you. She *misused* you."

"She didn't . . ." Brevity hesitated, before amending, "She didn't mean to."

Probity had been less defined growing up. The Probity that Brevity had known was a coltish question mark, the opposite of moral certainty. But she seemed comfortable in her own skin now. Her gangly limbs had grown into something wiry and strong, but the same wide eyes still scrutinized Brevity with a knowing gleam.

"But you're the librarian now. This is major, Brev." Probity squeezed her hands shyly. "I heard. We all heard, after it happened. I'm so proud of you. And I'm here to help you change things."

A flutter of unease intruded on Brevity's happiness. "That's why the corps sent you here, really."

"In a way, yes." Probity appeared able to read the alarm in Brevity's face and shook her head. "I volunteered, though. I've missed you. Are you— How are you?" Brevity let out a shaky sigh and didn't even have to put words to it. Probity made a tsking noise and guided her by the shoulder. "Enough work. Sit."

"But I was going to make tea—"

"I'll do it. Isn't that what you have your assistant for?"

"Hero's my assistant."

"Hero is a character and a book." A streak of awe shored up the pity in Probity's voice. "He's a treasure and a tragedy to be sure, but you can't expect him to care for you as I could."

"You haven't exactly caught us at our best, you know." Brevity allowed herself to be manhandled onto the couch with minimal argument.

"Then it is a good thing I'm here to care for both of you," Probity said as she placed the pot on the warmer. "You took care of me enough when we were young—won't you let me return the favor?"

"Oh. It's just—you came at an awkward time. I'm thrilled to see you—" And, gods, she was. Probity had been like a little sister as a half-grown muse. Following Brevity around, her fierce shadow. Seeing her grown made a quiet ache form in her chest, a kind of homesickness. "But . . . the ink, Claire . . . the Library. I don't know what to do."

"That's why I'm here." Probity's smile was firm with resolve. "To help you."

A distant voice in her head—one that sounded posh and stern and Claire-like—advised caution at such a grand statement. But this was Probity, as close to family as Brevity had ever had. Probity didn't lie—it wasn't in her nature. If she was here to help her, then she was. "After the fire, all the peop—all the books we lost. I thought—I thought we failed. But now, this ink—" She wasn't making much sense. Brevity sensed with relief that Probity didn't care. "It can't be just a coincidence. It *is* the books we lost, isn't it? The stories, I mean. Can we get them back? The stories that we destroyed?" Brevity asked, leaning forward. "Is it possible?"

"Destroyed?" Probity blinked. She stilled a moment, gaze flicking up and down Brevity with a new assessment before her hands came up in an aborted comforting gesture. Instead she fetched the steeped tea and pressed a cup of it into Brevity's hands. "Oh. Oh, sis. You didn't destroy them."

It was too much. It was all too much. The fear for the damsels, the ink, the argument with Claire, and now the appearance of her lost family, telling her the one thing she wished was true. Heat welled up and Brevity's vision blurred. "What do you mean? The books—"

The memory clogged her throat. She'd seen them. Seen the pages curl in translucent flames, been the last one to catch a glimpse of their words, ash on black. Heard the crack of leather, the smell like burnt flesh. And then she'd held small cold hands, as so many damsels faded away, drifting to death on a shiver of ash. She'd seen them *go*. And afterward she'd sobbed herself empty as they gathered and interred what ashes they could. Breathing in the soot of lost stories. Leto had hugged her, though he wasn't supposed to touch anyone by then. And then she lost him too.

Probity had wrapped an arm around her and didn't say a word. Brevity got herself under control, even if her voice was thin as paper as she repeated, "What do you mean?"

"You didn't destroy them," Probity repeated gently. "What happened was a travesty. That, that *woman*"—Probity's comforting pats turned a little more forceful as she mentioned Claire—"she was not fit to hold the title of a librarian. She barely is fit to hold the title of a human. The things she did, that she allowed to be done. But even she can't destroy a story."

It was true that Claire had sunk into a fierce, hurtful isolation when she'd taken the title of librarian. Hiding her own hurts, she'd become rigid with the rules and exacting in enforcing them. She'd been harsh and cold when Brevity had joined the Library. But hadn't they all changed since then? Brevity barely knew where to start, but old loyalty rose first. "Claire worked harder than anyone. She was a—"

"She treated you *horribly!*" There was earnest anger there, and Probity's voice was harder now than when she'd spoken of the books. "That's why you were sent here, wasn't it? For punishment. I can't imagine how hard it was. Sis . . ." Probity searched her face with a deep, earnest kind of sympathy.

Brevity started to shake her head. "But it wasn't—"

"But even a bad librarian can't destroy stories. They're made of stronger stuff than that." The smile on Probity's lips was brief before dropping into a darker expression. "Only the living can kill a story. Humans do it every day."

The animosity in Probity's soft voice was a velvet razor, the threat of which was impossible to miss. A cutting change, swift and harsh as a rockfall, came across her expression. But Brevity was distracted by what else she was saying. "You're saying the damsels—the unwritten books—are still alive."

Probity shook her head. "'Alive' is . . . a funny way to put it. No, the books are destroyed and gone, but the *stories* . . . the potential . . . that's preserved in the ink. And that's the powerful part."

Claire had said something similar, and the way the ink had swarmed and fluxed on the log page certainly seemed like a living thing. Brevity's gaze strayed to where the logbook rested, closed and inert on the massive librarian's desk. Brevity still thought of it as Claire's desk. "We could bring them back?"

"I thought that small, too, at first," Probity whispered, drawing Brevity's attention back. She was shaking her head with some kind of deep empathy. "We're taught to think that small. But seeing the ink work the wonders it did . . . that it exists is a miracle. It's a sign. You have the Library now—and the support of the Muse Corps. Think about it, sis! We can do more than just restore the way things were."

We. Being a "we" with the muses again; longing for that warred with the caution still echoing in Brevity's head. "Like what?"

Probity's bottom lip worried and caught between her teeth, seeming to hesitate over her words. She took a breath. "New books, fresh books. We would replace what the Library lost and more." There was a hopeful, sunrise kind of light in Probity's gray eyes, like her entire face was blooming. It brightened her, brought to mind old games and pranks they'd played, and made Brevity smile.

"Like, new stories? Brand-new? How could that be possible? Which humans—"

"It's possible." Probity clutched her hands in front of her, almost as if she were still that little sister. Sisters, sharing a secret daydream. "New stories, recovered stories. Who knows what else? But first we need a sample of the ink to experiment."

That snapped over Brevity like a flinch of frost. She straightened. "No more experiments. Claire and I already tried. You saw what happened. It rejected the paper straight out."

Probity thought about that for a moment, growing solemn and certain. "Then next time we don't try paper."

There were so many options, Brevity had trouble deciding which part of that sentence alarmed her more. As she passed Probity's shoulder, she caught a glancing wisp of emerald and periwinkle near the Library doors. That was a color combination she'd recognize anywhere. "Oh, Hero! Over here."

A moment later, the man himself appeared in the doorway. His step hesitated as he noticed Probity, but he continued over to them with a shake of his head. "I don't know how you always hear me coming."

His book might have rejected him, but he still streamed colors like any unwritten book in her eyes. Brevity chewed on the grin that threatened. "Just a muse thing, I guess." She turned her head to share her amusement with Probity, but a change had come over the younger muse. The excited look she'd had while explaining her dream to Brevity, the soft way she'd talked about the plight of stories, had turned pitying with the presence of one. Probity's eyes lingered on Hero as he approached, and she tensed from what Brevity could only guess were nerves.

"Everything all right downstairs?" Brevity asked lightly.

"Claire has the Watcher locking up artifacts," Hero said with a brief disapproving purse of his lips.

"Don't be afraid. She can't touch you anymore," Probity reassured him a little too intensely. Hero gave her an odd look.

"Ah . . . yes. The monster is dead. I can finally sleep soundly." Probity didn't appear to catch the droll twist of Hero's reply. She'd never been adept at sarcasm. Brevity quietly winced inside. Hero shrugged. "I suppose locking things up is what a librarian is best at."

"She is not the librarian," Probity said before Brevity could answer. She pinned Hero with a pitying look. "As a book you know that."

"Do I? Thank you for the reminder. But as *assistant librarian*," Hero said through a sharp-toothed smile, "I know how closely the Unwritten Wing and the Arcane Wing collaborate."

"Tea, Hero?" Brevity interrupted, before Hero could further sharpen his tongue on Probity's misplaced pity. She snatched the pot Probity had brewed off the stand. "Have some tea, Prob."

"No, thank you," Hero said while Probity accepted a cup. He gave Brevity a cautious glance. "I thought I'd spend some time in the stacks. Inventory, see if there's anything the damsels need."

Brevity wasn't sure which was more suspect: Hero volunteering for inventory or Hero concerned for the damsels. She was not stupid, but it was obvious Hero wanted an excuse to avoid Brevity and her guest for a while.

She nodded assent and pointed to the cart loaded with books. "Those go back to the children's fantasy section, please."

Hero approached the cart, glanced at a title, and made a face. "Imaginary-friend stories. Why are these even books? I *hate* it when they wake up."

"That's why we shelve them *quietly*."

Hero sniffed and kicked the cart ahead of him, in the direction of the stacks. "As you say. You're the boss." It never sounded the same when he said it. Less like a title and more like a reminder of what she wasn't and never would be. Had it been the same for Claire?

"He's forgotten his book," Probity said contemplatively into the silence Hero's departure left behind. "It's a terrible tragedy for one to carry."

"Hero's making the best of it." Probity hadn't precisely said anything malicious, but Brevity felt a surge of protective instinct. "He's learning fast."

"And moving farther and farther away from his story." Probity shook her head with a distant look in her eyes. "It'd almost have been kinder if he'd burned."

Brevity's stomach recoiled and brought her out of her chair. "Don't say that."

"I'm sorry. I know it's not what anyone wants to hear, but the truth rarely is," Probity reminded her, a pitying look in her eyes. "Think of it, sis. He'll never be written, and now he doesn't even have the company of his own kind in his story. He exists simply as a reminder of the Library's failure to protect him."

That pierced a little too close to the darker spots in Brevity's heart. "I'm trying to take care of everyone," she said softly.

"Oh, sis, not you." Probity looked far more abashed than she had when talking about Hero. She stood and touched Brevity's arm apologetically. "You are doing everything right. You are setting so much right. You shouldn't even be here. I simply meant he'll never have his story, a character without an ending. What kind of life is that? At least loss is decisive."

The oily feeling in Brevity's gut was a mix of horror and old wounds. There was some truth in what Probity said—there was always *some* truth, but Brevity had learned long ago that some truth was not all truth. "Stop it. You weren't there. The fire, when it took the books . . ." She gulped down the bile that threatened to rise and squeezed her eyes closed until her stomach behaved itself.

"You saw one fire," Probity said quietly. "I've seen them all."

Brevity opened her eyes to question that but stopped. Probity was already lost in thought, looking into the shadows of the Library but seeing something else.

"They burn them first, the stories. Humans always come for the stories first. It's their warm-up, before they start burning other humans. It's their first form of control, to burn the libraries, to burn the books, to burn the archives of a culture. Humans are the stories they tell. If you want to destroy your enemy, destroy their stories. Even if the people survive, it will be as if they never existed at all."

Brevity chewed on her lip. "Humans do a lotta terrible things during war—"

"War," Probity said, and it was caught somewhere between amusement and agony. "Shall we revisit the peacetime burning, then? Libraries censored and burned, the stories that died and were forgotten by accident, by neglect, by ignorance, by—and here, the most notorious peacetime murderer of all—by *piety*. Books burned because they threatened Bronze Age beliefs and scared old men in long robes. I'm not sure if humans have sacrificed more ink than blood to their gods over the years, but if not, it has to be a near thing."

No one liked to speak about the books that were lost, especially muses. Brevity knew it, had mourned along with the others as each precious story they'd ushered to the page was destroyed. Each story that'd managed to get out of the Unwritten Wing only to fall to nothing. It was like a midwife losing entire villages of children to war and ignorance. At least while they'd remained in the Unwritten Wing, they'd been possible. After a story was written and burned . . . there was only one fate for that. Each one hurt. And then each one had raged, and then . . . somewhere along the way . . .

"It's why you did what you did, wasn't it?" Probity glanced up, and it wasn't accusation in her eyes now; it was understanding.

To her credit, Probity's gaze didn't waver, didn't drop to Brevity's folded arms. The ghostly scars of gilt twitched, as if knowing it had been summoned. Brevity still remembered it, remembered when the loops and curls of magic hadn't been on her skin but in her hands, strands of pure inspiration, a human's inspiration. The giddy feeling of holding the seeds of a story. She had delivered it to unknowing humans a thousand times before, but that time . . .

That time she hadn't.

The betrayal had taken only an instant. Hands clutching, feeling the cool-warm flutter under her palms as she pressed the inspiration close to her chest. It'd fluxed, a bare moment of protest before finding her skin and flowing. No flash of brilliance hit her, no genius inspiration of her own—of course not; it wasn't hers—but the strands of inspiration had wrapped seamlessly over the skin of her arm and stayed.

There wasn't a law against stealing inspiration from a human, but then again, there wasn't a law only because it was unthinkable. Not just a crime; a moral travesty. Brevity had been expelled, the first muse to ever have her duty revoked. She'd been cast out and sent to the Unwritten Wing, where she could perhaps do no more harm and, the muses had likely thought, be tortured by the presence of stillborn stories she couldn't touch.

"So, you know," Probity was saying at barely a whisper, as if knowing she was intruding on Brevity's worst memories. "You have to know. We should serve the stories, not the humans. They've been a necessity for a long time, but they're flawed. Humans aren't worthy of the stories we bring them."

"What?" Brevity shook her head. "That's not—"

"You can't think of a different way it could be, but look at it, at least! The whole system is wrong. Why do we expend realms' worth of effort—the Library, the books, the muses, all of us—to try to entrust our most precious gifts to the most callous, plodding, destructive mortal creatures? Tell me how that makes sense!"

Brevity hesitated. "Humans are special; they can create stories—"

"And destroy them."

"But humanity, creation, takes a human soul."

"Does it?" Probity asked, and the question had such a fine razor point that Brevity stopped.

"What do you mean, 'Does it?'"

"Does it really take humans to make a story? Yes, they spin up the pieces, but they seem to need an awful lot of help from us." Probity paused and leaned closer, hesitant, as if there were a bubble between them that might break with the slightest wrong word. "What if we took them *back*? We could skip the middleman. What if the stories were ours?"

Brevity's world flipped. She took a shaky breath and shook her head. "No, when I stole the inspiration I didn't get any of the story. It's not possible."

"Maybe not from the inspiration. It's too distilled, the wrong form to work with. We'd need something closer to the end goal," Probity said thoughtfully.

Brevity stared at her. "The ink. That's why you were so excited about the ink. I already told you, it's impossible." When Probity said nothing, Brevity's brow furrowed. "But how would that even work?"

Not *could* but *would*. Brevity realized the mistake after she said it. Probity met her gaze cautiously, hopefully. "It would just take a small sample to try. I have some ideas, if you'd help me. You and me, Brev. Don't you remember how that used to be?"

That was the difficult part: of course Brevity remembered. She'd always felt better working with someone rather than alone. And helping train Probity had been the best of her memories as a muse. Working together, struggling together, wondering together. Probity had been so studious and good at anchoring down Brevity's wild leaps of ideas, the same way—oh, and there it was. Memories blurred from working with Probity to working with Claire in the Library.

"No," Brevity said, more to herself than anyone else. Even her own ears didn't believe it. "That's not what the Library is for."

"Sis." Probity touched her shoulder, looking at her with all the worship and steady belief of a child reunited with her hero. But they weren't the eyes of a youth anymore. Probity looked at her with the certainty of hope. "But what if it's what *you* are made for? Librarians have always been revolutionaries, right?" Brevity thought of the logbook, of Poppaea's rebellion and Gregor's skeptical pragmatism and Fleur's unorthodox means. She had to nod. Probity smiled. "Maybe this is *your* revolution. The system is broken; it's got to change. Maybe you're the one to fix it."

It was an alluring thought, one of stories and quests, but Brevity's anxiety was quick to remind her of the other way those stories ended. "But what if it breaks instead?"

"You can't break something that's already broken. Stop protecting things you could make better." Probity's hand slid down her arm, then dropped, hesitantly. She gave her a slip of a smile to soften her frustration. "Please. Think about it, at least."

# 8

# CLAIRE

Remake the Library. That's what they tell me, as if it should
be so simple. They tossed out the old librarian, as if chasing
off a wild dog, but left all the books. There you go: have at it.
Ha! As if books are all that's needed to make a library. My
people, we know libraries.

Stories are more than ink on pages. Libraries are more
than scrolls stacked upon shelves. There is something untold
here.

*Librarian Madiha al-Fihri, 603 CE*

QUARANTINE, CLAIRE HAD SAID, and she would have sworn it
echoed differently against the flat oak shelves of the Arcane Wing.
*Alone*, repeated back to her unsettlingly. It was a small mercy when
Rami set about the inventory and Claire could retreat to her desk.

The Arcane Wing hadn't had a proper office under Andras. The
demon had appeared to enjoy conducting the entire place like a lab. He
did any record keeping from the expanse of worktables at the front of
the collection. Or, more likely, foisted the more tedious tasks off onto
the abominations he called assistants. One of the very first changes the
wing had made for Claire's comfort, after lightening the aesthetic

gloom, was developing a small alcove along the back wall, past the empty rookeries. It was a cubby, really, just enough space for Claire's battered desk, chair, and row of shelves on the wall above that seemed to always hold precisely the record necessary.

It was a tiny space Claire could feel was entirely her own, in a place and routine that decidedly weren't. When she turned her chair just so, she could almost imagine she was in the corner of some distant library. It was usually a place to be alone.

Usually, when there wasn't a disgruntled-looking giant raven lurking on the back of her chair.

"Bird." Claire sighed and pulled a drawer open to scavenge some self-defense bread crumbs.

Andras had kept ravens—as experiment subjects, as hostages, perhaps both—when he'd been Arcanist. Not just any ravens—Odin's ravens. Ravens of Valhalla. Ferocious warrior-spies for the Norse realm. Gods knew what Andras had planned. Claire had been happy enough to free them in exchange for help reclaiming the Unwritten Wing. The raven women were welcome allies, and lethal and merciless against Andras's demons.

Afterward, they'd left with their leader, back to Valhalla. All except one old, lazy she-raven. She roosted in the rafters and showed up occasionally to peck at Claire and be a nuisance. She delighted in causing chaos. Claire had taken to just calling the creature Bird, since she'd never seen her transform into a human shape. Perhaps she had forgotten how. Perhaps she couldn't. Perhaps Andras had kept one regular, boring, mortal raven from the human world in the cages, just to have a go at everyone. That would have been his kind of humor.

*Trapped and cornered in a cage, everyone's the same feral animal, pup. Remember that.* The voice in her head was still there, her memory of Andras the Benevolent Mentor, not Andras the Buggered Traitor.

Claire fed the raven anyway, though she would deign to talk to it only when Rami wasn't around. He already worried about her sanity, after she'd survived witnessing Uriel face-to-face. He really was a fussy one, for a being that had seen epochs come and go. But he had a good heart, and she'd grown too fond to worry him.

"No, I haven't told him yet. And I'm not going to," Claire said to the reproachful look Bird gave her. She hadn't said a word about the whispers to anyone yet. It wasn't that she feared Brevity, Rami, or even Hero wouldn't *believe* her. It was just, given her history, the presence of voices no one else could hear after a dramatic event like a near-death staining might raise some alarms. Alarms were fussy things. Claire couldn't get a smidge of work done with them.

She found a broken biscuit behind a bottle of ink that satisfied Bird long enough for Claire to reclaim her chair. The sigh that pushed past her lips as she flopped into the dim of the alcove was not entirely intentional. Her stained hand came to rest, palm up, in her lap. It didn't feel different, besides a perpetually damp, chilly sensation that had her rechecking that she wasn't leaving wet fingerprints of ink on everything she touched. She hoped she still *had* fingerprints; it was rather hard to tell under all the black.

Bird resettled on the edge of the open drawer, biscuit crumbling between her scaly claws. Her feathers were fluffed into a dusty storm cloud that said she had no intention of taking the bribe and leaving Claire in peace. Bird destroyed the biscuit industriously, then set to snapping up a pen cap and rapping it against the desk. At least her random blats and gravel-filled squawks were anchors of solid, weighty things. Real things. Claire put aside the question of whispers and focused on the more productive question of the ink.

"Back to work," Claire muttered to Bird and the whispers.

No two of Andras's logbooks were the same. Claire drew one down from the shelf at random. The cover was bound in some kind of hide that was too heavy and metallic to be from any creature on earth. She found the index quickly and looked for any log entry dealing with an artifact or speculation of ink. When that came up empty, she broadened her search to any magical liquids, and that got somewhere at least. Claire spent the next three hours wading through Andras's spidery handwriting and parsing out his thoughts on chimera blood, arcane brews, ifrit tears, aqua vitae, and even the observable properties of holy water. An entry that was brief at best. What she wouldn't have given to have that in her inventory at any point of her tenure in Hell, Claire thought wryly.

There were entries on divine paints, dark visceral slurries, arcane potions, cosmic floods, and the blood of every impossible realm creature one could think of. But no ink. There was not a single record of any artifact of ink-like nature passing through the Arcane Wing.

Claire fell back into her chair and rubbed the grit out of her eyes with her good hand. The utter absence of a thing was nearly as telling as anything else she could have dug up. Telling *what*, though? A hot feeling threatened to well up in her eyes, and, *damn it all*, Claire hated to cry when she was frustrated. Crying, in general, was an indignity, but tears that came because she felt powerless to do anything else were the worst kind.

If she could just find a fulcrum, find a point to stand where the world made *sense* again, she felt she could manage. But everything had felt wildly askew from true since the Library fire. A slow, festering wound had opened between the Unwritten Wing and the Arcane Wing. And left unattended, it had burst—through the floorboards, through the tentative quiet—into the mayhem and confusion of ink that shouldn't exist.

And there was the wound. Claire mentally poked at it. It wasn't that she desired to be librarian again—she didn't want the Unwritten Wing back from Brevity—it was simply that she wanted to *understand* what had happened. It had never made sense, and her lack of understanding was threatening everyone. Everyone expected Claire to solve the riddle. Knowledge was what she excelled at. Yet she hadn't even been clever enough to keep from touching the stuff.

"... *naught is lost.*"

Claire sat up in her chair and glanced at the raven. "Did you hear that?"

Bird gave her a slow blink and released a rain of crumbs into her lap. She squatted into a fluffed ball and appeared to be considering relieving herself over the edge of Claire's desk. Birds really were awful pets.

But Claire had heard something. Or she thought she had. It was a bit like when you'd been startled out of sleep and your brain was still rewinding to catch up. It always left Claire with the sensation that she'd been jolted awake by a sound she more *remembered* hearing than heard directly.

This particular sound was a memory of a voice, young and with a formal accent that really only existed in Arthurian melodramas. Moreover, it was no voice Claire recognized. She pushed away from the desk—Bird cursing at her for the disruption—and emerged from her alcove.

The Arcane Wing was not entirely silent. Somewhere, far flung toward the entrance, she could hear the methodical thumps of Rami occupied with his work. She almost went toward the sound, but something, or the memory of something, made Claire turn and squint into the shadows of the rookery.

A figure crouched against the wall but slowly unwound itself as Claire's eyes adjusted to the gloom. A flash of brocade made her freeze and imagine for a ridiculous moment it was Andras, escaped and back in his old kingdom. But, no, Andras—or at least the idea of him—was imprisoned in a dagger Claire kept buried in the bottom of her own desk drawer, neglected and ignored. She blinked, and the figure resolved into a lanky blond man in a pit-sweated velvet suit that had been popular on the rock stars of Claire's youth. Then, just as she'd frowned at that, the figure's right pant leg blurred and jittered into the hem of a dress.

She stared, locked in place, as she tried to make sense of the effect. It was as if his—her?—as if *their* entire body had difficulty staying tuned to the same frequency. Hair buzzed from blond to red to black to pink. A blast of static seared away velvet into a cotton undershirt, a steel-ring cuirass, silk and feathers, some alien and organic armor, a gingham blouse. The figure made no threatening moves, or any moves at all for that matter. Perhaps they were entirely occupied with keeping their body together.

"Who are you?" The question came out mousy and frail in Claire's mouth. The figure simply stared at her (with blue eyes, now black, now orange) and began to walk away.

*Hold up.* Claire had enough narrative sense to recognize a haunting when she saw one. The whispers, the voice, the creepy dream, and now this every-person person. One did not live this long in a library without understanding the clear markers of Suspicious Nonsense. She was not about to go plodding off after some mysterious force like a complete fool.

No, she was about to go plodding off after some mysterious force like an *aware* fool.

She discounted the possibility of not following it right off the bat. She might have disregarded it, at one time, but she had learned what happened if one ignored a story in Hell: it got worse. She considered briefly the option of hunting down Rami, telling him what she was seeing. But that would have lead inevitably to apparitions that conveniently only appeared to Claire, and she'd rather skip over the unnecessary subplot of questioning her sanity, thank you very much.

If the figure was real, then Claire needed to talk to them. If it was an illusion, then it was surely a cause of the ink that had stained her hand, somehow connected to unwritten stories. And stories could always be counted on for an inevitable flair for drama. Maintaining a sense of narrative wasn't just a professional skill in the Library; it was a survival trait.

So Claire rubbed her stained wrist idly, prepared to be spooked, and marched down the aisle of shadows.

Floorboards creaked under her feet, and rows of shelves settled with a sigh as she passed by. It was all really a clichéd kind of effect, at least until she happened to glance at the artifacts nearest her.

Not all the artifacts of the Arcane Wing's collection were made from routine materials. Mortals were nothing if not innovative. There was a particular subset of items made from ghoulish materials—skin, bone, and other identifiable human parts. Claire kept this collection toward the back of the wing. Not because of any unusual power or danger, but because it gave her the willies. That's what she'd told Rami. In truth, the lines of finger bones and skulls reminded her too much of the underground tombs of Malta.

Her eyes skimmed briefly over the top row, where finger bones lay on the velvet in rows, like dead soldiers. Below that, several scrolls and tiny leatherworks—not a speck of cowhide in any of them; each had its own individual cubby. The scroll closest to Claire was a particularly tan shade of brown. The surface shifted just as her gaze landed on it. *A trick of shadows*, Claire thought, then: *Nerves*. And then she thought, *Oh*.

The tanned hide warped and puckered. A rolling shape rose out of the surface, churning like a fish under the surface until it began to take a recognizable topography. A cheekbone, the hollows smooth as the skin it remembered being. A shifting motion revealed a closed eye, the line of a nose, as if the scroll surface had thinned and something pressed in from the other side. Then: a perfectly shaped mouth. The lips were clear and detailed enough that when they parted around a single word, Claire could almost understand it.

Bones rattled. Each delicate finger bone shivered in its velvet bed. Shadows streamed across the ivory, words, or possibly images. Claire refused to look closely. A thump made her jump. The drum beside the scroll writhed, and a tiny, fragile hand tried to push through.

A blat of a cry startled her, and Claire stepped back abruptly.

Bird hunched over the nearest shelf, scouring her with pitiless eyes that said, *Pull yourself together.* Below the raven, a figure crouched in the shadow of the shelf, which sent Claire's pulse up again until she recognized the moon silver eyes.

"Not that," Rosia said in a whisper.

It took a moment to wrest her breathing steady, and Claire cursed herself before focusing on Rosia. "What?"

"You should be listening, but not to that." Rosia hopped forward with a birdlike jerk. Claire didn't flinch, which brought a pleased smile to the willowy girl's face. "You're not scared of me."

"Why would I be scared of—" Claire caught herself. "You shouldn't be here, Rosia. Go back to your home. There's something dangerous in the wing."

Rosia's head tilted and silver-dollar eyes blinked. "Dangerous to you, not me."

Claire hated to repeat herself. "What? I don't think you—"

"Ghosts don't scare ghosts," Rosia said simply before turning on her heel and walking off with a gliding step.

Claire blinked after her. Rosia was a damsel from a gothic horror—something crimson and spiky in the title, as she recalled. Claire'd *hated* ghost stories as a child, a fact she was just remembering now in the damning way things were forgotten in Hell. She'd hated ghost stories, always spending the whole story steeling herself for the scare, so that by the end she had given herself a headache. Knowing what was coming in a story wasn't always helpful. Sometimes it made it worse.

Still, Claire brooked no fears. She had a responsibility to watch out for Rosia, and at least the girl appeared to confirm what Claire was seeing. It was better than enduring Rami's skepticism. Onward, then. She did not run after the girl, but she upgraded her pace to a *determined* stride. Bird kept up with a kind of hopping glide from shelf to shelf.

The every-person waited for them by the well that the wing had erected around the ink reservoir. A low wood stack lined the edge of the liquid, making it more of a reflecting pool than a traditional well. The wing's aesthetic choices sometimes confounded even Claire.

Rosia stood in front of the every-person, hands clasped neatly behind her back as if they were having a polite conversation. The figure continued its static shifting, breaking up and reassembling. If the dead channel of a television could be a person, it might appear something like this one.

"Rosia," Claire hissed for her attention. "Get back from it."

Rosia didn't turn her head. "They just want you to listen."

"How do you know that?"

"I just wanted someone to listen, too, when I was a ghost."

Claire's mouth formed around several half responses before she shook her head. "This isn't a story."

"Are you sure?" Rosia lifted her hand, and the every-person mirrored. The static of its palm cycled through a number of skin tones and sizes before matching her own.

"Who are you?" Claire shifted her focus to the unknown threat. She drew to a stop a cautious distance from the edge of the ink. She crossed her arms in front of her uneasily. Not as if the finger bones had unsettled her. No creepy pronouncements from children with haunted eyes were going to get to her: heavens no. Impatience; that was what this was. "Ghost of sins past? Andras's vengeful shade? Do hurry up, whatever this is about. You're upsetting my charges, and"—she wiggled a few black fingers—"I'm on borrowed time, in case you haven't heard."

The every-person's head dropped to the side and briefly flickered to a rather annoyed expression. It turned, knelt slowly beside the pool, and began to extend an arm. Rosia eagerly crouched beside it.

"I'd really rather you *didn't*," Claire warned, stepping forward. After a moment she added, a bit resentfully, "Please." It wasn't as if she knew exactly how she would stop a phantom from touching the ink, but Rosia was her responsibility. Ink had attacked her as a human; who knew what would happen to a book? "It is not an experience I can recommend."

The every-person's eyes flickered to one perfectly arched brow for a moment. The static figure extended its hand over the surface, palm down but not touching. Claire had time only to take another alarmed step forward before the ink below its hand began to shift and roil.

"Look," Rosia breathed.

The helpless steps Claire had taken had brought her close enough to see it clearly. The ink wasn't moving; something was moving *across* it. Movement spiraled out from the shadow the hand cast on the surface. Claire caught figures and shapes. Then she caught a flash of blond and velvet that she'd seen earlier and gasped.

The figure was still, but the surface of its skin was in constant motion. The static flux of its appearance had picked up speed. Claire began to pick out a pattern in what had seemed random noise before. She caught a glimpse of the gingham-print dress on the figure's shoulder. It flickered and blinked, replicating all over its torso before slowly sequencing down the extended arm. The hand became slender and pale for a moment, and a new image spiraled out across the ink surface. A tall woman in a prairie dress strode purposefully through moonlit fields of grain, sickle in hand.

"Oh, how nice," Rosia whispered.

The stranger wasn't stirring up the ink; it was *communing* with it. Making some kind of transfer of . . . data? Memory? Claire didn't know what, but she needed it to stop right now. Rosia leaned ever closer to the pool's edge in the flickering shadow the every-person cast. Bravery and foolishness go hand in hand, and she was already displaying one of the two, so—

"Stop!" Claire pulled Rosia back with one hand and shoved the every-person by the shoulder to create space. She was half-surprised when her hand didn't pass straight through. The figure only straightened to its feet, so smoothly that Claire forgot to remove her hand. The constant change of texture beneath her fingers was alarming, but she gripped and twisted them around to face her. "Who— *What* are you?"

The every-person's arm lowered and it resumed its random jittering, but for one brief moment a single face resolved with dipped brows and begging eyes. Pleading, then hurt, then *angry*.

"They are us," Rosia whispered with a bereft note. "You're still not listening."

"They haven't *said* anything!"

"I'm listening," Rosia continued. "They're alone, sad. They want to be more. They *are* more, but everyone's forgotten. I'll remember, I'll listen—I'm more too."

"Don't touch—" A flicker of movement started in the corner of her eye. Claire focused on where her ink-blackened hand had gripped their shoulder. Armies of figures twisted and raced across the stain—across her *skin*. It was hers—*it was hers*—wasn't it?

Claire released her grip, flinching to stumble back and away from the shifting flow of strangers. Her breath was coming in gasps, so there was nothing left in her lungs when the every-person held its hand out to Rosia, who took it without hesitation. The every-person looked at Claire sadly, wrapped a protective arm around Rosia, and pulled them into the bottomless pool of ink.

"Ros—"

There was no splash, no ripple, not even more phantom figures dancing across the surface. The ink parted, creating a gap of space around Rosia as they passed, and closed over her head without a sound.

Claire rushed to the edge of the pool, heedless of the roiling way the ink churned as she approached. That was the only movement in the silence that followed as Claire tried to process what had happened. The space where Rosia had fallen was still as a mirror. No thrashing, no struggle of life. Rosia was gone beyond reach.

She'd failed to protect another damsel, another book. The sound that cracked up Claire's throat was a delirious giggle. The panic and terror were a film on top of giddy exhaustion, like soap on a bubble, held at bay until everything popped. She couldn't let it pop. She *couldn't*.

The ink had drawn away from Rosia. Claire replayed what had just occurred again in her mind to be sure. She forced the memory to advance, frame by frame. The every-person had seemed protective, and the ink had seemed to align with that. Rosia had been certain, and then she'd been gone.

Maybe not gone. Claire held on to that idea like a lifeline. Rosia was in there; she would get Rosia back. Because the alternative was failing, again.

Claire straightened from the pool as she recalled Rosia's words: *It wants to be more.* More what, then? More than a ghost?

It was then that Claire remembered that ghost stories usually had unsatisfactory endings. She had loss but no closure. She had an unsettled fear but no answers. She did, however, have a pool of questions. She would stop hiding from them.

*Ghosts,* Rosia had said. If it was time to hunt ghosts, she first needed to put her own to rest.

# 9

# RAMI

I have the wing to rights, as far as I understand it. The books sleep; the demons stay at a distance. Even Revka, the stone woman, seems to approve. Everything makes sense, except why this place should exist at all. And why in a place of suffering? The logbook is no help; it shows me words just cryptic enough to increase my questions.

I am in a world of damnation. I should not borrow trouble. But my mother taught me the viper that one doesn't follow to its hole is the viper that bites you.

*Librarian Madiha al-Fihri, 602 CE*

IT'D BEEN UNUSUALLY EASY to explain his absence to Claire. He'd found the Arcanist near the front of the wing, staring with some indecision at the doors. She'd jumped when Rami cleared his throat.

"Rami. Right," Claire said briskly, though Rami hadn't said anything that required agreement. "I have a task for you."

"Ma'am?" Rami had been gearing up to explain his absence, but Claire disappeared down the aisle at a brisk pace. Rami had to lengthen his stride to catch up. "Has something happened?"

"No!" Claire responded immediately and, if possible, quickened her pace even more. "No, of course not. It just occurred to me that there was an artifact overlooked that should go in quarantine."

Rami grimaced. "The waxed dragon scales? I apologize, ma'am, but it seemed like an edge case—"

"I'm not—" Claire paused outside her private alcove and gave Rami a querulous look. "I wasn't talking about the dragon scales. Not your fault at all. This one isn't on the official inventory, after all."

"Not—" Rami caught his breath as Claire pulled a key from her skirts and opened the bottommost drawer. Six months of disuse made the unoiled rails screech, and Bird complained from somewhere in the rafters above them. At the bottom of the drawer, the tip of a small blade poked out from beneath a tower of discarded paper scraps, like the fang of a viper. "Claire, are you sure? You said the safest place for that . . ."

"Was out of sight, forgotten. I know." It had to be the dimmer light in the alcove that made Claire look abruptly pale. Her gaze flicked around nervously before she appeared to remember herself. "But if this ink is a lingering threat from the coup, I want him secured far away from it." Claire studied an indefinite point on the desk. "And me."

"You?" Rami considered his accumulated observations and the nervy tension in Claire's face. "You mean you are afraid to touch it."

"Really, Rami! I hold a *cautious* misgiving about touching it, with my stained hand," Claire corrected, a shadow of her imperious self shaking her mood. She sniffed. "As if I would grant Andras the gift of my fear. He's unworthy."

"I agree." Rami stepped forward to take the dagger artifact that contained the essence of their fallen enemy—once friend, as Rami had understood it, though he had been no friend of any demon. Claire stepped back, knocking the arm of her chair against the wall. She hid the moment she flinched in a grimace.

"I'll wrap it and place it in the very back of the vault," Rami said slowly. The exposed blade was chill in his palm, but no colder than any polished metal. He hesitated at the alcove entrance, but Claire didn't meet his gaze. "Andras is gone and can threaten no one now. He's dead, Claire. Or as good as dead."

"Yes, well . . . the dead do have a way of making a nuisance of themselves when it comes to me." Claire's smile was too tight to avoid being a grimace.

"It only seems that way," Rami soothed as he tucked the knife away, watching as Claire visibly relaxed once it was out of sight. "I think we do the haunting to ourselves. Death keeps its own secrets."

Claire sighed, nodding defeat if not agreement. "We do. And Death—"

Her chin froze midmotion and her gaze sharpened enough to send a prickle of alarm up Rami's neck. "Claire?"

"Nothing. Nothing. Just a passing thought to consider." Claire straightened, and she appeared so much more her old self that Rami didn't dare question it. She made a shooing motion. "Get that in the vault, if you please."

IT WAS A CAREFUL matter storing what was effectively the Arcane Wing's most notorious prisoner in the archive vaults. Rami was grateful for it. It gave him time to formulate the careful way he would broach Hero's proposed lead with Claire.

"I'd like to look into some things," Ramiel said after finding Claire near the ink reservoir. She appeared to have gathered her calm again and had convinced the wing to repair the floor to something resembling a small—if incredibly gothic-looking—reflecting pool for the ink. She stared into it with what appeared to be expectation—as if the ink could talk to her. Abruptly, she nodded and took off for her alcove.

Rami followed and began to wrestle with the fear that now was a poor time to leave the mortal woman alone with her thoughts. "Claire?"

Claire looked up from the prodigious stack of books with which she had fortified her desk. For all Andras's duplicity, he'd kept exacting notes on every artifact in the wing, which Claire had only begun to sift through. "Things?" she said, as if no time had passed. "You've run across something like the ink before?"

"No," Ramiel said truthfully. "Whatever this is, it's unique to the Library."

"Then what do you hope to find that you can't share with me?"

"We intend to make discreet inquiries into the other libraries." Ramiel saw no reason to lie. Which was good because he had been told, repeatedly, that he was terrible at it. He had accepted it as a flaw of being burdened with a divine nature in Hell.

"And the last time I left the realm it was a minor scandal," Claire said with the grace of an understatement.

Rami smiled. "It was a minor scandal on our end too."

"Everything is a *scandal* to Heaven." On another's lips, that word might have made Rami flinch, but Claire had a clear-eyed way of looking at him that steadied him. Contentment, to be here of all places, was a radical novelty in Rami's life. Claire had no idea of the miracle that was. Instead she made a sour face, which was so familiar it dispersed Rami's previous concerns. "I have no idea how paradise realms can even get anything done with that much inefficiency."

"I believe it's viewed as ethics."

"*Inefficiency.*" Claire straightened the books in front of her before a thought occurred to her with a sharp glance. "You said 'we.'" She squinted. "Hero's dragging you along."

"For the sake of my dignity, let us say it's more of a strategic escort."
Ramiel didn't think he made a face, but Claire snorted a withering
kind of amusement. At least it served to center her. Her face took on a
more present kind of focus. She gestured, and Rami handed her the
teapot to refill her empty cup; then she offered him a clean one. The air
filled with the metallic drift of Darjeeling—perhaps with a Ceylon
blend? Rami had never developed the taste for it, but he knew his teas
now, evidently. Claire's personality was of such force that education on
such things came with her acquaintance. "From what I understand of
his logic, it is sound. I believe his intentions are in earnest."

"And has he gotten permission from Brev for these earnest intentions?"

"Not in so many words," Ramiel admitted. The teacup was pleas-
antly warm against the calluses on his palms. He took a tentative
sip—yes, still tasted like old water to him—while he fought the ridiculous urge to defend Hero. "He could have run before now, if that
was his intent."

"True." Claire's mouth executed a brittle twist that wasn't entirely
without fondness. "If I was still librarian, I'd be concerned."

"And as the Arcanist?"

"I'm recreationally skeptical," Claire admitted behind the rim of
her teacup. "Be careful. Hero isn't nearly as hard as he plays at being."

Rami sighed. "No, he's quite a bit sharper."

"He grows on you. Like a barnacle."

"A lesion," Rami suggested helpfully.

The laugh surprised Claire enough that it diverted into a cough.
Once she had regained her composure, she set her tea down. Her expression turned thoughtful as she appeared to search his face for insight. "I've grown to care about him, nonetheless."

Rami looked down into his mostly full cup. It would not be very angelic to scuff his shoes, no matter how much the dip in his stomach told him to. "I know."

Porcelain on wood clicked as Claire shuffled her undrunk tea aside to select a book from the stack. A patently false gesture, as Rami knew Claire never kept her tea on a reading surface for fear of spilling it. It distracted him from her next words. "Just as I care about you."

Rami startled. "I beg your pardon?"

He had no idea what his face was doing in that moment—Claire had a way of dipping around his guard. But whatever Claire saw made her lips quirk. She nodded smugly to herself. "All right. You may have it."

It wasn't *proper*. The thousands of years of etiquette Ramiel had on Claire escaped him in a confused noise.

"My pardon, I mean. For whatever foolishness you and Hero are about to get up to." Claire settled back into her chair, flipping through the initial pages of her book without reading them. "In return, I want both of you to come back. No heroics, and I expect you to ensure that you present yourselves again in one piece. Both of you."

Rami felt like he was missing an important undercurrent of the conversation. It wouldn't have been the first time. Humans were always evolving new ways of not saying what they meant. He had thought he knew most of them, until he met Claire. "Ma'am? I mean, Claire—are you feeling—"

"You're always so straightforward, Ramiel." Claire's smile was soft with exhaustion and, perhaps, fondness. "It makes it easier to return the favor. Let's just say this most recent threat has left me feeling inconveniently impulsive and tired of my own games. It has left me irresponsibly open to considering what I want." Claire slumped back into her chair. Two black fingers toyed with the tattered edge of a page. It drew attention to the ink stain against paper the color of old bone.

She pulled her fingers away as if they'd been burned. "Perhaps you should consider the same, Rami."

"What I want?" Rami echoed.

"Don't look so confused. You're not trying to get into Heaven anymore. You're surrounded by mortals and books and gods know what else. You're allowed to want things now. Give it a try; you might find it grows on you. Like a barnacle."

There was a precise conversation Claire was having, and there were the words Rami was hearing. He felt the two were rather removed from each other. Some vital part of his brain had gone into free fall, so he only managed an eloquent nod.

"Good." Claire turned her attention back to her desk. "Go. Be careful and bring both of you home."

"I'll see to it," Ramiel promised with some relief. And he did—promise. Hero might have been an ass with overconfidence in his charms, but Rami had sworn to protect all the residents of the Library. That included stunningly perplexing dead women and insufferable men with broken books.

# 10

# HERO

The Library is hiding something. I'm certain of it. But an immortal secret is not going to be solved by one soul. So I put forth the charge to you, future librarians: discover the secret of the Library's existence. Take what I've learned and add your own under the log index entry Myrrh. In my time, it was that which was sought after for medicine, knowledge, and purification. Knowledge purifies. We serve no one with ignorance.

I believe this little logbook can hold our secrets secure. And maybe one day, it will hold the truth as well.

*Librarian Madiha al-Fihri, 603 CE*

THE PROBLEM WITH BEING made from a book, Hero had decided, was that everyone thought they could read you. The firmly held belief that they could look at you, read you once, and know the entirety of your contents for eternity. That a book was simply the sum of the text on its pages.

It certainly felt like more than that, from the inside. Hero resented the simplification of it. The way Claire and Brevity nattered between them, dissecting terms with important capitalizations like Narrative and Story and Point of View. As if as a character his thoughts were prescripted, and he was merely a composition of cogs and bits to be taken apart and reassembled.

Granted, they never talked about *him in specific* in this manner, but being the exception was no comfort. It felt condescending, like a hall pass. At his heart he knew he was still a story. A story with a broken book, but a story.

He didn't know where that left him anymore. Not immutable but also not a cold assemblage of parts. Perhaps he was a draft, half-born but unfinished. Unruly and unfixable. Yes, Hero could definitely be that.

It was in this particularly sour frame of mind that Hero found Rami skulking around the entrance to the Arcane Wing.

"About time." Hero barely paused midstep to stride past the doors and down the hallway. He was gratified to hear Rami scramble to his feet behind him. Claire had done that trick enough to him. "I've bought some time, but if Brevity recalls me in the middle of an inquiry it'll be disastrous. We should get moving."

The transport office neared, then flew past them. Rami's heavy steps picked up.

"Don't we need to return to the Unwritten Wing?" Rami asked. "Or wherever this secret exit is that you found?"

Hero stopped and pinned him with a baffled look. "Dear gods, you think it's a *literal door*, don't you?"

Rami had too much dignity to blush, which was a pity, but Hero rather appreciated the way his glare turned self-conscious. "The warding of books was not a Watcher's concern in my day."

He said "warding of books" not quite the way one would say "mucking stalls," but it was close. Hero's lip curled and he leaned in. "It's entirely all right. I'll make sure you can keep up." He started off again before Rami could entirely respond. "Wards don't have physical weaknesses; they have *logical* ones. What we're looking for isn't a secret door; it's a secret loophole."

The loft of his lecturing air was not lost on Rami. "So, you cheat."

"Of *course* I cheat. Dear gods, what am I, a real hero? No." Hero waved away the absurd insinuation. "It's more about obeying the letter of the law than the spirit. Entirely appropriate. We'll use the Library's own processes, even."

"Definitely cheating," Rami muttered.

Hero suppressed a burr of irritation. He was being *incredibly clever* and his audience couldn't even appreciate it. Claire and Brevity had tried for hours to wheedle this secret out of him, and here he was, just handing it to the damned man and he couldn't even pretend to be impressed. Angels, really. And yet, Hero needed him for this next part.

"Voilà." Hero withdrew a small strip of paper from his jacket and flourished it under Rami's nose. "A hold."

"A what?" Ramiel snatched the paper out of Hero's hand with surprising dexterity.

"A hold request, for the IWL," Hero said, then helpfully clarified, "the interworld loan."

"I know that much," Rami said stiffly. Brows knit as he studied the sheet. Hero had taken the liberty of filling out most of the details. Title and catalog information for his own book, each detail triple-checked. Just two blank spaces remained. "Is this how you escaped the first time?"

"Sort of. It was easy, once I thought of it. Took a few months to convince a visitor to risk taking a slip back with him to Earth— suspicious lot, demons are—but, well, I'll show you." Hero shrugged and rifled for a pen. "Your signature goes at the bottom, of course, and—"

"Elysium?" Ramiel squinted at the sheet, then back up at Hero. "Why there?"

"Why not start with the Greeks?" Hero made a broad gesture. "I've had a lot of time to study the Librarian's Log lately. A shake-up—the last *big* shake-up—happened under the tenure of a Greco-Roman librarian. Claire and Brevity are astonishingly tight-lipped about it. Seems as if she tried to start a bit of a war. If this rebel librarian was sent packing to the Library wing in Elysium, we can get some answers."

Even Ramiel had to admit that the logic was sound. "But you're stamped, part of the permanent collection. Doesn't that mean you're not lendable?"

"Not to *patrons*. Not anymore, a shame." Hero made a face. It would have been so much easier if he was. "But the rules are less strict for esteemed *colleagues* of the Library. Like, say, an assistant curator of the Arcane Wing."

Ramiel began to crumple the sheet. "So that's why you need me."

"Only partially! Though I admit your charming company is leaving something to be desired." Hero stopped Ramiel's hands with his own. "You want answers, don't you?"

Whether it was the question or Hero's hands on top of his knuckles, Ramiel stilled. A complicated look washed over his face, but before Hero could blink to read it, it was gone. Rami yanked his hands free and took the pen. "I want solutions, to help Claire. We go, we ask if anyone's encountered such a thing as this ink before, and we get out. No games."

"No games," Hero repeated solemnly. Bless the sweet man, he almost seemed to believe him.

Almost. Rami shot him a reproachful look again and scribbled a signature on the bottom of the sheet. He allowed Hero to take it back along with the pen. "And now what?"

"Oh, now." Hero flashed a smile that was nervy and peaked with a touch of fear. He was already feeling it, that slow, seeping feeling, like he'd more than gone pale. He patted the square spot where his book always rested tucked into his vest pocket, just to be sure. Gods, Hero hated this part. "You know the way to Elysium, right?"

"What?" Ramiel sputtered, and was too shocked to stop him as Hero reached out, sank his fingers into Ramiel's dour, dusty overcoat, and came away with a fistful of gray feathers. His hand was so pale the feathers looked nearly black in comparison. His book, tucked inside his vest, felt like a hot ember pressing and burning a solid rectangle into his own chest.

"Never mind. Do your best." Hero's voice was faint, raspy as old paper even to his own ears. He clenched his eyes shut. This was his very *least* favorite part of cleverness. "I'll leave a light on for you."

The solid weight of the book turned cold. A heat raged through him, and his insides felt turned from solid to liquid to ash. Ramiel made a baritone squawk of protest, and Hero was swept away.

# 11

# HERO

Hell is a place for forgetting. Kind enough, really, because anyone who lands here has plenty they'd be happy to not recall. But makes you wonder, donnit? Where those forgotten memories go when they're gone from life and death? Maybe there's a life of "after" for memory too.

*Librarian Fleur Michel, 1771 CE*

PARADISE WAS NOT GOING according to plan. Not at all. Hero had expected to appear in some elegant version of the Library he'd just left—artful marble pillars, airy, maybe some grapes and wine? Surely at least a comfortable spot and refreshments to wile away the time in comfort until the angel found his own way to Elysium. But no, instead, he'd come to in tall wheatgrasses, which had fought back as he clambered his way out to the field's edge. Cockleburs clung to his jacket and were working their way into *other* places, and Hero was unimpressed with this realm's entire concept of idyll.

Paradise, it seemed, was distinctly rural.

The road was smooth with fresh stone pavers, out of place in the pastoral scene, and Hero paused to survey it. The road cut a neat line between a patchwork of tidy golden wheat fields and meadows luridly feral with yellow flowers. The greenery spilled right up to the edge of a cliff that sheared down to a bay that was a watercolor of impossible blues and greens. A far hill was crowned with the low outlines of a pale city, but nothing so grand and spiraling as Hero had expected.

Still, it was the most promising sign of civilization, the modest farm homes dotting the fields excluded. Hero set off toward it. He'd barely made it over the first rise when a rustle caught his attention above the gentle wind. A disturbance snaked through the wheat field on his right, something graceful and low to the ground parting the stalks. A subtle glance found a mirroring disturbance on his left.

Just once, Hero would have liked to enter a realm without immediately being challenged to mortal combat. Was that too much to ask? He sighed and forced his pace to stay slow and lazy, allowing the pincer formation to close in on him precisely as he came to a small stone bridge. At the foot of the bridge, he turned and scowled at the empty road. "Honestly, if you're trying to be subtle—"

A roil of muscle and fur glided onto the road, stopping Hero's breath. Two creatures emerged from the wheat. They might have been female lions had their fur not been distinctly metallic. Fine strands of gold, mottled with copper, flowed over the beasts' hides. Muscle, sleek and defined, rolled underneath with every sinuous step.

The lions came to a stop in the middle of the road and regarded Hero with unblinking eyes. They gave the distinct impression that they were waiting.

Hero's mind scrambled for the *what*. If there was a password for entering this realm, he didn't know it. There was likely a toll—there was always a damned price in these kinds of places—but he'd hoped Ramiel would catch up before he had to pay it. An angel with a flaming sword would not have been unwelcome just about now.

"Simon says?" Hero tried, then spun and broke into a run.

It was a short sprint across the bridge, made longer by anticipating the razor claws shredding into his back at any moment. Hero risked a glance behind him, but the beasts had followed at a mere saunter. Well, maybe they'd eaten recently. Maybe they were vegetarians. Maybe at this rate he'd outrun them—

A freight train took him at the shoulder. At least, that's what it felt like as Hero went down, tumbling with an unbelievable weight on top of him. He let out a shriek—an entirely manful, intimidating shriek, mind—and succeeded in rolling blindly away across the dirt. He came up in a clearing of trampled wheat, nose to nose with a third, very large, glimmering lion. This one was more copper than gold and had a rainbow sheen when the light played off the roll of its shoulders. Silver claws dug into the fresh-churned dirt as Hero rose.

His hand drifted immediately to his sword hip, but—no. Book and bind it, he'd left the sword back at the Unwritten Wing. He'd not wanted to raise any suspicion with Brevity, and he'd been so certain that traveling with Ramiel would have provided more than enough armament if needed. And it was needed, very much, right now, without an angel in sight.

"Damn the man," Hero murmured with a placating gesture. Raising his hand must have appeared threatening, because in a breath the lion launched itself in the air.

Hero dove to the dirt again, rolling as the beast raked the air where he'd been. He managed a lucky kick in the face, which set the cat back on its heels for a moment, but it was the only opening he was liable to get. Hero lunged before the lion could turn around, latching his arms around its neck in a way that he prayed kept the razor claws out of reach.

The lion's pelt had shone metallic in the sun, and Hero had expected a rasp of metallic needles as he wrapped his arms around the neck in a death grip. Instead, the fur was velvety, so soft it was almost slippery as the lion bucked. It howled its outrage, twisting. Hero didn't have long to develop a plan before the lion would discover this position brought Hero's legs into appetizing mauling range. On impulse, Hero tangled his ankles past the lion's haunches, wrenched his knees tight to the flanks, and rolled.

It wouldn't have worked if the lion had been firmly planted—lions were surprisingly hefty beasts. But Hero had caught it midstep, just enough to knock it off-balance. They hit the ground again and Hero threw all his strength into it, using the momentum to fling the beast away.

It was not expected. The beast tumbled across the beaten-down grass, and Hero heard a solid sound as the back of its head hit the half-buried boulder. Hero tensed on his hands and knees, dragging long fistfuls of air into his chest as he waited to see if the lion would rise again.

A crunch of dried grass interrupted. Over his shoulder, he saw movement. Two other cats, the damned beasts that had followed him across the bridge, had caught up. They sliced through the grass at a languid pace, but they no longer looked like the statues he'd mistaken them for before. A hungry ghostlight lit their gaze and followed Hero's slightest movements.

Hell. Hero could not catch a break. He made a furious sound in his throat and pressed shakily to one knee.

"Come on, then! Scabrous mongrels—coddled tabby cats—see if I don't scratch." His hand fisted in a gouge of dirt. Perhaps if he managed to fling it in the eyes of one . . . but then the other would be on him. It was a small chance, but he wasn't dead yet, if he—

A low snarl came from his back and—oh, strike that—Hero was dead. The initial lioness was not down for the count. The two beasts in front of him tensed, a shadow of movement flickered in his periphery, and Hero flinched his eyes shut. He would die, and it would probably be gory and *entirely* undignified, and the brutes would likely shred his book in the process and even Claire wouldn't be able to paste him together again, assuming she even bothered enough to try. And he'd die as *lion poop* and he hoped they choked on his binding and—

Copper heat brushed past his shoulder. A shadow shifted, and Hero couldn't resist peeking open one eye. His view was blocked by a wall of burnished fur and muscle. The lioness shifted in front of him, but her attention was not on Hero; it was on the two beasts that had been about to eat him.

Hero wasn't versed in the languages of cats. Or metal cat deities. Or whatever these blasted things were. But the air thrummed with tension as a wordless communication ensued. Finally, the ears on the two opposing lions flicked back, displeased as they dropped their heads and slunk away. They disappeared back into the grass, quick and silent as they had come.

Hero might have sighed his relief, but there was still one murder cat inches from him. The beast's fur twitched, as if sensing his speculation, and it turned to regard him with a baleful silver eye. Blood dripped down one side of its face, almost black against the copper fur. Injured, he supposed, when it had been thrown against the rocks. Hero's fault, then.

But while the cat had seemed intent on his demise earlier, now it just stared at him, as if considering whether he was worth the time. Hero grew light-headed from holding his breath by the time the lioness snorted, breaking the standoff. She turned and took two paces to the edge of the clearing. She paused, glancing over her shoulder impatiently. Hero got to his feet slowly, and the lioness made a satisfied sound and stepped into the grass.

After a few steps she stopped again, pinning Hero with another glance. As if she expected him to . . . follow her.

Follow the murder lion into the murder grasses and hope for the best. The residual adrenaline bubbled out of Hero's throat as a laugh. It was a ludicrous idea. And once upon a time Hero would have roundly ridiculed anyone who even entertained the prospect. That would have been before he followed a half-mad librarian into a labyrinth of a fully mad dead god, of course.

A murder lion seemed almost quaint by comparison, really.

Short of better options, Hero scrubbed his face, muttered curses to every god, librarian, and damned Watcher that had led him here, and stumbled into the long grass in pursuit of a lion.

The lioness led him across a wheat field and through a valley that Hero hadn't thought the island large enough to contain. She never allowed him to fall far enough behind to get lost, but she only waited with an air of indifference when Hero stumbled or struggled his way over a climb. By the time they reached the rise of the white-walled city, Hero had developed a fine film of sweat and grime and torn his velvet coat in three places. His favorite velvet coat, mind you. He was still picking an extra burr from the top of his boots when the lioness stopped.

Hero looked up and had to shield his eyes from the sun. Light reflected off the polished marble like a mirror, and it took a moment to identify the wide portico of the building he'd spotted from the road. A step into the shade gave his eyes relief, and he could make out that the veranda was scattered with low couches, invitingly outfitted with pillows. On each end table sat fluted ceramic cups of refreshments, which were being enjoyed by a small gathering of rather beautiful men and handsome women who paid Hero no attention. Only one inhabitant was looking his way, and when he registered, Hero's lip curled.

Ramiel, fallen Watcher of the Creator and glorified overstuffed bulldog of a git, did not so much sit on the couch as perch uneasily on the edge of the cushion. The fragile cup of wine looked practically toy-like between his calloused fingers, and he held himself with a still awkwardness. Probably entirely due to the company to his left and his right. A stunning woman, composed of lush curves, olive-gold skin, and curls the color of perfectly roasted almonds, reclined on his right, eyeing Ramiel with a look that could only be read as hungry. Her twin—brother? clone? had to be one of those—attended a fruit plate on the Watcher's left. Hero considered him even more beautiful, which was saying something, considering Hero *knew* beauty, thank you very much.

It might have provided an excellent opportunity to intuit Ramiel's preferences, if he didn't look stoically constipated trapped between them. His eyes jumped to the door and Ramiel nearly dropped his wine cup. "Hero."

"Oh please, don't bother yourself with getting up." Hero allowed acid to positively drizzle his words. Ramiel, at least, had the good nature to look ashamed and rushed to his feet.

"You told me to meet you in Elysium."

"Yes, well, obviously you have availed yourself of a shortcut," Hero said.

"Lord Ramiel is always welcome in Elysium. He is known here," the pretty man with the plate said with an earnestness.

"Others are expected to pass a hero's trial," his presumed sister cooed. She swept her glance over Hero in a clinical way that said he'd been found wanting. "Is this your friend, Ramiel?"

"Yes—no, I mean . . ." Ramiel's fingers fluttered along his goblet until he recovered enough to set it down and clear his throat. "Ah, Iambe, Pallas . . . Hero is an emissary from the Unwritten Wing."

"Oh, you work for the Library, then?" The boy, Pallas, asked with excitement.

Pallas wore a chiton that looked butter soft to the touch, if cut too short. It revealed a new inch of muscled thigh every time he shifted. It would have been unseemly to modern eyes if not paired with wide, guileless blue eyes. He was the kind of innocent that was expensive, and required resources for upkeep. Just the kind of beauty that Hero might have enjoyed flirting with once. But at the moment Hero could only find irritation at how closely the boy watched Ramiel. Perhaps that pastime, too, had been ruined along with his book.

"I am a . . . part of the Library, yes," Hero said instead.

"An integral part, even," Ramiel muttered, and Hero was too surprised to glare at him. That he'd chosen now of all times to gain a sense of humor was really impossibly rude.

Iambe nodded. "You'll be here to speak to Echo, then."

"Echo?"

"The librarian—*our* librarian. Of the Unsaid Wing," Iambe said, and tilted her head. "What brings the Unwritten Wing out of seclusion?"

"Just Library business," Hero said. He knew feigned uninterest when he saw it. Gods could only hope that Ramiel hadn't blabbed the entire predicament with the ink before he'd arrived. "Could we be brought to Librarian Echo, then? Or is there another *test* to pass?"

"Test?" Iambe laughed, gaze flicking briefly to the copper-colored cat that shadowed Hero's steps. "You arrive escorted by a Fury. They saw fit to let you live—how did you pull that off, might I ask? You're not the typical sort of hero we get around here."

"You have no idea," Ramiel muttered under his breath. Muttering. He'd done a lot of that since they'd got here. Hero ignored him.

"They ambushed me at the bridge—I didn't get much time to make an impression." Hero shrugged. "I wrestled that one, for little good it did me, and the others seemed to back off."

"You *wrestled* Alecto, in her feral form?" That appeared to draw Pallas into speaking again. His eyes widened and became even brighter, if that was even possible. "Alecto is the strongest of the pride—and ceaseless in a fight. She never gives quarter."

"Unless she finds something too familiar to her tastes to destroy." Iambe hummed. Her voice was light and syrupy, but her gaze picked Hero over with new suspicion. "She's the Fury of rage, did you know?"

"I didn't," Hero said, now uncomfortably aware of the she-beast in his shadow. He wasn't sure whether he was being escorted or stalked. "Perhaps she just took to my charms."

The lioness let out a low sound at that, halfway between a purr and a warning growl. It seemed to confirm whatever suspicion Iambe held. She smiled. "Have a trouble with your darker passions, Hero?"

The name might have been self-selected in sarcasm, but it sounded positively mocking when the Greek spirit said it. Hero stiffened, but Ramiel raised a hand before he could respond. "Peace, my lady." He took a half step, as if drawing Iambe's gaze from Hero. "You said we could be granted an audience with your librarian?"

"Yes," Pallas said quickly. He also watched Hero with a new shine, but it wasn't quite as carnivorous as his sister's. He leapt to his feet and fluttered a hand over his chiton before motioning to the open walkway that led inside. "Mother will be pleased for visitors."

"Yes, she gets so little good conversation these days." Iambe's laugh was sharp, as if she'd just made a joke. Pallas spared them an uneasy look as he held aside the curtain and motioned them inside.

# 12

# CLAIRE

The people to the south declared the time before now Jahiliyyah: a time of ignorance and darkness. If this place has really been abandoned and without care since the previous librarian, then that term may be appropriate. I understand enough now to imagine what damage might have come to stories left uncared for during that dark time. Muses abandoned without direction, books corrupting neighboring pages, forgetting themselves. The only reason no books were lost was because the entire wing was locked down.

Stories need a teller. Books need a reader. These unlived lives are nothing without humanity to anchor them, breathe life into the missing parts.

*Librarian Madiha al-Fihri, 609 CE*

BIRD WINGED ALONG THE shadowed passage ahead of Claire, coming to rest on the scarred triple-wheel carving that loomed over the door to the transportation department. Claire hesitated in the shadow of the arch. Granite-heavy footsteps creeped against the floorboards, punctuated by the glittering tinkle of glass jars. Walter resembled a small boulder crouched behind the counter when Claire entered the room.

"Miss Lib— Miss Claire! Ma'am." Walter punctuated his greeting with startled movements. He jolted upright, clutched the jar in his hands too tight, barely managing to set it down again before it could shatter. The whorls of nothing in his eye sockets appeared to spin particularly fast as he glanced around the small travel office and said again, "Ma'am."

"Am I interrupting something, Walter?" Claire paused at the threshold, hands folded in front of her as she took in the state of the office. The arching walls were peppered with shelves, which were lined with row upon row of clear glass jars full of colored smoke. That was usual. What was unusual was the zigzag of lines through the air. Colors exploded and skidded away from their jars like comet tails, twisting and knotting with others before fading into the gloom.

Walter's innocent look was composed of red teeth and bulbous scars, but it was authentic all the same. "No, ma'am. Just doing a bit of tidying up."

"Tidying up?" Claire stepped to the side as a spiral of persimmon orange floated toward her head. "Really, Walter, your jars are bleeding everywhere."

"Bleed—" Walter straightened so quickly a flight path of lime green had to divert around him in a tight corkscrew maneuver. The void in his eyes slowed nearly to a stop as he stared at Claire. "You can see that, ma'am? You never said ya could—" His gaze tracked down to Claire's stained hand and stopped. It was a peculiar feeling when something as large as Walter froze in place. "Miss Claire, I reckon you got a story to tell me."

A sigh welled up in Claire's chest, and with it every dreg of exhaustion she'd tamped down since seeing Rosia disappear into the ink pool in the Arcane Wing. Walter produced a stool from behind the counter, and Claire retold the tale with her hands folded carefully on the claw-scarred countertop, ink black over soft brown.

By the time she reached the argument with Brevity, Walter's brows had descended to nearly meet his nose. "You got yourself in a muddle."

Claire's lips quirked. "Well, if Death says it's a muddle, then it must be bad."

"I'm being serious. Serious as Sundays." Walter hunched over, squinting at her hand with an earnest intensity. He gestured to the line of inspiration holding back the black. "That stopgap the others jury-rigged. It ain't gonna hold forever, ma'am."

"And what happens when it doesn't? Since you seem to know so much about it." Claire regretted the question as the sorrow sank into the nooks and crevices of Walter's face. She cleared her throat and moved on. "That's not precisely why I came to see you anyway. I—"

"Why don't you make up with Miss Brevity?" Walter asked.

Bird made a noise that was akin to a goose being gently murdered, as if she was seconding the question. Claire's smile became strained. "There's nothing to make up, Walter. Brevity and I are fine."

"If'n you were fine, she'd be here with you," Walter said with solemnity.

"The Unwritten Wing have their own affairs, I'm sure. Brevity—" Brevity needed to be protected. Claire could not stand to be the cause of another ghost haunting Brev's eyes. She just couldn't. She pursed her lips around the words. "Brevity is too . . . *distracted* at the moment."

It was true, even if not *the* truth. Claire thought again about the assessment in Probity's first glance and the way the visiting muse was genial to Rami and Hero but curdled around the edges the moment Claire entered the room. When she'd been stained, it felt as if the visitor had helped against personal preference. The Muses Corps had never been her closest allies, even when she was librarian. But she hadn't believed she'd warranted *that* kind of loathing, professionally.

Which left something personal. Claire simply did not have the time or *temperament* to deal with the personal. She was not inclined to tease out why some random muse didn't care for her. It appeared she cared for Brevity with a sincere fondness from a long shared history. That was enough. At least it would serve to keep Brevity company while Hero and Ramiel jaunted off on Hero's half-baked excuse to get out of the Library, and Claire got to the real work of solving the problem of the ink.

"It is for that reason I am attempting to find answers," Claire finished, turning the strain in her voice into an overprecise tone that sounded wrong even to her ears. "I should have consulted with you sooner, Walter. I do apologize. Since Andras's coup attempt I have been . . . preoccupied."

"You been hiding."

"I've been working." Claire allowed the sharp edge to turn into a prickle now. "As you would know if you and the rest of Hell hadn't been mysteriously absent in our time of need."

"You wouldn't have wanted me there, Miss Claire," Walter said solemnly. "Not many people do."

"Walter . . ." Claire started but quieted as he raised his beefy hands.

"Nah, ma'am. I don't mean it like that. The nature of what I am—" His lips pulled tight, into a small smile that was unintentionally ghoulish. "No one invites me in, if they can help it. I'm glad I wasn't there."

"I understand what you mean." Claire knew they'd come right up to the cutting edge of losing Hero. Leto. Even herself. But the rows of bodies turned to ash drifted to the forefront of her mind again, like a cloud. "But Death was there, with, or without, invitation. We lost so many."

"Oh. I'm not supposed ta take sides," Walter confided in a whisper. "But I don't reckon those demon critters consider it much of a loss."

"I wasn't—" Claire frowned. "I was talking about the damsels. The books."

"Oh." Walter stopped and diverted a constipated look at his knuckles. "Right. Right."

Giant shoulders strained at the seams of his suit as he abruptly found a jar on the opposite wall that was an inch out of alignment. Walter was not a paragon of subterfuge even at the best of times, so Claire allowed him a full minute of nervous fiddling before she chased after him. "Walter. You don't know anything about the destruction of the books and this ink that's turned up, do you? Because we've been friends for a long time. I know a *friend* would tell me if he had information to help."

Walter's shoulders twitched up to his ears. His thumb assiduously blotted a speck of dirt off the jar named *Martha's Vineyard*.

"Walter?" Claire leaned her hands on the counter, precisely where he couldn't miss her blackened knuckles.

The narrow bottle next to that was labeled *The Isle*, and it swirled a sparky gold and cherry blossom pink. Walter tapped the glass and didn't meet Claire's eyes when he cleared his throat. "Mind giving me a hand a minute, ma'am? Them lower shelves get dusty and my knees ain't what they used to be."

Walter probably meant that statement literally rather than figuratively, but Claire was intrigued enough to duck behind the counter and join him in the tiny alcove of jars. "These here?"

Walter passed her a cloth in confirmation. Claire gave him a narrow look before beginning to wipe down jars that had destinations such as *Highever*, *Illeri*, *Minneapolis*, and one labeled, inscrutably, *The*

*Corn.* Claire knew Walter held pathways to more than just Earth, but she'd never seen these jars before. "Thank small favors that the Library cleans itself," she said, for lack of anything else. "I might have taken a turn homicidal if I'd had to dust books for thirty years."

"Library's all about preserving. I never minded a bit of dust if it kept things interesting," Walter said, seeming to relax into the chore. "After a while everything needs a good shake-up."

"How long *have* you been in this office, Walter?" Claire moved on to the next shelf down, which was headed by a primary-color explosion labeled simply *P. Town.* Claire was almost positive the colors swirled into a smile to wink at her. Next to it, a frosty void of black stayed mostly confined to a jar labeled *Terminus Systems.* The jars on the lower level seemed less used, quieter. The colors swirled and stayed mostly inside their glass.

Walter hesitated, because he was either reluctant to answer or reluctant to remember. "Not so long," he finally said. "Just you Library folk come and go so fast."

"Bjorn was here for *seven hundred years*," Claire pointed out.

"Ah yeah. Think he came around for a brew once," Walter said with a toothy grin.

Claire wiped down a couple of very old jars—*Kingston, Alexandria, Pax*—but her blackened fingers hesitated over a squat jar, almost empty, labeled *Summerlands.* She compared it to the other destinations on the shelf and had a thought that came with a memory of haunted leather and Beatrice's smile. Impossible things that wouldn't stay bottled. "Walter, it's not just colors out of their jars. I'm . . . seeing other things. What is it? Why am I seeing things now?"

For a moment, the hitch of his shoulders convinced Claire that he was going to shy away again, but eventually Walter wiped his hands with his rag and looked thoughtful. "Artists always got an abundance of soulfulness, ya know? That's why they got plenty left over, sloshin' around down here."

"I wouldn't have called myself an artist when I was alive," Claire said drolly. She hadn't allowed herself that: a daughter, a mother, a bookkeeper with quiet flights of fancy, yes, but not an artist. She didn't need a primer on what made librarians in Hell, but she could see Walter working himself up to—or around—a point.

"Yeh ain't supposed to be wearing that stuff." Walter cast a worried glance again at her hand. "It ain't natural, wearing other people's ink. 'Tain't natural at all."

"If there is a remedy, let's hear it." Claire had to suppress her urge to get testy. She sighed and straightened to standing again. "If this is unwritten ink—the stuff of the stories that we lost—then why attack me? What am I supposed to do with immortal ink?"

"Immortal?" Walter blinked and abruptly stopped his cleaning. His face formed a brief ravine of worry before he gently nudged Claire by the elbow. "People are always misusing that word around here."

"How so?" Claire frowned as Walter produced an empty jar from a cabinet and set it down next to a piece of paper. "Seeing as we're in Hell, I'd think—"

"'Immortal' is just a word for something you don't understand the shape of, yet. The boundaries, the end." Walter smoothed the paper with his calloused fingers. "No one would really want to be immortal. Forever is an awful long time."

"I'm not following," Claire admitted. "Are you talking about the ink?"

"I'm talking about *bloody everything*," Walter grumbled, before looking stricken. He tapped his knuckles together nervously, as if he'd forgotten himself. "Look. Say this piece o' paper is a bit of a life, yeah?"

"All right." Claire attempted patience as Walter folded the paper up neatly and dropped it inside the jar. He screwed the lid on and snapped his fingers, and the paper caught fire and smoked.

By rights, the lack of oxygen in the jar should have snuffed out the flames, but instead the smoke began to sully up the inside of the glass. Claire shook her head at the flagrant disrespect for physics, but Walter was moving on. "So everything inside that jar, that's a life, right? Whether it's paper or smoke or ashes or heat, it's all what we put in to begin with, yeah?"

"I'm with you so far."

"But say we take away the container." Walter moved with an uncharacteristic swiftness, flicking the jar off the counter with a finger. It slid and shattered on the floor with a crash. Claire flinched back, but the shattered glass evaporated before it could scatter. "Is what was inside gone?"

". . . Well, logically, no," Claire allowed. It was a peculiar thing to be schooled by Death.

"Then can ye point to where the life is? Or what it is?"

A single remaining shard of the jar rocked on the floor, turned dingy gray. The smoke had thinned and whispered away into the air almost immediately, and the remaining smudge of ashes was already getting lost in the floorboards. Claire didn't bother answering the hypothetical. "You're saying death is necessary."

"Nah, ma'am. Death just is. It's the container that gives it shape and makes what's inside important." Walter shrugged, suddenly seeming shy as he fetched a broom and began to sweep up the ash with surprisingly delicate movements. "Without a boundary that marks beginning and end, what matter would anything have? I reckon life inside a jar is special because of what it is under glass. Break the glass and nothing's destroyed, but everything changes."

"There's no putting the smoke back inside the glass." Claire frowned, folding her arms across her chest defensively. "I don't understand how this applies to the ink. I rather liked it when you spoke plain truth to me, Walter."

"I always stick to the truth, Miss Claire. Just sometimes . . . truth ain't what people want to hear."

"I've gotten rather a lot of that lately." Claire folded the cloth carefully between her hands. It remained spotless, no matter how she rubbed her inked palm against it. "If we can't restore the stories, then why does it linger? What could it possibly want?"

Walter returned to his place behind the counter, wiping his gnarled knuckles free of soot. He lifted his shoulders in a helpless gesture. "Can't rightly say, ma'am. I only know life and death. You and your books are the story experts."

Claire began to nod, and her mind snagged on the hook of that idea. She let out a soft oath. She'd been hunting ghosts, talking with Death, and staring at colors, when the reality was *right there*. The answers had been mocking her to begin with. She just needed a point of comparison.

Claire handed him back his rag and ducked toward the foyer before Walter could question it. "Thank you, Walter! I think I have a new hypothosis to test. You've been a brilliant help."

# 13

# RAMI

Myrrh. Not for the first time, I've wished I could talk to our fellows in other wings of the Library about this puzzle. We call ourselves brothers-in-arms, but in the end, it all comes down to secrets, secrets, secrets. I tried to explain my theories about the songs of books to Ibukun, but her interest ends precisely when I start talking of exploring other wings. "Hidebound"—now, there's a word made for Ibukun. It's only rules with her, yet she explains nothing. When I'm the librarian, I'll do better.

*Apprentice Librarian Bjorn the Bard, 990 CE*

THE SHADOWS MARKED A cool threshold from the sun that had turned everything golden and baked outside. Rami had expected a restful interior of white marble, but while the walls appeared faced with stone, it was a riot of color. Fluid, flat scenes flowed across the wall of the hall they were in. Countless iterations of men fighting men, men fighting monsters. He even caught a glimpse of lionlike beasts that reminded him of the feline Fury that shadowed Hero.

For all Pallas had claimed friendship, Rami hadn't visited Elysium since, well, the time of Elysium. Other paradise realms never sat right with him. He always grew uncomfortable, as if there was an itch between his shoulder blades he couldn't reach. He'd expected a tour; Iambe had just seemed the type to press the inherent superiority of her realm's art. But as they progressed through the decorated halls, she became as quiet as her brother. The temple air gradually shifted to something heavy and somber, like a tide coming in. Rami caught Hero's nervous glance. He, too, felt it, from the way his shoulders had tensed. But with the prowling shadow of Alecto at their backs, there was no recourse but to go forward.

"Has Claire ever mentioned Elysium's library?" Hero muttered.

"Not once," Rami responded, quiet and tight. He knew of Elysium only as another paradise realm, despite his brief past visits. Heaven's policy had been to avoid overtures of friendship with other realms. Uriel had run even the Gates under strict isolationism.

Hero replied with a grim nod that said he was similarly in the dark. Brevity had always been free with information on the other wings of the Library, and Rami had even sat in on some of the explanations she'd given Hero, since they were both new to aspects of the Library. But she had never mentioned this wing. Elysium was too close to another Greek domain—the muses. And it appeared even Hero had never had the heart to poke at that particular tender spot. That small amount of restraint softened the brittle edges of Hero, in Rami's mind.

They followed Iambe and Pallas down a spiral of stairs into what appeared to be a grotto underneath the building. Bright paint and marble quickly melted into raw rock face and a faint drip of water. They cut across a hallway that jutted precariously over a cavern of shadows before coming to an archway that spanned over their heads.

There were no great doors, not like Hell's Library. The threshold was marked by a gauzy shift of cloth. There was a spectral quality to it, moving with the unseen breezes that puffed and pulled from deeper inside. Iambe stopped just short of the arch with a disapproving air. She smirked at Hero and Ramiel before raising her hand and snapping her fingers twice.

From far away, deep past the veil, the staccato snap repeated itself.

"Really, sister. There's no need to be *rude*," Pallas muttered.

"*Rude*," came a faint voice past the arch.

That brought a smile back to Pallas's face. He brightened and pushed past Iambe. "It's all right, Mother! Please let us in. We've brought visitors of the Library—from Hell's Library."

"*Hell's Library?*" The words were repeated tone for tone, but somehow the voice managed to turn it into a question. Iambe rolled her eyes and looked as if she was prepared to say something, but a sharp gust of wind abruptly parted the veil of fabric. Pallas caught the edge and beckoned them inside.

Ramiel stepped past the arch and blinked. The space beyond had seemed another dark, gloomy cavern from the other side, but as they stepped through, a gentle light flooded his eyes. They were in what appeared to be a giant amphitheater made of stone. The walls were natural juts of slate, Corinthian, and swept up at a bowl-like angle. Green undergrowth, accented with tiny white flowers, only reached a meter up the walls before giving way to stark stone. Above them, a spider work of fine rocky tendrils, so thin it almost looked like bone, weaved a delicate trellis roof that held back the sky but allowed slants of light in. They created near-blinding spotlights of sunlight that hit long, strangely rustic towers of shelves and cast skeletal fingers of twilight.

"This is a library?" Ramiel breathed.

"Well." Hero looked disconcerted, trying to cross his arms over his chest even as he stared wide-eyed at the delicate path of flowers wound between each stack and the next. "Obviously not a proper one." The proud book of his first acquaintance would never have defended the Library. Rami turned his head to hide his amusement.

Pallas and Iambe, immune to the wonder, continued straight on inside and came to a stop in front of what Rami realized was a small depression in the stone filled with still water and bathed in a particularly bright sun spot. Rami and Hero trailed close enough to see the basin's surface was mirrorlike. Although Pallas and Iambe stood at the water's edge, only Pallas's figure appeared in the pond.

"Favorites as usual," Iambe muttered.

"*As usual.*" Now inside the Library, the source of the voice that repeated off the high walls was hard to place. It bounced around the canyon-like space, breaking into a whispered chorus until "*usual*" crumbled into a sigh of "*all, all, all.*" It faded into a serene quiet that raised every hair on the back of Rami's neck. His hand itched for his sword, but he was more disciplined than that.

Pallas gave Iambe a sympathetic nudge, then stepped forward, as if addressing the pond. He dropped to his knees and appeared to take a moment to get comfortable on the small patch of mossy earth. "These are my friends Ramiel and Hero, of the Unwritten Wing. Will you greet them in person, Mother? I don't mind."

"*Mind,*" the whispers repeated, like a warning.

Ramiel couldn't help but look at the pond expectantly. There was no movement beneath the surface, no change at all. Then, in the breadth of a blink, Pallas stood—no, that couldn't be right. Pallas remained, relaxed and kneeling at the edge of the water, but the *reflection* of Pallas was standing. The water shivered and mist rose, as if solidifying—or evaporating? It was impossible to tell. And then the standing image of Pallas emerged. It didn't rise from the pond, water streaming. The surface didn't change again at all. It *emerged*, as if stepping out of a panel. Or a mirror.

"What—" Hero made a sound of protest—whether protesting the creature, the entrance, or the entire situation was unclear—and took an involuntary step closer behind Rami's shoulder. It was distracting enough that Rami nearly missed the next transformation.

The new Pallas-figure touched its toes to the mossy bank and appeared to pivot on an unseen axis, fully standing on the basin edge now, as if gravity hadn't applied at all. It paused, head downturned to consider the identical form still kneeling by the pond. Fingers reached out, brushing through Pallas's golden curls before it straightened and faced them.

"Gentlemen, I present my mother, the cursed nymph Echo." Iambe's voice was droll and sharply pointed as a tack. "Librarian of the Wing of the Unsaid. And a lover of overdramatic entrances."

The mirror-figure flicked a level gaze at Iambe but remained silent, evidently not finding adequate words to repeat in her statement. Eventually her scrutiny turned back their way, and understanding hit Rami the moment he met her gaze.

Pallas's eyes had been blue, and Rami might have noted—just in passing, mind you—how appealingly the light caught and turned that blue to something like a paler imitation of the sky. It had an innate openness, a youth, that was unusual for immortals and long-dead residents of the realms. But those sky-eyes had been taken over, clouded. They felt grayer, infinitely older and weary, softening his entire face with an alien, remote regret.

"A possession?" Hero hissed under his breath.

"A reflection, you fool," Iambe corrected. She made a dismissive gesture to the still form of her brother. "Echo can only repeat what has been said, and can only appear as a reflection, willingly given."

"*Reflection willingly given*," the mirror-Pallas called Echo repeated, though his—her, at the moment, Rami mentally corrected—lips didn't move.

Rami tried to redirect his thoughts. "But your brother—"

"He'll be fine. Simply trapped in time until his reflection returns to him. Mother would never let *him* wither away."

"*Away*," Echo said wistfully.

Something else—something entirely silent and chalky with resentment—echoed between mother and daughter. Rami measured it and knew well enough that he wanted no part of that explanation. Some stories were not his to hear. He cleared his throat. "An honor to meet you, Librarian Echo. We would like to access your Library, by your leave."

Echo-Pallas tilted her head and regarded them for a tick of silence. "*Leave*," she said. Her eyes were on Rami, but the order was obviously for Iambe. To her credit, she barely flinched. She left with a shrug and one final sour look to her brother's still form.

Ramiel made introductions as brief as possible, since Hero was still staring aghast, as if Echo was the worst kind of demon. The sooner they moved on to business, the better. "We are searching for information on a past librarian of the Unwritten Wing. One by the name of Poppaea Julia. She was of your time, and seeing as this realm claimed her, we'd hoped we might find answers here."

Echo-Pallas appeared to consider. The soft voices were affirmative when they repeated, "*Here*."

"This isn't even a conversation." Hero's cheeks were still missing their color, but he appeared to have recovered his usual catlike disgust, at the very least. "We will get nowhere like this."

"*No. Where like this.*" Echo said, and Hero threw up his hands with a grunt.

"She's the librarian of Elysium," Rami insisted. "If there's anyone left who knew about Poppaea Julia, it's her. We have to try."

"*It's her we have to try.*"

Hero made a strangled sound. "See? This is an exercise in comedy."

He wasn't impatient; he was unnerved. Rami had learned by now to read around Hero's protests and simply ignored him. Echo was staring intently at them both. The replication of Pallas's faded blue eyes had grown sharper, and a keen intellect trapped in them was trying to get something across. Something important. "You do know something?"

Echo stayed silent.

Rami tried again. "Poppaea Julia, the librarian of the Unwritten Wing who rebelled. Did she come here after she was banished?"

Echo's chin drifted right, then left. *No.* But she was still staring at him, pinning him with her gaze. Hero began to grumble something, but Rami held up a silencing hand—a distant part of him noting with surprise that Hero actually *complied*—as he tried to run over what had been said.

"It's her we have to try," Rami repeated slowly. "Her, who? Is there someone else who knows more?"

Without so much as a blink, Echo turned on her heel, light as a dancer, and walked away. Rami furrowed his brow and risked a glance at Hero before gesturing after her. "We have to try."

Pure skepticism etched itself over every one of Hero's precisely handsome features, but he mimed his lips shut and raised his hands in defeat. They jogged to catch up with Echo, but it was obvious where she was leading them.

Into the sandstone canyons of the library of Elysium.

# 14

# HERO

The wings of the Library are multitude. What gets remembered and what gets forgotten? Books, poems, unsung heroics, regrets. It seems random, what the Library sees fit to preserve for eternity. What do these things have in common? Are they all creative acts, or fated in some way? What are the criteria of immortal survival?

The only thing I can see, from here, is that they're all innately human. Humans are the only mortal creatures that compose such ways to express desire, want, regret. Expression of the way things should be, or never were. That's a very human skill.

*Librarian Ibukun of Ise, 929 CE*

THE STACKS OF THE Unsaid Wing were not peopled by neat rows of dreaming hardcover spines. The spines in each square-cubed wood apartment seemed more scattered and dead than sleeping. Scrolls tumbled in a cascade out of one shadow, while a stack of tattered envelopes threatened to spill off a high shelf entirely. It wasn't all paper or parchment either. Hero caught a glint of sunlight between piles, engraved rings, carved bone. Knotted poesy crowns of flowers. Occasionally, a box appeared completely empty, but as he passed, a tendril of whispers reached out with a snippet of half-formed words. Hero knew better than to stop to listen.

Yes, the Unsaid Wing was an alien world compared to home. Compared to the Unwritten Wing. "Home," where did that come from? Hero was a character of an unwritten book. Unwritten books did not have homes; they had . . . prisons, he would have said once. Places where they were held. Unjustly. Illogically. Temporarily.

That was it exactly. The Library could not be a home, no matter what mad impulses took his brain, because that would make the Library cease to be a temporary stopping point. To stop would be to give up on his book, fixing his book, inspiring his author, or . . . or at least getting to live his story again.

No, Hero focused on the yellow tendrils that directed their path in the oddly smooth moss beneath his feet. He would always be far from home.

"These are all unsaid things, then? Words that were formed with intent but never shared?" Ramiel was saying ahead of him.

He was still trying to converse with the damned creature. Echo-as-Pallas floated along ahead of them, hair flashing bright in the patterns of sunlight. The edge of her chiton barely stirred in the breeze, as if the wide-eyed boy who owned that reflection had never existed, hadn't been left cold and crouching by the pool.

Yes, he could admit it. The librarian of the Unsaid Wing unnerved Hero entirely, because he was evidently the only one with a lick of *sense*. He was intimately aware of the idea of being fluid in identity and form. But when he'd woken up and made the gradual unfurling from book-shaped to human, it had been as natural as uncurling yourself from a long sleep. Every book carried a scar, a splinter of psyche, that was essential to its need to exist. Heroes, mostly, but sometimes a secondary character like a damsel, or even an object of desire. And sometimes monsters, antagonists like himself.

The sweet irony was, Hero hadn't realized he wasn't the protagonist until he woke, standing in a dusty, dimly lit hallway, with the weight of proof in his hands.

Hero or villain, either way there was no *question* what shape Hero would have taken. No choice, no abiding randomness of *opportunity.* The idea that creatures like this cursed nymph existed to just step in and out of another's skin—their reflection, rather—like pests rendering a tree hollow . . .

Everything should know their shape, in Hero's mind. His book was broken, yes, but he was still a *book.* He'd been shocked to not be the protagonist, but he'd long since adjusted to his nature as a villain. As long as he knew what he was, he knew the thrust of his story. Being nothing but what was reflected by others . . .

That wasn't a story at all.

"Letters, confessions, dedications . . ." Rami muttered again, slowing as he scanned the shelves. His profile was lit by the eerie, stone-split sunlight that suffused the entire library. It painted gold coins on his olive skin. "Remarkable. Humans are remarkable."

*Humans.* Not books. It was always the creators, not the created. Hero sometimes wondered why anyone bothered to preserve him at all. Still. Curiosity got the best of him. Hero drifted toward the nearest shelf and plucked a short scroll from the top.

"*I want you to know I never regretted it,*" he read under his breath. "*Not one moment of my life with you. No matter how the end comes now, choosing you was the best decision I ever made. You are . . .*" Hero frowned and rolled the scroll gently before returning it to the shelf with a huff. "What nonsense. Who would bother to save all this—this *sentimentality?*"

"I would have thought you'd understand," Rami said with a contemplative look. "Losing the chance for closure with people you may never see again."

Hero's step faltered. The square weight of his book burned in the pocket of his coat, weighty as a brand. The implication was obvious, no matter how gently Ramiel tried to put it. Hero had a whole world he'd been cut off from, the only one he'd known. The only one he'd been made for. He hadn't given it a thought at the time. Waking up was instinct. His book had been one world, the Library another. A simple journey. He'd always assumed going back would be just as simple—eventually. When he got around to it.

If he hadn't quite given up the idea of going back, he certainly couldn't see the road anymore either.

Ramiel's gaze was like a weight. "I—" Hero forced his chin up and his shoulders through a mechanical, well-practiced shrug. "It's not as if many would have missed me back home. Villains are not well-liked, even in their own stories."

Ramiel had taken too long to respond. Hero shook the lingering chill of old ghosts and looked up sharply. The Watcher feigned intense interest in the scroll in his hands. A glance said it was an unsent angry tirade, entirely unworthy of the sympathetic, soft look on Ramiel's stony features.

Hero clicked his tongue. "Right, enough of this heart-to-heart nonsense. Where's the monster gone off to?"

Echo drifted at the crest of the rise. *Rise.* Proper libraries didn't have *rises*, or hills, or moss, or sunlight like a song. Proper libraries had shelves and books, and an indexing system and calling cards like any sensible—

Oh dear *gods*, he was beginning to sound like Claire.

Echo didn't move as they caught up with her. Her face—Pallas's face—was just as dull as it had been since it stepped out of the pond. She extended one hand and pointed farther down. Hero followed the gesture with his eyes to another of the canyon-like stone towers, cubbies worn with more age than the neat slab cuts they'd seen so far.

"You have something about the Unwritten Wing here? In the actual archives?"

"*Actual archives*," Echo whispered, which Hero thought was rather cheating.

Ramiel exchanged a mystified look with Hero and nodded. "Well, we'll take a look, then—er, may I?"

"Aye."

Echo tilted her head back and forth, in a birdlike way that was entirely creepy, then began swanning back the way they came, leaving them in the stacks to presumably find their way out again.

Hero was entirely over the gimmick of this place. "Let's see what the vulture has for us."

Ramiel nodded, appearing to remember the task at hand past the wonder of the library. The Unsaid Wing had been cheerily empty upon entry, but as they wound farther back, the quiet lost the feeling of a living glen and took on the qualities of a held breath. Unwritten books were solid, held-together things, awake or asleep. But unsaid words were all fragments, sharp edges, like the shards of stone above their heads. The feeling of a precipice was too great. Hero kept glancing up at the sky, lost in lavender gloom and web work of stone lattice, as if the unspoken words would topple on them at any moment.

Folded sheaves gave way to rolled scrolls, which gave way to older, more eccentric materials. Unlike the words of the Unwritten Wing, these words were never meant for anyone but their intended recipient, so the artifacts felt no inclination to change, to demand to be read. An inherent laziness, in Hero's opinion. Finally, Ramiel came to an abrupt stop several shelves down.

"Poppaea Julia." Hero squinted through the blocky lettering on the shelf. "She's here after all. The librarian that challenged Hell."

"Supposedly," Ramiel said. "It can't hurt to look."

Hero made a noncommittal sound. This had been his idea, but after catching glimpses of the kind of unsent tripe this library held, he doubted they'd find anything enlightening here now. The first few minutes he spent perusing confirmed his instincts. "This is all human nonsense before the woman had even died. There's not going to be anyone with unsaid words for her *after* her death here. Nothing about the Library."

The complaint didn't slow down Ramiel in the slightest. He kept methodically examining shelves farther down, touching each scroll lightly, as if it was a treasure, holding it up to the light to read. His expression told the tales—Ramiel was not an expressive creature, but Hero had found himself gaining literacy in the way his arched brows knit in concern, the way the grim line of his generous mouth softened, just at the edges at small things. It was much more entertaining than the scrolls, at least, and Hero had to keep himself from staring.

"Here now," Ramiel muttered. His brows did a caterpillar dance. Code: astounded surprise in the language of Ramiel's face. Hero looked down to find the cause. The rolled papyrus in Ramiel's hand was not yellowed ivory like the rest of the collection. The bleached surface was too white for the human-made papyrus of the day. Fine emerald script, spidery as tattered thread, crossed the scroll in tight, orderly lines.

"What is it?" Hero relented and crowded Ramiel's shoulder to get a better look.

"Every unsent communication," Ramiel mumbled with a shake of his head. "They really are thorough."

Hero had no patience for slow reveals. Ramiel's hand was blocking the way, but Hero's eyes jumped to the blocky thick signature at the bottom of the page. "Revka . . . *Arcanist?!* As in *Hell's* Arcanist?"

"It appears so." Ramiel frowned as he unwound the scroll to read again. "It wasn't always a position held by a demon." Hero had a faint memory of Claire saying the same thing once. During one of the many obsessive attempts she'd made to train him to be a proper assistant for Brevity. Hero hadn't bothered listening, since assisting wasn't so hard and appeared to be simply doing what menial chores Brevity asked for. But it had been fun to watch the way Claire's dark eyes had sharpened into storms as she berated him.

Over Ramiel's shoulder, the text had taken on that wiggling, twitchy quality of library-to-library documents. Hero already felt a headache coming on—not that books could get headaches—but squinted his eyes determinedly until the ink resolved itself into a letter.

> *Librarian Poppaea,*
>
> *You are an imbecile. You are a knacker-eared, fecund-brained bastard of ill-cast winds. You are a fool's fool, a dunce among the blighted. I hate the day I ever learned your name.*

"Well," Hero said as he read, "this could be good."

> *And I miss you.*

"Oh, never mind." But he didn't stop reading.

The Library is in chaos. My own wing is in lockdown. Hell runs amok. And great wailing quakes of gods know what is the only indication I have that an Unwritten Wing even still exists. The Muses Corps, for lack of a better target, has been railing at me—me!—to do something, but of course there's nothing to do. Hell is hell. It's all very good to go on about the Library being an independent entity, but there's no one to stop Morningstar on a rampage. He can't get rid of us, I don't think. Not all of us. But, gods, it sounds like he's going to try.

What did you say?

What did you say, when you got this mad plan in your head? To challenge Morningstar for right to the domain? And then to claim authority, not on behalf of the Library—oh no, nothing as sensible as that—but on behalf of the BOOKS. Had you totally taken leave of your senses? Was my companionship so undesirable that you would seek to end your existence entirely?

I'm the Arcanist. My job is magical artifacts. As a golem, I am an artifact. Artifact and Arcanist. My domain is working with materials. As you used to say, things. Finding things. Keeping things. Fixing things. Yet I don't know how to fix this.

I know you, Julia. I know what your first concern would be. "But are the books well?" you'd ask, voice getting that endearing fleshy squeak that humans do when distressed. I'm sure that'd be your first question. I wish you were here to shake. Of course the infernal books will be fine. You could drown the whole Library and the essential part—what makes the damned things so valued—would be left. I don't know what that would even look like, but the unwritten books will outlive us all. The curse of unwritten books is to never truly live but exist forever.

*I wish librarians had been half as cursed.*

*Where are you, Poppaea? When it failed, where did he send you? To your Blessed Isles, the land of heroes you spoke of? To Tantalus? Or to oblivion? Surely, what qualities you share with your damned books mean oblivion isn't in store for you. The written and the writer are the same, after all. Perhaps Morningstar sent you to one of your books, to rejoin what you've missed for so long. Maybe you'll be caught in your own story, ready to be read. I think you'd like that, really.*

*You used to tease me, sweetheart, about emotions. How stoic golems were, how passions must move so slowly through clay. But I am angry now, dear one. Angry at you. How could you abandon your post? Abandon our shared duties, our routine of care and curiosity?*

*How could you abandon me?*

*I may be mere clay and magic, not like your precious books. But I thought you'd cared for me all the same.*

*Come back, Julia. This can't be the way your story ends.*

*I'll read every book until I find you.*

> *Arcanist of the Arcane Wing, Revka bat-Rav*

"A tragedy." Ramiel's murmur was like ground gravel against Hero's skin. He must have stared at the papyrus long after reading it. Hero felt queer, like he was slipping between the loops of thick script.

"More self-pitying nonsense." Hero shook his head and tried to focus on what had nagged at his attention. "I would have thought a golem would have been more practical."

"Nothing more practical than loss. It's a natural product of time," Ramiel said quietly. Hero struggled not to wince. Of course the stoic old wart was still haunted by his own losses—Hero couldn't imagine what it'd be like to be born in literal paradise and lose it. Hero hadn't been born in paradise. If there was an opposite of eternal contentment, Hero had woken to that. He'd been born with a burning *want* in his chest, a hunger-pang sense of something missing. He supposed his author had put it there, though he'd never thought to hate her for it.

"Well. She could have done something about it besides bellyache," Hero said weakly.

Out of the corner of his eye, he caught Ramiel's glance at him, his expression softening to something dangerously near kindness. "Like a suicidal run at your own author and burning your own pages?"

"To be accurate, I didn't burn my pages. She did. Authors are innately cruel like that." Hero shrugged. He welcomed the opportunity to bicker. He held no illusions about his own mistakes and failures, not when they'd been performed so openly in front of all the Library. But the memory jogged through him. Hero frowned and tugged until Ramiel released the scroll into his hands. "But there was that line—"

"About cruelty?"

"No." Hero chewed on his lip as he scanned the page. "There! *The written and the writer are the same, after all.*" He read aloud. "What does that mean?"

A bemused look settled on Ramiel's face. The confusion curdled the half smile that Hero had noticed earlier. A pity. "I'm afraid you're asking the wrong one. I never worked with your Library, not like Claire and Brevity. I know souls, not books."

Yes, everyone loved to remind him how different Hero was. "Yes, I'm aware how unhelpful you are." The huff came out a little harsher than Hero meant it, but the riddle had sunk its claws in and now he couldn't shake the feeling that it was important. "The written and the writer . . ."

"You books do have a documented affinity for your human creators," Ramiel tried.

And because he tried, Hero bit back the barbed reply that welled up. He settled for pinning the Watcher with a patient look. "And you have an affinity for swords and filthy raincoats. That doesn't mean you *are* one."

Ramiel took that with the same graceful acceptance he took every harsh word Hero had for him. It was infuriating, really. That had to be why Hero couldn't stop. The Watcher's brow furrowed as he scrutinized the letter again. "What qualities you share . . . it appears at least that this Arcanist was convinced that books could not be destroyed."

"If that was the case, we wouldn't have spent the last months with Claire and Brevity walking around as if we'd kicked their puppies," Hero muttered.

"Their grief is natural, and sincere."

There was a guilt in his chest that ached every time a stray comment caused the librarians to get that haunted look in their eyes. The defense of the Unwritten Wing had been his strategy, his. And it'd failed. If he'd fought harder, perhaps—but no. Hero had a policy about mistakes and failures. The guilt could stay and ache, but he wouldn't pick at it. He had enough scars, after all.

Hero rolled the scroll closed impatiently. "Either the Arcanist is mistaken, or the librarians are. The existence of this damned ink supports the scroll's claim. It's not as if we can ignore that." The scroll closed with a snap, and Hero caught movement out of the corner of his eye as he shelved it. The damned metal lioness stirred to her feet at the noise. Its gold eyes emitted a faint light as it tracked Hero. He tried to ignore it and began to pace. "Shame this golem woman wasn't still Arcanist instead of Andras. We might have gotten some answers."

"Or not had the question to ask in the first place." Ramiel watched Hero with nearly as much concern as the cat. "I wonder what happened to her."

Hero dismissed that with a wave. "Perhaps she got rusty. Surely your wing keeps some kind of record." Hero paused midstep and turned back to Ramiel. "Of all the . . . Could the answers be in there?"

"The Arcane Wing?" Ramiel blinked. "Doubtful. If such knowledge was recorded, surely Claire—"

"Claire has been preoccupied with not drowning in the history of her regret," Hero said, not ungently. "She—she can't see straight since the coup. You know that. That's why she needs us."

*Needs me*, Hero wanted to say, but no, he did not believe in kidding himself. Ramiel had stepped in when Claire had been forced to reposition herself as the Arcanist, shoring her up with an implacable calm, a peace when all that Hero could offer was flippant distraction. They were both walking, nettling reminders to each other of what they once had been. Ramiel kept Claire standing, and Hero kept her on her toes.

Hero's opinions on that were grudging and unresolved, so, as he did with all unpleasant things, he ignored them.

Ramiel nodded thoughtfully, as if Hero had merely commented on the weather. "Claire has been sequestered with the few documents the Arcane Wing holds. So, you are suggesting we should return, then, and search the wing on our own?"

"Yes—no." Hero's gaze strayed to the scroll he'd just put away. He led the way down the corridor the way they'd come. He listened but couldn't hear the copper cat's paws stalking across the moss behind them. "There's one more thing we should investigate while we're in this realm."

"In the library?"

"No," Hero said. "But perhaps it's adjacent. The golem mentioned the muses—they're a Greek creature, too, right?"

# 15

# CLAIRE

Myrrh. First thing I did was investigate the material evidence. No, not the stories or characters—everything has been quiet on that front. But between my lessons with Bjorn, I have been conducting a clandestine study of the paper. I'm not so dead that I have forgotten haggling with the ragmen for my linens. Not yet. Provenance! Everything comes from something. Pages are made and remade: that's the story I'm interested in.

First observation: there's no sizing, no coating over the paper to keep it from absorbing ink too quickly as it dries. Which would seem impossible. What surface is made to absorb everything? What ink?

The coating a paper has to keep ink from soaking in immediately and feathering is going to be unique to the environment. A flour-based size works admirably in the dry desert but quickly turns to rot in humid countries. What are the material concerns of an immaterial, immortal library?

*Apprentice Librarian Fleur Michel, 1736 CE*

TO A MODERN EYE, ink looked like water. Colored water perhaps, like poorly brewed tea or the garishly colored sugar drinks of her youth.

Claire knew better. She had been alive at the turn of that era, when the incendiary grit and gristle of war had led to a boom of new technologies, new ways of doing things. She'd started school learning her letters with fountain pens, but by the time she'd matriculated into the workforce, all the modern workplaces were driven by the plastic milled barrels of ballpoint. When it dried up, a pen was tossed, not refilled. What a wasteful idea that was. Ink became something that was a minor component of the pen, not the fuel for it.

There wasn't a lot left that Claire could remember of her life on Earth, but she remembered the language of inks. The viscosity and flow, the way some inks dried on cheap paper, feathered and bone bleak, while others went onto fine vellum paper like a sigh, changing from dark to light in a single stroke. Inks had temperaments, personalities. And inks left marks, smudged fingers, smeared words, lost meanings.

A sound, like a weaponized rusty hinge, broke her concentration. Something pinched the end of one of her braids and pulled. It was a brief tug, a demand for attention. Bird cocked her head, regarding her with one flat eye and obvious accusation.

"Right, attributes." Claire sighed, remembering to straighten her back for the first time in hours. The ache was a welcome change of pace. "It is slow to dry. A supernaturally high viscosity." Claire ticked off the characteristics on her stained hand again. Bird appeared to listen intently but might have just been watching for treats. "Iridescent sheen when wet, but dries to a matte finish. Waterproof, tamperproof, smear-proof. Obviously." Her blackened fingernails felt chalky to the touch.

The secret was here, in the evidence. Her talk with Walter had told her that much. She just needed to verify her hunch. Ink did not exist without the book. It could not be replicated, borrowed, or transplanted—though gods knew she'd tried countless times when attempting to repair Hero. A book could only hold the ink it remembered. A book was paper and ink together, existing as the story slept.

So, without paper there should *be* no ink. The books lost to the coup had burned, a tragedy that she was almost grateful she only remembered as aftermath. The haunted look Brevity got when talking about the burning was enough. The stories that had been preserved in those books died, trapped in so much ash. The ash that had been everywhere. Claire had spent days afterward afraid to wash her hands. It felt sacrilegious; it felt cruel.

She adjusted the bright light over the worktable, as if that would reveal anything more than her own reflection. The Claire in the ink was cast in shades of black, staring out at her from the pitiless surface like an omen of what was to come. Claire rubbed her clean hand against the gooseflesh that crept up the back of her neck. There was barely enough liquid in the bowl to coat the bottom, but light didn't penetrate it at all. The ink had a lubricated loll when Claire tilted the bowl from side to side. That might explain why it never dried, no matter how long it sat. No film developed like on her skin; no pieces flaked away. Just an infinite, oil-slicked black, swallowing the light and every color in the spectrum and giving back nothing, nothing at all.

"An unknown variable requires caution," Claire muttered, feeling ridiculous for having a raven as a lab partner. There was nothing to be learned by glaring at her reflection in this bit of ink. She carefully set the dish aside and dug around for gloves to prepare a new sample.

All Claire wished to do right now was hurtle the damn sample into the bin. This was Claire's problem to solve. The only thing she could *do* was solve it. If she didn't understand the ink, then what good was she?

"Enough experiments." Claire sat back, glaring at the table. She'd put off the thought as long as she could. "Jars, ashes, ink . . . it's all nonsense. I need a comparison."

A comparison. The idea lightninged through her, less like an illumination and more like a shock. Sharp, cutting, and then gone. If the ink had once been books, then it had once been damsels too. Rosia had led them here, under a compulsion, a connection. She'd called the ink "they."

Claire had been so determined to keep the ink from the Unwritten Wing, but she'd been going about it wrong. It was important to keep the ink out of harm for the *librarian*. Not the wing.

"Books know stories. Walter, you're a genius." Claire had to speak to the damsels immediately.

Claire straightened from her slump and grabbed several empty sample bottles. It was a risky experiment and would require fresh bottles. "Bird, watch the artifacts for a spell."

Bird croaked and tilted her head at Claire's hurried movements, bleak eyes tracking her hands for any sign of an edible treat. "Later," Claire reassured her. If the damsels held the answers she sought, she'd give Bird the whole cracker box.

THE DOORS OF THE Unwritten Wing drew her to a stop, yet again. It was a ridiculous hang-up. Claire needed to obliterate her memory of them in her mind. She stopped down the hall from the doors, and a shiver of cold drew across the nape of her neck like a clammy hand. Surely the doors hadn't been this towering. Brevity must have darkened the stain, giving it a glow of amber and red that only served to remind Claire of fire. She could almost still smell the ghost of smoke on the air, the grit and sulfur presence of never afters and poor ends. Lost stories. She had a visceral memory of how the wood boards had

squelched ever so slightly under her feet as she left, waterlogged with
the last-ditch efforts to save the stacks.

If the doors had been closed, Claire would have turned around
right then. It would have been too much to reach out and touch, to
relive the feeling of blasting through those doors into a sanctuary in-
vaded. The sear of ash, the fetid exhale of demons, ink, and blood.

But the doors were open, as they should have been. Claire forced a
purposefully deep breath and caught the scent of old leather, paper,
and the faint not-unpleasant ripple of anise that existed in the back-
ground of all of Hell. No ash, no rot.

It wasn't a hard task to slip into the Library, once Claire could get
past her own ghosts. Claire kept her eyes carefully focused ahead,
diverting them only long enough to ascertain that the librarian's desk
was empty. Brevity must have been somewhere in the labyrinth of
stacks, deeper in the Library and perhaps in comfortable conversation
with Probity. Recalling old times. Claire would be here and gone before she could bother them.

The stacks had remained largely organized the same, thank goodness. If Claire focused very carefully on the end of each row, she could
pretend not to notice all the little differences. Like the reflection of
cheerful faerie lights off warm cherrywood. Or the things that remained so achingly the same, like the soft constant susurrus of sleeping unwritten books. It was constant and soothing, like waves on a
smooth shore.

It was impossible to tell which hurt worse.

If there was one thing with which Claire was experienced, it was
the alchemy of turning pain to usefulness. By the time she reached the
small frosted door of the damsel suite, the ache had become a stone,
and stone had become certainty. The more it hurt, the surer she was.
This was the right choice, the correct path of action. She would get

answers here. She would know, and in her knowing, the world would make sense again.

And if the world made sense again, she could *fix* it. For Hero, Rami, Brevity. For all of them.

It was the resolution Claire needed to place her hand on the latch. The metal was cool, grounding as the ache of stone. She rapped her knuckles twice on the frosted glass before letting herself in.

A pocket of air heavy with tea and fresh linen enveloped her with warmth. The damsel suite had always been several degrees more to the side of cozy than the rest of the Library, and Claire marveled again at how even this had changed under Brevity's care. She'd had the opportunity twice before, but now she had the luxury of being neither injured nor harried. She stepped into a well-appointed sitting room. Well, perhaps the sitting rooms of Claire's era wouldn't have been quite so lined, wall to wall, with bookshelves, but it was still decidedly homey. A glimpse of small hallways and open doorways said there were even *bedrooms* now, which had never before occurred to Claire as something an unwritten book would need. A small fire licked the hearth in the corner, and the sight of it made Claire's heart constrict for longer than she would admit. Flames, in such proximity to the book-lined wall, opened up a scab in her chest that had never quite healed.

When she'd woken up earlier, she'd been preoccupied with her hand, but now she was here with a goal in mind. A few damsels were scattered in pockets of activity through the lounge. Repeatedly, gazes flickered up, taking Claire in with a guarded glance, then turning back to their focus. At one point, Claire had felt more boogeyman than librarian. Now she felt like neither.

"Child." Claire turned to see a damsel finally extract herself from conversation. The woman who approached was not the typical cut of damsel—young, pretty according to the standards of her era, with a blank look in her eyes that quickly rubbed off like bad varnish after a taste of the independence that the damsel suite offered. The woman who approached was older, silver hair cut into a businesslike pixie and stout body swathed in a kind of housedress that was meant for comfort.

"Claire," she corrected automatically. Andras had been fond of pet names, and Claire had developed a distaste for them. "Just Claire is fine."

"Of course, Claire." The woman took the correction with good grace. "They call me Lucille. Granny Lucy, mostly, but I don't imagine you allow yourself such luxuries as elders." Claire wasn't allowed more than a moment to consider whether that was a compliment or not before Lucille was nodding to the nearest seat. "What brings a former librarian to us?"

Claire preferred to remain standing. If anything, the damsel suite was more homelike, more welcoming than ever, but Claire felt on edge. The vials in her pocket were chilled weights, and her mind noted every crack and hiss from the fireplace like a snake ready to strike. She cleared her throat. "There's a line of inquiry I believed you all might help me with."

Lucille had begun to lower herself into an armchair in that ponderous way arthritis sufferers did, but halted midmotion at that. A calculating expression flicked across her face, then was dismissed as she finished settling into the chair. By the time she straightened her baggy skirt, she'd become a picture of grandmotherly care again. "Well then, a welcome change to the rare dramas that brought you to us before. Have a seat, dear. Would you like a cookie? Summer baked brownies, but"—Lucille lowered her voice to a fond stage whisper—"he uses *carob*. He's from some hippie romance," Lucille supplied, as if the unwritten book's genre explained everything.

"It's better for you," a pale young man muttered with a shrug as he set down the plate of chocolate squares she supposed must have been pulled from some unwritten cookbook. Summer gave Claire a single once-over that spoke volumes of judgment before leaving them again.

Claire resisted pointing out the fact that none of them precisely needed to eat in the Library, let alone *carob brownies*. She was disliked enough in the damsel suite as it was. Still, the vials clinked restlessly in her breast pocket. "We've discovered the source of the disturbance that was drawing away damsels."

"Oh, well done, Claire dear!" Lucille enthused over her tea.

Using a pet name *with* her name was just impertinence. Claire bit back a sour response behind a smile. "Yes, I'm collaborating with the . . . the librarian—" She stumbled through the half-truth, glad Brevity wasn't here to see how difficult that title was for Claire to say. "But I'm reluctant to decide a choice of action until we understand the nature of it."

"How nice of you to think of us," Lucille said. She sounded sincere enough, though "nice" wasn't the mood when Claire took the temperature of the room. None of the damsels met her gaze, but there was a prickle on the back of her neck. It was a paper-cut feeling of unwelcome, despite Lucille's smile.

Claire was being handled, bugger it all. The realization came on her in a flush of irritation. She was being handled, by this old woman, and she was *so tired* of being handled. In the Unwritten Wing, Brevity trod around her like an abandoned puppy, and even in the Arcane Wing, supposedly her own domain, she had to deal with Rami's stoic kind of fussing. Hero poked and prodded with a fraction of the venom he once had. Whether because they considered her dangerous or because they considered her fragile, Claire was always being *handled*.

And she was tired of it.

"I came here for *answers.*" Her voice was sharp and discordant over the hum of the room. Things quickly turned silent. Claire withdrew the vials of ink from her pocket and set them down—next to the ridiculous brownies—with a precise, cold clink. "About this."

Ah yes, they couldn't ignore her now. A dozen gazes drew to the table. The ink bobbled in each vial like a viscous raindrop, leaving an oil-sheen rainbow in its wake. Claire raised one sample above her head. "Tell me what it is."

Lucille hadn't moved. "Why would you think we know more than a librarian, child?"

"Because it's *part* of you and your books, as far as I can deduce. I wouldn't have found it without your meddling," Claire answered. She paused, seeking but not finding a polite opening for what she needed to ask. "You are the instigators of this situation."

"Instigator? You make it sound as if we were at fault."

*You were,* a seething voice in the back of Claire's mind raged. *You fought, like you were mortal, like you were* human. *And worse, you were cruel enough to die, you foolish, foolish things.* There were many things over the years that Claire had learned to soften on, to forgive. But breaking Brevity's heart—giving her a foundation for hope and ripping it away—that was never going to be one of them.

It was an ugly, unthinking grudge. So Claire kept it bottled inside her, with other dark things. It leaked out to a razor in her voice now. "I reserve judgment. Fault will be decided, I suppose, by your cooperation with the facts."

Lucille appeared to take a moment, as if weighing the taste of Claire's anger on her tongue. She shook her head slightly and busied herself with the platter of ceramic ware beside them. "I have never been afraid of the truth, Claire. Though it has never done me a bit of good.

Hiding from an unpleasant fact doesn't make it go away, does it?" She paused, steel in her eyes as she met Claire's gaze. "Tea?"

"No, thank you." It was a testimony to Claire's mental state that her stomach roiled at the thought of drinking tea with this woman— this *character*. She'd been a fool to think they might help her. She'd begun to think of them as damsels, as people, like Brevity insisted. But these women weren't like Brevity, not even like Hero, who'd shed ink like blood to prove his humanness.

Was that what she required? That everyone must bleed for her before they mattered? The memory of black wounds made bile rise in Claire's throat, but a thought came with it. "Ink," she muttered.

Lucille's placid gaze wavered until she sat the teapot back down with a sudden clink. "Ink over tea? You have odd tastes, child."

"No, you *bleed ink*." Claire remembered the way black liquid had seeped through Hero's velvet coat, too thin and slow drying for blood. She remembered the aftermath, after the fires and ruination, peeling the smoke-ragged clothes off him to inspect his wounds, fingertips coming away smudged with familiar stains. Her lungs were squeezed by a hot, clenching kind of urgency. "Characters in your form bleed ink, not blood. I've got an unidentified substance that I *need* to identify, obviously connected to your people in some way. All I need is a simple sample for comparison."

The room had gone quite still again. Claire hadn't noticed how false the room's quiet murmur was until it died. Perhaps because, at some point during her explanation, she had stood. Her hand had found the work scalpel she kept in a skirt pocket and held it high. It caught the light and shone like a threat.

"Claire," Lucille said, soft as lead. "There's no need for that here."

"I think there is." Claire's voice threatened to wobble in her throat.

She tried to shore it up with that bottled anger, but all that came to her summons was an increasing sense of desperation. "I need answers. It's my job to *have* answers. I can't protect them without answers."

"And who protects us?" Lucille didn't move from the chair but simply finished her tea and folded her hands in her lap.

The question bit, gnawed at the tender, guilty shadow that was Claire's past. But the possibility—the hope—that the answer was in front of her was too much to ignore. She swallowed and lowered the hand holding the scalpel—not to put it away, but for a slightly less overtly villainous posture. "I'm not the Unwritten Wing's librarian anymore. Your protection is not my responsibility."

The lie tasted like ash, but Lucille nodded acceptance. "As you wish. Here. Come, then. If you want blood, you know how to draw it." She put her hands heavily on the table and pushed to her feet, slow and ponderous. She stretched out an arm and met Claire's gaze. "Not the first time you've hurt a character, is it?"

"I'm not doing this to hurt," Claire said, trying to feel for the truth as it passed over her tongue. Wasn't she? She needed answers, but wouldn't it be a relief to take an answer from a book—willing or unwilling—and for a moment feel like she was certain of her role again? Her fingers wrapped tighter around the handle of the blade to steady her doubts as she reached for Lucille's arm. "Not that I have to explain my actions to you. You're certain you'll be able to hold on to this form?"

Lucille narrowed a level gaze at her in response. Eyes blue and unfilmed by age despite her appearance. "I'm not one of the lost young ones. I've known myself for a long time, child. Your little knife doesn't frighten me."

Claire nodded once and took hold of Lucille's arm about the wrist. A distraught murmur shivered through the room, vague distressed words that faded because the damsels followed Lucille's lead. Her skin felt the age the book was portrayed to be, human and papery thin under her fingertips. As Claire's would have, had she not died in middle age. Humans turned to paper and stories in the end, given enough time.

But not here. Her fingers were strong, and Lucille held still. She didn't need to pick a vein on a character—any prick would bleed. Claire glanced up once but received no encouragement from Lucille's cool gaze.

She brought the scalpel down in a practiced motion, a small diagonal cut. Black liquid welled along the line, and Claire dropped the scalpel to the table so she could snap up an empty vial to catch the bleeding ink.

Claire pointedly ignored the wash of disquiet that started at the sight of spilled ink. It wasn't squeamishness, no—the damsels who had survived the slaughter of the coup attempt were far beyond that. No, the gazes Claire felt on the back of her neck were hostile. Taking a scalpel to Lucille had brought back too many close associations with Claire's past treatment of books.

Mistreatment, she supposed, as she retrieved her instrument to press down harder around the wound to get a viable sample. Which was fair, she brooded, as she examined the black liquid as it dribbled across the glass of the vial—a red sheen, hmm, not exactly like the mystery ink. Not at first glance, in any case, but as Claire stared she felt like more colors bubbled beneath the surface. The others didn't understand the stakes. Claire needed answers. Needed them for—

"Claire!"

Brevity stood in the doorway, a shadow of a muse at her back. The naked horror on her face made Claire's hands flinch away from Lucille despite herself. But not before she carefully and precisely corked the sample.

# 16

# BREVITY

The poor boy thinks me mad. Yoon Ji Han is too polite to say it, of course, but he would lose his knickers at the gambling table. It is obvious that he thinks he's humoring me. Mad . . . now, that's a peculiar term, and, saints, don't they love applying it to women. Women have a special facility for madness. We're encouraged to go mad over the littlest things, because if our anger caught and held on the big things, we'd shape the world.

It's acceptable to be mad; it's dangerous to be angry.

The secret is that I am both.

*Librarian Fleur Michel, 1792 CE*

BREVITY HADN'T NEEDED AN explanation of the situation, when two damsels had stumbled, red-eyed and panicked, out of the depths of the stacks. She'd been idly doing log work while catching up on gossip from the corps that amused Probity, but Chiara and Becca's entrance stopped the conversation dead. Brevity knew the damsels by sight. Becca's cheeks were flushed with distress and she had a vise grip on Chiara, who looked prepared to punch someone. Or anyone. That might have been status quo for Chiara, but Becca's face had Brevity slapping the logbook closed and grabbing for her pen.

Probity was a beat behind her. Perhaps it had been because they'd been reminiscing, but a pang of familiarity struck Brevity as Chiara led the way into the stacks. Running here and there, Probity behind her like a loyal pastel ghost. It left Brevity with a kind of vertigo, feeling like the memory of two people at once. Brevity the cocksure muse, ready to inspire the world. That'd been easier than Brevity the librarian, hesitant and unprepared for whatever emergency had the damsels so upset.

The path they were taking was familiar; they were headed to the damsel suite. The thought of another threat there made her heart bottom out. Brevity glanced to her side, but Probity kept pace with fierce determination, not even breathing hard as she nodded. "Whatever you need. I've got your back."

That helped both versions of herself solidify together, if only for a moment. Brevity took a breath and followed Chiara through the suite door with determination. She could handle this, any situation; she was prepared; she could handle this just as well as—

"Claire!"

Brevity felt it like a strangling kind of montage. Scalpel pressed to a bleeding wound on a thin arm. Lucille's resigned way she stifled a flinch at the pain. Claire's expression as she turned, some kind of dull pragmatism. And the ink. The ink seemed to drown out everything, smeared across paper-fragile skin, welling at the incision, smudging Claire's fingertips, dripping . . .

No, not dripping or smudging; that was a different memory, a different time. Brevity sucked in a breath. "What are you *doing?*"

Claire was occupied with the vial of gore in her hands, stoppering it with a calm that sparked rage in the pit of Brevity's stomach. Claire looked up. "I'm doing my job. And you?"

There was a guarded reserve there, a waver that said she knew, she *knew,* she was doing something wrong. It was too familiar: the stiff line of Claire's back, the distant, flat look as she lifted her chin. Brevity knew that look, *knew.* It was the way Claire always looked when she felt it necessary to do something cruel.

Brevity steadied herself by application of her nails into the palms of her hands. "Step away from Lucille, Claire."

Claire flinched as if slapped but drew herself up and took half a step apart from the older woman. "I have what I need, in any case."

"And what would that be?" Probity asked lowly. She'd brushed up to Brevity's shoulder, a small gesture meant to be supportive. A soft horror colored Probity's soft voice, and her eyes were wide. "What use does a librarian have for blood?"

"Ink," Claire corrected sharply. "It's Library business."

"Library business is not *attacking* people!" Brevity hadn't meant to shout, but the sick feeling bubbled up through her throat. Many of the damsels stood in their places, still as stone. Becca was already helping Lucille wrap a clean towel over her arm. Lucille was too stubborn to return to her book to heal, but she'd be fine—Brevity knew this, but the fact was too quiet to drown out the recoil that Claire had *bled* a character. She'd damaged a book. Even now, after all that had happened. Probity laid a steadying hand on her shoulder and Brevity remembered herself. Yes. She was the librarian now. "We should talk about this, Claire. Outside."

Claire opened her mouth, then closed it. Her lips paled into a fine line and she busied herself with wiping the ink off her fingers onto her skirt. "This is quite unnecessary," she muttered as she swept up the vials in one hand and strode to the door.

Probity made a show of stepping aside with a sad shake of her head. "That's the librarian's call, not yours."

If Claire's footsteps faltered, just once, she covered it by turning stiffly back to Lucille. "Thank you for your cooperation." And she swept out the door.

Brevity made to follow but hesitated. Lucille was being tended to, and the other damsels only cast her a reproachful look before slowly drifting back to their small groups. Brevity deserved their judgment, she supposed. She was responsible, for all of them. It had never felt like such a weight until today.

Probity caught her gaze and placed a gentle hand on her shoulder. "You are the rightful librarian," she said quietly. There was a fervent belief in her voice, one Brevity couldn't find in herself. She clasped onto it and strode into the darkness of the stacks.

CLAIRE WAS WAITING FOR her, leaning up against the wall under a silver section placard that read MODERN NONCANON TRANSFORMA-TIVE WORKS. Her arms crossed like a shield in front of her chest, her head turned upward, studying the bobble of the faerie light. Brevity had always found the silvery way it lit the shelves enchanting, but now it painted Claire's face like frost, making her seem like a cold, removed thing.

"What happened?" Brevity asked, tight and controlled.

Claire blinked placidly at her, though a nervous energy twitched her ink-stained fingers. "Nothing to alarm yourself about. I am following a line of inquiry that needs a sample, and Lucille volunteered—"

Heat rose in a spike in Brevity's chest. "She didn't volunteer. They *never* volunteer!" She bit down hard on her lip as Claire's expression dropped. Brevity shook her head. "No books volunteer for your scalpel. Especially not the damsels; they know the risk of being shelved. Whatever Lucille did—"

"You think I *attacked* her?"

"It wouldn't be the first time!" Brevity threw out her hands. "Boss—Claire," she corrected her slip. No, Brevity was the librarian now. She had to do her job. Protect the books, even from Claire's misgivings. She was keenly aware of the weight of Probity's worried gaze on the back of her neck. Guarding, also judging. "I kinda thought—Hero and all—you'd come around. Figured some stuff out."

Claire flinched as if she'd been struck. "I don't need to *figure things out.*" She pulled two vials of ink from her pocket, wielding them like a key. "I *know* unwritten books; don't presume to chide me just because now they call you librarian—"

"I *am* the librarian." The words surprised Brevity, the sureness with which they appeared on her lips. But it was true; it was *true.* The books looked to her; Probity came to *her* to collaborate on behalf of the Muses Corps, not to Claire. No one expected Claire to protect the books, to fix the gaping empty spaces in the shelves of books lost in the fire. And when she failed, it wasn't Claire who would suffer the painful silence of the Library. Brevity drew herself up. "And as the librarian, I require you to explain your . . . 'line of inquiry' and why damaging one of my books without permission was necessary."

*My books. Without permission.* She sounded like Claire had sounded as librarian. Those were cruel, unnecessary barbs. Brevity had known that when she'd said it. Claire stared at her with an alien expression. Loss, Brevity realized too late. As long as Brevity had known her, Claire was a creature of certainty, even when she was dead wrong. She never looked lost, adrift. Even as her expression shuttered, reassembled into something more familiar, it felt wrong.

All of this felt wrong.

"It should be obvious enough to a *librarian.*" Claire's words were clipped and sharp as glass. She held up one vial in one hand, then the other. "This ink is of unknown origin and had a . . . peculiar response when applied to the logbook. You yourself argued for experimentation, if you'll recall. A sensible course of action is to compare it to the primary source of ink we understand: the wounds of unwritten characters."

*"Understand"* was an overstatement, in Brevity's opinion. Librarians knew how to correct corrupted text, how to herd the text around the page of an unwritten book to help maintain the integrity of the story. But that was curation. That was editing. Ink unattached to a book felt like a tool of creation. Or destruction. Ink could be both, to written words. Brevity saw the potential—it was why she argued for experimenting to understand if this substance could restore lost books—but the hard look in Claire's eyes said she wasn't thinking about creation.

Brevity couldn't hold that gaze. It hurt too much. She diverted to the vials in Claire's hands. Just ink to Claire. But Brevity saw the colors. Lucille's familiar tangled skein of tawny gold and violet spilled light from the right vial, twining like lazy mist between Claire's fingers. Unwritten books always reached for Claire, for humans. The left vial was different. The colors that reached from the mystery ink were numerous, like a rainbow put through a blender, chopped into static.

Probity had an intent expression at her side. She could see it too. Carefully, Brevity reached out. Claire's eyes narrowed, and she half expected her to snatch her hands back, but she allowed Brevity to carefully pick up each sample. She held Lucille's up to the light, as if to examine it. The threads of color still wisped through the air, back to Claire. No interest in Brevity's nonhuman touch. It'd been that indifference that had troubled Brevity during her time as a muse too. Humans created; muses only inspired.

But Probity thought that could change.

Her stomach fluttered at the thought, so Brevity quickly switched to studying the ink from the Arcane Wing. The static cloud of color flickered when she held it up, and Brevity half expected it to lash out. The spectrum churned and subsided, drifting like a fragmented cloud around the glass.

Not reaching.

"Slight differences," Brevity said carefully, as if just admiring the sheen of the ink. She brought her hands together. The glass vials had begun to warm against her palms, along with a quiet, persistent treachery of an idea.

"They are different," Claire allowed. There was an intensity in her eyes as she tried to catch Brevity's interest. "I know you want to try to restore the lost books, but until I can fully test these inks, it's too dangerous—"

"Tests." Something like emotional vertigo tilted through Brevity. She wanted answers; she wanted redemption; she wanted hope. But if it was Claire's job to experiment and understand unknown artifacts now, it was Brevity's job to preserve the books first. It felt like a mirror of their previous argument, and wrong. "The damsels are not here for you to *test* on."

Claire sighed. "Brev, I don't mean it like that. You know I wouldn't—"

Brevity clenched her hands together around the vials. "I know you've stayed away from the Unwritten Wing for months"—*leaving me to pick up the pieces*—"and now you finally return, only to *damage* one of the books in my care. The books aren't here for your whims, Claire. Not any longer."

Too far, too far. Claire's cheek twitched and her back straightened. Her voice dropped to a strange softness. "You don't have to remind me of my failures, Brev."

"No," Probity spoke up, just as soft, backing Brevity. "But she does have a duty to protect the Library from them."

Wrong, this was all wrong. But Brevity had only one way forward—

Claire had only *left* her with one way, no matter how much she hated it. "The Arcane Wing has claimed jurisdiction over the unbound ink. But Lucille's ink is part of her book. I can't allow it to leave the Unwritten Wing." She rolled the vials in her hands before stiffly holding one out. "Any further ideas you have should be run through me. But in the meantime—"

"Oh, don't worry," Claire interrupted lowly. She snatched the vial back and shoved it into her pocket. "I won't be needing any further help from the Library in this matter."

*You're the Library too. Unwritten and Arcane against Hell, remember? Stop. Think this through.* Misery welled up in Brevity's stomach as Claire strode away, disappearing into the shadows of the stacks as quickly as if she could shadowstep.

# 17

# BREVITY

Myrrh. When the log revealed these entries, I knew Fleur had to have taken leave of her senses. Any logical person would—there's no need for a fanciful conspiracy when a god-demon has absolute control over the realm. I set about disproving Fleur's conclusion with hard application of facts.

I couldn't. There are irregularities that make no sense. The pages of the Library's books have no detectable composition or construct. Books exist on the shelves with text already on their pages. Should one try to annotate or correct an unwritten book with any ink other than its own, the ink wicks away into the paper like water into a sponge. Nothing stays but what the book was born with. This explains the difficulty of repairing damaged books, but not why. Stories change and are changed by the reader. What are unwritten books made of or connected to that resists exterior alteration?

Could Fleur actually be right? How is that possible?

*Librarian Yoon Ji Han, 1801 CE*

PROBITY MAINTAINED HER SILENCE the long way back to the librarian's desk. It was a sympathetic kind of silence, the kind of quiet meant to soothe and shore up. The wrongness stayed with Brevity, but at least with Probity here she didn't feel alone. It allowed her to go through the motions of checking in on the damsels, reassuring them that they need not worry about scalpel-wielding former librarians for the rest of the day, and withdraw. The damsels had knit a community out of their limbo status in the Library, and it was tight as a fist. As cordial as Brevity was with the residents of the Unwritten Wing, she knew there was a distance she could never cross as librarian.

The desk was lit in a sleepy puddle of lamplight, like always. A teapot sat on a warming stone, a convenient magic as old as the Library. She'd brewed strawberry and rose hips this morning and likely still had half a pot waiting for her. The urge to shake off the unease was so strong she nearly called for Hero before remembering he was away. Instead, she reached the chair behind the desk and all but fell into it.

"You did the right thing." Probity had come to perch just on the edge of the desk, right where Brev used to sit to check up on Claire.

Probity was more graceful than she was; the stacks of paper didn't shift or become displaced. But it served to remind Brevity of the ache beneath the ache. "Did I?" Brevity said, and sank back with a sigh. "It doesn't feel right." The levels of *not-right* ground at her frayed edges.

"That woman had to be stopped." Probity was somber with her certainty. She chewed on her lip a moment, and it was such a familiar habit that Brev almost smiled before Probity spoke again. "You made it sound as if she had done such a thing before."

Brevity grimaced. "I'm sorry. We shouldn't have subjected you to that . . . discussion." The Library certainly had not put on a good show since Probity arrived. It wasn't the impression she wanted the muses to have. It wasn't the impression she wanted her *friend* to have. "You're aware Claire was the librarian before me. She was a great librarian, and

I learned everything from her. She just . . . ran the wing with a firmer hand than I can do."

"Abuse should never be in a librarian's repertoire." The censure in Probity's tone was streaked with horror. "To cut into a book like it is some kind of . . . kind of *melon*. It's grotesque. Books are to be treasured, not dissected."

It was, perhaps, a very good thing that Probity had not perchance visited while Claire had been in charge. When she put it that way, it did sound awful. "It wasn't like that," she insisted quietly. The urge to defend Claire was innate, and righter than the rest of the muddled thoughts in her head. She picked at the threadbare seam of the armchair as she searched for the words to explain it. She'd replaced Claire's rickety old seat with something comfier, but not without some guilt. "Humans and their stories . . . it's a complicated relationship."

"An abusive relationship." Probity hugged herself absently, as if she could ward off the thought. "It is a good thing you're the librarian. I miss you terribly, but seeing you here . . ." She trailed off, suddenly looking small and earnest.

"This is where I'm supposed to be." It was true. Was it possible for the truth to comfort and wound at once? Brevity rubbed her eyes. "This has turned into such a mess, sis."

Probity's distant look melted a little. "I was wondering if you were ever gonna call me that again."

A clot—of emotion, of exhaustion, of longing, of worry—formed in Brevity's throat that she couldn't get words around, so she just smiled wearily. "Normally I'd have Claire to ask for advice, or Hero at the very least to suggest the worst possible option so I could rule it out. But he's gone and—"

"The book is gone?" Probity interrupted.

"Off researching what we can about the ink from our end. He co-

opted Rami, said he might get lost in the stacks for a few days, but . . ."
Brevity waved her hand. "I suspect he's found a loophole to sneak out
again to other realms. Don't tell Claire. Hero will come back; I think
he'll always come back now."

"I won't." Probity had a troubled look. It seemed to take some effort
to shake herself to focus again. "I mean, of course I wouldn't tell that
woman anything. Do you think she'll try—"

Brevity was already shaking her head. "No. I think I . . . Gods, Probity, I hurt her. I was just so upset that she could *do* that, after all this
time. After everything—" Brevity stopped herself. No good trying to
explain Claire's winding history with the unwritten books of the Library, not now. "There was something weird about her too. And instead of fixing it I messed it all up."

"We can fix things," Probity promised. Brevity shook her head.

"Humans are complicated. There're these *emotions* and it's . . .
tricky."

"So we don't fix the humans," Probity said quietly.

There was a thread of intensity that tugged Brevity's head up. Probity was still sitting on the edge of the desk, hands folded in her lap.
Still small, still soft, but *more* somehow. Burning with an intense certainty, the kind of look Claire got when there was trouble. When the
solution would be the kind of insanity that Brevity had trouble saying
no to.

"What?" Brevity echoed.

"We don't fix the humans. The books—that's what's worth saving.
You said it yourself back there. That's your duty, isn't it? And if we fix
the unwritten stories, the humans will sort themselves out." Not that
Probity seemed to care about mortal problems. She faltered, chewing
on a lip before pressing forward. "Have you thought about what I proposed earlier?"

More than thought about it. The possibility burned a hole in Brevity's pocket. "Maybe."

Probity hesitated, allowing the silence to draw tight between them until she could be certain of what wasn't being said. What Brevity couldn't say but was ready to consider. Probity nodded once, expression easing. "'Maybe' is good enough to explore the possibility. If we can just find a way to get a sample of the unwritten ink the Arcanist is keeping."

"I might . . ." Brevity began slowly. She took a breath, squeezing her eyes shut before committing to the door she was about to open. "I might already have the answer to that."

Brevity inched her fingers into her pocket and withdrew a single vial of ink.

It took Probity a moment to register it. Not the whipping, reaching tendrils of gold and violet that would have been Lucille's ink. Her dark eyes narrowed, then widened as she recognized the static cloud, the chopped-up color of error and loss, as it roiled off the ink inside.

"The unwritten ink," Probity breathed.

"I switched them," Brevity confirmed, embarrassed at the guilt she felt. Claire would notice eventually, but it would take her a while, not seeing the colors of the world as muses did. "One experiment—one. Just to see if your idea works. And the books have to be protected—"

"We won't be needing the damsels for this, or any of the books," Probity reassured her, face blooming wide and hopeful. "I have volunteers—muses. Oh, sis, we can do this. We can *do* this."

Probity made a delighted sound and launched herself off the desk. Brevity barely had time to pocket the vial and plant a smile before the hug. It felt warm. It felt sincere. It felt hollow.

They could do this. A quiet voice in the back of Brevity's mind just worried what, exactly, they would have done.

# 18

# HERO

Stories are as old as us. No one culture holds claim to the creation of the first stories. The origin of stories has often been attributed to something divine—gods, the Fates. The Greeks and their muses, though, that's something more fickle. Muses aren't divine, or necessarily benevolent. Their purpose, their gods, are the stories. Anything is justifiable, anything is expendable, in service to that.

*Librarian Gregor Henry, 1977 CE*

THEY FOUND IAMBE LOUNGING with a lyre one hallway over from the stairs that led to the library. She plucked at the strings less like she was playing music and more like they'd offended her. When they asked after the muses, her laughter was bright and vicious.

"You wouldn't want to step foot in the home of the muses," she said after she'd recovered herself.

"Why not?" asked Rami.

"Muses don't have a home; they have a well. A well of possibilities." Iambe's gaze darted to Hero. Her eyes were cruel and delighted. "Your sweet little book wouldn't be quite himself."

"This isn't my first after-realm trip. I can take it." Hero crossed his arms.

Iambe just looked amused. "They would eat you alive, little hero."

"Be that as it may," Rami cut in before Hero could think of a witty comeback. "We have questions to which we need answers. Surely there is a way to gain an audience with one of their number?"

Hero still didn't know what he'd done to earn Iambe's disdain, but evidently it stopped at irritating scruffy angels in overcoats. She tilted her head, then gave a graceful shrug. "You can go to their little wishing well and make a wish, if you like. If Mother's thimble of madness wasn't enough, I suppose you can drown in it." She rose and began to walk through the columns and into the sunlight. Alecto the lioness padded after her, pausing just long enough to stretch and give a very feline glare at Hero before following.

Rami's brow knit in a question, but Hero just shrugged his shoulder. "In my experience, this job is ninety percent following or waiting for inscrutable women."

Rami nodded as they set off in Iambe's wake. "What's the other ten percent?"

"Oh, blind terror mostly."

THE SUN WAS NO lower in the sky when they followed Iambe outside, along a large promenade. Plump white pillars cast long rivers of shadows across the stone. Alecto let out a low growl as they reached the end and began to descend into a garden. The large cat sat down as if offended, obviously disdaining to go any farther.

"What's her problem?" Hero asked.

Iambe shrugged as she stepped over the cat's tail swishing with vexation. "The Furies do not care for muse territory."

Hero was not too proud to taunt a murder cat, especially one that had been menacing him since he landed. He'd be glad to be rid of the pet. He formed his mouth into a pitying moue. "Afraid, kitten?"

In response, the cat took a lightning-fast swipe at the back of his hand. Pain bloomed, and Hero cursed and stepped back, cradling his hand.

"Are you all right?" Rami asked.

"Do stop taunting the Furies." Boredom laced Iambe's voice as she gestured. "This way."

The cat had taken a sharp rake of skin off the back of his hand. Hero dabbed the bleeding ink off with the hem of his coat. "May you host the most heroic of fleas, beast."

Alecto didn't even have the grace to look ill-tempered. She gave him a slow, content blink and relaxed into a sprawl in the spot of sunshine.

"Hurry up," Iambe called before passing through a curtain of diaphanous fabrics that diffused the light of the gardens beyond. Hero gave one last reproachful glance at the cat, wondering what would shy off a literal living avatar of anger. Alecto gave away nothing else. Rami followed him out, and Hero just caught the edge of the swaying curtain before stepping into the light.

"Oh, I'm going to be ill," Hero moaned under his breath. He stopped short enough to cause Rami to collide with him. It must have carried in his voice, because Rami grunted and rubbed sympathetic circles on Hero's back.

When Iambe had described a well, Hero had assumed a tidy cistern, or at worst a looking pond, as Echo had used. But the marble steps led down into a terrace transformed. There was no well, or cultured pond—the terrace *was* the pond. Water surrounded them on all sides, as if they'd stepped into a bathysphere of mirrors. At least, Hero had to presume it was water. The substance was perfectly clear, like liquid light, and appeared simultaneously thin as a soap bubble and deep as the ocean. It went on to forever and to naught. And when Hero tried to focus his eyes to make sense of it, he found himself staring at countless reflections. He took a step across the marble, and a thousand similar Heroes took a step at a half-second delay. Rami's arm moved at his back, and a repeating visual echo of Ramiels followed suit. Each movement sent his brain into riot trying to make sense of it.

Hero squeezed his eyes closed as vertigo threatened to upend his stomach. "No one . . . move." He focused on swallowing—very carefully. "If you please."

Iambe's sandals clicked on the marble, and though he had his eyes closed it was as if Hero could *feel* the reflections. "I did warn you."

"And your guidance is appreciated, spirit." Ramiel managed to sound mild and unaffected. His voice was a low, stabilizing presence, as sturdy as the hand at Hero's back. "But we came to speak to the muses."

"And here you are, master angel." Iambe swept one arm—dear gods, how did Hero *know* that; his eyes were closed but he could feel the motion against his skin; this place was horror—and laughed mirthlessly. "The well of the muses. It's where our realm brushes against their realm and we can hold congress. It'll be up to you to catch their attention."

With that, Iambe appeared done with them. Hero opened his eyes just in time to see her walk briskly to the surface of the water surrounding them and disappear in the slender space between two reflections.

"I can't say she was eminently helpful, but at least we're here."

"You've been here before?" Hero asked. It was a reasonable question. Rami might have been a newcomer to the Library's fractious staff, but he was also a fallen angel, ageless in ways that Hero didn't care to think about. He talked about the Fall of Lucifer as if it had happened last Tuesday.

So it surprised him when Rami shook his head regretfully. "I was long fallen by the time the muses rose to prominence. And while we were not exactly forbidden from it by the Creator or Morningstar, visiting other realms was . . . discouraged."

"I wouldn't have thought you'd give much care to what Lucifer condoned," Hero said, though every curious nerve in his body wanted to ask about the other one, the Creator. The maker of angels had seemed a contentious point between Ramiel and Uriel, his Heavenly colleague that had tried to invade the Library, leading Rami to stand against her. Hero didn't believe for a minute that there was a singular creator—too many seemingly contradictory realms rose, coexisted, and fell based on the fancies of humans—but anything that had won the devotion of such a rare creature as Rami had a certain amount of fascination for Hero.

But Ramiel was strangely silent on the topic, at least with him. Hero had become adept at, by turns, charming or antagonizing information from people, but whenever the subject of Heaven's god came up, the only thing he could draw from Rami was a distant look of loss. For some damned reason that look on Rami's face always made Hero's stomach hurt, so he had stopped prodding.

Lucifer, however, was different. Rami was always happy to mutter about Hell's erstwhile leader. Rami puckered his lips as if he'd tasted something foul. "I don't care a whit for the Deceiver. But if I had any hope of receiving forgiveness from Heaven, I judged it best not to exhibit an interest in realms other than Heaven and Earth." He looked around him. "So this is new, all these reflections of us and—oh."

Rami's voice did a missed-stair kind of lurch. Hero followed his

gaze, but at first all he could see was what he'd seen before—hundreds
of mirror images. Upon focusing, however, he realized that an identical
"mirror" wasn't quite accurate. To his right, he and Rami appeared in
the glass surface of the water much the same, but Hero had his arm
in a sling. In the image just below that, Hero appeared to have a dagger held to Rami's ribs, as if he'd brought him here by force. In a distant, tiny reflection behind that, Hero wasn't there at all and it was
Brevity staring back at him. Each mirror iteration bore a difference.
Some were slight—Hero's scar was gone; his coat was a different
color—and others were great. He caught a glimpse of a tiny reflection,
almost translucent with its not-thereness, where neither Hero nor
Rami appeared but the well was polluted with smoke.

"What trickery is this?" Rami wondered uneasily, but Hero
grasped it in an instant.

"Possibilities. It's a well of possibilities, every alternate possible way
this moment could have gone." Hero caught a glimpse of another reflection where neither of them was present, but a familiar figure in a
gentleman's clothes and a gentleman's malevolence stared back at him.
The image rippled, disappearing quickly, but not before Hero could
shudder at the victory in Andras's demon gold eyes.

Every possible way the story could have gone was here. If Rami had
refused to accompany Hero, if Hero had never returned to the Library,
if Andras had succeeded in his coup. Since he was a character, the book
part of his nature made him keenly aware of how every story could
turn on the knife-edge of any decision. But standing in a bubble, sepa-
rated from all his other fates by a mere slip of time, he was terrified by
the fragility of it. Reality took on an unstable quality, soap-film thin
and ready to burst.

"Remarkable." Rami swiveled his head around as if the imperma-
nence of their own existence was not about to *fall down* on their

damned heads. The angel shook his head in wonder. "If this is just a touch of the muses' realm, then surely they'll have the answers we need."

"Yes. Confidence. That is *exactly* what I draw from this too," Hero said blandly. He straightened his shoulders, not quite able to shrug off the sense of unreality, but he could make a good show of it. "We'll need to gain an audience. I'm not fond of the idea of being trapped here or wandering into the wrong reflection."

"Iambe said we would need to attract the muses' attention."

"And this is why you were clever enough to bring me," Hero said. The smile he flashed was perfect and perfectly fake. "Attention is my specialty."

Claire would have frowned, Brevity would have laughed, but all Hero received from Rami was a thoughtful nod. How infuriating. "Good point. Your charisma is an asset here, no doubt."

Well, maybe not entirely infuriating. Hero blinked, trying to realign his world around an unexpected compliment. It was a feeling he was not accustomed to, especially from earnestly serious men like Ramiel. "Yes, well—"

"What do you propose?"

Hero scrutinized the question for cynicism, for mockery, but found nothing. Rami patiently waited for his lead. Him! Hero was more accustomed to having to wrest control of a situation out of other people's grasps with trickery and guile. He abruptly strode toward the bubble surface, hoping that would cool the warmth in his face.

His reflection approached him in turn. This Hero was very similar to him, lip curled and cocksure. Behind the mirror-Hero, Rami's reflection kept watch with a soft expression on his face. As if that version of their working relationship had the opportunity to be based on more than the resentful, grudging necessity of acquaintances.

Hero didn't have the courage to glance over his shoulder to see if that reflection rang true. It would bother him if it didn't, and then it would bother him that it bothered him. Instead, Hero withdrew his book from where he'd carried it—miraculously unshredded so far—in his vest pocket. He flipped to the first page—blank, of course, but that would do for this purpose—and began to recite out loud. "Once upon a time . . ."

He expected a snicker, at least a skeptical comment from Rami, but his audience remained quiet. Hero cleared his throat and began again. "Once upon a time, there was a rather devastatingly handsome prince who, through entirely no fault of his own, was trapped in a high, high tower by a horrible, misguided sorceress with an atrocious tea habit and questionable fashion taste."

Rami made a stifled sound that interrupted him—which was good because Hero really wasn't sure what should happen next. "The reflections," Rami said in a whisper.

Hero risked a glance from his book. The mirror-Hero in front of him hadn't moved, but there had been a slight shift in his neighbors. Each copy of Hero and Rami trapped in the surface of the bubble had turned to stare, intently, in Hero's direction. The weight was unnerving, but Hero scrounged for more. "The prince, in addition to being devastatingly handsome and gifted, knew his kingdom needed him. So, one day he was *horribly* clever and escaped the tower without alerting the willful sorceress."

"Keep going," Rami murmured. Hero felt movement in the reflections, but he knew better than to look. He screwed his eyes closed in thought. "His quest to save his kingdom took him to a dangerous fa-erie realm known as *Seattle*, the denizens of which were too scruffy and its weather far too damp for the likes of his pages—er, delicate skin.

There he met the lady of the lake, a fair goddess who the prince believed could save him from the sorceress's evil spell. But the lady had been . . ." Despite himself, Hero paused, frowning to himself as he tried to pick a word. ". . . she'd been *ensorcelled* by the realm and forgotten her power. So corrupted was she that she rejected our prince, drove a dagger through his heart when all he was guilty of was being entirely too charming and clever. Then the cruel sorceress, more of a witch really—"

"Hero," Rami interrupted.

"Shush, Claire will never hear this. It's fine. I'm almost—"

"No, Hero. *Look.*"

His eyes snapped open in time to catch a blur of movement over the surface of the bubble. The reflected pairs were moving, swirling around the mirror-Hero in front of him like water down a drain. The movement threatened to make Hero ill, but one by one, the Hero and Rami clones shivered into a single pair.

Hero forgot his tale and studied the reflection in front of him. This Hero was certainly tidier than his current state. Familiar copper hair was trim and clean, and this Hero's coat was not sliced by lioness claws. But the biggest change was in the alien differences of his face. This Hero's eyes were soft, muddled somewhere between regret and pity. His cheek was smooth and devoid of scar tissue. This Hero had not been tortured by Andras for trying to defend the Library. This Hero likely didn't trick himself into smelling smoke, hearing the tearing of pages in a silent room. Hero rubbed his own jaw, and the raw ridge of flaws was almost reassuring.

In the bubble's mirror surface, Rami approached. He had a worried look, but then, Rami usually defaulted to some somber version of concerned. The angel reached out in the mirror, and Hero almost flinched until no pressure came on his own shoulder and he realized it was only mirror-Ramiel's action, not his angel's.

*His angel*, Hero quickly decided, was a problematic thought he would stow away for later.

The Ramiel in the mirror gestured, saying words to the other that Hero couldn't hear. A worried look, soft edged and fleeting, passed between the two before they looked back, over their shoulders, into the distance of the reflection. Hero saw nothing at first.

"Someone's coming," Rami said, and Hero squinted. A speck in the mirror, which Hero had first mistaken for a flaw in the surface, was growing larger. It elongated into a slight figure, and Hero couldn't keep his lip from curling as he caught sight of a pastel froth of lace and a fluff of bangs.

"Probity," Rami rumbled. He'd repositioned himself at Hero's side. "I take it from your presence that your business in Hell is finished."

Probity clasped her hands in front of her skirts, wide eyes looking soft and full. "Not at all. I just popped back to report on the Library's cooperation. How strange a coincidence to find you here."

"When we left I don't believe the tenor of conversation was *cooperation*, specifically," Hero said.

"Thankfully, Brevity sees sense much more easily than you books do." Probity's cheerful voice tugged with an undertone of tension. Her amicable smile tightened, just at the edges. "I've known Brevity my entire life. She understands the importance of what I'm trying to do. She's been nothing but helpful. And why wouldn't she? We both have the best interests and well-being of all books at heart. Even yours."

"Even *me?*" Hero pressed a hand to his chest. "What radical ideas you have."

"I'm a muse. You're a *book*. Do you even know how special that is?"

Probity's clasped hands flinched as if she'd suffered a stab of emotion. "We love all books and do not judge between the written and unwritten. Everything we do is for you." Probity spoke as if the reminder was aimed inward rather than at Hero. She tilted her head, and her brow furrowed with pity. "How is it, Hero? Do you still feel your story?"

A sourness welled up in Hero's throat, but Rami answered instead. "He's well. We are fine." There was a gritty grind under those words, more of an unvarnished edge than Rami usually had. Hero looked from muse to angel, but Rami's frown gave nothing away. "We are actually on a quest for the Library. We were hoping the muses could provide answers about the forgotten librarian and the makeup of books."

Probity paused, and her face softened. "The makeup of books? You don't know what books are made of?"

She paused, and Hero grudgingly shook his head.

The sorrow that flickered across Probity's face seemed genuine. "Oh, sweet creature. To not know yourself." Then a glint in her eye turned harder, angry. "It's wrong. It's more than wrong. The selfish librarian has done more harm than even I could have anticipated."

"Claire has given everything for the Library." Hero's voice was sharp. It was a surprise to feel Rami bristle beside him too. But then his brain caught up with his mouth, and a little guiltily he added, "As has Librarian Brevity."

"Not everything. She could never give enough to make up for what she has done. Humans can't understand the real meaning of sacrifice." Probity no longer looked at Hero like a pitiful rescue. Her mouth thinned into a fine line, as if she was steeling herself. "Even a broken book is still loyal to the woman instead of the true librarian," she said. "She's not *worthy* of your devotion, little book. I wonder if you would be so fond of your human librarians and authors if you knew how many books just like you they've turned to dust. They're a parasite on the Library."

"Watch your tone," Rami said, low as a threat.

"I mean no disrespect, Master Watcher." Probity held up a placating hand, but the new tension in her shoulders wasn't reassuring. "I do respect the work you do, securing and passing judgment on muddled mortal souls; it really is a wonder."

"I'm no judge," Rami objected, and Probity tilted her head.

"Well, you should be."

"Yes, humans are terrible. Not like you muses," Hero said archly. "Tell me again, where were you on the day a demon came to burn us all? The only muse I recall seeing on the battlefield was Brevity."

Probity flinched. "The Library fights its own battles," she said before adding, a little softer, "I would have come if Brevity had called me."

"So help now," Rami said. "What do you know that we don't? What do you know about the ink? Why did it remain when the books were burned?"

Probity didn't answer for a moment. She took a step forward, closer to what seemed to be the film of water separating them. "You really don't know, do you?" Her voice was wondering. "But how could the human not know? Not recognize . . ."

She trailed off, and the silence tripped past Hero's last remaining bit of patience. "Not know *what*? If you will not help us, then why should the Library 'cooperate' with you?"

Probity tucked her arms around herself until her hands disappeared in the volume of soft knit. She chewed on her bottom lip, and the prospect of something sadder that Hero couldn't guess. "I'm trying to save you, little book. Whether you believe me or not. That ink represents the best opportunity to save stories that I've seen in all my many years. It deserves to be used, not locked up in a dusty vault. That ink is the heart of a story. Every story. I'd give *anything* to protect that."

"Then tell me what that *means* so we can fix it!" Hero threw up his hands even as he felt exhilarated. *To save stories.* The moment he'd laid eyes on the unknown substance, a quiet voice at the back of his mind had whispered a possibility. That ink could repair his pages where the Library's efforts had failed, so Hero could see his story again after all. That was what Probity was hinting at; it had to be. That ink was the *key.* The hope he'd kept firmly buried began to worm its way up his chest.

Probity appeared torn, debating before speaking again. "I've told you enough to unravel the lies the Library has told you. Anything more and you'll run back to that cruel human with accusations. I might have even said too much already." A sigh drained out of her like a surrender. Her eyes turned wet, and she diverted her gaze to the ground. "That can't happen. It can't. Things are too important, and moving too fast now for it to happen, no matter my own feelings. You wanted to escape Hell once, didn't you?"

Hero was too preoccupied with his thoughts to notice the sudden change in Probity's tone. At least, not until Rami gripped his shoulder in warning. "We will be missed, should we not return soon," Rami said carefully. "We'll be on our way."

"Hell, one of the judgment realms." Probity seemed to be considering to herself. "Really, they are all so very much the same. One damnation is the same as any other. I wonder how those are connected."

"Muse . . . perhaps we can speak to a different representative before we go," Hero said carefully.

"It's for the stories. It's . . . Brevity would do the same if she were here. I know it," Probity whispered. Her voice wobbled, but her hand was firm as she raised it in front of her face. Rami jerked Hero back another step, but there was nowhere to precisely retreat to. Probity's smile looked distinctly unhappy. "I'm sorry. Really, I am. But there's no point in that. You were never here."

Probity's fingertips tapped against the film of water, and there was a soft pop. Rami's fingers dug into his arm, Hero drew a sharp breath, and the entire sphere of space dissolved into stars.

# 19

# HERO

Myrrh. I did not hold with my senior's suspicions. At least, not until Librarian Ji Han was gone. Now nothing seems right. But I am not a scholar. I'm here because I am a failed storyteller—what can I know of books?

Demons; demons I know. I caught a lesser infernal trying to sneak into the stacks again today, and this time I questioned him: why are Hell's creatures interested at all in the Library? He seemed to not know himself, except the Library had always been here, and the books were irresistible to their kind, coveted by even the great dukes. Jackals.

Hell was born with a library, or evolved one soon after. Men condemn themselves to Hell, but who passes judgment on mere books?

*Librarian Ibukun of Ise, 791 CE*

HANGOVERS WERE, TRULY, CREATIONS of the devil. Hero felt he could say that with authority. His head thudded, dull and constant as a drum. He was under no encouragement to open his eyes, or remove his cheek from the warm wood surface supporting it.

"Hero."

Someone leaned over him. Someone with a voice like bourbon in a cut-crystal glass. Excellent, and matching the big hand that tentatively wrapped around his shoulder and gave him a shake. "Hero," the voice said again.

"Shan't. Go away. Guards—"

"You don't have guards." The voice paused, and an amused tone crept in. "Well, besides me."

"Then you're dismissed. Go join the rebellion for all I care."

"Hero—"

"But haul yourself out first. That's an order."

Another pause. The hand left his shoulder and Hero idly leaned for the missing warmth. There was a huff of a laugh. "Did that kind of order even work in your story?"

"I—" Hero's sleepy mind tripped on that, and unfortunately it brought him fully awake. His eyes sprung open and he bit back a yowl as light weaponized itself like blades into his headache. Between squinted eyelids, he could just make out the uneven grain of a wood table that was battle-scarred but clean. Raising his head brought the world to a proper perspective. They were in a large room, cluttered with candles and a cheerful melancholy. Other figures were clustered in small groups at tables identical to his, but talk was subdued, words drifting through the sweetly spiced air like memories.

"Where the hell are we? I mean, obviously *not* Hell, but . . . and *why* does my head feel as if I was kicked by a gargoyle?"

"You'd be a lot worse if I hadn't lent a hand. I believe the muse yanked the realm right out from under us back there." Ramiel sat in the booth across from him. "Sat," however, might have been a bit of a stretch, as the stubby, broad angel looked afraid to breathe for fear the bench would give up the ghost. "Dropped us straight into nothing, and with as long as we fell, you'd have arrived as so many paper scraps if I hadn't had a hold of you. I'm not certain we were supposed to survive the trip."

"And you brought us here?"

Rami looked abashed. "We . . . woke up here. On the floor."

"Probity. That harpy reject is *dead* when we get back," Hero muttered. He rubbed his head tenderly, which at least kept Rami from correcting him on the lineage of muses.

Ramiel made a sympathetic face instead and grabbed one of the cups in front of him. "Here, I think the tea helps."

The pot was a slender silver contraption, and Hero watched with amusement as Rami attempted to pour a cup the way most men might approach defusing a bomb. The liquid ended up in the proper container, for the most part. Hero took the offering and made a face as he brought it to his nose. "Tea. Why is it *always* blasted tea? Where're the realms with magical coffee elixirs? Wine? A decent sherry? At least Valhalla had ale."

"That'd be a question for Claire," Rami demurred. Hero noted he didn't pour a cup for himself, so surely he agreed with the sentiment.

Hero resolutely gulped the tea. It was the precise golden color of the light spilling from the candles, and had a sweet note to it. Perhaps licorice. "Where the blast are we anyway?"

Rami's gaze flickered over the room in a way that said he'd already spent time culling any useful details from it. "I'm not certain. Middle Eastern and Persian influences, that's for certain. No one's bothered us so far, so they must be used to new souls."

An active realm, at least. Not a cannibal realm that would attempt to eat them at the first opportune moment, at the very least. A well-fed realm might wait until the *second* opportune moment.

Hero missed the Library sometimes.

The tea was helping, at least. He took another determined sip. The tearoom—because that seemed the only thing it could be—was warm and subdued. Some of the inhabitants had the scruffy appearance of having not slept in a couple of days. On the other hand, a Persian grandmother bundled in a bright red blanket worked on some kind of yarn art in the corner, pausing occasionally to warm her bony hands on a mug idling by her side. Everyone seemed lost in their own thoughts or quiet conversation, all waiting for something.

In Hero's experience, there was nothing good worth anticipating in these kinds of realms. "We should get out of here."

"Yes, you're right." Rami nodded tightly, perhaps because any grander gesture would have risked tipping the bench. "What do you propose?"

Rami's eyes were somber, intense, and Hero found himself pinned under their focus. There was no mockery, no doubt, just patient attention.

"Why do you do that?" Hero asked. The question was suddenly pressing, urgent as anything else he could accomplish.

Rami turned to meet his gaze. "Do what?"

Hero's mouth felt dry and awkward. "Take me seriously. Why do you take me seriously?"

That received a raise of one thick eyebrow. "Should I not?"

No. No one should have taken Hero seriously. Earnest regard had weight, had consequences, had familiar ties and responsibilities. "The others don't. I work very hard on the frivolity, you know. It's hand-crafted, artisanal even. But you ignore it entirely." Hero realized he was staring but only seemed able to drop his focus from Rami's eyes to his chin. "I want to know why, I guess."

Rami's serious expression muddled with a kind of softness at the edges. He considered before speaking, "It's a fair enough question. I mean, I can see you're vain; you're arrogant and irresponsible—"

"Flatterer," Hero muttered, but Rami wasn't going to be derailed.

"You choose to behave as a *beast* sometimes. And you're very hard to tolerate, let alone like," he said firmly. Then he paused, a complicated look ill settling on his features until it drifted off again. "But then there's who you are when you're taken seriously, treated with respect and thoughtful consideration. You're insightful and kind. I like that man."

"Nobody *likes* me," Hero said, a little aghast.

Rami stopped, and a very un-Rami-like smile taunted the shape of his lips. It was a soft smile, and if he wasn't careful, someone would accuse it of being *fond*. Not Hero; Hero knew better. But still. It was a dangerous smile, with what a less cautious fool than Hero could read into it.

"You might be surprised. You seem to have found a home in the Library, at least."

Hero sniffed. "Only because I can't return to my book, so I can't be shelved."

"You really think so?"

"Of course," Hero said with a certainty that had been there a moment ago but was disappearing fast as Rami frowned at him. He managed to break the gaze, turning his head to fish through the crowd for anything, anything else to talk about. His attention lit on a tall figure who slipped through the tearoom with a peculiar kind of familiarity. The figure was dressed in a long tunic and flowing pants, belted loosely at the waist. They were broad-shouldered and thick-hipped, moving with the kind of surety that described a comfort in their own skin. The figure cut a sure path through the quiet crowd, saying a word here or there. Each time, the figure would withdraw, and the table would soon get up and leave through the curtained doors at the far end of the room. Some left with purpose, but many with reluctance.

They stopped at a table not too far away, close enough for Hero to hear. "Last call," the newcomer said quietly.

"Can't we stay, Sraosha?" asked an old man wrapped in gold-embroidered finery.

The figure called Sraosha smiled, and when they shook their head, there was no malice in it. "Why would you want to stay? You've got family waiting for you across the bridge."

"I do." The man didn't seem comforted and suddenly looked at his hands. "I hope I see them."

Sraosha didn't say anything to that but placed a hand on his shoulder. "Everyone crosses the bridge sometime. Your family is waiting."

The man nodded and drained the last of his tea in one ponderous motion. His grip was white-knuckled, but after he finished, his courage seemed restored. He nodded to his companions and left at a march toward the door.

They left their cups behind. Sraosha swept their hand over the table, and in a moment it was refreshed with clean cups and a steaming pot of tea nestled next to a comforting candle.

Hero glanced to the side to see if Rami was observing all this. He was, frown pinned with a particular kind of concern. When Hero looked back, Sraosha had turned and spotted him.

They approached the table at a glide. "Last call," they said quietly.

Up close, Sraosha struck Hero as likely fluid in gender presentation, but not in the slender androgynous fashion. Loose linens, a long braid of hair, but that wasn't it. Wide shoulders, wide hips, and a stance of distinct ease. They had a solidness to their presence, an undeniable individuality that drew the eye. It struck Hero that most people were not so much *themselves* as this creature was. It was an intimidating authenticity, and Hero drew back just a little. "Oh, no, thank you."

That appeared to amuse their host. Sraosha tilted their head, considering. "No, I suppose you missed your call before now."

"Kind host," Rami interrupted, raising a placating hand. "I'm afraid there is a misunderstanding. We're not souls awaiting judgment. Hero and I are representatives of the Unwritten Wing of Hell's Library."

Even after all this time, Rami still had trouble with the H word. His brow always did a microscale twitch as he stumbled over the word. Hero usually delighted in drawing it out, even if there was no time to do so now.

"Yes, I am aware who you are, Ramiel of the Watchers." Sraosha ignored their surprise by turning their attention. "And you, Hero of the Lost Book."

Hero's mood curdled. "I know precisely where my book is, thank you."

"Oh?" Sraosha tilted their head. "Is that the when? My apologies. It is easy to lose track in the tearoom."

Unease sifted up through Hero's confusion, though he couldn't place a finger on it. Thankfully, Rami knew when to step in. "If you know us, then you'll know we are not meant for this realm. We arrived here by misstep, and we can be on our way if you simply indicate the way out."

Sraosha tilted their head to the exit with a practiced gesture. "The exit is, of course, that way." They paused, studying them both. "But the only way is the bridge."

Hero suspected very much that he did not wish to avail himself of the bridge. Bridges in after-realms, in his experience, had a troubling way of leading to grief and bloodshed. Symbolism was a bitch. "I don't suppose you have a gently sloping path."

"The bridge is quite comfortable," Sraosha said. They appeared to scrutinize Hero for a moment. "Human souls find on the bridge only what they take with them."

"How lucky that I am *not* one," Hero said. "Souls sound like rather pesky things."

"There's no other exit out of this realm?" Rami interrupted before Sraosha could say something irritatingly vague and profound again. "Surely there is."

"On the far side, past the bridge," Sraosha offered with a gentle lift of their hand. "Once you cross, the judges might be happy to grant you audience and passage to your realm."

"Judges are not usually our most ardent allies," Hero reminded Rami. The irritated look he threw reassured him that the angel was *well aware* of the trouble Hell's Library dragged around with them like a tin can on a string.

"There's no exit from this side? Not even for nonhumans such as us?" Rami pressed. Hero was again reminded of the nightmare that was the abandoned realm of crocodiles and labyrinths. They'd fallen through a gate that had remained open. Ramiel himself had been there, still struggling to fulfill his role as avenging angel and barring their path. He'd taken away their only route back, and Leto, their youngest companion, had sacrificed himself for it.

It seemed like the kind of thing Hero should hold a grudge about. He knew himself and was very aware of his deep capacity to hold grudges. It was his favorite pastime. But every time he tried to rip the scab off that memory, instead of anger he got something different. He remembered clutching Claire as they'd scrambled over the crocodile god's back. He'd tossed one wary look behind them, expecting to see this malevolent angel that had been dogging them. Instead, shadowed in the doorway of the arch, he'd seen a worn man in a shabby coat, with the saddest eyes he'd ever seen. Hero knew what it looked like to be lost and far from home.

Neither Hero nor Rami could go home again. It'd been hard to fault him for trying.

Sraosha shook their head. "This tearoom is simply a resting place for unjudged souls. Some dead refuse to cross the bridge without a loved one; others simply need to accept their death and summon up the courage to cross." They paused, a thoughtful look coming upon their confident features. "Strange that you should fall here."

"We had help." Rami flicked a glare toward the ceiling, as if he could have struck Probity from here.

"Nonetheless, there's nothing for ones such as you to gain by waiting here." Before they could protest, Sraosha straightened their shoulders, pulling up authority like a cloak. "Last call."

A faint hiss brought Hero's attention down to where steam was sizzling out of the teapot. When he inspected his own cup, it was dry as a bone. "You're kicking us out? Bad form!"

"I am encouraging you to move forward." Sraosha began their ritual of wiping the booth table.

"What happens on the bridge, Sraosha?" Rami asked, intent as a hunting dog. "How can we pass it?"

Sraosha pursed their lips. "I suppose most souls arriving here would already know that much, so I may explain. One is guided through Chinvat to pass beneath the judgment of Divine Mithra and Rashnu."

"Chinvat?" Rami stared. "This realm is a realm of Zoraster?"

Sraosha tilted their head. "It is a realm for those who know that truth, yes."

"What judgmental nonsense is it this time?" Hero lifted his shoulders when Rami frowned at him. "What? I'm an atheist."

"Atheist?" Rami was aghast. "You *literally* live in Hell. You have met *literal* gods."

Hero sniffed. "Yes, and I didn't find myself that impressed."

The way disbelief lit Rami's gray eyes was simply *delightful*. "You weren't impressed—"

"*Honored* guests," Sraosha cut in, before Hero could bait a further reaction. "This was your last call. If you are so curious about the Chinvat, perhaps you can see it for yourself and continue your debate. Outside."

Their host's tone brooked no argument. Rami threw Hero one last exasperated look before standing and nodding to the door. "One last question. This realm's judgment, what is it based on?"

One of Sraosha's brows inched up, as if Rami had asked if the sky was blue. "The primary virtues, of course. Good thoughts, good words, good deeds."

"Oh hell," Hero muttered under his breath. It was like the entire afterlife was built to menace him for the simple happenstance of being his story's villain. It really grew old.

"Thank you," Rami said without sounding as if he really meant it. Sraosha herded them between the low tables effortlessly. Hero noted that new souls had appeared during their conversation, looking around with disorientation before nervously taking a cup of tea in hand.

They pushed through the heavy doors of the tearoom, and Hero began to wish he hadn't gulped his so quickly.

The sky was a forbidding and violent oil painting. Dark carmine

reds swirled and roiled against indigo, lashed with occasional blooms
of orange. It felt too thick and vibrant to be air. The clouds churned
like undertow, threatening to pull them up into it. Navigating the roil
like agile fish were figures on winged mounts. At least he assumed they
were mounts; Hero saw them only by their silhouettes, inkblots
against the oil sheen of the sky.

"We should be cautious. Stay close," Rami said, drawing Hero's
attention back to the earth. The tearoom had emptied them out onto
a simple paved square. It was the kind of open area you'd find in a his-
toric village, pavers too uneven and chalky to be modern. It was also
clogged with people. Young and old milled around the square, mostly
single but sometimes in tight, anxious groups. The majority were
dressed in the same kind of bland fashion Hero had observed humans
preferred these days, though some of the older ones were embellished
with heavy gold jewelry and brightly threaded coats and dresses. Burial
wear, Hero realized. The crowd simmered with a roil of emotions—
not violent, but erratic and volatile—that must have been what put
Rami on high alert.

The crowd milled, though more or less reluctant progress seemed
to be made in the direction of the far end of the square. From a distance, it appeared more as a wall than a bridge, so steep was the incline
toward the sky. But the details gradually resolved as Hero and Rami
were inexorably jostled closer.

The bridge was composed of embers of color, shimmering sparks
that somehow supported the heavy traffic stumbling across it. It stood
in stark contrast to the rough cobbles and appeared to arch up nearly
to the clouds, like a moon bridge, before dropping again to a distant
cliff.

It spanned a mist-choked nothingness of a ravine, so devoid of the oil-paint colors above that it was nearly white. Wind currents stirred movements here and there in the depths, though Hero could make out nothing else from this distance.

"Good deeds." The voice was so close behind them it made Hero jump, though Rami was calm enough to have heard the approach. Sraosha stood with their feet planted in the crowd, seemingly unmoved by the press and jostle on either side of them. Souls seemed to shy away. They studied the bridge briefly before looking back to them. "Good deeds, that much I can grant you."

"You're one of the judges," Rami said.

Sraosha nodded. "Your shadows cast enough tales for me to be certain of that much. I can grant you the judgment of good deeds. But good deeds only. For the other two, you will have to face the divines." They gestured, and Hero twisted to follow the line of their arm up, up, up.

The blots of indigo, which Hero had previously mistaken for storm clouds, had gained shoulders. Two impossibly large figures flanked the sky above the bridge, obscured in clouds and roiling twilight. They were so large it was impossible to discern whether they looked down on the bridge or away, or if the petty world escaped their notice entirely.

"How can they even *see* us, let alone judge us? It'd be like you discerning which are the very kindest ants in an anthill!" Hero was done; he was completely *over* the idea of being judged, cast in a role, given a title, measured up, inevitably found wanting.

His outburst gained the attention of the crowd, and souls cast them dreadfully reproachful looks before skirting a wider berth around them. Rami gestured furiously for him to quiet. He looked nervous, but Hero was past nervous; he was scared. And when Hero got scared, he got philosophical. "What even are *good* thoughts and words anyway? Who decides what is good? And good for whom?"

Philosophical, and a touch dramatic, granted.

Sraosha was unflustered. "To ask what 'good' is. Yes. Perhaps you are right: you don't belong here." With that, they bid them farewell and slid back into the crowd toward their tearoom.

"Have you never heard of the *trolley problem?*" Hero hollered at their back. Granted, he himself had never heard of the trolley problem until one particularly boring night inventorying the unwritten morality narratives section of the Library, but he was a book; a god of moral *conscience* really had no such excuse.

"It's all right," Rami said. He wasn't bothered by Sraosha's words. His attention was focused again on the bridge. "You'll pass through just fine."

Hero stopped short. He scrutinized Rami's profile but couldn't detect a hitch of sarcasm. "You've got to be kidding me. I'm a villain! Worse, I'm not even human."

"See, you didn't mention good or evil a single time in that statement." Rami focused on Hero with a hesitant smile that did terrible things to the outrage in Hero's chest. "You are a *good* person, Hero. You fought for your fellow books; you've risked much to make it this far and help your friends. Even Sraosha had to grant that those were good works."

"Oh, I've done my fair share of wrongs."

"A minority. Your words have more sting in them than real malice most of the time, and good thoughts . . ."

"Aha," Hero said when Rami paused. "Let's not lie to ourselves; we both know my mind is filled with rotten schemes."

Rami's smile persisted, even as it softened at the edges. "I never cared for the puritan notion of policing a man's thoughts. I think the weight of a man's life lies in what he *does* with it. Reasons and heart are important, but it's your actions that have long-reaching effects."

Hero blinked. He leaned forward and pinched Rami's cheek until he grimaced. "Are you sure you're our Watcher? Or maybe you've seen him around? Tall, dark, and endlessly broody?"

"You are taller than me," Rami muttered, rubbing his cheek.

Hero arched a brow and opened his mouth to respond before a noise rose from the crowds near the bridge. He half braced himself against a pillar to see over the turmoil of heads.

Something was happening on the bridge. A segment a few yards from the entrance had begun to shrink, rainbow material flaking away rapidly on either side. Souls crossing the bridge scrambled, peeling backward and forward to escape, but the decay seemed to follow. Finally, like frantic schools of fish, the crowds on the bridge parted, backing away from one old man who was rooted with shock as the bridge narrowed on either side of him.

Even the dead still had a sense of self-preservation. The man regained his senses and lurched ahead, hands outstretched for the crowd. There was a hesitation, a perilously hung moment when it seemed someone—anyone—in the crowd might reach back. But a groan, far and deep, shook the bridge under their feet, and the edges disintegrated faster. The man reached the edge of the crowd, but panic had set in. Someone shoved; the man stumbled back with a cry.

The rainbow section he stood on had narrowed to the size of a tea table. The doomed man swiveled, but it was obvious by now no one behind him would risk their own eternal soul to assist. Froth of mist churned to either side of the bridge, but whatever moved in the ravine stayed out of sight.

The bridge had crumbled to a balance beam beneath the doomed man's feet. He swayed once, twice, trying to keep his balance, but his arms pinwheeled and signed his fate. His fall seemed silent at this distance. A gout of mist lashed up into the air as the man fell through, then nothing. The crowd was quiet for the count of one breath; then a susurrus of murmuring returned. More subdued.

The bridge quickly rebuilt itself, filling out again to be a uniform shimmer. Sooner than Hero had thought possible, migrants planted their feet over the space where, moments before, a soul had fallen to the dark.

"Hero." Rami said his name, but not for the first time. A hesitant hand wrapped around his elbow. In a moment he would shake him; in a moment Hero would be sternly reminded of their duty; he'd have to shrug and pretend nothing had happened and—

"Are you okay?"

The question was like an unexpected drop into cold water. Hero tore his gaze away from the bridge. Rami had angled himself to create a kind of buffer from the crowds, and all of him was focused on Hero. Shoulders turned, serious face emanating concern. It was a question asked in earnest, and it shocked him so much, an earnest answer fell out.

"When have any of us been okay?" Hero focused on relaxing his hold on the pillar until color returned to his whitened knuckles. He constructed a shrug and a smile in much the same way one might erect a barricade. Brick by brick. "No offense, dear man. I think I preferred the crocodile."

"That's not happening to you."

Hero huffed. "Of course I wouldn't beg so inelegantly—"

"No, Hero. Listen to me." The weight in Rami's tone forced Hero's head up again. Rami's gaze flickered over his face, as if searching for a key. "That *won't* happen to you. I won't let it. We will force our way across the bridge if we have to. I am not leaving you behind."

"I believe you," Hero whispered and found it *true*, despite all logic. He did. He believed Rami. He believed *in* Rami. It was entirely foreign ground to Hero. He allowed Rami to help him down off his vantage point.

Rami continued to study him. "Ready to do this?"

*Absolutely not.* Terribly, terribly unready. Hero flashed a brittle smile. "To storm a magical drawbridge? My good Ramiel, I was *written* for that."

# 20

# HERO

So much frivolity and fuss over the human soul. You've got to wonder why. What makes the stick-around-ness of a human more special than, say, a muse or a demon? But all the realms seem intent on hoarding the stuff. Gathering souls, preserving souls, rescuing souls, judging souls, eating souls, if you wander into the wrong neighborhood.

Let me tell you, from someone with lifelong experience owning one, a soul's not that shiny on the inside. A grand bother, it is. We spend half our life worried about preserving it, then the rest of it worried that we haven't spent the currency well enough. Better if we never knew we had one, in my opinion. Life is for the living; leave worrying about souls for the dead.

But there was no chance we'd be that sensibly ignorant. Not in a world so lousy with stories.

Souls: pesky, powerful stuff.

*Librarian Fleur Michel, 1784 CE*

HUMANS WERE RIDICULOUS CREATURES, in Hero's expert opinion. They always saw what they wanted to see and ignored the rest. No creature edited its own reality so viciously as a human. After watching a man get sacrificed to oblivion, a rational creature might rebel, decide that three gods and a judgmental bridge were a poor form of moral government. A rational creature might at least *consider* whether any paradise one has to sacrifice others to get into is worth the price of admission.

But no, not humans. Even in death, they picked and chose a comfortable sort of truth. Humans milled in organic clumps, hesitating at one end, before making the slow progression to the other. It was impossible to walk the bridge quickly. Its sharp incline seemed designed to force a soul to slow down and consider one foot placed in front of the other, the lean of the body against the grade. The glimpses of mist and cinder caught beyond the translucent path.

Hero didn't allow Rami to hesitate when they reached the point where stone translated to shimmering bridge. He dragged them over the threshold and kept walking. If he was going to pass this damn judgment, he was going to do it his way. Hero preferred having a *choice* in his dramatics, thank you very much.

They passed under a lacquered arch, and Hero didn't allow himself to look down until his foot landed, solidly, against the shimmering glass-like substance of the bridge.

It held, souls continued to mill around him, and Hero let out a breath he'd been keeping stoppered in his chest.

Rami stopped at his shoulder, asking a silent question. Yes, Hero would be okay. He could do this. He nodded, still gazing at his feet, and pressed on.

The arch of the bridge was strenuous, and by the time they'd nearly crested the middle, every muscle in Hero's legs burned, but his hope was rising. The bridge remained, stable and wide, under his feet. Though, nonetheless, Hero stuck precisely to the center of the crowd. The traffic on the bridge was brisk, now that it seemed stable, and if the gazes of the two giant gods shadowing the sky fell on him, he couldn't feel it.

It was all going perfectly well, so when Rami's chin jerked up, it was like a siren. "Hero."

It took an extra second of scrutinizing for Hero to see it. To his right, past Rami's shoulder and caught in glimpses between souls, the far edge of the bridge had begun to dissolve into sand.

"Maybe it's someone else," Rami whispered, and shoved Hero ahead at a faster pace, to place distance between them and the disturbance.

A shiver, like sand cascading over glass, told him the effect was keeping pace. Hero's stomach dropped. "Or maybe not."

A cry broke out near the disintegrating edge, and a murmur began to spread. Humans saw what they wanted to see, yes, but when presented with an immediate threat, crowds could turn like lightning. Souls began to jostle behind them, and Rami caught Hero by the arm as someone shoved past.

The disturbance spread. In a blink, Rami had drawn his sword. "We need to *move*."

Hero nodded, and they dove through the crowd that had begun to cluster and back away from the edge. A scrabble of feet behind them said that the bridge was melting away from both sides now, and then there was a scream.

Hero looked back just in time to see a bramble of humans fighting near the ledge. "It's her! It's got to be her!" another woman shouted with a girl in her grasp. The next moment existed in only two things: a puff of displaced mist, a smothered scream.

"No," Hero whispered.

"Holy light, she pushed her." Rami's voice was hoarse, then hard. "We need to get out of here."

Hero saw what he meant. To either side of his section of the bridge, the edges hadn't slowed with the sacrifice; if anything, they sped up. Sand spilled away beneath scrambling feet, and the voices turned accusatory. Anger snapped over the crowd like a waiting storm, and another figure slipped over the edge.

"Back! Get back!" Rami swung his sword in a short, controlled arc.

Hero winced. A furious man with a sword might have kept panicked souls at bay, but it also drew twice as many eyes. An undertow of accusation hardened through the crowd, until it was just Hero and Rami isolated on the swiftly shrinking section of bridge.

"Let us through!" Rami swung his sword again with increased desperation. Hero saw the embers of anger on Rami's face, saw the sand and the bridge unraveling faster, faster. Hero was falling, but Rami—he wouldn't let Rami fall again.

"Stop." He gripped Rami's elbow as he prepared to swing again. Muscles bunched and jumped under his fingers. The bridge had narrowed to the size of a narrow staircase now, forcing Hero into Rami's space. "Just stop."

"What?" Muscles jumped again as Rami stared at him in dismay. "We can't give up."

"I'm not giving up," Hero said, and he took Rami's confusion as an opportunity to step under his guard and shove. Rami stumbled— toward the crowd, toward the section of bridge that wasn't disappearing. "I've just figured out how the game is rigged."

The bridge shrunk to the width of a dinner plate. Mist churned, thickening and clinging to the evaporating edges like thorns in wool. Hero refused to calculate how far down it was. There was no wind, but something warm and decay sweet wafted up from the dark. Sweet, perhaps like anise. Gods, let it be anise.

"What game?" Rami cried. He had one foot on the narrowed plank of bridge, but the other hesitated, anchored on the stable section. He had enough sense to know that he shouldn't give up the ground gained, probably believed he could pull Hero to safety. Still.

Heaven appeared to make angels as stupid as heroes. And Hero knew how to deal with those.

"The trolley problem!" The width of a dinner plate had narrowed to a single plank. Hero rearranged himself sideways and steely kept his eyes off the mists. "Claire told me there's no real answer, but I think I figured out my own."

The plank had become a bar and was headed toward a tightrope. How lucky that Hero had been written with excellent balance. How unlucky that he'd been written desperately afraid of heights. His breath was being slowly squeezed out of his chest. Rami reached out again but Hero held up his hand.

"The one or the many—it's bullshit. The only way to play is to declare the game rigged." Hero tipped his head back, because it was always better to be angry than terrified. "Rigged! I won't sacrifice myself, and I am *through* with people sacrificing themselves for me! So, what now, you so-called divine judges? Well?"

As if in answer, Hero felt the pressure beneath his toes narrow and the edges of his toes flex on empty air. He made the mistake of looking down, and the nausea of panic made him squeeze his eyes shut. "Oh hell."

"*Hero.*" One foot held Rami's weight on stable bridge, while all the rest of him seemed stretched, attempting to span the space. He looked anguished. "I understand. I respect your answer, and you. You are a singular creature, Hero. The gods are wrong, if they can't see your—"

"Don't start with the sympathy now, or I really will throw myself off this bridge." Hero's eyes stung and leaked; it was ridiculous he could notice that seconds from oblivion. His knees swayed out from under him. "Instead of just fall."

"That's the thing about falling . . ." Rami's voice had a current of calm that made Hero look. Rami had put away his sword. His face was overcome with an intense look of concentration as he appeared to gauge the disappearing bar and take an unsteady step across it.

"Rami—"

"That's the thing about falling," Rami said again as Hero's foot slipped off the edge. He just had time for his stomach to do a loop up his throat before he felt weightless. "None of us ever fall alone."

Hero caught the impression of arms locking around him tight, cool feathers against his cheek, and a shriek of something slicing free through muscle and sinew as they tilted free of the bridge, and the mist had them.

# 21

# CLAIRE

Myrrh. I wanted to be the one to figure it out. I admit it. Might be why I've held on for so long. I'm a foolish old man, and after the first couple of centuries here I thought, hell, this would do it. This was why I was here. I would be the one to kick down this house of questions. The song of the books—I thought if I listened long enough they would sing to me too.

But my apprentice is here and I'm still no closer to the answer. Smart as a whip, for a Norman. Well, leave the glory to her. I can keep on mulling about it in my cups in Valhalla. They'll have to allow a doddering old man his thoughts.

*Librarian Bjorn the Bard, 1711 CE*

IN RETROSPECT, CLAIRE HAD never appreciated Brevity enough. This was a fact she was aware of already. It was a given that Brevity was a better, smarter, more loyal assistant than Claire had deserved. But thank gods that, up till now, Brevity's good intentions had aligned with Claire's own.

Because when she put her mind to it, that muse was *devious*.

Claire had the ink in an examination tray, under a magnifying glass, before she realized the switch. And she could hardly complain, because a sample of unwritten damsel ink *was* what she'd been after in the first place. Not that it had revealed much. The damsel ink sample lolled in the clear tray, leaving behind isolated droplets in its wake. It dried—slowly, but it did dry—adhering to paper and fingers and flaking away harmlessly as ink should.

Claire should have been more concerned about the vial that'd been swapped: the vial of their unwritten ink. It was right that the Arcane Wing should keep account of the ink, at least until they understood it fully. Claire should return to the Unwritten Wing and call for fair play. But every time she collected the intention to do just that, Brevity's horrified face came back to her. Claire had taken Lucille's ink and Brevity had looked at her like she was a monster. Brevity, the cheerful woman who had stood by her side through almost thirty years of mishandling the Library. She'd seen Claire at her worst, but Claire had found a new way to step over the line.

Claire had been scared and acted rashly; she had. She could admit that much. But she didn't want to face her again right now. Brevity was the one person who could cause that uneasy, oily feeling of shame in Claire's head. And there was enough interfering with her thinking as it was. For instance, there appeared to be a soliloquy going on past the open doors, just outside of eyesight.

"Bird," Claire said without looking up. The sound of dusty feathers fluffing up and resettling told her she'd been heard. "Is there a Shakespeare knockoff in the hallway, yes or no?"

Hard claws tapped softly against metal as the raven shuffled along her perch on the back of the opposite chair. She cocked her head sideways, then made a sound akin to a tuba in mid-childbirth.

"No, that's what I thought." Claire sighed, but the phantom sounds faded, as they always did when she had Bird to confirm or deny. If the price of mental clarity was talking to birds, Claire would take it. If the ink eating her arm wanted to communicate, it could damn well just spell it out.

A new noise replaced the old and increased too quickly for Claire to get Bird's opinion on the matter. Giant footfalls echoed up the hallway before shoulders large enough to block the light filled up the doorway.

"Walter?" Claire stood, ignoring Bird as she shot into the air and screeched her displeasure at the racket. The large gatekeeper had to duck his shoulders just so to squeeze through the Arcane Wing's double doors.

"Sorry about ta interruption, Miss Claire. I wouldn't have bothered you but the other one was real sure you'd know what to do."

The opportunities for Claire to know the correct thing to do were infrequent lately. She was about to tell Walter as much until he turned clear of the doorway. Hero was cradled in Walter's scarred hands and unmoving. His face was pale and drawn but Claire couldn't see any injuries until she caught sight of his foot, smearing ink down the side of Walter's faded shirt.

"Sweet harpies," Claire swore under her breath. "Set him on the couch, Walter. Foot on the ottoman, please."

Rami drifted in after Walter, looking every bit a ghost himself. Claire observed him out of the corner of her eye as she busied herself with finding clean thread and needles in the bottom of the drawer. He seemed unhurt, which allowed her to focus her anger at *someone* at least.

She shoved a bowl of water and a pot of salve in Rami's hands with enough force to slosh his coat. "Wash the wound while I try to find something more delicate than *bookbinding materials* to sew flesh."

Walter handled Hero with a tenderness that would have softened Claire's heart if she had been in a better state of mind. As it was, the giant wisely retreated as she stormed past. Perhaps some surgical equipment was in the worktables. Enough artifacts in the wing were made of flesh and hide that there had to be something.

When she finally returned with a suture and a suitable needle, Rami had managed to get Hero's damaged boot off and had cleaned the wound. It was a slice up the side of his foot, shallow but vivid. Rami held pressure with a clean towel and the weight of a hangdog expression. Claire sighed and carefully picked through Hero's jacket.

"Explain," she said into his breast pocket.

In turn, Rami appeared to address Hero's foot with a hoarse voice. "We fell afoul of the bridge in Chinvat."

"Chinvat?" Claire found what she was looking for, set his book to the side, and glanced up with a frown. "Why would you go *there*?"

"We didn't start there. We started in Elysium," Rami said, and Claire kept her peace until the whole story had been haltingly reported. Elysium, the Unsaid Wing, Hero's grand idea to go poking at the muses as if they were an information desk. Claire pulled on a pair of clean gloves—no coming near an open wound with her inked hand, certainly—and resisted the urge to rub her temples.

"He twisted up his foot in the fall," Rami concluded quietly.

Walter had been conducting a very thorough examination of his toes but finally cleared his throat. "Miss Claire, if everything's ready, I left the office empty—"

Claire pulled herself together enough for a polite smile. "You can go, Walter. We've got it in hand. Thank you for your help."

It was true. Hero would be fine. Hero's *book* was fine, and that was the extent of her knowledge. Claire was not a surgeon, but the cut seemed worse than it actually was. Rami had cleaned the wound with the expertise of a combat medic. He should have been the one to stitch

Hero up, but instead he hovered like a very guilty kind of storm cloud. Claire pursed her lips as she threaded a needle. "You should have taken him to Brevity, you know. She's the librarian."

Rami had the grace to look ashamed. "I know. But . . ."

"I'm not the librarian anymore, Rami."

"No," Rami said quietly. "But you are . . . to him . . ." His brow furrowed, as if digging for the word and coming up short. He reverted to watching Hero. "He's yours."

"Hardly. He's Brevity's assistant."

"You know that's not what I mean."

The wound closed easily enough with one stitch, maybe two. Claire finished a stitch and held the tension in the thread long enough to meet Rami's troubled gray eyes. "No, you sweet, stupid angel man. He is not." Rami's worry transformed into confusion. Claire hid her smile in an inspection of the stitches on Hero's foot. The ink had already faded, and the skin was pulling together nicely. He'd be sore for a couple of days, but mobility wouldn't be an issue. Even outside their books, characters were remarkably resilient. "Hero and I both have a particularly checkered history when it comes to romantic entanglements between unwritten books and authors. I'm not saying the attraction isn't there. But the pull between an author and a book—even a character—is too messy. I care for him, I will continue to care for him, but I will lay no claim on him. That's not what love is."

Rami was quiet a stunned moment. "You're saying—"

"I'm saying nothing but that Hero is not mine. At least, he is no more mine than you are. You should see to your own feelings. Ah! No, no use denying it. I see it there behind those atrociously serious brows. Hero has that effect on people."

A groan like a rusted hinge forced Claire's attention from Hero's foot to his face. He'd regained some color but restrained his glare to the thinnest of squints between closed eyes. "Do I get a say in this?" he croaked.

"No." Claire finished trimming the stitches and flicked his big toe gently. "You should really learn not to eavesdrop on private conversations."

Hero grunted and groggily rubbed at his temple. "You should learn not to conduct private conversations over my unconscious body."

"You should learn to stop swooning like a silly—"

"You should both learn to stop taking such self-sacrificing risks!" Rami threw up his hands, looking between Claire and Hero as if they were some horrifying new form of torture Hell had devised just for him. His gaze flicked between Claire's gloved hand and Hero's foot before he appeared to settle his ire on Hero. "You don't *anger* another realm's gods while you are *in* the realm!"

"I learned it from watching her," Hero mumbled.

Claire sniffed. "Oh no, you did this one yourself."

"He jumped *with* me," Hero insisted.

"I *fell* with you, fool. You didn't even know where you would be sent! You had no way of knowing whether falling in that abyss would send you to our Hell or that realm's equivalent."

"I smelled anise! It was a reasonable wager!"

"Wager! Don't take that kind of risk on a *smell*—"

"Gentlemen!" Claire had to clap her hands to get their attention. She got twin abashed looks in response, one light and narrow, one dark and broad. They really were going to be the death of her. Claire shook her head and began returning her instruments to her drawers. "You are going to have to continue this . . . whatever this is . . . elsewhere. Hero's obviously recovered enough to be a petulant child, so, Rami: please help Hero up to the Unwritten Wing so he can inform Brevity of his poor choices and the sorry state of things."

"I don't need help," Hero said as Rami stooped and gently heaved an arm over his shoulder. His color appeared to peak in his cheeks as Rami hoisted him up to as polite a bridal carry as possible. "I don't need to be *carried*! This is an insult."

"And I don't need you splitting that paper cut open before it heals and getting *ink* all over the halls. We've had enough spilled-ink problems as of late."

"*Paper cut?* Are you mocking a man wounded in the line of duty, warden?"

"Always." Claire made a dismissive wave with her good hand. "You heal like a hero, at least. I don't want to see you down here again until you've earned Brevity's forgiveness."

Hero threw her a dark look, still a bit pink in the cheeks as Rami carried him out.

# 22

# HERO

The best of humanity can be found in Hell. I'll fight any theologian on this fact. Hell is a place you sentence yourself to, which by necessity requires a solid bit of self-reflection. Or, at the very least, a death's-bed awareness. Mortality has a way of forcing one to be honest with oneself; none of the frivolous barricades we erect in life withstand it. You find the failures here, but you also find the strivers, the yearners, the eyes open enough to see the distance between where they are and where they could have been. Hell is a place for the dreamers that have woken up, and the books still asleep.

In both ways, Hell is a place ripe for stories.

*Librarian Gregor Henry, 1933 CE*

THE CEILINGS OF HELL were an underappreciated bit of architecture. All the shadows and mismatched beams—wood, stone, was that an arch of bone there?—blurred into a smear beyond Ramiel's chin. Which Hero had a very good view of. Because he was being carried. Like a child.

"She is being vindictive," Hero pronounced, and plucked irritably at one of the feathers that cushioned his cheek.

Rami's steps didn't slow, even when he jostled his elbow up to shift Hero away from his chest. "Can't imagine why."

"Don't get cute with me," Hero muttered without heat.

"Then stop with the feathers. That tickles."

"Tickles? Angels are *ticklish*?" Hero took any opportunity to be delighted, especially since it distracted from the hot throb in his twisted ankle. "Who would have guessed? Wait until I tell the demons."

Rami slanted him a look, which from this angle was heavy with long-suffering tolerance. "As I've told you before, I'm technically a Watcher."

"Angel, old-as-dirt proto-angel . . . I fail to see the distinction." Hero startled as Rami stopped abruptly and was forced to clench a hand in his trench coat for balance. "Except possibly a proper angel wouldn't be flinging me about—what's that frown for?"

"The doors." The frisson of unease in Rami's voice made Hero crane his head around. The ceiling had been all very much the same, so it was some surprise to see they were in the foyer of the Unwritten Wing. Rami had stopped near the gargoyle, who was napping by evidence of the snore that emanated, in a couple of frequencies adjacent to reality, from his alcove. If Hero twisted his head further, he could make out the upside-down curve of the Unwritten Wing's doors.

Which were nearly closed.

"That's peculiar." Hero wasn't alarmed, not yet. He was, however, getting a crick in his neck. "Put me down, will you?"

Rami hesitated, which gave Hero the opportunity to flop back against his chest a little too heavily and pin him with his best royal disdain. "I twisted my ankle; I didn't *lose* it. And I can already tell the scrape is healed closed. I'd rather not fall on my head while you're wrestling with the doors with your hands full. Put me down and stop acting like a nursemaid."

Rami relented, which allowed Hero to almost forgive him for the way he nonsensically set him down as if he were made of blown glass. Hero thumped his bandaged foot down to prove a point and hid the grimace of discomfort as he turned toward the door.

He cleared the small distance at a limp but hesitated with his hand above the silver curve of the door pull. Doubt flickered in his stomach. He silently willed the doors to swing on their hinges. There were many reasons why the wing might close its doors, but only one reason to lock them.

A shift of movement signaled Rami coming up behind him, cautiously, likely one hand on the pommel of his sword to charge in and save the day. It was a ridiculous thought, and enough for Hero to grasp the silver handle and yank with more force than necessary. The door parted open on silent greased hinges, and Hero thrust it aside to hide his relief. "There. The doors probably closed on a breeze by accident. Let in some fresh air, Brevity?"

His voice thudded into the well of quiet as heavy as a stone dropped in a pond. The lights were on, and across the expanse of the lobby Hero saw the productive kind of clutter that the librarian's desk had when she was working. But a chill kind of quiet frosted the air without a response, and no one stirred from the stacks.

"Librarian?" Hero tried again at a louder volume. A feather-soft touch brushed his elbow and nearly sent him out of his skin. His injured ankle filed another complaint, which he focused into a glare.

Rami raised his thick brows in apology and pitched his voice low. "Did Brevity have external business when you left?"

"Not that I knew of. She was chattering away with that traitorous muse. The stacks have been quiet and she's been so preoccupied I wouldn't think—" Hero's gaze fished over the long shadows of the Library. It was possible Brevity was on some errand deep in the stacks, so deep she hadn't heard Hero call. But he trusted the instinct that told him that wasn't the case. The wing wasn't just quiet. Quiet had a mild flavor, a pause. Vacancy, abandonment, was heavy and deep. The back of Hero's neck prickled. "I should check on the damsels."

He made it two limping steps before Rami caught his elbow and used his momentum to spin him away from the stacks. "No, I'll check on the damsels. Perhaps Brevity left some kind of note in the logbook."

"I am the librarian here," Hero objected in a mostly confident tone. Assistant librarian. Technically.

"And only librarians can make sense of that grotto you call a desk," Rami said simply. He had that implacable Watcher look; that *I've waited millennia; what's another one?* placid stare that made Hero want to dig in his heels. If one of his heels didn't hurt right now.

Hero straightened his shoulders toward the desk, chin too high in the air to notice when Rami was satisfied enough to disappear between the rows of books. His ankle was a brittle complaint by the time he reached the desk, and Hero flopped down in Brevity's armchair gladly and let out a slow, measured sigh.

The quiet was less forbidding, just knowing Rami was there among the aisles. It was funny, how companionship did that. Like how just *knowing* there was a campfire to return to made the night feel less dark, even when you were far from it. Hero had spent enough cold nights stumbling around in the dark to know. Or had he? He'd been a rebellion leader, and then an ill-prepared king, then a bad one, in his story. Did it count? Were those memories any fainter, less accurate, less painful, for having happened between pages he could no longer return to? Just because something—supposedly—didn't really happen didn't make it less real.

It wasn't worth consideration, as things stood now. And Hero prized his consideration highly as a means of survival. He straightened and reached for the logbook, even as he kept an ear tuned to the quiet of the stacks. Certainly he would hear a scream or whatnot if something was amiss. A barrel-chested brute like Rami would have to have good lungs and all.

Leather scraped against wood as Hero pulled the logbook into his lap. It was heavy, heavier than its size suggested. Heavy with ink and paper and an eon of librarians. Hero still felt like an impostor flipping the cover open, and he resented it. Why shouldn't he read the nattering chicken scratch of librarians long dead? Sure, they were human, but he was a *character*, which counted for something. He hoped it counted for something, beyond the fraying thread of doubt in his gut.

The most recent entry had been Brevity's, reporting the existence of the ink and the arrival of Probity. It went on, but Hero stopped reading when the paragraph started to be peppered with "I" statements. It was the habit of the librarians of the Unwritten Wing to empty their hearts to the logbook. It was also the habit of the librarians not to pry into the entries of their contemporaries. Hero had scoffed at that, until he happened to read Brevity's first entry after the destruction of the books during the coup. He hadn't been able to meet her eyes for days.

He might be a villain, but he wasn't a sadist to anyone but himself.

Instead his index finger tapped at the blank of the page, where an explanation, an answer, should have existed. There was no one around to judge him when he put his feet on the desk. Brevity hadn't closed the Library and hadn't recorded a reason for her absence. That either meant it was too trivial to note or it'd come upon her so suddenly that there hadn't been time.

Hero would assume the former, at least until the next disaster.

He didn't have to wait long. Rami emerged from the stack depths, but not alone. "The damsel suite is as it should be," Rami reported before stepping aside. "Mistress Lucille offered her help—"

"Oh, delightful," Hero muttered, tilting the logbook up in order to better slouch behind it. The damsels had made overtures after he returned to the Unwritten Wing. He was supposed to feel a kinship, a commonality with them, other characters who had woken up from their books. Other unwitting residents of the Library. But the line from them to their books was unbroken and secure. Hero's wasn't. He wasn't book *enough*, not really. The damsel suite felt like a pantomime in a foreign land that he was supposed to call home. A language that was supposed to be in his blood but felt borrowed on his tongue. Too much a book to be a person. Too much a person to be a book.

"Hero," Lucille said in the tone of wearily beset older relatives everywhere. Hero crept a glance over the top of the book. She had narrowed her gaze onto where the heels of his boots rested on the desk.

"Auntie!" Hero rearranged his expression and trilled with a wiggle of his toes. "So good of you to be concerned about my welfare, as always."

"I understand you were injured."

"Only a bit twinged. Nothing the restive embrace of the Library won't fix." Hero twisted his heel again, just to see the crow's-feet around Lucille's eyes deepen. Paper crunched beneath the friction. "I don't suppose you've seen our librarian recently? Puppy-dog eyes, terrifying with a returns cart, blue all over?"

Lucille's lips thinned. "Not since she chased her predecessor out of here."

"What would Claire be doing here?" *Without us*, Hero said in a glance toward Rami.

"Taking her pound of flesh, so to speak." Lucille's fingers tapped at her forearm. "Up to her usual tricks, without her assistant to keep her in line."

The furrow in Rami's brow deepened and— Really, only Hero was allowed to cause that dismay in him. Hero frowned. "Ramiel is much too smart to try to herd that woman. Claire makes her own decisions."

"At the expense of the Library," Lucille said, dropping her eyes to Hero's heels on the desk again. "I wonder how much longer we can afford it. Or you."

She had the mortifying power to continually make Hero feel like a scrawny farm bumpkin again. As if he were twelve years old, mud on his face and pig shit between his toes. Hero's feet hit the floor with a thud, and he stood to make it seem like his idea.

"An inventory would be appropriate." Lucille sat herself down on the edge of a divan, looking for all the world as if she were preparing to order a cup of tea. "And would ease my concerns."

"I was not aware that your concerns extended beyond your little island of misfits."

"No one is an island. Especially here." Lucille folded her hands, and the faint rasp of her aging paper skin sent a chill up Hero's neck. She pinned him with a placid stare. "Stories have a way of entangling."

Rami interrupted the silence with a grunt before Hero could conjure a response to that. "An inventory would be prudent," Rami said to the floor. "If the acting librarian agrees?"

It took effort to keep the snarl from his lips. Rami was trying to be supportive, in his way. But under Lucille's gaze the reminder of his supposed authority felt wrong, like a sliver wedged under his nail. Hero flung the logbook back onto the surface of the desk and flipped through the pages until he hit the inventory page. The pen was already flourished in his hand before he had a chance to hesitate with the nib inches from the page. The flutter in his gut was a nuisance. He'd written in the logbook before; he'd do so again. He'd never commanded the Library before.

And he could think of no sensible reason why it would listen.

Self-irritation acted as the best kind of lubricant to movement. Hero scratched out the order swiftly, dotting the period at the end with a vicious flourish. His hand cramped around the pen, which he found he couldn't quite put down until, after an insufferable pause, the book began to hum with a rustle of paper. The opposite page began to fill up and scroll through an impossibly long list of titles.

"There." Hero flung himself back in the chair and lifted his chin to Lucille. "Happy, Grandmother?"

"As happy as you are." Lucille smoothed the thin polyester of her housedress over her wide hips and got comfortable. "Oh, my dear. I appear to have forgotten my tea."

"I'll see what I can find, ma'am." Rami straightened and made an awkward scan of the desk before heading back into the stacks.

The tea caddy, the silver cart that Brevity kept overflowing with sachets and chipped cups, was three paces behind the desk, in the alcove with the sleeping tapestries. It was not among the shelves. Hero could have told him, were it not for the way Lucille's gaze sharpened on him like a whetstone. "The elderly are so absentminded," Hero tsked over the hum of the logbook running inventory.

"That boy is older than most of the damsel suite put together." Lucille pinned him with a weighted glance. "You should leave the Arcane Wing well enough alone. Come back to the Library."

"I'm the assistant librarian. And part of Special Collections." Hero dropped his head back with a dramatic flourish. "I couldn't be more entrenched in the Library if I tried."

"You can't, though. Try."

Lucille was watching him when his head snapped back up. "I beg your pardon," Hero said in his most *I absolutely do not beg your pardon* tone.

"You can't try," Lucille repeated simply. "I'm sorry, child; it's not as if you have a choice in the matter. Is that why you make everything you do seem as if it's both the largest imposition and also done at your forbearance? Fancy way you have with that."

It took Hero a beat longer to arm his words than it should have. "As if you have room to speak, *damsel*."

The wattle of aged skin on Lucille's throat shivered as she chuckled. "Oh yes, heaven help you if you thought you were one of *us*. But rest assured—you're not. You'd be welcome with us, of course, but . . . well, we have chosen to stay in the suite, instead of going back to our books. It's a slim choice, but a choice all the same."

"I make my own choices. I'm a *librarian*, aren't I?"

"If that's what gives you purpose, my dear." Lucille hummed gently. "It is all right, is all I'm saying. We all understand you do as you must."

A sharp poke at his thumb interrupted Hero's thoughts. He hadn't put down the pen, and the tines of the tip prodded into the flesh of his thumb with a smear of black. A moment, just a flash really, of another time came over him. Claire being swallowed by black. And then, before that, a damsel bleeding and turning to ash. Tasting ink on his tongue and dark at the edge of his vision.

Hero shook it clear, but instead of feeling better it made him feel precisely too aware. Aware of the walls, suddenly too close; the air, a little too warm. "I could . . . I could run."

"Only as far as they let you, sweetling." Lucille sighed, and her earnest pity was worse than her scorn. "So you've convinced yourself you don't want to."

"I *don't* want to." The ink wicked along the fingerprint of the broad side of his thumb. He rubbed it, only succeeding in smearing it larger as it began to dry, leaving his skin feeling tight. No matter. It would wash away as if it'd never been there. "I chose to stay. To help."

As soon as he'd said them, the words took on a familiar echo from Chinvat bridge. The wind had dragged its nails through his coat and across his skin. He'd balanced on his toes, terror in his throat, and told himself he would not play their game. He'd spite the gods; he wouldn't play their game, and he'd *choose* to fall.

As if anyone chooses gravity.

"You are a help," Lucille said while precisely not saying a thousand other pitying things. "But when someone stays with you because they don't have any other choice, that's not a kindness. The damsel suite is always open to you, when you need a home."

It was strangling; it was falling; it was enough ripping sensations to tear Hero apart. His ink-smeared fingers clenched under the desk, but just then the logbook chimed a reprieve. "I'll make my *own* way, thank you," Hero said with every bit of acid stored up in his throat. He bent over the desk and studied the inventory with far more scrutiny than the single line—*all books accounted for*—required. It gave him the moment of privacy he needed to stop the twisting fear building in his chest.

"Nothing missing?" Lucille said after the silence turned awkward.

"None. Does that satisfy you?" Hero drew himself up to his full height. It was so much easier looking at people from the narrow parapet of his nose. "Rami!" he called, without turning to look.

After a few moments, he could hear the familiar heavy trod of angelic work boots. Hero tried to not let the relief play on his face.

"I couldn't find the tea cart," Rami apologized as he left the long shadows of the stacks.

"You're a sweetheart for looking. Never you mind." Lucille rose slowly with dignity, playing up her age in a way that made Hero strain to not roll his eyes. "There will be a kettle on in the suite."

"Oh . . ." The heavy brows on Rami's olive face did a complicated twitch as he stepped aside for Lucille to leave and glanced at Hero. He was canny enough to step carefully over the frost in the air. "But the inventory?"

"Satisfactory." Lucille patted the angel's arm as she passed. "The rest of it is no business of mine, of course. You boys tell the librarian I'd appreciate a visit when she gets back."

Hero's lip was curled. It took an effort to straighten out his expression as Lucille left and Rami turned a questioning gaze back to him. He took a tentative step on his injured foot and was pleased that only the rotation of his ankle twinged in protest. He could work with that. "Rami, I do hate to be a bother, but—"

"What can I do to help?" Rami asked, as Hero knew he would.

Hero rewarded him with a warm smile that was shockingly earnest. Some of the doubts Lucille had left in his chest began to recede. Choices, and the power to make them—Rami lived his life so effortlessly that way. It would be impossible for Hero to keep up, at least as he was. His smile brightened. "Could you do me a favor and mind the desk for a bit—in case Brevity comes back? I would hate to miss her in the hallways."

Rami frowned. "I thought you were to rest—"

"And I shall. But first, I just have one small errand." And Hero forced his aching feet to walk straight and true, out of the Library.

# 23

# CLAIRE

The story and the storyteller are never far apart, in my experience. Authors and their books maintain a relationship that is the best and the worst of us.

Once a book is out in the world, the author pretends to let go. Stories, after all, are for the people who need to hear them. We have to let go of a story, give up the reins, when we ask it to be read. We pretend it's like making any other product, bread for the hungry or coats for the cold. But what no author admits is that it's not like that at all. Stories are not made of flour or wool. Stories, real stories, are made with a sliver of yourself.

The *purpose* for stories is what readers will make of them. But the reason, the desperate need, is a splinter in the author alone. A good story gets under your skin, because that's where all good stories start.

*Librarian Bjorn the Bard, 1313 CE*

IT WAS A HABIT of the Library to keep count of days in a mortal fashion. Hell had nothing so simple or precious as sunrises and sunsets, but it *felt* late when Claire finally looked up from her reading.

She'd found a dusty historical in the back of Andras's cluttered shelves. Some sixteenth-century creation that appeared to confuse demonic summonses and keys of Solomon and faerie poppets, of all things, into one volume of nonsense. However, it must have had a grain of truth, powerful truth, to end up down in the Arcane Wing. Claire had set herself about finding it, on the off chance it related to the ink.

Reading garbled conspiracy theories by long-dead Scotsmen; this was how far Claire had fallen. But the ink held no answers, Walter had no answers, and the Library shunned her. As tragic as it was, this was the best lead she had in the time left.

The shimmer of blue itched above the curve of her arm. It had thinned to no more than a width of fine yarn, and frayed to scratchy, twitching threads. Claire rubbed an idle hand over it, but it did nothing to quell the itch or the hourglass running empty in her mind. The border on her skin was growing more distinct, ink-stained skin south of the line chill, with a dry clamminess that its northern counterpart didn't have.

The wing was quiet, and grit had worked its way behind her eyeballs. She rubbed over her face furiously before startling as the door gave a labored groan. Hero appeared hesitantly in the gap, looking slyer—or perhaps shyer—than usual.

"Warden? Are you about?"

"Where else would I be?" Claire called, and glanced once at the page to mentally mark the place she'd left off. Hero was nothing if not a reliable distraction.

Hero closed the door behind him, pulling another creak from the hinges, which made every one of Bird's feathers puff as she cracked open one beady eye. Claire fluttered her hand, forcing Bird off the table and clearing a space as Hero approached at a slower pace than normal.

He favored the instep of his right leg and tried to hide it with a lazy stroll.

He paused to trade one sour look for another with Bird, then precisely pulled out a chair on the opposite side of the table from the raven. "Another book? I would have thought you'd read everything in here three times over already."

"Some books give up more on closer read," Claire said, not bothering to explain her desperation as she carefully closed the old book on her lap. "How's the foot?"

"Handsomely turned, as always," Hero scoffed, and wiggled his ankle, mostly hiding his grimace. "It did no lasting harm."

Meaning, Claire read with familiarity, he was injured and in pain but willing to ignore such problems until they went away. She nodded, having no room to speak on the denial of injuries. She allowed a streak of her usual reserve back into her voice. "I hope Brevity talked some sense into you."

"Brevity . . . yes . . ." Hero paused, fishing his gaze around the room before shrugging off a not-quite-response. "Surely you know that would be a lost cause."

"Entirely." Claire put her book down and crossed her arms. "So, what do you want?"

"Want?" Hero's theatrics were so familiar that when he put a hand to his chest, a disconcerting warmth rose through Claire's. "Perhaps this is simply a social call to express gratitude."

"If you thanked me every time I stitched you or your book up, I'd never be rid of you."

"Said as if you wouldn't miss me terribly."

An answering smile pulled at Claire's mouth, though she stifled it. A smug expression told her Hero had picked it up anyway.

"Said as a hypothetical because yet again here you are. But not to thank me."

Hero, reliably, appeared to change the subject. His gaze drifted to the thin cotton gloves on Claire's hands. A shadowy wash of black and a thin line of blue were just visible below her right elbow. "I didn't have time to ask earlier. How is it holding up?"

Claire followed his gaze, and the back of her knuckles itched. She tugged at the long cuff of her glove carefully until the stain was covered. "Unremarkable, if you'd believe it. A tight feeling, now and then, like the skin is chapped, but nothing that warrants complaint."

*Nothing physical*, she silently amended. She did not mention the whispers, the dream of Beatrice, the filter of colors that filled every shadow. The cold slowly settling into her stained skin went unsaid. She definitely didn't mention the phantom visit from the every-person. If Hero was allowed to play at health, then so was Claire. It only seemed fair.

"Fascinating." Hero hummed to himself as he craned over the table as if Claire's hand was some kind of intriguing bug. But a small nit of worry was a strange fit between his brows. "It's growing, though."

"Is it? It must be too slow to even notice," Claire evaded, not quite meeting Hero's eyes. What Walter had said—or not wanted to say— was not reassuring. But there was no reason to worry the rest of them with fates that might or might not be inevitable. "I haven't noticed a change. No cause for concern."

"Is that so." Hero's eyes narrowed, and if he noticed how the thick blue-gold line around her arm had thinned from a wide band to a thin ribbon, he didn't say so. "It's an interesting experiment, at least—and I've come with a comparison study."

He was attempting to sound aloof but hadn't quite contained the way his fingers drummed on top of the table nervously as he did it.

Claire's stomach swooped at the proposal of another experiment, but it was obvious he was about to propose something important. "Really?" Claire put away her book and crossed her arms. "Well then, do continue, scholar Hero."

"Simple. Considering how little we know about this ink, comparisons are in order."

Claire rubbed her temple. "I've already tested the ink thoroughly, Hero."

"Not compare the ink—compare the material. It certainly had an enthusiastic reaction before. So it only makes sense that we should try this mystery substance against as many materials as possible to discern its nature."

"To discern its nature," Claire repeated, amused. It wasn't often that Hero tried to cover up his own concerns with anything other than grand arrogance. It was endearing, if endearment could be highly suspicious. "We've already tried it against paper and, inadvertently I'll admit, librarian skin. What else do you propose?"

"My book. Try the ink on my book," Hero said. "See if it can do what my own ink can't."

"What?" Claire recoiled, and all her humor fled her. "Have you taken leave of your senses? You saw what the ink does to a book!"

"To a *logbook*. An artifact solely of the Library, not an unwritten book that was meant to be made real."

"I don't see how that makes a difference."

"And I don't see how we have the time to debate it!" Hero had dropped his intellectual air. He braced his arms over the table as if it was all that held him up. "I think it makes all the difference in the world. What is an unwritten book, Claire? What's it made of? Where's it come from? Where do *I* come from?"

"What a silly question. That's—" Claire's mouth started working before she could quite come up with an answer. He'd come to her for answers. Her insides churned. "Well, stories come from their authors, of course—"

"It's *more* than that," Hero interrupted, pushing away from the table. He raked a vicious hand through his hair. "I admit it; I took this recent investigation as an excuse to get out of the Library, but also to find *answers*. But all we came back with were more questions! Everyone talks about the books of the Library as some sacred thing. The books must be preserved. The books are immortal, the letter said, but *why?* None of the artifacts in the Arcane Wing are. We destroyed enough baubles fighting Andras to prove that. And why Hell? Why are we here, in this realm of all places?"

Claire felt lost in the torrent. It wasn't just questions; it was the obvious agony of not knowing. Hero's face echoed the blinding panic that had taken over her every moment since the ink had appeared. She couldn't face it, so instead she looked down as she shook her head. "None of that has anything to do with this ink business—"

"It has *everything* to do with it." Hero's shoulders had wound up to his ears. "I can feel it. That ink is *kin*, Claire. Or as near to it as books get. You said yourself, you thought the ink had pulled back from hurting Rosia! I'm a character, as much as she is. I know it won't reject me."

"Like your own story did?"

Hero stopped, tight as a wound spring and trembling with a warning kind of tension. "Don't."

Once, Claire might have persisted. That Claire had hurt a lot of people. She chewed on her bottom lip. "I'm sorry. But there's no way, Hero. It's too big a risk."

"It's the only risk that's going to lead to answers. We *need* answers. We're running out of time." Certainty straightened Hero's shoulders. "You can peer at that ink under a microscope all you want—

and knowing you, you have. But you're never going to understand it from the outside. Ink isn't made for a bottle. It's made for . . . me."

"We don't know that, Hero."

"I do." Hero took a small step. He hesitated only a moment before raising and placing his hands on Claire's shoulders. "I can't go back to my book. That's all I know. And it's going to slowly drive me mad not knowing if I ever will."

A bramble of distress tangled in Claire's throat. It felt like loss, and it felt like fear. "You're really that determined to leave us? Leave the Library, I mean. What about Rami?"

Hero's lip twitched as if he'd been stung. "Don't you mean what about *me*, Claire?" He made a sucking sound with his teeth. "Jealous?"

A laugh, exhausted and inappropriate, bubbled past Claire's messier emotions. Hero's surprised blink only made her chuckle again, and feel infinitely tired. "No, not jealous, Hero. Selfishly sad, maybe. But not jealous. You heard me before. I can't be to you what Rami is. Or what he could be if you allowed him."

Hero looked caught between insult and vulnerability. His hands flinched back abruptly. "Ha, I don't know what you're even talking—"

"*Yes*, you do. And so does Rami. So be gentle with him."

"I—" Hero stopped and studied the floor, the pale skin beneath his long lashes slowly turning as red as his cheeks. "That's not what this is about."

"Then what?"

Claire wavered, and Hero pressed on ahead. "This ink is the answer, Claire. I know it. You know it. Help me do this."

Claire's breath caught, then snagged on a question. "Why me?"

Hero blinked. "Why? Well, of course you, since you have possession of the ink in question—"

"Do the others know about your idea? Does *Rami*?"

Hero was not quick enough to hide the guilt that wrung across his features.

Claire nodded. "You rotten creature, with your talk of feelings earlier. Yet you have snuck down here precisely when you knew our overprotective guardian angel would be out."

"Hardly! As if I care one whit what that tedious man thinks of me. I simply was trying to avoid what would surely be an exhausting explanation of my logic and having to endure the subsequent dramatic objection and . . ." Hero stopped his huffing, cheeks a little flushed. "You said it yourself: he's overprotective."

"Right. And you look to *me* to play your villain, again."

"You've never been my villain, Claire." Hero risked a look at her. "I've been yours. I don't want to be. I'm—I'm trying to help. *Help me* get us answers."

"Help." Her chair creaked as Claire leaned back with the full weight of her skepticism. "And what do you think he's going to do when he finds out you went behind his back and I *helped* you?"

"Nothing," Hero said as if stating the obvious. "He worships you."

"He . . ." Claire's stomach did a small revolution of wrongness, and she marveled at how it flipped around a small burst of warmth. "No, he doesn't. He's a literal divine being. That's *grotesque*."

"I'm not going to quibble about definitions with you. He admires you, then. With great depth of affection," Hero conceded with a shrug of his shoulders.

Claire closed her eyes and groaned at the rafters. "Hell and harpies, no one is that stupid, even in Hell."

"Absolutely no one at all," Hero agreed, with a small curious smile that grew soft at the edges. "Will you help?"

The whole conversation had her off-kilter. Claire suspected that was Hero's intent, but her resolve was crumbling all the same. "Promise me one thing: this isn't you running away."

Running away from the Library. From Rami. From her.

Hero shook his head. "It's not."

"Lying is not becoming, Hero." Claire studied her hands. "Not that you care what I think."

The floorboards creaked. "Don't I? Lying is not becoming, Claire," Hero repeated lowly. He waited until she raised her eyes, trading her a shy smile before plowing on in a rush. "I want to stay. I haven't had a thought about running away or even returning to my story in ages. I want to stay more than anything. But . . . I need a choice. No one will believe—Rami and you won't; the damsels won't—no one will believe I am here to stay. None of that will ever really matter until I have a choice. I need to *choose* to stay here, warden. And I can't do that with a book that rejects me." Hero held her eyes steadily. "This is the opposite of running away. You have to believe me when I say that."

She did. She hated it most when she understood him as completely as her own reflection. Each of them represented the greatest injustice of their lives to each other. Hero, the books Claire had never gotten to write, the failure that had punished her to Hell, and the betrayal that had left her alone. Likewise, Claire was the librarian who kept books quiet, and one of the human authors every book turned to like sunlight. It wasn't easy, making peace with the wound inside your heart, but she and Hero had managed, in their own halting ways.

Help had been a foreign concept between them once. They'd started out hunter and hunted, librarian and book, but even after she and Hero had come to some kind of accord, what they'd done for each other had never been help. It'd been a simple alignment of priorities, happening to point their shared rage in the same direction, instead of at each other. It'd taken the deaths of hundreds, damsels and books, to cement their places at each other's side. She couldn't be to Hero what Rami was, but that didn't make what they were any less important. What Hero was to her required a harder word than "friendship," a word with teeth. Family. *Hers.*

He couldn't be hers. But there it was: he was hers, and Brevity was hers and Rami was hers and no matter how tightly Claire held on, she felt like she was losing them all. It made a kind of sense, an aching kind of sense, to try loosening her grip. Maybe she owed him that much.

Hero was staring at her. The emerald in his eyes was closer to malachite, dark and intense and gritty with a kind of vulnerability that obviously scared him. "Please, Claire," he said again, softer.

Her resolve broke, and a rush of breath left her. "We can . . . try." She bit her lip, almost snatching the words back before she shook her head resolutely. "Okay. We can try. I don't believe this will work, but I'll help."

Hero took a sharp breath, snagged on the apex of surprise. He went pale with it before color flushed back into his cheeks. Claire was idly amazed at how much she'd learned the tells of Hero's emotions. He nodded. "Okay. Thank you."

"Please don't do that."

"What?"

"Thank me." Claire began to clear her work surface, adjusting the light. "You've already asked for help. And said 'please.' I don't think my poor mortal heart can take it." She risked a glance at him with a surprised smile. "Your adventure with Rami has changed you."

Hero sniffed. "Change? Me? Never. I am constant as the sun."

"And just as insufferable." Claire patted the tabletop. "Get your book out and press back the pages like I showed you. I'll go see if I can coax the ink into a nib. I still hold that this is the worst idea."

She was halfway to the shelves when Hero muttered, barely audibly, "All our best options usually are."

# 24

# BREVITY

There's been a political fracas here in Hell. Suddenly, the Arcanist is a new demon by the name of Andras. He is polite, generous with his time, and professional to a fault. I don't like him.

My apprentice will accuse me of being unkind. He is not wrong—I am too well trained to be a warm person. But that is not the source of my dislike. Gregor hasn't grasped the basic truth of the realms yet. Hell and other realms are filled with a compelling cast of personalities. Demons, muses, jinni, spirits, and ancestral forces. Creatures that can feel, covet, love, hate. The truth is this: they are not human. Humanity isn't defined by feeling, or the facsimile therein. Humanity is defined by fragility. We are a cherry blossom, and they are the frost.

Frost melts, but it is the blossom that dies.

*Librarian Yoon Ji Han 1804, CE*

PROBITY HADN'T HESITATED. ONCE Brevity finally agreed to her experiment, it had been a swift cascade of consequential actions. The only delay had been on agreeing to a time and location.

"Not in the Unwritten Wing," Brevity said firmly.

"But, sis, it's the simplest—"

"No." And Brevity wouldn't budge on this, even for Probity. "We can't do this anywhere near the books." It felt wrong. Even aside from all the logistic concerns, the idea of unlocking inspiration in a muse by using the ink, with all the unwritten books of humanity looking on, made Brevity uncomfortable. It felt disrespectful, like she was sullying the Library. But Probity wouldn't understand that—there was no such thing as the Library, as a thing greater than its parts. The only concern Probity understood was concern for the books and for Brevity. So Brev stuck to logistics. "It's too big a risk if something goes wrong."

"No stories are in danger. Nothing is going to go wrong," Probity insisted with certainty, but she relented. "I doubt you're going to feel comfortable taking it outside of Hell, sis. Is there a room?"

Finding a room in Hell turned out to not be as difficult as one might imagine. Hell was a vast realm, and since souls sent themselves where they needed to be, one might say attendance had dropped over the centuries. Damnation was too constant an idea to ever die out entirely, but it could fall out of fashion.

An empty hall proved the best option, improved by its adjacent location to the transport office. Brevity had fabricated an especially urgent emergency for Walter, emphasizing the absolute need for privacy, and Hell's gatekeeper had been sweetly agreeable about vacating his office for a spell. At least he had after Brevity had taken the time to explain the human concept of a "smoke break," which seemed a redundant concept in Hell.

Brevity hesitated upon returning to her desk for her tools and the tiny vial of unwritten ink she'd hidden at the back of a drawer, shrouded beneath linen thread. The logbook lay open with heavy accusation. Brevity picked up the pen half a dozen times, precisely uncapping it and drifting the nib over a fresh page before putting it away again, untouched. A sense of duty found the seams inside her and tugged. As librarian, she should close the wing as a safety precaution, especially with Hero still gone. As Probity's sister muse and co-conspirator, she should do as little to raise alarm as possible.

In the end, the wing stayed open. The books stayed quiet, the damsels stayed unaware, and Brevity stayed her hand, hovering over the handle of the great lobby doors. She left them half-open, creaking on the hinges of her own doubts. It wouldn't matter. This wouldn't take long.

The architecture of Hell was pasted together with lost things and tragedies, bits of buildings and spaces that have had the worst of existence visited upon them at one point or another. That meant a lot of Hell was an absolute drudge through muddy battlefields and concrete corridors that smelled like chemicals, but evil happened in beautiful places as well. The long room chosen for this experiment was splintered with cathedral windows. Through each piece of colored glass, Brevity could make out the light of a different scene. Sunlit squares fit for a hanging, shaded porticos to decide who was and was not human, cloistered confessionals that turned human love into sin. It made for a pretty kind of twilight in the hall, painting coins of color all over the stone floor. Brevity loved color; she might have enjoyed it under better circumstances.

As it was, she didn't care for the way the multicolored light spilled rainbows like oil slicks off the vial of black ink in her hands. Probity had departed to fetch her muse co-conspirators, and Brevity was left to pace nervously. Electric ghosts of worry crept up her nerves, bunching her shoulders near her ears.

This was the right move. Or, rather, it was the necessary move. Claire had made this necessary, refusing to collaborate on the nature of the ink. It was Brevity's responsibility as librarian to *fix* this. She thought Claire would want to fix it, but Probity had been the only one to suggest a solution. Brev felt a little guilty about blaming Claire, though. She'd been absent since the accident, but that would be expected. Claire would rather die than have anyone see her injured or suffering.

If this worked, they could figure out an equilibrium with the ink and stop the stain on Claire. In a way, Brevity needed to save Claire just as much as she needed to save the books.

Brevity had a lot to make up for.

The carving-crusted doors at the end of the hall creaked, and Probity came in, leading a pair of wide-eyed younger muses in her wake. They had matching heads of scarlet curls, one tanned pink and the other orange. Brevity squinted, trying to place them, but Probity warmly started through introductions. She had her elbow crooked around either muse's arm familiarly. "Gaiety, Verve, you know of Brevity."

"The exiled muse of Brevity," one breathed, while the other held a hand to her mouth. "It's an honor to meet you, ma'am."

"Oh, really? I don't . . ." Doubts, formerly niggling, swarmed up as the two younger muses stared at her with something approaching awe. Brevity struggled not to fidget. "You heard about me?"

"I took them under my wing . . . same way you did for me," Probity said, eyes diverting and voice dropping off at the last part. "I try, at least."

"Probity is the best," the one with orange skin announced. Probity had called her Verve. She bounced on her toes eagerly. "She's told us all about your rebellion. How we can save stories. Is that the ink?"

"It's so beautiful," the pink-skinned boy named Gaiety whispered.

"Oh . . . well, it is . . ." Doubt swamped Brevity out of nowhere.

Probity's eyes sharpened, as if she could sense the waver in Brevity's tone. She extracted herself from her sibling muses and put a hand on Brevity's shoulder. "Gaiety and Verve are here to help us."

"You volunteered, right? To test this ink?" Brevity didn't precisely think of the question before she asked it, but she felt better as the two younger muses nodded with confusion. "And you understand we aren't sure what will happen?"

"Of course they volunteered." Probity's hurt was evident.

"We'll be the first muses to create our own stories." The one named Verve was appropriately ambitious, with a glint in her eyes.

"We aren't certain of that, actually."

"We understand the risks. If we can create the stories ourselves, we won't need to entrust them to humans who burn books," Verve said. "It's worth it."

If Probity had been an enthusiastic activist for this cause, these two were true believers. It was tempting to be swept up in the wake of their certainty. "I'm not sure—"

"Anything is worth it for the sake of the stories," Probity said. "We're not weak human souls to be overwhelmed like the librarian. Muses are connected to the Library by nature. I'm certain we'll be fine."

"I am certain you're certain," Brevity said weakly. But it made sense, and again the thought of the black creeping up Claire's arm strengthened Brevity's resolve. "As long as we have precautions in place."

"Of course. No one wants to protect the stories more than us. We're well away from the books of the Library." Probity tossed an expansive gesture around the silent hall before directing the red-haired muses to the center. "There and there. Are you ready to go? Let's change history."

"Will it hurt?" Gaiety fidgeted as he took his place. Evidently Brevity's unease hadn't gone entirely unheard. "You said this could end humanity's book burnings."

"It will. I've seen the power of this ink," Probity soothed, and touched each of their cheeks with a motherly fondness. Brevity marveled at how neatly she avoided answering the first question—or perhaps not. Either way, the younger muses appeared calmed, then awed as Probity took the vial. Brevity's anxiety crept up again as Probity uncorked it, holding the glass up to the light. "But we'll be cautious anyway. Just a drop to start. One drop, and we'll create the first story born of a muse. We won't need humans. We'll save the future of every story ever written."

*And unwritten,* Brevity wanted to remind her, but Probity was already gesturing. Gaiety and Verve held out their hands. Probity didn't hesitate. She precisely tipped the vial to flick a droplet of ink into each palm.

The ink didn't sink immediately into the skin, like it had with Claire. In fact, it seemed repelled at first. Tiny amounts of the dark liquid beaded, then skittered over their palms like oil on a hot skillet. It raced over their knuckles, black lines starting to coalesce and swirl against their sunny-colored skin.

"Focus," Probity soothed when Gaiety and Verve began to shift nervously.

"It might be working," Brevity said quietly. The ink appeared to be stretching, thinning out into long lines. Perhaps it would take shape and simply mark their skin like the inspiration Brevity had stolen. She clutched one bare forearm at the thought, but the ink showed no sign of settling down. It raced across the back of Verve's hand, and Brevity frowned.

"Did you see . . . ?"

Probity's gaze snapped to her. "See what?"

"Light," Brevity muttered. "We need more light." She grabbed the edge of Verve's tunic and dragged her over closer to one of the windows. The stained glass depicted some long-forgotten saint, looking forlorn and wearing a mostly white robe, which cast the clearest amount of stolen light. "There. It's leaving a trail."

She pointed as the droplet of ink wove its way around the orange skin of Verve's knuckles. The skin it passed felt lightened, pulled to a paler shade of tangerine. The ink moved quicker over the back of her hand, appearing to pull color with it. The ink stayed bleak and black, even in brighter light.

"It's cold," Gaiety said softly. The ink was doing the same to his rose-colored skin. Pastel tracks stood out where the ink had slid over the surface and up his wrist. A glassy tone in his voice made Brevity uneasy.

"I brought a blotter." She began to reach for her bag. "Maybe we should—"

"No." Probity's hand was on her wrist. "I suspected this would happen. It's a good sign, see? The ink isn't sinking in like with Claire. It'll work. It'll work," Probity repeated, quieter. "Just a moment longer."

Brevity hesitated, for just precisely that moment, and a small sigh of air brought her attention back. The ink had sailed its way up Gaiety's forearm, and its pale track disappeared under the hem of his sleeve at his elbow.

Gaiety struggled for breath.

A streak of alarm shot up Brevity's neck. "Are you—"

"Cold," he mumbled between clenched teeth.

"Look," Probity said, with a distant kind of awe.

Brevity followed the line of Probity's attention to the neck of Gaiety's tunic. His skin was naturally darker there, a sweeter rose than pink. But as she watched, it paled before her eyes, fading from almost red to pink to a pastel kind of coral, until it started to turn white.

"Shirt off!" Brevity batted at the muse's shirt, alarm rising. When she managed to pull the shirt over his head, the dot of black ink had not grown but was racing in increasingly more frantic patterns over his chest. "What's it doing?"

"Absorbing," Probity breathed, sounding almost faint with disbelief. She lifted a hand, hovering over the small liquid bead as it swept and swooped over Gaiety's fading collarbone. "It's absorbing bits of him."

"We need to stop this!" Brevity turned and ran for the bag she'd left in the corner. She came up with the pad of blotter sheets, but Probity was already stripping Verve to see the same thing there.

"They aren't absorbing the ink, like the humans; the ink is absorbing them." Probity's voice was full of awe. "But absorbing what parts? I wonder. Where does it end? What does it take and what does it leave behind?"

"Probably not healthy parts," Brevity said. She ran back over and attempted to smack the blotter down on the ink, but the droplet beaded and darted away every time she got near. Gaiety was nearly white by now, and Verve had turned a sickly shade of yellow. "We've got to stop this now."

The ink fluted up Gaiety's neck, creeping like a gnat beneath his skin. Brevity brought the blotter sheet up again but hesitated. Gaiety opened his mouth and a strangled creak slipped out. Past his lips, his teeth were white. And so was his tongue, and the long white nothingness of his throat. Brevity couldn't stand to see any more; she pressed the blotter page against his face as the ink darted out of his mouth and toward his hairline.

The sheet fluttered as Gaiety sucked in rapid breaths, and Brevity held it there, uncertain how long was needed to capture the ink. His hair was draining of its normal pigmentation, fading swiftly from scarlet to something weak, like blood-tainted water. Abruptly, the breath rustling beneath the sheet stuttered, then stopped. Brevity exchanged a worried glance with Probity, who looked uneasy despite her earlier confidence.

She pulled the blotter sheet back, ready to slap it down again if the ink moved.

No ink moved. Instead, Probity let out a short scream.

Gaiety's formerly rosy complexion was entirely an off shade of ivory. And the skin was an unblemished expanse. It was as if the blotter sheet had taken the features of his face as well. There was naught but smooth skin where the valleys of his eyes had been, and his mouth was no more than a divot in the pale clay of his skin.

Probity leapt back, horror taking over her face. When her eyes met Brevity's, they were wet, and she shook her head rapidly. "I didn't—this isn't possible. I didn't mean—"

Brevity stepped back as Gaiety lunged forward, pale hands already swimming into translucent claws. It was as if all of the muse was being absorbed by the ink, turning to paper and ice.

"We need to fix this! There's got to be a fix." Probity sounded pleading now. She held up her hands, and the abundance of lace at her wrists gave away her tremors.

Brevity shook her head. "I think we can call this experiment a f—"

They had forgotten about Verve. A white shadow streaked past her head, launching itself at Probity. They went down in a tumble, but the ink-blotted muse was fast, and rabid with movement. She smashed Probity's face into the floorboards and leapt toward the end of the hall before Brevity could even act.

Gaiety made a creaking, breathless kind of sound, as if protesting his sibling leaving him behind. Brevity was already running. "Stay with Gaiety and keep him calm. I'll go after her!"

"Sis!" Probity called, but Brevity didn't look back. She had to keep her eyes peeled on the retreating ghost, a flutter of pale skin in the gloom of the hallway.

It canted through the door of Walter's office, and Brevity groaned as she heard the clatter of shattered glass. She burst through the archway just in time to see billowing red and purple smoke—which travel jar had been shattered was difficult to tell, but she would have so much apologizing to do when Walter got back—and, just beyond, the retreating shape of Verve disappearing through the main door. Brevity skirted the smoke, saying a silent apology to Walter, and ran after her. They were in familiar hallways now, and Brevity gained on the maddened muse, but as they vaulted the stairs up a level, Brevity's heart stopped.

She knew this path, and knew exactly where the feral muse was going.

The Library.

Brevity struggled to catch up, but the muse was fleet on pale white feet. It shrieked a hunger-pang sound that made Brevity's teeth hurt and hurtled itself down the hallway. It made it past the gargoyle, who just blinked sleepiness in several dimensions. Some guard dog he was, but then again Brevity supposed there was no reason to ever bar muses from an open library. Verve scrabbled at the doors, leaving deep scratches in the wood as she rushed into the lobby.

"Verve, stop!" Desperation gave Brevity a burst of speed. She hurtled past the entry and flung herself at Verve with just enough momentum to snag her by the ankle. The washed-out muse went down, hissing and snarling. Brevity clamped down and tried to drag her back, but

Verve's claws shredded at the rug as she went. She couldn't allow her to reach the books; above all else, Brevity knew with entire certainty that she could not allow anything with that kind of hunger to reach the books.

Brevity dragged Verve back at the cost of the rug. The younger muse was almost completely white now. Washed out and almost translucent in the weird light of her eyes. The only color remaining was the faintest wash of pink still clinging to the tips of her long hair. Unlike Gaiety, she'd retained her facial features, but the bead of black ink swirled hazily from eye to eye, occasionally making a detour down to slash black across her lips. It was the only sign of life in the face that had been so hopeful and eager to help moments ago.

Brevity's heart clenched but she didn't let go. "Verve, you gotta snap out of it."

She didn't appear to hear. Verve lunged across the carpet again, hands straining toward the shelves of books as if she were a dying man reaching for a mirage. She croaked again, hungry and keening. It was all Brevity could do to sit on her back until Probity arrived.

Probity had managed to procure a strap from somewhere and had belted Gaiety's thin arms to his sides. The faceless muse twisted and writhed, as if suffocating in his own skin. It hurt to watch. Brevity looked away to twist around and begin to roll the shredded rug around Verve's sides. "What *happened* to them?"

Probity's face was tear streaked, and she looked stricken. "It's—it's like the ink took them, all of them. Sucked them dry. Why would it— It shouldn't have been able to do that."

"Seems like that shit is doing lots of stuff it isn't supposed to be able to do lately." Brevity thought again of Claire and blanched at the thought of Claire without a face and leached of color. It almost seemed a blessing now that the ink had stained, giving rather than taking.

"This . . . we can fix this, though. Right?" Probity looked at her as if she had answers instead of an armful of rabid muse.

Verve bucked again beneath her, spitting her anger and forcing Brevity to pin her shoulders down. "It's like they turned feral."

"Not feral . . ." An idea brightened Probity's reddened eyes. "Not feral, hungry. The ink drained them, and now they're struggling to fill themselves back up. They're hungry for what we're all hungry for."

"Human stories," Brevity supplied. She looked toward the stacks worriedly. Liquid tendrils of color still washed out from the books, but they seemed to recoil from where Verve writhed on the floor, staying out of reach. The books knew danger as well as Brevity did. "But we don't *eat* stories! Muses transport stories and inspiration to humans all the time. Look, she's already gnawing on the rug."

"Maybe it's not about what a muse wants, but what the ink wants," Probity mulled it over. "If they can get enough to satisfy what they've lost, then perhaps they can get control over the ink."

"No part of this is *in control*! Probity, please, listen to me." Brevity's hold on Verve was slipping. Probity came over without being asked, expertly twisting the other end of her strap around Verve's neck until it appeared she had two feral ghosts on a leash. Brevity backed up onto her knees, aware of every muscle in her arms screaming. "Listen. The experiment failed; this was a terrible idea from the start. Muses aren't *made* to control stories. That was my mistake when I tried to take inspiration for myself too." Her hand went self-consciously to her bare forearm again. It still felt naked and raw. "We can appreciate stories, protect them, help them get written, honor them even. But we're not human. Muses are conduits. If we try to hold on to them, we'll just hurt ourselves."

Trying to steal the inspiration gilt and bind it into her skin had hurt, but being driven out of the Muses Corps had hurt worse. She almost felt an empathy for the husks of Verve and Gaiety. She'd had everything ripped away once, and felt that emptiness, the overwhelming ache to fill it with something, anything.

She'd been sent here, to Claire, and the Library. Learned how vulnerable and fragile stories are. It wasn't enough to have inspiration. It took a special kind of alchemy to bring a story into existence, and that was so easy to destroy. Brevity shook her head. "We have to get them out of here before they hurt a book."

"Yes," Probity said slowly, but she made no move to drag her captives away. "But . . . what if we gave them one?"

Brevity pivoted, mouth agape. "What?"

"What if we gave them a book? Just one." Probity was warming to the idea, scanning the shelves thoughtfully. "There are so many. We could pick one that was never going to be written anyway."

"No!" Brevity felt like she was trembling. "Of course we can't! These are books!"

"But what if this is it?" Probity began to pace, tugging Verve and Gaiety at the ends of their leather straps. Verve still randomly lunged toward the stacks, and it appeared Probity was edging closer. "What if this is what allows them to gain control of the ink? What if they can eat a book and then write it themselves? We can take the stories from the humans before they can destroy them. We can fix this. We'll be saving them."

"Saving them by destroying them." Brevity stepped back. Probity looked taller, rail thin and pale in her own way, as if the ink was taking hold by proximity. "No, we can't do that." She shook her head. "We aren't stealing stories, let alone trading them for our own."

"You don't understand. It's *stories*. It's everything. How can you not understand how important this is?" Probity abruptly veered away from the lobby and across the small expanse of space to the stacks. "Look, let me just prove—"

Verve and Gaiety were a froth of claws at the end of their leashes. Brevity didn't stop to think; she leapt to her feet and threw herself in between the feral muses and the shelves of books. "No."

For a moment it felt like Probity wasn't going to stop. Verve lunged, making a guttural snarl at the end of the leash. Her pale lips were peeled back, and all the color had been seeped away from her gums, making her teeth look elongated and bone sharp. She threw up her hands, now tipped in claws, and slashed at Brevity's arms. Pain laced up her elbow. Brevity closed her eyes and resolved not to flinch.

Verve's breath was hot and smelled of boiled rubber. When Brevity opened her eyes, the muses' claws were an inch withdrawn from her nose, though Verve strained enough to make the leather creak.

At the other end of the strap, Probity had rooted her feet in place and was leaning back to counteract the tension of the two creatures. Her lips were pressed thin, and when she met Brevity's eyes they were full of a complicated kind of pain. "I want to save them, sis. I want to save *you*. You shouldn't be stuck here. You could be the librarian that *fixes* things."

"A fix that sacrifices someone is no fix at all." Brevity held still. She was aware that Probity could release the straps, allow Verve and Gaiety to hurtle into the stacks. She might be able to wrestle one, but she couldn't keep both of them from the books. She needed Probity to see it. "The humans have destroyed enough books for their own ambition, right? I thought you told me we could be so much better than that."

Probity flinched, and her voice began to shake. "Don't compare me to them. Don't compare what I'm trying to do to the millions of books tossed aside, burned, left to rot in the—" A small gasp stopped her, and Verve's claws swayed close to Brevity's cheek until Probity caught control of the leash again. "That's the answer."

A foreboding rose in Brevity's stomach. "Probity?"

"That's it! There's a giant supply of books that no one will miss, because they've already been forgotten! We protect your treasured unwritten charges and we change the system. And we have humans to thank."

Probity yanked on the strap with surprising strength and began dragging the ink-maddened muses away from the stacks. Brevity only got a moment's relief as Probity began to make her way across the lobby to the door. "Probity—where are you going with them? You need to take them back home; perhaps the other muses can fix—"

"I will fix it." Probity tossed a small smile over her shoulder that was meant to be reassuring. It failed, in part due to the desperate redness of her eyes. "I'll fix everything, sis. Don't worry. I won't make you regret the faith you've shown in me. There's plenty of books for them in the Dust Wing."

"The Dust Wing," she whispered, and the dread grew. The Dust Wing wasn't just a tomb for books; it was a tomb for stories. The Dust Wing had no librarian, because these books were not destined to be curated, cared for, or read. A book only fell to the Dust Wing after an existence on Earth, after the very last copy of its story had been destroyed, the last lines from its text forgotten. Humanity had buried almost as many books as it had never written. The Unwritten Wing was the largest annex of the Library, but a close second, its shadow twin, was the Dust Wing.

Brevity's heart stuttered, but Probity was waving a hand, grasping clots of light from the lamps she passed by as a nonsense scent of cardamom binaries and ripe hope rose in the air. She whipped it around her and the leashed muses like a cloak, once, twice. She glanced to

Brevity, and a kind of vulnerability flickered in her eyes. "Will you come with me?"

Brevity sucked in a breath, unnerved by the sudden silence only punctuated by her own pulse in her ears. She was trembling, unable to process the horror chasing relief in her veins. The Dust Wing. Probity's desperation to hope. The horror of the desiccated muses behind her. The threat to the books. Her past and her present collided in front of her, spiraling out into a dozen different directions and taking a different piece of Brevity's heart with them. It all came down to one question, in the end. Was she a muse, or was she a librarian?

"Please," Probity whispered to the floor. "I don't want to do this alone."

Brevity stumbled forward, pulling on her own puddle of light with one hand while taking Probity's with the other. Her sister muse smiled, shy and soft. Probity stepped into a false sunbeam, dragging Gaiety and Verve with her, and they were gone.

## 25

# CLAIRE

The Library is a misnomer. Think of the wings: yes, there is the Unwritten Wing of books, but then there's a wing of sagas, unsaid words, poems, songs—and the cursed Arcane Wing on top of that! It makes no sense. What is the mission of a library? We're not a lending library, so it must be a mission of archiving and preservation. What, then, is the common quality shared through out the entire catalog? What makes books, scrolls, letters, songs, worth the attentions of eternity?

What, precisely, are we preserving?

*Librarian Ibukun of Ise, 900 CE*

THE ARCANE WING CURATED books. Not nearly as many or as varied as the Unwritten Wing, but a few leather-bound manuscripts from the world of humans managed to find their way there. Letters poisoned with crude curses, folios with victims pressed between the pages, and a handful of bleak spell books that had somehow stumbled on actual power between the folklore and nonsense. If the Unwritten Wing was humanity's potential, the Arcane Wing was humanity's shadow. Anything that grew dark enough, weighty enough, eventually succumbed to the gravity that the Arcane Wing held at its core.

It made for dreadfully dull reading material, but it also meant the Arcanist was kept supplied with a steady selection of bookbinding materials. Claire selected a dip nib and blotter but also gathered extra pages, paste, and thread out of an abundance of caution. The ink hadn't damaged the logbook during their first experiment, but she wasn't willing to take any further chances with Hero's book.

Hero was ready by the time she returned, arms full of supplies. He'd laid his book precisely under Claire's work light, and an oiled shine rolled off the edges of the emerald cover. Claire had a memory of rebinding with that color. She'd simply chosen green to match his irritatingly bright eyes. And then Malphas had interrupted. That book had been her last official act as librarian.

And now she was going to tamper with it again.

The cover had taken on a well-loved burnish, worn at the edges where it rode around in Hero's breast pocket daily. There were discolored segments in the leading edges of the parchment, just the width of a thumb, where Hero had obviously paged through his own book more than once. Claire could imagine him, brows furrowed, trying to make sense of the writhing text. Trying to force it into familiarity. Trying to read his way home.

Claire knew that ache.

Hero hovered to her right, shifting from one foot to the other with an uncharacteristic restlessness. Lining up the supplies within reach was a simple task, but Claire made it a methodical process in order to take her time. "You're certain?"

Hero grimaced, then nodded. "Yes, and please don't ask me again."

"As you wish," Claire said. She found the first blank page and slipped the corners under the page rests. A small pot of the unwritten ink was secured in the inkwell, and she unstoppered it carefully. Her gloved hand trembled as she set down the cork, and Claire forced herself to pause and close her eyes until she felt steady.

"I trust you, warden. You should know that." Hero's voice was quiet; when she opened her eyes he had finally come to lean on the edge of the worktable. His longer fingers were splayed on the surface, a breath from hers. He looked at her reverently until she met his eyes, then nodded. He turned his face resolutely away from the book as if bracing himself. "Whenever you're ready."

Claire polished the nib of her pen. It shivered under the light, sharp as a blade. When the point touched the surface of the ink, the channel flooded with unnatural ease. The pen drank up ink and when Claire pulled it away from the well, a bleak teardrop clung to the tip like blood on a fang.

*No lasting harm to the logbook.* Claire kept repeating that in her head, which was the only reason she was able to shake off the loose ink and dread. The palm of her right hand itched, as if the stain could sense the nearness, anticipate what she was about to do with it. Claire took a deep breath and lowered the tip of the pen to the blank expanse of parchment.

Writing was a chemical dance between the ink and the surface. Cheap paper would suck the life out of an ink, leaving a flat, feathered line. The materials used in the Library were both infernal and divine, in that the paper was a smooth and faultless cream that embraced ink gently, letting it dry and sheen to perfect brilliance. Which was what made ice shiver up Claire's spine when the ink slid across the page as if a plug had been pulled. Claire lifted the nib, trying to break the flow, but black lines writhed across the paper. Corkscrew shapes twisted, then lifted *away* from the sheet, creating tiny black ribbons in the air.

A gasp broke the silence, but Claire couldn't spare a glance for Hero. She acted fast. Three decades in the Unwritten Wing taught one to take unruly words in hand before they spiraled out of control. She snagged one escaping serif with her nib, pinning it back to the page. She abused the tines of her pen, pressing until they began to separate, but it forked the ink in two. That weakened it, allowing her to carefully, so carefully, drag the squirming text back to the top of the page.

It was a chapter page. Claire knew the general shape of it from the rest of Hero's book. A chapter heading. The ink didn't fight her as she draped it into position, trying to coax it into taking shape. A thrill thumped once in her chest as the ink snagged on the page and began to form the graceful arch of a drop cap. A *T*. It squared off, then crested into another symbol, *h*.

"*There was* . . ." Hero's voice creaked, as if he was afraid to say it. Claire looked up. He had his hands braced on either side of where he leaned on the table, concentration lining his face. "*There was* . . ." he said more certainly, and as he said it, Claire saw the ink snag and shape the words on the page. Hero bolted upright, hands in the air. "There was! That's how it starts! Claire, I *know how my story starts!*"

The unrefined joy was like sunshine in Hero's voice, no snarl, no sharp, cutting end of his humor. Just triumph. His smile was effervescent. He let out a whoop and spun around in place. "It's working!"

A tangled kind of relief spooled out with Claire's breath. "You mean, *I* am working," she said, instead of the lingering worry she had. She couldn't constrain her matching smile, however. "Now, focus, Hero. One sentence does not a book make."

She brought her attention back to the page with a surge of confidence. She dragged the ink precisely over the words, and Hero was a kinetic celebration out of the corner of her eye, unable to contain his delight.

"*There was a* . . . Oh, do keep going, warden. We're getting there! I knew it would work!"

He sounded giddy as a child. Claire bit down on her grin as she refreshed her nib in the inkwell and brought it back to the page. The *a* went down easily, and the ink even appeared to settle into the page, calming into a dry sheen that didn't twitch and jerk out of alignment. A *w* appeared, then an *h*.

"*There was a man who* . . ." Hero's voice faltered. "Who. Who are you?"

The flurry of activity out of the corner of her eye had stilled. Claire looked up. Hero stood by the table, one hand still raised in mid-celebration. A startled look of alarm was on his face, but it slowly drained as she watched, and all color was lost from his cheeks.

A breath caught in Claire's throat. "Hero?"

Emotion melted off Hero's face, smoothing even the small lines around his scarred cheek. His eyes were blank when they met hers. "Who are you? Who? No." A tear blinked down his empty expression, watery and faintly smoke-colored. "Who?"

Ink was flowing in the corner of her sight. Her knuckles went white around her pen as Claire looked down. The ink had continued writing, line after line of neat manuscript text appearing, growing more jagged and irregular as it went. Claire clutched the pen to her chest, nowhere near the paper, but still the words kept repeating over and over: *There was a man who who are you who are you who are you who who who who who.*

It occupied every line on the page, and then the serifs of each letter turned jagged, as if spawning their own contributions, written at an angle. All repeating the same word, *who who who.* Ink began to sop the page, puddling in the work light.

Hero made a gagging sound. Black sputtered across his lips, as if he was spitting up blood. But it was so much worse than blood. The liquid was black and staining, spiderwebbing down his chin and across his skin.

Her heart roiled into her throat. Claire threw the pen away from her and grabbed the blotter, already loaded with a sheet. She slammed it down on the surface of Hero's book, but when she lifted it, the blotter was dry, and black crept across the page like mold. It began to soak into subsequent pages.

"Who, who, who . . ." Hero's voice was a gurgle between gasps for breath. Black consumed his neck, turning his clothes sodden with ink. His hands grasped at Claire's shoulders until the infection reached his elbows and he yanked back. Hero shrank to his knees, holding a hand up to his face. One emerald eye melted to pine, then tar. The remaining eye teared up, and his gaze flicked to Claire for one flickering moment. *"A choice, ward—"*

Ink swarmed his eyes and his face went slack. Desperation clawed a whimper out of Claire's throat. Careless of the ink, she ripped out the sodden page with her gloved hand. But it had spread to the next page, and the next. Parchment began to disintegrate, melting together with the ink.

And when Claire looked up, the same horror had begun on Hero's face. His high cheekbone, the right one, unblemished by scars, crumpled first, followed by his nose and the socket of one black, unseeing eye. His body caved in on itself. A wordless gulf filled Claire's chest and somewhere, distantly, a raven was shrieking. Hero's book, pages, binding, and all, melted into a bleak slurry. Claire clutched it on instinct, but it dripped through her hands with a sharp, cold heat. Used up, it didn't even appear interested in staining her this time. When she looked up, she was alone.

Alone, except for a blot of ink, wet upon the carpet.

# 26

# RAMI

Forgetting is its own kind of awful magic. The longer we are down here, the more things melt away. It's unnerving, but I try to remember that entropy doesn't apply in places like this. Nothing is really destroyed; nothing is lost for good. It cheers me to think maybe our memories go where forgotten books go. Silent readers to keep the silent books of the Dust Wing company.

It's a nice story, at least. No one is forgotten, and no one is alone.

*Librarian Gregor Henry, 1917 CE*

RAMI WAS A MAN used to routine and duty. Two things that had been sadly lacking since they'd returned from the Chinvat bridge. Hero had left him the duty of the Unwritten Wing, but Rami felt ill at home there. Yet, when he'd left, Hero seemed troubled by a private errand. It only felt supportive to make an excuse to stay out of his way. He suspected Hero was seeking out Claire. He understood there was a deeper tie between book and former librarian than he, or anyone, understood. He was glad of it.

But the problem with being an angel—albeit a discredited one—in

Hell is that there were few places he actually wanted to be. He was restless. Despite his promise to man the desk, he stepped out and returned a couple of times to the Unwritten Wing, thinking to see if Brevity had returned, update her on their progress. But the Library was quiet when he got there, all as he had left it. Rami had waited as long as seemed polite in the lobby, but when the damsels had started poking their heads from the stacks with curiosity, he'd left.

He'd stopped by Walter's office and had an uneasy conversation with the gatekeeper about human smoking habits, of all things. It disquieted Rami, knowing what Walter was. He was quite used to dealing with immortal forces and personifications of powers beyond his kin, but usually they were not so affable and obsessed with felines.

So, eventually, he'd run out of excuses and had to return to the Arcane Wing, hoping Hero had finished his business by now. The Arcane Wing had an essential quiet to its nature. Claire tried to soften the hard edges of nothingness with the soft patter of pages and the busy-making sounds of tea preparation, but Rami recognized that, at its core, the Arcane Wing was a place of silence. He knew silence, respected it in all its natural variations.

Perhaps that's why the moment he crossed the threshold into the wing, he could tell this silence was all wrong. No one was visible up front, among the worktables and paper-stacked desks that Claire maintained.

Claire's stray raven was picking through some toppled teacups and paused long enough to cock her head at Rami's entrance. She grackled, low and warning, and took two hops to the end of the table before taking flight. She paused, perching just on the end of one of the shelves, as if making sure Rami was taking note of her path before taking off again.

The silence, between muted beats of feathered wings, was alarming. Rami took another quick look around before jogging down the shelves after the bird.

He found the raven after a few moments, paused between two tall racks of amulets. He heard the muttering before he saw Claire, pacing back and forth with a rather alarming bramble of talismans and arcane specimens in her hands.

"Claire?" Rami tried, carefully.

She looked up, and her cheeks glistened. Tears tracked down her face, fresh and raw, even though her expression was gaunt and empty. She distantly seemed to acknowledge Rami's presence and shoved a handful of her selections into his arms. "You're here. Good. Take this and fetch the Persephone seeds."

"Claire," Rami repeated, worrying at the way she paced and seemed to stare past the shelves. The raven came to land heavily on her shoulder and bleated in her ear. An action that would have normally caused an aggrieved snarl and shake-off. Instead, Claire's shoulder just sank under the weight and a small suffering knit between her eyes.

"Claire," Rami said again. "What's all this for?"

"An expedition. A mission, a—a rescue mission. A retrieval." Claire's voice was cracked and abused, possibly from crying. She waved her hand with a frown twisting up her face, breath coming a little fast. "Don't ask questions. You're my assistant; you'll assist. I don't keep you around for questions."

"You keep me around because I choose to stay," Rami corrected gently. A complicated expression stung across Claire's face, full of hurt. She turned away abruptly.

"No more questions. We are going to search the realms one by one. We can start with wherever you and Hero went to last."

"Chinvat?" Rami recoiled at that. The bridge was a place he never cared to visit again, especially not with anyone he cared about. He tried not to get distracted. But a certainty fell like a stone in Rami's chest, settling in with old intuition. "Where's Hero?"

"Gone," Claire said, never quite meeting his eyes. She pulled another rather blood-crusted set of pearls from the shelf and flung them over her shoulder like a bolero.

Every jolt of movement, so alien on calm and measured Claire, wedged deeper dread into Rami's stomach. He had to ask anyway. "Where? Gone *where*, Claire?"

Claire's knuckles whitened on the string of pearls until Rami feared she would break them. She held still, hunched under the wings of the raven on her shoulder. She slid to the floor, staring intently at nothing through wet eyes. She took a breath that sounded like it hurt and quietly said, "I don't know."

Rami's pulse quickened. "What happened?"

Claire was already shaking her head. "It's not—I didn't. I *didn't!*" The last came out ragged, on the tail of a hiccupping sound that Rami guessed was Claire's attempt not to cry again.

Rami fought the urge to push her. He knew Claire's past, the secret she'd kept from everybody. That she'd attempted to leave the Library with one of her characters, and her mentor had died at her hands in the botched attempt. His fear rose at what that meant for Hero and he felt the ground slipping beneath his feet. He took two slow breaths. He'd had experience with trauma, too much experience, really, both personal and professional during his tenure at Heaven's Gates. Panic could be felt without being acted on.

"Please, so I can help you," he said quietly. She tried to stand. The raven launched herself off Claire's shoulder, and Rami replaced the bird with his hand to steady her before she stumbled.

Claire's throat worked before she could speak. Finally, her forehead came down on his shoulder, light and then heavy all at once. He caught her as she crumpled against him. "He wanted to be fixed. He was so certain I . . . I was stupid and weak."

The words came out in a halting tumble, snared between sharp gulps of whatever misery existed between not-tears. When the extent of the loss had been relived, she managed to pull back and rub her face harshly. "I ran to the Unwritten Wing, of course. Hero is stamped; he's special—he's in Special Collections. That means Brevity could IWL him if—" *If he still exists,* Rami's mind supplied. Claire's words firmly dodged that. "But Brevity's not there—no one is—and if I'm not the librarian anymore I can't recall an IWL and I can't face the damsels, so—"

Rami felt gutted as he slowly rubbed her back through another racking shudder of not-panic. Claire was not-crying, not-panicking, not-self-loathing. She was full of nots, which Rami had always known. He admired humans who went on in spite of the nots. She took a deep breath. "So we'll search the realms one by one. Start with the Libraries, fan out from there. Someone would have to notice if a character . . . or a damaged book . . . appeared without warning."

"You're certain he would have been sent to another realm," Rami repeated, gently but with a point. He wondered if she noticed when his voice wavered.

"Yes," Claire said immediately, then: "No." She looked down at her blood-splashed pearls as if the answer would be there. "I don't know. But he has to be somewhere."

"But if you leave without permission again, defy Hell once more—"

"The Hellhounds will have to keep up if they want me. Besides, I'll be about the Library's business, retrieving books."

"You are Arcanist, not librarian. What's more, you're injured," Rami said gently, and Claire turned a flinch into a frown.

"I don't care if I'm Hell's goddamned janitor." She narrowed her reddened eyes, which showed too much white and wildness. "I'm going to find him, Rami."

Rami remembered Hero's face on the bridge, pale and defiant. Certainty as sharp as the razor edge of bridge beneath him, and the memory cut. Hero didn't *have* to be somewhere, but Claire couldn't operate on that possibility. Rami realized with a searing ache that he couldn't either. He nodded and released Claire to juggle the baubles in his hands. "What do you want me to do with these?"

Claire already looked distracted with her own thoughts again. She was staring down the aisle. "Take them back to the front table and pack them in the satchel I've laid out. Take whatever else you need."

She strode down the aisle deeper into the collection without looking back. The Arcane Wing wasn't for looting—Rami knew he should remind Claire. The items in the Arcane Wing were locked away within the control of the Library for a reason. She'd used the Arcane Wing as an arsenal once before, but that was when the threat was in Hell. This would mean taking the artifacts out of the realm, and potentially out of their control.

But if it would save Hero, he'd loot it empty.

He looked down at the items in his hands. A tangle of tarnished chains held together a bramble patch of brooches. There was a dented crown, a scroll sealed with a fang, and at least eighteen ways to inflict death and mayhem between his palms. Rami didn't like this, but he disliked imagining Hero's fate even more. He took a steadying breath and carried the items back to the worktables.

Claire's pet raven was waiting for him, hunched like a vulture over a leather satchel. Rami made a shooing motion as he approached, but the bird continued to worry at the leather strap.

"Off with you." Rami set down his load and tried to gently scoop the bird into the air as he'd seen Claire do a number of times. She took a stab of his palm for his trouble, which distracted Rami long enough that by the time he finished cursing, the bird had hopped to the other end of the table with the dented crown in her beak.

Time felt as if it were running askew. Rami pressed down his fear and quickly packed the other items into the satchel. "I'm going to need that."

The bird honked a particularly vulgar response and fouled the chair beneath her.

"Don't care much for you either," Rami muttered. He made a move to grab the crown, but the bird hopped to the next table over. Rami sighed, resisting the urge to skewer the bird on the end of his sword, and studied her instead.

The bird was a sullen mess of feathers and terrible attitude, as usual. Her beak clicked as she worked over the thin metalwork of the crown in her jaw. Rami didn't precisely recognize the piece, but the collection of the Arcane Wing was huge. The crown was a swooping circlet of gold, with a shape that resembled branches, or elk horns. Each crook of metal was crusted with emerald and rose agate, which reminded Rami of Hero's copper hair.

Rami's mind betrayed him with the image of Hero in a crown, crooked with that ironic smile that saw all of Rami's flaws. Hero lived to prod at regrets, which Rami supposed was what drew him to Claire and Rami over Brevity. Early on, Rami couldn't understand why Claire tolerated him. His first impression of the character had been a boy playing at being a man. His second and third impressions hadn't fared much better, but Claire had trusted him, so when Hero came to Rami with an audacious request for help, Rami had imagined shepherding the boy out of trouble.

Rami had been quite wrong. It'd been Hero who knew the questions to ask in the library at Elysium, and Hero who'd kept his cool as the Chinvat bridge judged their souls and found them wanting. It was a ridiculous judgment. If the judges of Chinvat had half a level of discernment, they would have tossed Rami off the bridge for all the wrongs his soul carried, instead of focusing on Hero.

The raven squawked again. She flicked her head and improbably tossed the crown across the room. It landed somewhere near the door with a crash that made Rami wince. He shook his head as he went to fetch it. They didn't have time for this. They never had time, but Hero was lost somewhere in the afterlife and every realm seemed to have a murderous obsession with punishing—

"Souls." Rami's fingertips froze above the crown. The realization staggered him like a punch to the gut. He jerked straight and stared at the raven. The bird was watching him expectantly. "Lost souls."

The raven clicked once, the most approving sound Rami had heard her make. Ramiel, the angel, had been granted certain gifts, gifts he retained even after being exiled from Heaven, retained even here in Hell. Rami was a shepherd of souls. His mind was still reeling when Claire emerged from the back of the archives, carrying a cloak and a particular gray dagger. She looked drawn and resigned as death, but she paused and tilted her head when she caught sight of Rami. "What now?"

"Arcanist . . ." Rami carefully measured each word, uncertain when the idea forming in his head would give out beneath him. It was too fragile to say out loud yet. "What would you say if I thought I could track where Hero's gone?"

Claire's fingers jumped along the dagger. Rami prepared for the questions, for the inquisition of Claire's logical mind that would poke holes in what was surely a false hope, but none came. Instead, Claire considered the crown at his feet before raising her gaze with a hungry kind of certainty. "I'd say, when do we leave?"

# 27

# HERO

There is no library of secrets. Secrets cannot be kept or curated. Secrets have no need for a library, but each library
needs secrets. Books are a secret hidden in plain sight. *Read
me, they say. Look at me. Turn my pages. Touch my spine. Read
my words, and content yourself.*

Every book is a secret that only readers know.

*Librarian Ibukun of Ise, 904 CE*

HIS TONGUE TASTED LIKE wicked death itself.

Hero's first awareness was that he was gagging. He coughed, and
his lips felt slippery. His body recoiled with the force of his next cough,
and he smacked his cheek into the gritty, solid surface beneath him.
Everything was black. Everything was black and melting and he
couldn't breathe, couldn't hear for the screaming in his head. He couldn't
see. It took him several long moments to consider opening his eyes. It
took him several long moments to remember he *had* eyes.

When he opened them, it wasn't much of an improvement.

It was dark, dark enough that it took a minute until Hero's eyes
began to adjust and pick out the vagaries of his surroundings. Long
panels of flat ground stretched out in front of where he lay prone. His

arm protested as he reached out, but the surface felt smooth beneath his fingertips, with a dry grain. Wood, perhaps. It had to mean he was at least somewhere civilized. He rolled to his knees, feeling a slick, oily ache both inside and out.

Civilized, Hero amended, but abandoned. The light was practically nonexistent, but a diffuse glow came off the dust that sifted through the stale air. It painted the space in twilight that was one step above midnight. The light-tainted dust was everywhere, drifting around Hero in spectral blooms. It cast weirdly soft shadows on the dark crags and unidentified shapes that surrounded him. Hero might have thought he was trapped in some deep, stalagmite-strewn cave, if it weren't for the paneled floor beneath him that reminded him of the Library.

The Library.

Hero's hand went to his coat. He ferreted over the pockets with rising panic until he located a familiar rectangular lump in an inside pocket. He had his book, safe and sound. But a barb of memory trailed the relief. The pen nib hovering over a blank page, a clot of black on his lips and a rotting feeling behind his eyes, hundreds of voices almost but not quite drowning out Claire's scream.

The ink. Remembering felt like falling. He could recall it now, the drowning sensation as his throat filled with ink, the eerie warmth as it swept over his skin like a whisper, the whispers, like an ocean surf, washing over him until the question rotted through him inside out.

*Who are you? Who are you?*

Bile scaled his throat, centering him enough to slow his breathing. The ink hadn't accepted him at all; it had rejected him and done *something* to him and his book. Sent him somewhere, wherever here was.

He got unsteadily to his feet and breathed in another luminous cloud that made him cough. The soles of his boots scraped invisible grit against the floor, and it echoed across the space like a growl that was quickly snuffed out. Silence, silence so complete that Hero's own breath was a bleat in his head.

Unease curdled in his stomach, but Hero shoved it aside with the rest of his aches. His book was part of the Unwritten Wing's Special Collections. He would find his way out, or at the absolute worst, he would be recalled when Claire reported he was missing.

The scream echoed in his head again and Hero winced. He could only guess what the others might think, what Claire and Rami might think. That he'd planned it, that he'd run away. Claire's disapproval would be *insufferable*, but he could make it right. He could make it all right as soon as he made his way back to the Library.

The resolve forced his foot across the floor, feeling for a path. It caught on what might have been a rock, and Hero stumbled directly into the crag to his left with an audible groan. Even braced for impact, it was not the hard collision with rock that Hero had been expecting. Hero righted himself and tentatively ran his fingertips over the surface.

A thick layer of the barely glowing dust was on everything, but beneath it his fingers found a pliant leather. He followed a seam until his fingertips hit a ruffle of pressed fibers, leaves that fluttered under his fingertips. It was a feeling he'd had opportunity to familiarize himself with lately, and such a shock that he gasped in a breath. His lungs filled with dust and sent him coughing to his knees again, dragging part of the pile down with him.

It stirred up enough dust to illuminate his lap when he'd recovered. Enough to see what was in front of him.

Books—piles, acres, caverns, *a mass grave* of books. Piles, jumbled as if they'd dropped from the ceiling, waved and crested around him with no rhyme or reason. Books splayed on their spines, pages bent, covers torn; others appeared completely untouched. All sharp edges made soft by the colony of dust muffling everything.

Abandoned books had a scent. It clung to Hero's tongue and gilded his lungs with dust and regret. It wasn't precisely an unpleasant smell, no hint of mildew or rot. These books hadn't been abused, but simply forgotten. Gauging by the dust, Hero might have been the first creature to set foot in this place in centuries. Altogether, it gave Hero a terrifying suspicion of where he was.

The Dust Wing of the Library was not mentioned many times in the Librarian's Log. And when it was, it was mostly under the emotional subheading of NOPE. It was the wing to which books that were written but forgotten, lost, or destroyed were consigned. A graveyard of humanity's stories. No librarians to care for them, no patrons to peruse the stacks, simply the books and the dark of oblivion.

When Hero had read about it, he'd enjoyed the feeling of delightful horror. A boogeyman for unwritten books. An idea to give one a delicious shiver before going about one's day.

The reality was far colder.

The ink should have *created* something with his book, not damned it. Not sent him here, where no books return from. It was illogical, and Hero gratefully grasped onto the irritation in preference to other, darker emotions curdling in his chest. Illogical, an affront he would have to complain about at length when he got out of here.

When he got out of here.

The charade of that idea required movement. Hero stumbled to his feet. He picked a direction, trying and failing to chart a way through without stepping on any books. It was impossible. Canyons and hillocks of books stood in his way in any direction. Leather covers slipped under his toes, and pages crinkled and tore under his heels. Little destructions, tiny deaths passing in silence for those already long forgotten.

He'd half expected the damage to stir something up. Wake up a book. Surely these poor blighted creatures couldn't be so lost that they wouldn't try to send out a character to save themselves. But as Hero struggled through a leaning arch, the only thing he could hear was his labored breath, and that would definitely drive him mad before the dust did.

So, he started to mutter under his breath the first thing that came to mind.

"Once upon a time there was a man . . ."

Hero's eyes had adjusted to the gloom by now and could make sense of the terrain. It wasn't all leather-bound books here, not like the Unwritten Wing. With no readers to reach for, each text arrived in its original state as on Earth. There were books and folios, scrolls and hides, stories told in tribal knot work and stories etched in bone. Though they were few, bits of hypertext even drifted mist-like among the higher columns of rubble. Leto had told Hero only enough about the internet to give him a vague idea, but even humankind's most prolific, infinite libraries still let stories slip through the cracks of time.

Hundreds, thousands, millions of stories. Lost like Hero was. He tucked his chin in his chest and tried again.

"Once upon a time there was a very handsome, clever man who was unfairly called a villain. Although he did nothing but speak common sense and see what needed to be done, his acts of charity were never understood and therefore he was a villain. It was all quite unfair, so one day he said to hell with the rules and . . ."

A sigh shattered the silence, which had been so complete, the slightest noise sounded like a gunshot. Hero jolted, plastering himself to the cliff face of books so hard he was enveloped in a cloud of dust.

He coughed, and his eyes watered as he took in a lungful of neglect. For a moment, faces appeared in the haze. A chin, wide eyes. An open mouth. When he wiped his eyes and could finally see again, they were gone. It'd been a trick of imagination, wishful thinking. He couldn't start dredging up ghosts now, or he'd never get out of here.

Hero cleared his throat again. "Once upon a time there was a man . . ."

It was a story. It wasn't his author's story, not even his book's story; he couldn't even remember how that started anymore, but maybe this was more important: it was *his* story.

"Once upon a time there was a man who made very bad mistakes. No, that's not right. He made very bad *decisions*. And so was a very bad man."

A rise of crumpled hides dropped off to a slick descent of scrolls that Hero had to navigate on his hands and knees. He half slid, half fell to the bottom, bringing half a dozen scrolls down with him and a scattered shower of papyrus flakes. When he managed to unbury himself, he realized he'd slid to the foot of a clearing, bordered on all sides by massive, cresting waves of forgotten books. It would be a long, fruitless struggle up in any direction. As if Hero even *had* a direction. Shadows played at the tops, fluttering between drifts of hypertext fragments like blackbirds. It gave him the feeling of a hundred eyes, being watched. Or perhaps, being listened to.

The weight of it caught up with him. Hero sighed and sagged down onto a rubble of tablets.

"Bad men are not wrong, you see. But simply bad, bad at being an expected kind of man. Bad at playing their role in stories. So this man had a thought to change the story, for he was also a very foolish man."

The dark was descending now. Like ink seeping across paper. The illusion dragged the memory out of him, the ink rotting across his pages and the way Claire's face turned to him etched with horror. The shadows were drifting down the rubble, swaying and coalescing with the glowing dust to take spindly, drawn-out shapes. Hero shook his head and closed his eyes, as if that had ever worked to make phantoms go away.

"He set out to change the story, but that's not how stories work. He changed instead. Entirely by accident, and not always for the better. And it came to pass that this very bad, very foolish man wasn't quite sure what kind of man he was anymore."

A breath of sound fluttered around him again. It was airy, but not quite a sigh. More like an intake of breath. A scroll shifted against the toe of his boot, and when Hero opened his eyes it was his breath that snagged. Half a dozen figures stood at the base of the cliff. "Figures" was the only term to use, because there was nothing else definable about them. Their faces lacked the definition of skulls, their lips no more than a faded smudge of ink. Crumpled shadows where their eyes should have been. Their spindly legs faded out to nothing just above the dust-creased paper. Figures, gone fuzzy with no one to clearly hold them in their mind's eye. Stories, lost with no one to read them.

They didn't move, and neither did Hero. When he was able to breathe again, it wasn't fear that swept over him, but *sympathy*. A deep, infinite sadness at the loss and the slow kind of death that awaited him, and all books, here.

"And with no one to tell him otherwise, he clung to his story," Hero said in a whisper. "Because story was all he thought he had. And that's how . . . how he got lost. Somewhere along the way of searching for a story, he'd wandered off the path and into the dark woods. And he discovered perhaps what he had wanted wasn't a story at all."

More figures multiplied out of the drifts, creating a slowly shrinking ring around him. They drew close enough that Hero's voice took on a confessional nature by necessity. He studied the torn pages at his feet and wrapped his arms around himself, tight. He barely noticed the square press of his book into his ribs anymore. He'd wandered so far off the page.

"A very bad man had made mistakes, and bad choices, but they'd led him into a life. And a life, while also a story, is also something quite different."

The light grew until it was almost a half twilight, glowing dust collected and limning the silent audience around him. A shiver, more of a bare impression of fingertips than an actual hand, curved under his chin and raised his face. The figure in front of him was slightly more distinct than the others, perhaps younger with less dust on their book. They had holes for eyes, but somewhere inside the socket of black there was a flicker. Almost color. Navy against black, Hero thought. They'd had blue eyes once.

"A life is a question." Hero paused, but there was no recognition. No flicker of kinship. The figure waited. Hero wet his lips. "And the what happened?"

A whisper, almost like long-coming release, ruffled the air frost around him. The charcoal smudge that was the figure's r trembled, then parted. The glowing dust increased, swirling ir as figures opened their mouths, drew in breath.

And Hero listened.

# 28

# CLAIRE

If I am to remake the Library, then it follows that I am to remake the librarians as well. No use modeling ourselves after the human equivalent—in my time, the only reason I had the education I did was because of the wealth and status of my family. Even then, I would never have been made a scholar in charge of learning. Scholars are more hungry for control and the blessings of the powerful than for knowledge.

So this is my charge: We will be librarians. True to the books, but even more important, dedicated to those who have yet to read them. Understand that our duty does not end at the edge of a page. Stories must serve the living, not the reverse. If knowledge is freedom, then we must be chain breakers. If there's one thing I learned from the specter of my predecessor, it is this: to be a librarian is to be in rebellion against time, against the world.

*Librarian Madiha al-Fihri, 612 CE*

IRE WASTED PRECIOUS TIME with another visit back to the Li-
. She couldn't quite believe Brevity had abandoned them—it—
¹oned *it*, Claire corrected. She couldn't believe that Brevity would

abandon the Library, the books, the damsels who relied on her. It wasn't like her, not the Brevity Claire knew. Thought she knew.

But there was no denying the dust. Brevity's books lay open. The tea that had been merely abandoned earlier had now grown cold and silt sifted. There was a muddy boot print on the blotter. Brevity hadn't even locked up the Library—the logbook was buried underneath a dynasty fantasy she'd been repairing. Claire pulled it out by the edge and studiously ignored the feeling that she was snooping. She'd had thirty years to stare at this book; she'd earned the right to updates.

The book fell open on her lap, fluttering to a specific page with an almost lazy murmur of pages. The latest entry was written in Brevity's loopy, shy hand:

> Log entry number whatever. I'm not even sure I should be writing this down. Is it muse business or Library business? I'm not certain anymore, and there's no one to ask. Maybe that's why I'm writing it here.
>
> It almost feels like reporting to boss again. Claire. She doesn't like it when I call her boss anymore. If she would just talk to me, we could be doing this together. Probity is so certain that this ink will unlock muses, turn us from conduits to creators. She's so certain. I'm not, but isn't it worth the risk? Isn't it what's best for the books? We could get them written, remake what was lost. If ink is what remains of the lost books, then I want to give them that chance.
>
> Claire's isolated herself. Hero's not here. Probity's like a sister; I shouldn't feel alone. But it's like she's seeing past me, six months into the future or six years into the past. When I'm here. And trying.
>
> I'm trying. I have to try.

Claire smoothed out the parchment under her fingertips before closing the book softly and returning it to its proper place in the bottom right-hand drawer. The faerie lights that lined the fronts of the stacks held back the gloom with a cheer that she didn't feel. The Library was a sigh, without a librarian here to draw a new breath. The books beckoned, tempting Claire to wander in. She could make up a purpose, to speak to the muses, to do a patrol of the stacks since Brevity had left them so abandoned. But there was only one book she was looking for, and she wouldn't find it here.

*If only Claire would talk to me . . .*

Claire retrieved the log, picked up the pen, and was writing before she could think whether it would even work. She was part of the Library, but not the Unwritten Wing's librarian anymore, and this was the Librarian's Log. But she wanted—needed—to take a step toward bridging that gap and fixing what she'd been too self-pitying to notice had been broken in the first place. She pressed the nib to the paper and experienced a watercolor of relief and bitterness as the letters streamed out behind it.

*I have made many mistakes, but I will try to right them before it costs the Library any more. Ramiel believes he can track our lost character and his book. The Arcane Wing will dedicate every resource to this attempt, in assistance to the Unwritten Wing. We will find him.*

"Claire?" Rami hesitated at the threshold, as if realizing she was in a conversation that was both crucial and silent.

Claire hesitated, then signed the log.

*I'm sorry. I will do better. You deserve better.*

*Arcanist Claire Juniper Hadley*

She straightened more slowly after she set down the pen. Her gaze trailed along the desk to land on a familiar scalpel that Brevity had been using in repairs.

Claire shoved it in her skirt pocket on impulse. "You are certain you have a trace?" She raised her chin, as if Ramiel's mysterious certainty wasn't all that was keeping her together at the moment.

"I am." Rami held up a puff of silver clutched in one fist. The feather looked less substantial plucked from his coat, but it was imbued with a kind of light that wafted it in a decisive direction.

She didn't have permission. She was injured and stained by malicious ink. She didn't believe it could work. She had responsibilities. She had fears. There was an abundance of reasons why she should sit this one out. But it had been her hands that had caused this. Her hands that had cut down a man, stamped a wrist, woken the Library, held a sword, wiped away pages turned to ash.

Color whirled like a wet smear every time she turned her head. The tourniquet of inspiration on her arm was a mere bead of blue now. The ink did not feather or thin beyond it, but glistened. She was carrying the stain of what her hands had done in her skin. It was time to see it through. She owed Hero that much at least.

She tucked her clean hand in Rami's elbow. "Let's be off, then, before the damned fool gets the idea to run away."

Rami nodded softly, giving her a look that said her defensive calm was as thin as rice paper. He made sure Claire had a tight grip on his arm, then held up the feather and blew on it as if it were a dandelion. He closed his eyes, and an undeniably soft look came over his face, one that made an echoing ache in Claire's chest. It was a familiar look to read. He was thinking of Hero, and she'd never stopped.

The feather trembled, and light muddled off it like smoke, swirling briefly around them both before appearing to catch a breeze. Claire had focused on the feather so much, she barely registered the shuffle and shift of movement behind her until a familiar downy touch brushed her outside shoulder. Rami's trench coat had parted to reveal—or perhaps become—an impossible fractal of gray wings that Rami *certainly* had not exhibited before. They arched over her head protectively, and Claire had just enough time to give one gasp of wonder before they flexed, and the solidity of the Library spiraled into smoke and light.

TRAVELING BY ANGEL WAS a quite different experience than traveling by mist, raven, or ghostlight. The roads between realms that Claire was familiar with were meandering, as all deaths were. Dying bodily was fast, fast as a snapped neck, a stopped heart, but *death* was a ponderous logistic of the soul. Claire had assumed all travel in the afterlife was the same.

Claire had assumed wrong.

The Library did not so much fade from around her as shatter. There was a pulling sensation, and the world—multiple worlds— appeared in fractals around her, as if she were trapped inside a giant prism, each glimpse of reality only a shard, and sharp enough to cut. Metal spires of buildings, burnished shields of longhouses, reedy beaches and sun-bleached stone, pearl whites and dried blood and silver and brass and gold. Claire didn't have time to fear, because she was being pulled along, dragged by Rami's presence at her side, which she felt more than she could see. They were spiraling through time and space and either one could reach out and shatter her at a moment's notice. She was subsumed in potential. It was positively *terrifying* and enthralling, and the last remaining jagged edge of Claire's reason released something in her chest that felt dangerously close to joy.

So when the fractal shard of shadows took them, it felt like being split in two. The transition from light to dark was a wallop, and threw her from Rami's grasp. She hit the ground at a roll, surface flexing and sliding beneath her until she came to a stop. Claire sucked in a breath and came up coughing.

"Claire!" Rami's hand landed heavily on her shoulder. "Are you all right?"

A serpent of dust and decay had coiled itself around Claire's throat. She gagged, forehead pressed against her palm as she tried to force a breath. She finally could croak, "Nothing about that was all right, but thank you."

"I'm just glad you held on." When Claire looked up, she could make out the dimmest distinct blur that was Rami, against the dark. Somehow, light was seeming to drift and settle on his outline, at least enough to see that his wings were gone, folded back into his trench coat or his subconscious or wherever fallen angels kept their wardrobe these days. "Those paths aren't made for humans."

"So I gathered." Claire grumbled again, in order to clear her throat. "The poets continue to get everything about Heaven and angels wrong."

"They do." Rami sounded infinitely relieved to be complained at. He stayed crouched by her until Claire was drawing somewhat regular lungfuls of dusty air. "We are here, though I can't say where here is, precisely."

"That would require being able to see," Claire muttered.

"I'm managing," Rami admitted mildly. Why, yes, of course an angel could see in the dark. She sniffed.

Claire finally managed to get her feet under her and try to assess their surroundings. It did not bode well that a being as old as Rami didn't know where they were on sight. From the slip and shuffle of the material under their feet, they had landed on a great heap of something or other.

Similar monstrous bulks were just barely illuminated in the gloom. The dust floating through the air appeared to be its own light source, well dispersed but utterly insufficient for the task of lighting their surroundings. Claire held on to Rami's offered hand for balance as she turned her attention to the ground. She reached down and ran her hand over the slippery bits beneath her feet.

Leather, scuffed and rotted at the edges enough to come away with her fingertips. And then paper, fragile as ash and torn just as easily. Claire took in a sharp breath. "It's a library."

She couldn't make out Rami's expression in the dark, but the gentle snort was unmistakable. "It's in shambles. Who would allow a library to reach such a state?"

"No librarian or book lover, that's for certain." Claire was preoccupied with trying to chart the slope of the pile they were on top of. It seemed to stretch on forever, but a downward slope grew slippery until her feet hit a puddle of damp. A familiar bloom of mold and mashed pulp hit her nose and Claire gagged again. "Oh gods, the poor books."

"Hero has made you empathetic," Rami said quietly, and Claire was coughing too much to deny it. She shook her head until she could breathe again.

"Water, dust, mildew, time. Gods, *this* should be Hell's Library. It's torment for books." She fished a mostly dry page out of the pile and squinted with futility. "Rami, grab the opal from my bag; it's crusted to a finger bone—don't ask. Catholics are weird about their relics. There you go—that's better."

Claire pinched the dry bone between her fingers so she could bring the gem welded to the end up to her eye. Her vision illuminated, as if someone had turned on a dim light, though everything was narrowed to the pinpoint of a single pane of cut stone she could manage to see through.

The page was like tissue in her hand, and Claire held it up, trying to make out the words. The ink on the page was old, and the language something full of sharp joining lines that Claire could only guess was Assyrian. It didn't change for her. Claire took a breath and bent down to grab a different sample, this one a mostly complete scroll. She unwound it, struggling to be careful as a dread rose in her. The text on the scroll ran top to bottom, possibly an ancient form of pinyin, but that was Claire's wildly uneducated guess. In her wing, books translated themselves.

The scroll dropped out of her suddenly nerveless fingers. She lowered the gem from her eye, dropping the curtain of shadows around the room again. It hurt to breathe.

"Claire?" Rami's voice was soft at her side. "Do you have a guess where we are?"

"We don't have to guess." Claire's voice was unsteady. "Though I'm not surprised now that you didn't recognize it. No one comes here; no one should be here, least of all Hero. Rami, this is the Dust Wing."

The understanding registered as a startle of breath in Rami's otherwise solid-as-stone presence. He shifted, and Claire supposed he was uneasily scanning the half dark, trying to catch any movement. "Hero is here?"

He sounded uncertain, as if he suddenly wanted to doubt his own tracker skills. That would surely be a more comfortable thought than the idea of Hero here, injured or dying or lost in a mausoleum of forgotten books.

Claire didn't allow herself any such comforts. Concern was raw in her throat. "Of course he is. Your abilities led us here, so here is where we will find him. We will find him." She repeated it, mostly to herself, despite the way it undercut her certainty.

Water soaked through the toe of her sneakers. Claire straightened, squinted against the dark until she could be certain she wasn't about to walk off a cliff, and strode off in a random direction. "Get your little feather out, angel. We are going to find him."

THEY MADE THEIR WAY in the dark, stumbling over gullies of shredded parchment, swamps of rotted paste, led by the slender waft of the feather in Rami's palm. Rami said nothing, but Claire's head was filled with an unending scream.

"The trail leads this way," Rami said, starting up a precarious-looking slope. Claire took a step to follow but halted as a shiver came over the air. A thunder of falling books rang out behind them, accompanied by an unholy screech. Abruptly, the ground beneath them shifted. It didn't move, not in the physical sense, but the books beneath them shivered, throwing the accumulated dust up into the air and painting the dim world in an incomprehensible fog.

Perhaps it was a matter of familiarity; perhaps it was an instinct honed after three decades in the Library; perhaps it was a sympathetic echo between unwritten writer and unremembered books, but Claire knew in an instant that there'd been a loss. A book of the Dust Wing had been further disgraced, dismantled, destroyed. She pivoted, wheezing and straining to see through the dust, but nothing else moved.

Until the scream. It was wordless, cut off, but it was also, undeniably, Brevity's voice.

Claire spun to Rami, wide-eyed with alarm. "That was Brev."

Rami didn't question it, didn't ask how she could possibly be certain. And for all that, for his stoic, buoyant belief that held her up like a life raft, Claire loved him a little more. He nodded and measured the drift of the feather in his cupped palm.

"Go. Find Brevity. Do your duty."

Claire's heart jumped, and she felt torn in two. "But Hero—"

"I'll find our wayward man," Rami said with a gentleness that seemed to expand his care for the entirety of the Library. "He can't be far. Go. You need to do this. I'll find Hero and we'll find you."

If the soft gravel of Rami's voice had been an ounce less certain and made of stone, Claire couldn't have done it. If his eyes had been a smidge harder and not full of love—for her, for Hero, for what horrible mistakes had brought them here in the darkness—Claire couldn't have trusted it. But he touched her face in the light-limned dust and she impulsively went to her toes, pressed a kiss to his cheek, and flung herself down the bleak, slippery incline.

# 29

# BREVITY

A reader doesn't mark his life by days but by memories. A book doesn't mark its life by pages but by readers. We are made up of those whom we touch.

*Librarian Claire Juniper Hadley, 2017 CE*

THE WIND AND WEFT of light left them suddenly, and Probity's grip on Brevity's hand twitched her forward a moment before Probity's magic swept closed at their backs. Goose bumps immediately pricked at Brevity's bare shoulders.

It wasn't dark. No place that held stories could be dark to a muse, but it was *dim*. Dimmer than it should have been. The books beneath her feet were quiet as pavers. Instead of lashing auras of color, they merely glowed, weak. The light of their story barely dribbled over their surfaces. Brevity hadn't thought stories could wither, not like this.

But then she looked up and realized all she had thought was wrong.

They were in a forest, of sorts. Everywhere, books lay open on the floor and their pages were unstitched, folded and torn until wafts of barely connected paper drifted up in a fine column, freed of the sensible logic of gravity. Every couple of feet, another mutilated book bloomed paper that drifted in place like a sea of kelp on an ocean floor.

Brevity gasped, and the nearest frond shivered. Against the dark and the dim glow, it was like standing in a forest of ghosts and bone.

"Is this the Dust Wing? Who did this?" Brevity turned and found Probity watching her. The ink-bleached muses were animated since they stepped through, straining at the ends of their makeshift leashes to lunge for the nearest drifting tendrils of paper.

"No one's allowed in the Dust Wing, of course," Probity said, completely ignoring the contradiction in her presence. She hesitated, then covered the hesitation by yanking on the leashes impatiently. "The books do this to themselves."

"No way." A frond of shredded paper drifted close enough to brush Brevity's hand. She startled away. "It's mutilation. No one would do this to themselves."

"Not even a character who woke up to find themselves entombed in the dark for the infinite reaches of time? Even books can go mad with enough isolation; you know that." Probity gave her a sad, pointed look.

The idea refused to sink in, then settled on Brevity like a layer of cold iron. Books can go mad, like anything sentient, Claire had told her once. It was why every wing of the Library required a librarian. Not just to keep the books from escaping, but to curate, and attend.

No one could tolerate oblivion alone.

"Why?" Brevity whispered brokenly. The book at her feet had split in two, pages lost long ago.

"Because humans are agents of decay," Probity said. Her voice had been soft, gentle, but hardened to steel. "I've been trying to tell you since I arrived, sis. Humans are the reason the Dust Wing exists. We gave them the power of creation—something only *gods* have—and they spit on it. They don't deserve it. It's time we take it back." And Probity let her hold on the leash go slack.

Gaiety and Verve stumbled and appeared to pause, noses in the air—well, one nose, since Gaiety's face was blank—before lunging. They tore into the nearest fronds of damaged paper with a gluttony of violence. The sound of shredding and chewing covered Brevity's cry, and Probity held up a hand when she started forward.

"Careful, now, best not get between them and their meal."

"They're not meals; they're *stories*. We're supposed to *protect* them."

"Humans sealed their fate long ago. They're not stories; they are just corpses." Probity's eyes glittered in the twilight as she intently watched the pale muses rip shreds of paper and bring them to their faces. Verve swallowed greedy mouthfuls whole, but Gaiety made a grating noise of frustration as his hands encountered his ink-erased face. Probity stepped forward, a scalpel suddenly in hand, and sliced across Gaiety's blank chin. A gap appeared in a bloom of black ink, and scissored razor teeth beyond. Probity stepped back, satisfied. "It's a worthy sacrifice if it shifts the power in the right direction."

"Your direction," Brevity clarified. She shook her head, feeling helpless as Verve followed the frond of paper and began to try to gorge herself on the book whole. "Prob, this is against everything we are."

"I've heard that before," Probity said, anger inching an edge into her voice. She broke her intent study of the ink-sopped muses to frown at Brevity. "Didn't they say the same thing when you took a stand and kept a line of inspiration for yourself?"

"That wasn't a stand! That was—" Brevity clasped her bare forearm. A vile feeling roiled up in her throat, but it was all pointed inward. "It was an act of desperation. A mistake."

"It *wasn't*. Don't you dare say that!" Probity yanked the leashes as she turned, entreating, toward Brevity. "I can't believe she made you believe that! This is all because of that old librarian; she's *human*, Brevity! She's not your friend!"

"I can understand the doubt. All appearances seem to indicate otherwise," a gravely amused voice came from behind her. A waft of paper parted, and a silhouette struggled through the darkness, taking care not to step on fractured books. "Yet here I am, for some reason."

"Claire!" A tangle of contradictions flooded Brevity. Relief, worry, then abject horror that Claire was here, at the center of Probity's ire.

"You shouldn't be here." Probity's tone was streaked with ice.

"None of us should," Claire said pointedly. "But I'm trying to atone for my mistakes."

"Atone? Your sins are many, human. Valiant of you to try." Gaiety and Verve lurched on their leads again, having shredded and consumed every book within reach. Probity tilted her head, considering for a moment. "How about I lend you a hand?"

The leashes fell from her grasp, and the cold that rushed Brevity's veins seemed to slow time. Gaiety torpedoed in the direction he'd been pointed—straight at Claire. Verve, however, still had eyes and a hunting instinct. The feral muse darted away and quickly disappeared through the forest of dead books. Gaiety crashed into Claire, claws out. Claire barely managed to grapple at his wrists. Protect the books; protect the human. Brevity had a moment, just a moment, to decide what to do.

# 30

# HERO

I'll explain this once, and only once, because just writing this down gives me the willies, frankly. The Unwritten Wing is where stories exist before humans know them, but there's a wing for after as well. A wing for after, when stories die. When the last copy of a book is burned or the last fond memory of a folktale fades from an old man's mind. When pages are used for scrap and fodder. When gold embellishments are ripped off as bounty of war. When the light on all possible pages of a story goes dark, that's when a book's life ends.

But like humans, that's not the end. The afterlife for a lost book is quiet, and final. An eternal sleep in the Dust Wing, never to be read again. No books wake up there; nothing stirs. It is perhaps the most final kind of death in all the afterlife realms.

The death of a forgotten book.

*Librarian Gregor Henry, 1974 CE*

HERO HAD NEVER BEEN a reader. Not in his own story, not outside it. Naturally, he *could* read, but he saw it merely as a convenient conveyance of information, a transportation device for the skills necessary to operate in the world. This opinion had only been reinforced upon waking and realizing he could scan any book other than his own and acquire skills that would have required years of mastery otherwise. It was handy, sometimes, being a creature of creation.

But it meant he had never understood reading. Not in the way Claire and Brevity seemed to revere it. He revered *being read* as a character of an unwritten book. Quite a lot. Though evicted from his book, he knew the singular awareness of life he felt being seen, being experienced. But he'd never been quite sure what the reader got out of it.

He came to an understanding in the Dust Wing. He was lost in a sea of dust and decay. Staying here would surely mean drowning, but stories reached out and offered him a life raft.

It was not like taking skills from a book, as he had before. Nor was it like as he remembered living his own story. It was not even reading, not with his eyes. Stories filled him like water into a sponge—first he absorbed; then he overflowed. As he listened—as he received—story after story. Each one passed through him, yet left something behind. A suspicious voice, a desiring ache, a fierce demand, a lungful of bittersweet victory.

It was like recalling well-loved music; it was like training swordplay into your bones. It was like the meditative wistfulness of hunting. It was like the euphoric agony of running. It was like everything and like nothing, and it seeped deep into Hero's bones. He was the first reader the Dust Wing had had in—well, perhaps ever, and every book that hadn't yet withered to the point of madness stretched out to him, eager to be known.

It overwhelmed him. Hero had always made a point to avoid other books—he would never be caught in the damsel suite. He'd always held the uneasy fear that the presence of other characters, from unwritten books like him, would only remind him of what he could not do, could not have, could not be. Perhaps the ink had weakened him and poisoned his resistance, but he found the opposite was true. The Dust Wing poured its stories into him, and he felt nourished, not washed out.

Claire had tried to explain what listening to a book's song was like, the lingering sense of possession even after a book was closed, but this wasn't that at all. Hero wrapped the stories around him like armor, not to become someone else but to see what he recognized in the mirror.

The only thing he lost was time. When he came back to himself, he was midway through a close-cut ravine of tablets and clay. The light-giving dust was thick enough here that he could see a couple of feet around him, and dust was like a thin layer of muted slate gray snow beneath his feet. The sharp cliff face of tablets to either side was jagged, not worn down by time. Hero supposed that was only logical; no natural formations of time and weather held sway here. It looked more as if a towering pile of tablets had grown until breaking under its own weight. It had split and crumbled, creating walls of jagged and tumbling artifacts that reached over his head.

Like in the Unsaid Wing, the form of the text felt unnatural and wrong to him. Books should be friendly to the reader—an enticing voice, paper, or even a flat-screen. These tablets were the wrong sort and unfriendly to the core. Not many spoke to him here, and his head was filled with only a susurrus of whispers. The silence might have been what drew his attention back. It was the only reason he heard the slow, ponderous grind of footsteps.

It was enough of a grounding sound to alarm Hero into action. He hunkered down against a spill of clay, just grateful that he'd been here long enough that the dust had frosted even his bright hair and clothing to dullness. The steps grew nearer, and only at the last moment did he think to snatch up a heavy clod of stone that must have broken off some greater slab. It was more cudgel than sword, but Hero hefted it anyway.

There was no helpful shadow cast in the dark, but the whispers receded in their own kind of warning. A broad figure emerged from a gully in the ravine, making their way, Hero noted, with a purposeful kind of shuffle that was more surefooted than he'd managed. Hero could only track his movement by the way the dust shifted in his wake. He'd been here long enough for another living creature to feel foreign, and the thought struck an absurd panic in him. As soon as the figure moved under him, Hero leapt with the rock over his head.

It was not an elegant attack—Hero found himself embarrassed by the raw sound he made to ease his frayed mind—but Hero had enough experience in combat to be efficient. Which was why when a fist closed around his throat and the world inverted, his back hit the ground with a grunt of surprise.

He flung his knee up, catching his assailant in the gut. The grip on his collar didn't loosen, but the curse he heard stopped his intentions of a follow-up move.

"Hell" was the word, and Hero had heard it said often enough with self-righteous judgment and disdain to place the voice.

"Rami?" He felt a subtle trace of feathers brush past his nose, and there was no containing his relief. His voice sounded cracked and thin as paper to his own ears and his eyes were alarmingly hot. "Ramiel?"

The hand at his throat let go and appeared to hesitate a moment before patting down his collar. "You're a rather hard man to find," Rami finally said.

The dim light shifted as Rami backed off of him, but Hero felt plastered to the ground. He entirely ignored the sharp point of rubble that was beginning to make inroads into his ribs. "How—you—what the hell are you doing here?"

"Are you injured?" Rami's voice sounded sharp, and he'd ignored Hero's sputtering entirely.

"Only my pride." Hero allowed Rami to clasp his arm and pull him to sitting, relishing discovering the warmth of Rami's hands all over again as they steadied him by the shoulder. He didn't try to stand. "I thought—" He stopped, words clotted up in his throat like chalk. He hadn't thought. He'd known he was alone, would be left alone, and had only survived by not thinking. His head was full of other people's stories; his own felt distant. "This is the Dust Wing," he said instead.

"Yes, I had begun to suspect as much," Ramiel said with that straight-faced calm that he used when he was amused. Then he asked again, "Are you injured, Hero?"

"Me? No. I—" Hero paused, considered the fragment of his thoughts, then tried for something more honest. "I would be very glad to get out of here." His voice came out smaller than he'd intended.

"That's the plan." Rami shifted to a crouch, and Hero briefly lost track of him in the gloom. A day ago, he would have ridiculed the panic that spiked up in his gut simply by losing contact with someone he knew logically would not leave him, but that didn't stop him from gripping the feathers of Rami's trench coat and not letting go when he found them again. "Claire and I split up, but I should be able to find her."

The questions stacked up behind Hero's tongue. He sputtered. "Claire's here?" No one should be here. No one came to this place. No one came for these books, least of all him. He shook his head, trying to order his thoughts into a way this made sense. "How did you find me?"

"I tracked you," Ramiel said with a curious kind of tone that made no sense to Hero. He moved on before Hero could question it. "I don't think we're alone in here."

"We're not," Hero said with a vague gesture to the broken tablets.

"No, I mean—" Rami gave a helpless shrug. "We should get moving."

Hero wasn't about to argue that point. Rami pulled him to his feet, and if he noticed how Hero clung a little too tightly to the back of his coat as they skirted their way down the embankment, he was circumspect enough to not say so.

They had nearly made their way out of the clay tablet canyons—Hero could see scrolls and wood panels encroaching, like sedimentary layers of an archaeological dig—when they heard a third pair of footsteps up ahead.

Rami held a hand up, though it was really unnecessary with Hero inelegantly clinging to his side. He took a tentative step into what seemed to impossibly be a *darker* puddle of darkness. "Claire?"

Rami kept his voice pitched low. There was no response, but the footsteps didn't slow or increase. Hero felt a chill prickle over his neck. Rami tried again. "Claire? Brevity?"

*Brevity's here too?* Impossible. This was an impossible place to be in the first place, let alone by *choice*, and certainly not for Hero's sake. Hero wanted to ask, but he bit his lips instead to keep quiet. The footsteps were not heavy, but as they got closer Hero could make out a messy slurry with each step. As if something was scrabbling through paper and scrolls.

It grew closer, skittering around the corner. Hero felt Rami lean forward, squinting into the darkness. He jerked hard enough to throw Hero backward into a stumble. The sound of the sword clearing its sheath reached him, and the igniting of the blade threw light into the darkness like a grenade. Hero was momentarily blinded and paralyzed as he blinked away the stars.

Rami's broad shoulders were silhouetted by a white fire. It set each feather on his coat in contrast and for just a moment, Hero swore he could have seen wings. "Rami?" His voice was dry as paper.

"Stay back, Hero." Muscles twitched under Hero's fingers and tension sung through Rami's shoulders, translating down to the arm that held a sword pointed steady. Hero leaned around him and had to hold a hand up to block the light in order to see what threat had caused such a change.

He almost missed her. So pale she was almost drowned out by the light of Rami's sword, the girl hunkered just outside the brightest radius. Her shoulders were clenched up to her ears, one strap of her bleached clothes hanging off. Hero recognized the scrappy, eclectic kind of fashion mayhem. Brevity wore clothes like that.

He jolted forward. "Rami, that's a muse—"

"No, it's not," Rami said as Hero grabbed his forearm, and really, his blade didn't even waver. It really was unfair, angels in general. Hero latched onto the trivial thought, because it was easier than what his eyes were trying to tell him was in front of him.

The girl did look like a muse of an indiscernible age. But muses were full of color—even serious, intense Probity was painted in mint and sunshine colors. But this one was pale as bone, and just as sharp and thin. The light flickered over her and it almost seemed to pass through her, as if Hero could make out smudged impressions on the other side. That was impossible, but then so was the face she revealed when her head tilted up. Beneath ivory straw hair she had a blank expression, grayscale eyes glazed with a hunger-pang gloss. Her mouth was the only contrast when a snarl pulled back her lips to reveal rows—rows—of black, jagged teeth.

"Stay back," Rami warned with a sway of his blade.

The creature paused, glassily considered the sword point, and slowly closed her hand around it. The holy light leapt from the blade to her knuckles, but instead of burning, it danced over her bleached skin before twining up her wrist. The muse's razor-tipped smile widened.

Hero wasn't written to curse—his author had probably thought it too lowbrow—but what slipped out as the white muse stepped forward was a very heartfelt, fervent "Shit."

Rami's grip on his arm tightened. "Run."

They ran. Dust-dry scrolls crumbled beneath their feet as they scrambled. Rami's lit sword made shadows jump and frenzy around them with every step. They heard the muse's steps lurch into a ragged run behind them. The thought hit him that they had no way of knowing whether she was alone. Hero remembered the predator behavior of the lion Furies in Elysium. Every wild flinch of dark shadows could be another one of those things springing a trap. The image hit Hero hard: a white demon launching itself at Rami, black razor teeth tearing feathers and closing around his unprotected throat.

The sick fear kicked Hero forward, pulling him ahead as the scrolls crumbled and gave way to the canyon of clay tablets again. They fled past the spot where Rami had found Hero, and were running blind.

Broken piles of shards rose around them, like menacing walls of teeth. Teeth behind them, teeth to either side. There was no time to consider their route. Hero didn't remember this path through the slate canyon, and he worried that at any moment the terrain would drop off or close in entirely.

Almost as he thought it, the teeth on either side of them began to draw closer, closing like a maw. The path beneath them began to slope up. The clay pieces were precariously balanced, and Rami with his heavier feet and frame was slowing down. Hero had to grab his shoulder as he stumbled. Clay shards clattered down the slope and momentarily masked the sound of the muse in pursuit. Hero's pulse wedged itself between his ribs for a nice panic attack.

"Climb, you great, dull bastard," Hero muttered, dragging on Rami's coat. The angel took another step and a cascade of clay dislodged beneath them, dragging them both down.

Rami arrested their slide by planting his sword. "It's too steep."

"Then sprout some goddamned wings and *fly*," Hero growled. "I don't think that creature behind us is coming to give us a boost."

"I keep telling you, not—" Rami winced as he stumbled hard to one knee. "Not that kind of angel." He pressed to his feet and glanced above them. The blade lit them from beneath and threw his eyes into complete shadow. "It narrows and levels out up ahead. Make it over the crest and there's enough space to lose her."

"Fantastic. After you, then—"

"It's too steep," Rami repeated grimly. Hero couldn't see his eyes. Why wouldn't Rami move so he could see his goddamned eyes? "You go up that way. I'll find a different way around."

Rami had never endeavored to be a believable liar, and in Hero's opinion it was far too late to start now. He scoffed, but the sound was buried in the loud crunch of clay. The bleached muse came into view at the bottom of the rise. Hero had a moment of hope. "Perhaps she'll have the same difficulty—"

The phantom girl scrambled again, then launched herself into the air. She cleared several meters, grabbed a ledge of clay jutting from the cliff side, and hung there like a gargoyle. A feral, hungry growl filled the air.

". . . or not," Hero finished.

"You should go," Rami said. There was a cracking sound. The tablets appeared to start to disintegrate and wither everywhere the muse touched. Hero shuddered and had to suppress the memory of black ink rotting him from the inside, how it felt to melt away like that. The muse tracked him hungrily. Her perch wouldn't hold for long, and she was already eyeing the distance between them.

First the bridge, now this. The tumult of fear in his chest boiled over into a desperate kind of anger. He grabbed the lapel of Rami's coat and hauled him an inch from his face. "Listen here, you noble idiot, I don't have time to argue with you. You are an *angel* and angels do not sacrifice themselves for shitty characters of a broken book that is a dime a dozen anyway."

Rami's face was close enough that Hero could feel the warmth coming off his breath as he huffed. "We can't both make it—"

"Maybe not. But angels do not give up and die in filthy trash heaps like the Dust Wing." Hero hesitated, and it felt like a sudden narrowing. The stories he'd let pass through him had left him hollowed, clean. Nothing mattered but the shadows of the second in focus, as if everything else had been a slow blur turning on this decision. Here. Now. Hero became aware of the breath he took, drawing in the air as it left Rami's mouth. Even that was warm. "Angels don't *do* that. But books do."

Rami's mouth dropped open. "What—"

Hell with it. Hero chased that breath and sealed Rami's lips with his own. He swallowed the words, swallowed the questions, swallowed the consequences and anything but the hot relief of finally, finally feeling right outside his story. Rami's lips were shock-stiff for half a second before turning supple, all-encompassing, and giving as infinity. Soft. Soft! Hero marveled. Such a stony, hard face, to have such soft lips.

Hero might have closed his eyes and died like this, but he caught a blur of movement as the muse launched herself at them, pale hands like claws. Hero already had Rami off-balance and by the lapels, so the turn felt natural. He waited until the last minute to shove him away, clear of the claws and teeth that descended on Hero's shoulder.

Hero fell backward, and his ears were filled with snarls as the muse grappled with him. Teeth needled his shoulder, and something trickled under his skin, worse than blood or ink. Rami gave a hoarse cry from somewhere in the dark, but Hero and the muse creature were made of lighter things. He ducked and threw her off, leaping for an outcropping of slippery shards that led her farther and farther up the cliff wall.

Away from Ramiel.

The monster took the bait. It snarled and spurred after him until Hero ran out of options. The ledge was an isolated jut, and the accumulated clay began disintegrating to sand the moment the muse touched down. Past her feet, Hero could see light flickering like a will-o'-the-wisp through the dark as Rami tried to reach them.

"Nasty thing, aren't you?" Hero touched the wound at his shoulder. He slowly backed up until his back hit the cliff face. He watched as the muse grew from her crouch, a bit of clay melting in her hand. She brought the sandy remains to her lips. The pieces clicked together for him. "Or just hungry?"

Slowly, Hero reached into his vest pocket and withdrew his book. Every limb in the muse went rigid when the green cover of his book came into view. Hero held it to his chest warily. "That's why you're here, isn't it? Hungry for a good story. But the dried-up old bones in this place aren't satisfying your appetite, are they? No, you want something juicy and fresh."

He stepped to the left, then the right, and the muse tracked the book like it was mesmerized. It made a parched, hungry little keen. Hero sighed. "Pathetic, aren't you? I—"

This was *Hero's* revelation; it was really atrociously rude when the muse interrupted. She snarled and lunged, clearing the distance. She slammed Hero against the jagged cliff face, and claws scissored down on his throat.

The world became oblivion and black teeth as Hero grappled to keep hold of his book. Ink was filling his throat instead of air. He could smell the fast decay of leather and glue. The fight was inelegant; it was messy; it was stupid and ugly and contrary to every forgotten story that coursed, like fire, through Hero's veins.

He wrenched the book over his head. It startled the muse just enough to loosen her grasp on his throat, and Hero gagged a breath as he swung his arm down. "Choke on it."

He swung for her face and punched the spine of his book straight into her open teeth. The scream that filled the air was thin and felt as if it went on forever. Hero couldn't say in the moment if it was the muse's or his own. Her weight was off his chest as she rolled away.

Numbness crept across his skin, from shoulder to throat wound. It felt colder than blood or ink or even ice. He couldn't move from where he fell. The Dust Wing's stories surged and seared through his fading pulse. Lurching sounds of ripping, tearing, and ragged, wet swallows came from somewhere nearby as his book, his world, his life, his essence, was gnashed between rot-black teeth. And Hero stared, in his last moments, at his empty hands cupping the dark.

# 31

# RAMI

What is a story without want, without need?

Moreover, what is want, what is need, without a story?

*Librarian Gregor Henry, 1896 CE*

RAMI HAD LOST HIS wings in the fall. They all had, all the Watchers that had been cast out. Lucifer, when he'd rebelled, had been allowed to keep his wings. Rami had never thought that was very fair. But Watchers had cast their lot in with humankind, sympathetic to their plights. It was some kind of divine justice, he supposed, that they be earthbound with them.

It felt like a sin, then, that he would trade every human on Earth for the wings he needed to reach Hero right now.

He saw them clash and saw the open way Hero welcomed the attack. He saw the struggle, hands locked over the book, before they fell beyond sight of the ledge. There were horrible ripping sounds, and then there was silence, which was even worse.

And Rami couldn't fly, couldn't even leap with the agility and grace that Hero had. He could only claw, one bleeding hand over the other, up a cliff of broken words with his heart held in his mouth.

He reached the outcrop in a breathless pain that had nothing to do with the air in his lungs. He made sense of the tableau he saw in pieces. The muse creature was near a crumbling ledge, hunkered over an empty space that had been a book. It raised its head sluggishly at his approach and its eyes were eerie, whiter than white. They were the white of snow on fire and made the black on her cracked lips more profane by comparison. She licked the ink off her pointed teeth with a delicate air.

The ignition of flames along his blade made her pupils shrink. Rami hadn't been aware of the moment he'd drawn it, but he was entirely in possession of the moment he decided to use it. The muse snarled, pale eyes streaming. Fissures formed along her skin, a colorless kind of wrongness revealing her fault lines. She lurched, but a full belly made her languid and slow. The tip of his sword caught her under the collarbone. Rami drove it home. She exhaled a long, relieved breath in his face, tickling his nose with the scent of leather and new paper enough to sting his eyes.

When she fell, she'd changed from snow and bone to a paleness the consistency of spun sugar. Rami didn't care to watch her melt away. He sheathed his sword and turned to the shadows that clumped on the opposite side of the ledge.

Hero had fallen on his side. The sight made the remaining strength in Rami's legs fail him, and he reached the limp body on his knees. His velvet coat was torn, and the ragged edges were muddy with ink-dampened clay dust. It made a stiff kind of death shroud that cracked when Rami turned him and pulled him into his lap with shaking hands.

A well of despair narrowed his focus. For a moment he didn't see, couldn't see, Hero's face. He saw ink stains on chapped, feral lips. An attack made sluggish by story. A pale concave belly that would fade and rot and take the mashed remains of a book with it.

Hero's hands were cupped, reaching. Always goddamned *reaching*, he was. For more, more, more. That should have been Rami's first hint, shouldn't it? That he was more than paper and ink and unreal dreams. The desire; the desire to know more, more, more. To *be* more. Hero had been screaming it, with every moment and every breath, but Rami hadn't seen it. It'd been so much easier to pretend to judge him.

"You didn't know, you didn't even . . . get to know." Rami wasn't sure what he was confessing, to Hero's forehead. There was a multitude of truths that Hero hadn't known, and several Rami hadn't had the time or the courage to say. And it wasn't *just*. He could whisper them now, into a dead man's hair, but what good would that do? Would it end anywhere that mattered? Would another letter appear in the Unsaid Wing to be forgotten, sniggered over by some later souls?

Souls. The word made Rami bleed inside. One thing, then; one thing he had left that he could do. The prayer for a soul's rest was cracked on his lips, and each word tasted like ash. He folded Hero's arms one over the other and crossed them gently over the wounds on his chest.

The prayer was all he had left to hang on to, and Rami was so lost in it that he almost missed the pained gasp. He nearly dropped Hero when cold arms flinched under his own, and a different prayer was answered.

"God's *tits*, that hurts." Hero's voice was thin and broken. It appeared a momentous effort to curl his fingers away from the wound at his shoulder. He dragged in another lungful of air without opening his eyes.

"Hero." Rami was dumbstruck with the obvious. He froze, wanting to reassure himself by touching Hero's face but not certain the hallucination would hold up. "Are you—you can't—your *book*—" Rami glanced over his shoulder in the bizarre impulse to confirm that the muse hadn't died and kindly reassembled Hero's book in the process. There was only ash swirling across the ledge.

When he returned his gaze, Hero's eyes were open and he made a small groan. "My book again. Claire's going to kill me. I—" Finally, the realization appeared to catch up with him. His eyes widened, glossy with shock, and his dry lips made a speechless moue.

"It's okay." Rami curled his fingers gently and prepared to reassure him. That his book was still gone and he was still here was a miracle, if an angel ever saw one, but it would be a shock and any normal man would reel to make sense—

"Oh gods, I *kissed* you," Hero whispered.

"*That's* what upsets you?" Rami struggled not to shove the man out of his lap, if only because he was afraid to let him go.

"Well, I didn't even ask, and that's really unacceptable. I'm a villain, not a coward." Some of the color came back to Hero's eyes as they ticked over Rami's face. "Though I didn't anticipate you'd be *this* upset, or that I'd be here to see it."

"Hero . . ." Rami searched for what came next and came up empty. It took effort to leave a several-millennia-old immortal speechless, but damned if he didn't manage it. Rami swallowed and finally allowed his fingertips to touch the familiar scars on Hero's cheek. "Your book."

"Oh," Hero said, closing his eyes, then opening them again suddenly. "*Oh.*"

He struggled to sit up, so Rami braced his arm beneath the injured shoulder until Hero could turn himself around. He surveyed the ash-smeared clay with a lost expression. "She took it, ate the book—"

"I killed her."

Hero balanced on that fact until it became too heavy for him. He sagged against Rami completely. His weight was welcome and grounding for Rami, honestly. Someone that heavy was not going to fade away on him, not yet. "It's gone," Hero said faintly.

"It seems that way."

"And I am still . . . here." Hero held up his hand and inspected it, though Rami knew he didn't have the dark vision that Rami did. Hero's fingertips squeezed over his eyes before hesitating at his own lips. "I'm still here."

"You are," Rami repeated firmly, and would repeat until they both believed the impossible fact. "How do you feel?"

"I feel . . ." Hero's thoughtful expression did a complicated kind of acrobatics. "I feel it. There's a . . . an empty space, but then there's so much noise." He risked a guilty glance at Rami. "She took the book and there was— I fell. And then I . . . I listened. To the books. It was so loud, and then everything turned black; I heard whispers and my bloody hand *hurt*. And I got mad." He paused, running a thumb along the deep scratch that Alecto had given him, what seemed like several disasters ago to Rami. Hero looked rueful. "Mad enough to get lost in the stories. I may have gotten into a spot of haunting before you showed up."

"That would figure." Rami measured Hero with caution. There would be quiet, later, when losses came back to a man. Hero would need to be watched. But they could be there for him. *Rami* could be there. "Are you feeling able to move? Claire ran off to face another one of those things, I think."

That brought Hero's head up. He nodded quickly. "My shoulder hurts like murder, but I'll manage." He accepted the hand Rami held out and pulled to his feet lightly. He pretended to dust flecks of clay from his coat, but Rami caught the way his gaze slid uneasily back to where the muse had died. "Claire's here? How? How did you even find me?"

Rami hesitated. It wasn't the time, it wasn't the place, but damn if he was going to withhold truth from Hero again. "I tracked your soul," he said simply.

"My—" Hero did a double take. It was really a wonder his head didn't twist off. His confusion stirred a quiet fondness in Rami's chest. "I have one of those? I can't! I'm a—" His gaze flickered back to the ashy ledge uneasily, and he whispered in a more subdued tone, "I didn't think I had one of those."

"I think you do," Rami said, letting all his faith and certainty warm into the words. "I know you do."

A small knit appeared between Hero's brows and a ghost of confusion, a mere slice of the shock and the shifting of self-identity that Rami knew would come later, came into and went from his eyes. He followed Rami down off the ledge and slowed to match Rami's heavier pace with an uncharacteristic sedateness. He would have a lot to think about, Rami supposed.

"One thing . . ." Hero muttered as they reached the bottom. Rami braced himself for existential questions he could not answer. "It happened, didn't it? I kissed you?"

Surprise was another thing an old immortal was not used to. Laughter bubbled up in his throat, riding on a wave of his remaining fear and relief. He didn't laugh, but he turned to hide the softness of his smile. Hide the way his cheeks warmed. Thank goodness Hero couldn't see in the dark.

"Yes," Rami said with as much dignity as he could muster. "I believe that did happen. Right before I kissed you."

Hero joined him on the ground, landing with more agility than any near-death survivor had a right to. He was smiling when he looked up, searching Rami's face before nodding once. "Claire. Brevity."

Rami nodded. "Let's go get them."

# 32

# CLAIRE

> The secret isn't about books at all. It's about people.
> *Librarian Gregor Henry, 1942 CE*

CLAIRE'S WORLD HAD NARROWED to pale claws and void-like needles of teeth. The creature snarled and spit in her face as its claws passed narrowly over her skin. The glove covering her inked hand was slippery, and it was difficult to keep her grip. Claire stumbled backward, and her foot shifted unsteadily against the slide of books. To keep her mind from panicking she tried to understand what she'd seen. Brevity, Probity, and two pale creatures on leashes. The monsters appeared vaguely humanlike but devoid of color. As if someone had reached down and merely sketched in a black-and-white negative of a person in their place.

They had been mutilating—no, *eating*—the books. The horror of that was all that Claire's mind had been able to take in before Probity had unleashed her pets. Claire had only the foggiest speculation of what they were, but from the way they'd swallowed pages whole, she suspected nothing good would come of the monster discovering the ink beneath her glove.

The creature had nearly succeeded in catching the hem of her glove with a razor finger when it was ripped away. She heard an inarticulate howl of rage wherever it had landed; then Brevity was there, pulling her to her feet. Horror, or regret, had paled her features almost as much as the other creatures'.

The similarities occurred to Claire all at once. "Those are muses?"

"What's left after the ink," Brevity said in clipped tones, as if already bracing herself for the worst. Claire hadn't been the only one driven to experimentation, and she had neither the time nor the inclination to judge. The beastly muse had gained his footing again before he lunged, clawing at Claire's hand.

The back of Claire's glove had torn, exposing the ink-stained skin to the air, and the muse zeroed in on it as if he could smell it. Claire backed up to put space between her and the creature, and he leapt an inhuman height through the air. Paper fronds of the dead books snagged and curled around his limbs like seaweed, but the muse had no interest in lesser snacks now that he'd found a prime source.

"I knew it," Probity said more to herself than anyone.

Brevity was somewhere to Claire's right. "Knew what?! Probity, we have to stop this!"

"Stop it? Sis, don't you see? This is an opportunity! We have something better than an unwritten book or the dead things of the Dust Wing. This is justice."

Claire couldn't spare the attention to see what she was doing. It was just enough distraction that she was too slow when the ink-bleached muse moved again. Claws snagged the fabric of her skirts and pulled Claire to the ground. Claire had a moment of enough awareness to shield her ink-stained hand against her chest before the feral muse was on her.

Torn and moldered books slid underneath her. A torn chain of paper caught on her throat, and Claire had to writhe it off so she could breathe. At the very least, the creature seemed to have no interest in mauling the rest of Claire—just her hand. He grappled with her, trying to flip her onto her back, and screeched his frustration in her ear. His breath was fouled with an acrid mix of pulped paper and the sour sweetness of rotted fruit.

There was arguing going on above, and a fretting sound she assumed was Brevity struggling to reach her, but the creature was a weight that ground Claire's cheek into the rubbish of books beneath her. The leather of an ancient and moisture-ruined cover stuck to her skin and delaminated away from its book like a bloated corpse. The most Claire could do was keep her hand curled, tucked beneath her breast as the muse's claws pierced their way through the skin and muscle of her back.

"Claire!" A familiar voice cut through the haze of pain and replaced it with the cold shock of alarm. Hero's voice and the clatter of footsteps confirmed Rami was with him. But Hero was a character with an unwritten book in tow. It'd be like introducing blood into shark-filled waters. Claire writhed but couldn't twist enough to see more than the muse's claws.

"Stay back!" Her voice sounded hoarse and small, smothered into the floor. She felt choked on dust. "It eats books!"

"Claire—" Hero's voice sounded closer. She felt the weight shift on her back, as if the monster was about to take note of the same fact.

No. A wild protectiveness seared the exhaustion out of her veins. *Not him. Not if we got him back.* She shoved against the floor, dislodging the muse off her shoulders at a moment of imbalance. She ripped her glove off as she stood and exposed her stained palm to the air. *"You can't have any of them."*

The pale creature had skidded to his knees, ripping the tangling fronds of books with his teeth. He had half turned toward the direction of Hero's voice, but he caught sight of Claire's arm and froze. Claire was close enough to see the way a shiver passed over the surface of his featureless face.

"You can't have them," Claire repeated again. "But it's the ink that's done that to you, isn't it? Developed a taste for it?" Claire shakily raised the scalpel to her arm and slashed down. "There's plenty here. Come, then."

The blade bit into her skin, precisely severing the thin floss of blue that hemmed black in. Claire barely registered as the inspiration flaked away from her skin and fluttered to the ground. Line of inspiration tourniquet broken, a cold flooded up her arm. Claire didn't want to see, but she looked down anyway. Bleak, inky liquid swarmed up her biceps and disappeared up her sleeve. She felt the odd kind of frost-prickled warmth slam into her ribs, ripping the breath out of her as it spread. It swept up her shoulder and chased goose bumps up her neck. Claire felt it when the ink seeped, a film of taint, into her eyes. Her vision went blurry, then dark and buzzing with multicolored serpents of shadow smothering everything.

Everything except the cold that seized her as the ink wrapped around her brain, and her heart, and she lost herself in a scream.

# 33

# ????

ONCE UPON A TIME.

No. That's not how the story began at all.

Start again.

From the beginning?

Or the end. It matters not to us.

Who is us?

Once upon a time . . .

. . . Something is missing.

Something is missing. Once upon a time. Something is missing. Once upon a— Something is missing. Something is missing. Once upon— Something is missing. Something is missing. Something is missing. Once— Something is missing. Something is missing. Something is missing. Something is missing. Something is missing. Something is missing. Something is missing. Something is missing. Something is missing. Something is missing. Something is missing. Something is—

Do you want to hear a story?

# 34

# HERO

Myrrh.

Huh. Well, that just figures, doesn't it?

*Librarian Gregor Henry, 1941 CE*

HERO RAN INTO A charnel house of horrors. Books were flayed everywhere he looked, paper entrails twisting suspended in the air as if from butcher's hooks. Many of the dead of the Dust Wing rested, content with their tombs and dust, but not here. Here was where stories had gone destructive and turned on their corpses instead.

He had hesitated at the sight when he and Rami had broken through into the clearing where they'd tracked Claire and Brevity. He'd hesitated, and that'd been enough. Claire had shouted, the scalpel had impossibly cast one sliver of light in the dark, and then the corpses around him ceased to matter.

Hero dived into the viscera of paper and gore. Bile rose in his throat every time he crushed a brittle spine under his heel, but he hurtled himself forward. He tore at the paper skins that tangled him. He would tear at his own skin next.

Ink swallowed Claire, between one breath and the next. No, "swallow" was too natural a word. It *absorbed* her, leaving behind a bleak

Claire-shaped figure stained so dark it was impossible to make out against the darkness. The sight stopped him cold, just a step away. Her warm brown skin swallowed shadows, until even the ruffle of her uneven skirts and the small clasps at the tips of her braids turned pitiless black.

He lurched into motion again but was stopped by Rami's hand at his hip. "It's ink," Rami reminded him. As if Hero could forget, forget the feeling of his own skin decaying and crumbling in on itself, the feeling of drowning in ashes, smothered and lost. As if he could forget the way Claire had screamed, which was why he needed to reach her *right now*—

It was a testament to how weak he was that Brevity broke past Probity first. The ink-bleached muse had fallen and struggled to get to his feet. Brevity scrambled across the bowl of shredded parchment but was still too far away when the muse zeroed in on Claire. It sniffed the air and clacked its teeth. Brevity lunged, tackling it around the ankle and dragging it to the ground with her. The muse fell, outstretched claws passing within a whisper of Claire's unmoving obsidian face.

Brevity wrestled it back, biting back a yelp as the stained muse spun around and turned his claws on her. The sound drew the first lurch of movement, though everyone but Hero seemed too busy to notice. Only Hero saw as the black statue that was Claire twitched her limbs. Her head tilted at a sharp, mechanical angle, while the rest of her appeared to move with the sinuous nature of the ink itself. When her head turned its bleak gaze in Hero's direction, his skin chilled surely as if a naked blade had scraped along it.

"Help us," Hero whispered. To himself, to Claire, to gods he didn't believe in. None, at least, would hear and answer prayers in the darkest corner of the afterlife.

The ink that had subsumed Claire appeared to shudder in its

depths and gave a slow blink. She turned its attention to the feral muse wrestling with Brevity on the floor. She stretched out one arm, garnering everyone's attention. Hero half expected the ink to drop from her fingertip, but she opened her mouth and spoke.

"*You.*" It was Claire's voice, but splintered and shadowed by something else. The presence of *something else* was heavy in the air, but it felt like the shadow of an eclipse. Not a single entity, but crowding nonetheless. Like a swarm of blackbirds. It clotted the air and made it difficult for anyone to move as the ink-stained Claire took one step, then two. Black pools bloomed beneath her feet, as if the ink was spreading, but always retracted as she stepped away again.

Hero had an irrational urge to reach out and touch her, to grab for the footfalls of ink. What would happen now, Hero wondered, if that ink touched him again? Nothing good seemed to come of it, but would he be stained like a human, or bleached like a muse? What was the wick of a story, when you've already burned your book?

Brevity had the feral muse by the shoulders and was struggling valiantly to pin his arms back, but the creature outweighed Brevity by at least a stone, and it almost lurched free as Claire stopped in front of it.

Claire appeared to study it, its bleak, expressionless face like a statue carved out of ebony. "Listen," the many voices whispered. A black fingertip pressed to the middle of the pale creature's forehead. The ink-bleached muse began to shriek.

"You're hurting him!" Brevity attempted to pull the muse she'd just been wrestling back, but Rami lurched forward and stopped her.

"No, she's not. Look."

The point where Claire's finger brushed the muse's forehead had begun to darken, as if bruised. Hero followed the shadow beneath the muse's bone white skin and drew a breath. Like ink dropping through water, the muse's natural coloring was returning. Orange skin, sunrise red hair. Slowly the color seeped in, pushing the white and black ahead of it like a wave. Ink pooled at the point of contact and hesitated at the surface of the muse's forehead for just a moment before the surface tension seemed to break. The ink flew up Claire's finger in a veiny line, black on black, and the muse fell backward.

"Gaiety?" Brevity startled as she grabbed him, as if he was lighter, less weighed down with snarling muscle and hunger. A perplexed look crossed her face as she hesitantly lowered the muse to the ground, but he didn't rouse.

"What did she do?" Probity dropped to the other side, checking over the unconscious muse with an urgency that bordered on mothering. Brevity let her take Gaiety out of her arms, and for a moment Probity clasped her hands. It struck Hero as almost like an embrace, or a good-bye.

"Dear god . . ." Rami breathed the words like a curse, or a prayer. It took a moment in the dim spectral twilight to see what he meant. Ink wept from Claire's eyes, skidding down her cheeks briefly before being absorbed again by her skin. Her lips parted, and liquid, viscous and darker than blood, tumbled over her lips.

She'd taken in Gaiety's ink, but this was even more than that. Ink had stained, then soaked Claire, and now she was suffused with it. She didn't blur and turn pale like the muses. She didn't absorb and rot into nothing like a book. She was human—the paper of her soul was primed for stories. But she was trying to hold on to too much of it.

"Claire." Brevity shoved to her feet but was stopped by Probity's grip on her arm.

"Don't," Probity said firmly. There was sympathy there, but at a remove. The kind of look you gave when someone lost their goldfish. "You can't help her."

Brevity twisted her arm free. "I have to do something."

"She's a lost cause!" Probity struggled, not able to keep hold of Gaiety's body and Brev both. Her voice threaded with pleading. "But you're not."

Brevity stopped, and the moment held its breath around her. Hero's voice felt stopped up in his throat. Claire was dying, or worse, behind them. But Brevity's sibling muses were here, alive, not drowning in shadow. He had a deep, wounded familiarity with being a heart caught in two places. He couldn't bring himself to pull anymore. There was a coin-flip moment of doubt as he watched Brevity's eyes, but the coin landed true.

"If I don't help her, I am." Brevity shoved to her feet. She didn't look back, despite the twist in her expression. Hero began to breathe again, but tides of ink writhed and sank like eddies across Claire's frozen form. Brevity ran and threw open her arms.

Her fingertips slid into Claire's palm, and their hands closed as if on instinct. For a moment Brevity glanced to Rami and Hero, wide-eyed, until ink began to invade across her knuckles, beading across her skin and leaving colorless flesh behind. She stifled a gasp.

"Sis! Stop!"

"I'm not letting go." Brevity's lips moved around the whisper, words falling slightly out of sync with the sound. Propane blue began to wither and dry to cornflower on her cheeks.

"We have to do something," Hero whispered, and the helplessness that raged up in him threatened to burn him up whole. "Anything."

Rami's head came up, a thoughtful expression on it. "Okay."

He started forward, sending a spike of terror through Hero's chest. "No! No, no, no. That ink messes up everyone it touches."

Rami shook his head, gently taking Hero's hand off his shoulder and holding it in his. "Not me. I figured it out. Didn't you?"

"What?"

"Souls," Rami said, a gentle smile breaking over his features before he let go of Hero's hand and ran toward Claire and Brevity. He swept something up off the ground, something that glimmered thin and blue. Only after he slapped it on Brevity's arm did Hero recognize it as the inspiration gilt that had protected Claire. It was a thin thread, but Rami returned it to Brevity's forearm like a talisman.

Then Rami dropped to his knees in front of the two women, pressed his hands to each of their cheeks, and appeared to begin to pray.

# 35

# BREVITY

Myrrh. Myrrh. MYRRH, sod it! Souls. That's what they didn't want me to know. Librarian Poppaea rebelled in order to acknowledge and free the fragmented souls of books. It didn't work, obviously. Perhaps Old Scratch thought we librarians would be more compliant if we thought it was just books and magic. The devil obviously has never met a bibliophile. Rebellion is in a reader's blood.

Stories are slivers of us, all of us. What makes a story real is the soul of the author. We're humanity, splintered into the stories we tell ourselves. I doubt the old demon would be pleased to know I've rediscovered this. I'll need to feign ignorance; perhaps we all will. But future librarians need to know.

The logbook keeps a librarian's secrets, until they're needed. Well then, old book. It appears we have work to do.

*Librarian Fleur Michel, 1782 CE*

THE BRUSH OF RAMI'S palm on her cheek had been the end. Or perhaps it had been the words, echoing long after her sight faded. Guttural, heart-piercing prayers, colliding like wayward meteors in the dark. Maybe the end had been long before that. All the paths led to here and now.

When she could see again, the Dust Wing was gone. Everything was gone, replaced with . . . color. Not the rainbows-and-unicorns kind of color. No, the miasma that swam around Brevity and clogged her throat was the spectrum of light off the surface of something dark and deep. There was no breaking the surface here. This was oil slicks and crystalized lava. It was like breathing bismuth, with its rainbows of geometry shaped by very old, old things.

Brevity floated in a world of specters and in a sea of ink.

A darker blot loomed, growing larger like a whirlpool that the world turned around. Brevity let the current pull her, for lack of another destination. The shadows grew, and eventually she could make out a solid thing, a sliver darker than ink at the core of it. The piece at the axis was fragmented and melting. It was a kernel of an idea, an unfinished shape that lost edges, gained edges, until it was nearly impossible to discern what was underneath the roiling black.

Nearly.

The air felt punched from Brevity's lungs. "Claire." A familiar jut of stubborn chin gave way to long braids that dripped and melted like candle wax. Brevity tried to swim forward through the air, but it was harder now. As if the colors were swirling through her, not around her. A furious dog paddle drifted her in the right direction. The effort sent little eddies that ate away at and disseminated what was left of a shoulder. "Oh, boss."

The kernel of Claireness rotated like a tumbling asteroid in the void. Her face was carved out of obsidian, cold nothing instead of warm, beautiful brown. Only the shifting ridge of eyelashes told Brevity that her eyes were opening.

Brevity let herself drift, afraid even the slightest current would carry more of Claire's core away. Never mind the way her limbs felt increasingly light and gauzy, as if she herself was being erased. "What have they done to you?"

"A gentle colonization." Brevity flinched and just barely stopped herself from twisting at the voice. Rami stood as if on solid ground. If solid ground were at right angles with any sense of up and down that Brevity's brain had. The ink swirled around him, ruffling his feathers like a breeze, but didn't appear to sink in. He studied her for a long moment, face growing graver. He held out a hand. "They're being less careful with you."

Brevity reached out and trembled with the certainty that her fingertips were not going to stop at Rami's palm, but he clasped around her wrist with a precise kind of confidence and pulled. Brevity fluttered toward him as if she weighed nothing at all, and when he set her feet gently to the ground—his ground—it felt more like sticking to the filmy surface of a bubble than standing.

The puddle that made up Claire, thankfully, did not stir at all. She didn't appear to notice their presence, or if she did, she simply chose not to care. Brevity swallowed down the feeling of impending grief. "I can see the ink, but . . . the books like me. They wouldn't do this to us. What is this?"

"Souls," Rami said quietly. "The heart of any story is a little, tiny sliver of an author's soul. That's how any story is made."

"What?" Brevity blinked rapidly, trying to hold on to that thought. It felt important somehow, the way dream revelations felt important right before disappearing upon waking.

"Later." Rami's voice was hard and grounding. "All you need to understand is that the ink is slowly taking over Claire, piece by piece.

Trying to bury her under its own existence. We need to anchor her before I—before I try what I'm going to try. Otherwise we could lose her too."

"Okay." Brevity took a deep breath and held a little tighter to Rami's hand. "Right. Claire?"

With Rami's anchoring influence, the black core appeared to be turning in a slow orbit. Claire's face began to turn away without stirring.

Right, it wasn't just Claire in there, and it certainly wasn't Claire in control. Brevity needed something the ink would respond to. Something that would get its attention, and also Claire's.

"Do you want to hear a story?" Brevity breathed, through searing tears that felt like they were flooding her throat. "I promise it's a good one."

There was no color inside the ink that had smothered Claire; too much was going on beneath the surface. But there was a ripple, however faint. The wax-wasting drip of her hair slowed, as if cooling.

"A story. A soul for a story, and a story for a soul." Rami's voice was thoughtful and he was nodding when Brevity glanced back. "Try it again."

Brevity swallowed and focused on Claire, the familiar outline she could still pick out through the black. "This is a story of a woman who lived in a library."

The edge of the puddle had a questing tendril that stayed reaching toward Brevity even as the center turned. She chewed on her lip. "There was a woman who lived in a library, not because she was a great reader. Not because she was a great writer. Not because she was anything special at all, but because she'd lost the way of her own story."

Claire didn't stir, and with the melting slowing, she looked more like a statue wrought in ebony. She was drawing out the ink, not Claire.

Rami shook his head, and Brevity grasped desperately for something to separate the two.

It wasn't fair. Claire was the storyteller, not Brevity. The only story Brevity ever had, she stole. This was all on her shoulders, and they would all die here in the ink because Claire wouldn't listen. "You're so stubborn," Brevity hissed through clenched teeth. A watercolor of frustration took on the bold strokes of anger and Brevity let it. "She was so stubborn, this woman in the library. She was selfish and mean and lashed out at anyone who tried to help her. She wielded a blade against books and words against everyone else. She was so wrapped up in her own self-pity, so certain of all that she'd lost, that she couldn't see all she had gained. All of us that were right there, right there in front of her and hurting and confused and scared just as much as she was! We were right there!"

Brevity's eyes were full of tears. Perhaps that's why she couldn't make sense of the way the ink moved over Claire's skin now, rippling, shifting, almost drying into black scales. Half-fractured and curled in on herself as she was, Claire looked like a dragon's egg ready to hatch—or rot away. Brevity held on to her anger; it felt solid in her chest. It was the only thing that kept her pinned here—wherever here was—besides Rami's hand.

"She was selfish and cruel, and she acted like it was because she was smarter, stronger, than everyone else. But she wasn't. She was just stupid. So stupid she couldn't see the friends that surrounded her, the women who were not her enemies, prisoners, or rivals, but friends. She was so stupid it took the deaths of hundreds—hundreds of god-damn wonderful people—to realize it. It was your fault, Claire! Okay? I'll finally say it. It was *your* fault, and none of this would have happened if you had just talked to me! And not—"

A shiver, starting somewhere distant and rolling right through

Brevity's chest, stole her breath. Black scales began to flake and peel. Beneath, just beneath, were the tiniest freckles of brown skin. Distantly, Brevity realized Rami was praying. It seemed fitting, trapped in her own confessional. "I blamed you, Claire. I said I didn't but I did. And then when there might have been a way to fix it, you just—you just gave up. When it was no longer your job to care, about the books, about me, you just gave up." The world spun, as if she'd lost touch with the ground again. Which was strange, because Brevity couldn't even feel her toes. She was fairly certain it was her turn to melt. "I'm here to make you decide, right now, whether you are giving up on yourself or not. You're not a story, Claire. You're a human; you're my human. And if you end, I'm ending with you."

She couldn't feel Rami's hand. Everything was color. That's what black was, wasn't it? All color, all the potential color of the world together, minus light. Everything and nothing at once. There was no wall between the air in her lungs and the air without. Only the low, steady pulse of Rami's prayerful words in some angelic tongue. The ink was ignoring her now, passing through her the way she herself passed away, in favor of drifting along the currents of Rami's words. Black peeled away to reveal a brown cheek. Claire was under there, surviving and wonderfully human in every way Brev was not.

Brevity would never be human; she was a muse. So as the language of the spheres rolled through her head, she did what muses do. She let go of the allure of story, let inspiration and ink fall through her fingers, and fell to Earth.

# 36

# HERO

Going mad is an excellent defense. Nothing is so discounted,
dismissed, as an eccentric woman speaking the truth.

*Librarian Fleur Michel, 1792 CE*

"NO, NO, NO, NO . . ." A keening sound shook Hero out of his shock
and pulled his gaze away from Rami. Probity rocked on the ground,
holding Gaiety to her chest, but her attention was only on Brevity. She
took sobbing breaths and straightened. "No. I can fix this. I *won't* let
her do this." Probity abruptly lowered her unconscious younger muse
to the ground. She started forward with intent in her wet eyes.

Hero drew in a breath and had Rami's sword raised and leveled at
Probity's throat before he exhaled. The muse's reddened eyes narrowed. "Get out of my way, book."

"I don't have one of those anymore." Hero's quiet admission startled a reaction out of Probity. Hero hardened his jaw and kept himself
and the blade between Probity and the others. "I don't think I get to
be a story without a book. Then again, I haven't been sure what I am
for a while. I've tried and thought I was winging it, you know." His
smile was a snarl, but it wasn't directed at Probity. "I was a loyal as-

sistant for Brevity. I was a clever rival for Claire. I tried to be a questing hero for Rami. An angel that needs a hero—imagine that."

Probity made an impatient noise and tried to brush past the blade. Hero twitched his wrist. It was a tiny movement, but just enough to flick the tip of the sword into the soft of Probity's palm. She drew back with a hiss, and Hero waited. He waited calmly, silently, until Probity raised her chin and met his gaze with glittering hatred in her eyes.

"I've tried to be a lot of good things for each of them, in every way they need to be loved. But if you threaten them, if you take one single step closer . . ." Hero's breath broke. He slid his foot forward, relishing it as Probity jumped back a step at the end of his blade. "For you, for their sake, I will be the wickedest and worst monster. That's a promise."

Muses were always in motion, so when Probity held still it was an unnatural sensation. Her breathing was fast as she tried to get her emotions under control. "What happened to Verve?"

"Who?" Hero tilted his head. "The other monster you created? We encountered her in the stacks. I fed her my book, and she died."

"You fed her . . . ?" Shock, horror, and a flash of grief cycled quickly through Probity's expression before settling into a wary realization. "You really mean your book is gone. A character surviving past its book. That's an abomination, if not impossible. You are a monster."

"I could be. As I said, I am still discovering what I am." Hero's brittle smile cracked as he flicked the blade again. "Your experiment has failed, muse. Take your people and go. The Library isn't your plaything."

"My people." Something of the anger withered and died in Probity's eyes as she repeated the words. Her gaze went past Hero's shoulder to Brevity again. She took her next breath like one would take a punch in the gut. "She . . . I'd hoped . . . But you're right."

The hostility deflated out of the air then, but Hero kept his sword leveled as Probity crouched down, slung the unconscious Gaiety in her arms. She started to turn, then stalled. When she looked down Hero's blade, it was as if it wasn't even there. "Do me a favor, monster."

"Nah," Hero said, but Probity didn't miss a beat.

"Tell her . . ." Her lips worked a moment before she found the words. ". . . tell her . . . ideas never die. Just . . . tell her I said that. That I still say that."

Then Probity appeared to fold the air around them like origami until they disappeared in a displacement of dust.

Hero hesitated, frozen in place a moment longer. His pulse thudded in his ears, and he half expected some new threat to emerge out of the deep shadows of the Dust Wing. But nothing moved except the fragile drift of tattered and tormented books. It was so still that Hero's eyes stung. It must have been the dust.

A small grunt behind him reentered his thoughts. "Rami?" Hero lowered the sword, not quite entirely dropping his guard as he glanced behind him.

They were a trio of statues, Claire painted in an oblivion of blacks and Brevity's blue skin as pale as a robin's egg. Rami knelt between them, a hand on each of their faces. The concentration knit his face, as if he was doing personal battle with the ink. Hero felt a strangling feeling in his chest at the thought he was going to lose them, all three of them, right here and now. He couldn't do that. He could bear to live without his story; he could bear to live as a servant of the Library; he could even bear to live as an abomination without a book. But if the Fates took these three maddening souls from him now, he would give himself over to the despair and eternity of the Dust Wing for good.

Then Rami drew a breath and whispered a single word: "Peace."

The invading pallor in Brevity's skin retreated and appeared to swirl, absorbing into the thread of inspiration twined on her arm. Dapples of brown caught Hero's eye as the ink appeared to dry up and flake away from Claire. Both women fell like deadweight, Rami sagged, and Hero just managed to sweep forward to support him. It ended with the four of them entangled on the floor of the Dust Wing.

They were a tiny island of warm skin and wheezing breaths in the center of a tomb. Hero struggled to right Brevity against his shoulder. He distantly noted the tear of paper beneath his heel as another Dust Wing tragedy, but for a moment—just a moment—he didn't care. He didn't *care* because Rami's chest was heaving and Claire was unconscious but drooling against his feathered trench coat.

When Rami managed to pull himself together and met Hero's gaze, there was no way to hide the relief that burst onto Hero's face with a grin. "You did it, old man."

"I didn't—I did, but . . ." Rami paused, bowing his head for a moment, and Hero realized he was late recognizing the tears on the Watcher's cheeks. "So many souls, Hero."

"Souls?"

Rami's look was searching when he finally met Hero's gaze. His brow still set with worry and streaked with dust and sweat. "That's what the ink is, the fragment souls of books. Remember what the golem's letter said? *The written and the writer are the same.* Books and authors are made of the same stuff." Rami shook his head wonderingly. "I wondered, as an angel I can reach lost souls, and then it seemed too dire to not at least try . . ."

Rami trailed off, but the logical leap was too much for Hero's mind to make. Books didn't have souls. They had characters and pages and story, and good ones might seem *soulful*, but books were—Hero was . . .

Hero wasn't sure of anything anymore. He looked away. Most of the jet-black ink had flaked away from Claire's skin, even if a mythical kind of oil-slick shine clung to her tangled hair. She seemed merely napping against Rami's chest, more peaceful than Hero had ever seen her. "Do you think they knew? All this time?"

Rami considered and shook his head. "I don't know. But I do know we should get them out of here. Let's go home." He lifted Claire easily, even if he was slower to get his feet under him. Whatever he had done had worn on the angel as well. Brevity was light enough that Hero had no such trouble.

"I'm—I'm glad you're okay," Rami said quietly. He took his time drawing a feather. It made a complicated pattern through the air in what Hero assumed would be a means to travel back to the Library. "I heard part of what you said. To Probity."

"Did you? How distracting." Hero shifted Brevity in his arms and stepped closer under Rami's arm without quite looking him in the eyes. "Of course I'm fine. Always fine."

Rami was terrible at telling lies, but not at reading them. Hero could feel the weight of his concerned frown as feathers and the frost-clean smell of Rami's angelic magic kicked up through the dust. His voice was soft and lost in Hero's hair. "I'm glad. I was afraid this—this was going to change things."

*It already has,* Hero wanted to say, but the Dust Wing folded in on itself and the sweep of Rami's sheltering magic stole the air from his lungs.

# 37

# HERO

I still feel the place in my chest where my story should be.

—My book. I meant my book. Where my book should be.

That's what I meant.

Where is a goddamn eraser for this log?

*Apprentice Librarian Hero, 2020 CE*

HERO KNEW HOW STORIES began. *Once upon a time.* After hundreds of Dust Wing books passed through him, he even understood how stories end. *Happily ever after.* Except when not. Nothing had prepared him for the agony of the middle. The hollow pocket against his heart where his book should be was a great, aching question mark. It was an end; it was a beginning; it was wrong and completely foreign terrain.

If this was what it was like living outside a story, Hero thought maybe death had been kinder. He had these thoughts as Rami swam them in and out of the dark, tripping across nowheres and in-betweens until the familiar glass zoo of Walter's transport office took shape around them. He walked down familiar hallways and thought of endings and beginnings and the terrifying watercolor of unknowns that spanned the two. He thought of Rami and Claire and Brevity, and the fragile way they kept going on after the end. And then he said the exact opposite of what he was thinking.

"Well, this is familiar," Hero pronounced as he followed Ramiel through the doors of the Arcane Wing. Rami strode to the nearest couch and laid Claire down with a painstaking gentleness.

An elbow shifted into his ribs. "I'm *awake* this time." Brevity's words were a slurry of exhaustion. She'd started to stir not long after they'd reappeared in the transport office. She looked pale and grumpy. "Put me down, please."

"My pleasure." Hero picked the armchair and carefully extracted himself until Brevity was in a somewhat comfortable sitting position. "It's my personal policy not to coddle suicidal idiots."

"I would say everyone present falls under that classification," Rami said with a level look in Hero's direction.

"I saved your life." Hero had begun making tea without realizing it. He stopped, glared into the teapot in his hands, and chose a relaxing chamomile. Claire would hate it when she woke up. When.

The water had heated to a near simmer by the time Brevity heaved herself up on her elbows, as if taking stock. "We should be in the Unwritten Wing."

"I didn't think it prudent to bring you in proximity to the books until I knew you were all stable," Rami said evasively. "How's your arm?"

"You mean before you knew if I had developed a taste for story flesh or not," Brevity said, and deflated back into the armchair. She stuffed her arm under a throw pillow before adding, a bit sullenly, "I haven't, by the way."

"As the sole remaining representative of the Library who has not gone under an existential transformation—"

"I didn't transform!" Hero squawked.

"—*or* existential crisis heretofore unknown by our understanding of the universe," Rami continued smoothly, "I feel comfortable ordering all of you to sit down and *stay down* until I can at least create a concise record of this disaster."

"Not as if anyone can read your chicken scratch," Claire mumbled into the couch cushions. She slit her eyes open and grimaced at the light. As if in response, the lamps of the Arcane Wing dimmed a notch. She squinted with a sour expression. "What are you lot staring at?"

"Boss! Oh—oh gods. I'm so glad you're okay." Tears started to well at Brevity's eyes before the look suddenly dried up into stricken. Her shoulders started to creep up toward her ears. "Claire—"

"You have nothing to apologize for, so don't you dare." The harsh edges fell away from Claire's tone. She made an aborted attempt to sit up before consigning herself to the couch. "You were doing what you thought was best. That's what a librarian does."

"I lied to you. I tricked you," Brevity insisted.

"And I allowed a damsel to come to harm, entered the Library, and promptly terrorized the damsel suite without asking." Claire's mouth twisted and for the first time she looked down at her unstained hands. Not a trace of the ink remained. She rubbed her thumb against her forefinger. "That wasn't right. I'm sorry. We were both operating under stressful concerns."

Moisture returned to Brevity's eyes, so Hero hurried along to a different point of relevance. "All the same, making an enemy of the Muses Corps would be a bother."

Brevity took the distraction. "Probity . . . ?"

"Left. Along with Gaiety." Hero hesitated, sending a questioning look to Rami. There was a lot to disclose, now or later. He sighed when the angel shook his head grimly.

Brevity's face crumpled. She mulled this over with a distant sorrow. "She won't go back to the muses, not with Gaiety. I can't see them tolerating something like that. Verve and Gaiety were so loyal to her, I don't even know how much she told them. I—I think Probity had her own ideas about stories, ones that no sane muse in the corps would ever have endorsed." Her mouth twisted, bitter. "Which is why she came to me."

"From my brief acquaintance, she seemed to trust you and hold you in high regard," Rami said.

Brevity's smile was thin with skepticism, and Hero couldn't stand the tedious cycle of self-blame a moment longer. He flopped onto Claire's couch noisily and began to pick dried mud from his coat. "At least now I can officially say I've seen a more odious place than the Unwritten Wing. You've been grandstanded by the Dust Wing, ladies."

He waited for Claire's sharp rebuttal, or at the very least a dismissive noise. When none came, he turned his head. She had tucked her legs to her chest and was nearly swallowed by the pillows Rami had piled around her. That, and the vulnerable uncertainty in her eyes, gave her a more delicate appearance than she normally allowed. Delicate—not breakable—like a fine blade. She studied him with disbelief. "You're really okay."

Claire never asked questions, not really. She wielded challenging statements and demanded verification. Hero cleared his throat and studied the ragged tear the muse's claws had made in the shoulder of his coat. These stains would *never* come out. Ink and stains and gods knew what else. He was going to have to ask Brevity if Hell had a tailor soon. "I'm here, aren't I?"

"You are. I hadn't been sure you would be," Claire said with unnatural quiet. Some of the tension left her and she unwound herself from her seat to straighten her shoulders. She held out a palm. "Hand it over, then."

Hero was familiar with that pose, that posture, that steel in her eye as sharp as a scalpel. His stomach dropped, and he found his filthy cuff fascinating again. "Hand over what?"

"Your book. Let's see what a muck you've made of it this time and how many hours of back pain and labor I—" Claire paused. "That I or Brevity is in for to fix it."

It was under his nails. The damned clay was under his *perfectly nice* nails. He cast about for a file, but of course Claire wasn't the type to keep appropriate grooming products on hand.

"Hero?" Claire said.

"I—" Hero cleared his throat and had to count to three before he had the courage to raise his gaze to meet Claire's. His insides felt a little hollow. "I don't have it."

Claire's eyes flew wide. "You *lost* your book?!"

"I didn't—" Hero started, but Claire was already halfway off the couch, though she didn't let go of the arm for support.

"Of all the irresponsible— How are you still sitting here if you left it in the Dust Wing? You grand fool, we need to go back immediately and—"

"Claire." Rami caught her before she could stumble away from the couch. He firmly guided her back in a way only Rami could get away with. "He didn't lose it." Once she was seated again, he glanced at Hero. His tone was sympathetic but unforgiving. "Tell her."

Rami's eyes were encouraging, and Claire's were confused. A phantom of panic threatened in Hero's throat. It would change everything, everything he didn't want changed, he realized. The thought descended like a shock of water. Being a broken book—Claire's pain in the ass, Brevity's assistant, Rami's . . . dear gods, whatever he was to Rami now.

He didn't want any of it to change. He didn't want to run away, or fix his book, or be anything but what they accepted him as. He glanced to Brevity for reprieve, but her look was curious as well.

The mud on his coat had somehow coated his tongue and Hero had to swallow again before he could start. "There was a struggle, with the muse in the Dust Wing. She . . . consumed . . . my book."

"What?" Brevity startled to her feet, and she was at least steadier than Claire was.

"It's gone," Hero said to the floor.

"That's impossible." Claire's voice was oddly clipped, like she'd dug her fingernails into the shreds of her logic. She shook her head. "Explain yourself."

By the time Hero had haltingly described his version of events, the chamomile had gone so oversteeped even he wouldn't try to serve it to Claire. Rami had interjected corrections a couple of times, and picked up on what he saw when Hero fell. Hero had gotten to the part where he'd kissed Rami and chose editorial discretion to skip quickly over it with a rush of heat in his cheeks. Rami sat there just looking calm and supportive. Damn the man. Claire had started out with interrogative interruptions but had slowly dropped to silence.

No one was eager to jump into analysis, which made Hero grateful. He managed to listen to the tick of the Arcane Wing's cursed clock count a dozen more seconds before Brevity sniffled hard. She was wiping her eyes furiously but saved a watery grin for Hero. "It sounds like you almost—I woulda never forgiven myself if we'd lost you in there."

"Maybe you did," Hero said ruefully. His book was gone; that was the part a librarian should have been worried about.

"We didn't. You remain. Just as the ink remained." Claire had wrapped her arms over her chest as if she was holding on for dear life, but there was a distant look in her eyes. Hero could feel Claire's mind turning like an astrolabe, aligning events along some unknown mental star charts. She broke the spell with a blink and focused on Rami. "When you said you thought you could track Hero to the Dust Wing, was it—"

"Souls," Rami finally said the word that made the entire room feel like a released breath. "That's how I track anything. And it worked. I began to consider the idea after I read that line in the Unsaid Wing. The old Arcanist said *the written and the writer are the same.* And then the soul bridge in Chinvat tried to pass judgment on Hero, and . . . well."

"Stories—she meant stories. But if they're made of the same stuff, then that means stories are made of souls—" Brevity's eyes went wide as saucers.

"No," Claire whispered, and Hero's heart dropped. He felt irrationally disappointed as she started shaking her head. It shouldn't matter, her reaction. But somehow it did, because they were talking about what *he* was, and she was and . . .

"I would have known. I would have had to have known. Gregor would have *told* me. Or the log—" Claire straightened as if she'd touched a live wire. "The well. Rosia. I need to see the well."

"You need to rest," Rami started, but Claire was already teetering to her feet. The angel sighed and lent his arm. Claire charged down the aisle toward the back of the wing as fast as her battered body allowed.

That left Hero with Brevity. Luckily, his librarian was much steadier on her feet—and much more sensible—than the previous one. Brevity accepted a hand up but followed them at a sedate pace.

"You're you, Hero," she said, just loud enough for him to hear. "Claire just needs to work it out in her own head."

The upside-down feeling in Hero's head eased an inch. Brevity did that—saw the rough edges her people rubbed against one another and tried to smooth them. It was a remarkable trait, but Hero couldn't remember anyone ever acknowledging it. He tried, but his throat was already clogged with so many things, he could only nod. "Did you know?"

Brevity shook her head slowly. "I didn't—at least, I didn't think I did. I didn't put it together." She chewed on her lip. "Maybe Probity had."

Hero had too many emotions roiling like a pack of rats in his head to hold on to one more. He hesitated, then said, "She said something, before she left."

Brevity looked up, full of trepidation. "What'd she say?"

"She said to tell you"—Hero took a moment to recall the words exactly—"ideas never die."

The silence in Brevity's eyes as she quickly looked away spoke volumes. Hero was literate in those silences, so he waited it out.

"It was something we said, back then. We thought we were invincible. We thought we could do anything. When I was a muse, we . . ." Brevity chewed her lip raw. Claire appeared to be having an argument with her black bird ahead of them. At least if she was that irascible, then Hero suspected she'd recover all right. "Muses are obsessed with humans. But we're not taught to care about humanity as *people*, just as creators. The end creation is what is important. Ever hear of an artist wrecking themselves for their art? That's a bad muse. And internalized capitalism."

"But you're not like that," Hero pointed out, and Brevity rewarded him with a tired smile.

"Nah. I was always curious about humans. Then I got kicked out and actually had to *deal* with one. Woof." Brevity pulled a face, but it was riddled with fondness as she glanced after Claire again. "Humans are a tough nut. It's obvious—at least to me—that a story is essential to the person who tells it. No matter how cliché or common your story is, it's *you* telling it, right? We understood that essential connection, but we didn't care much about the soul. Few muses care much what happens to the human after the story is told." Brevity fell quiet. "But taken too far, that's how you get folks like Probity."

Hero had a dozen questions queued up behind his tongue. He had a soul? Or just part of one? Was it his creator's? Every book was made of a soul? What did that mean—for anything? He felt starved for answers, but they caught up and all of Brevity's concern focused on Claire.

A well of shadows trumpeted out of the floor and cupped a basin within. The reservoir of ink at the back of the Arcane Wing remained, with one significant change. Claire's knees banged into the ledge as she dropped down. Hero's chest clenched as she leaned precariously over the edge with a gasp. "Rosia."

The others rushed to join her—and if Hero secured a firm grasp on her shoulder to keep her from tipping in, it was purely out of professional concern, of course. He needn't have worried. The interior of the well dropped away to a smooth concave of stone. The ink was gone, and left not a dab behind.

In its absence, instead, curled up tight as a seed, was a girl. Rosia lay on her side, arms pillowing her head. She didn't move. Claire jerked forward and Hero was glad he had a grip on her shoulder.

"No," Rami said from behind them, already moving past to drop down the slope of the basin. "Let me." He crouched down as he approached Rosia and reached out. His fingertips were still a breath away from her cheeks when her eyes blinked open.

A tick in Rami's shoulders put Hero on alert. Whatever he saw in the girl's face startled him. Rami stepped back as Rosia stretched, unfurling like a spring leaf. She rose to her feet, still facing away, full of an alien grace that her coltish limbs hadn't had before. She tilted her head one way, then another, as if releasing a crick in her neck. As if, a suspicious part of Hero's mind supplied, she was limbering up for a fight.

But when Rosia turned, pivoting on the ball of one foot like a dancer, her expression was relaxed. Her gaze, as it flicked around to each of them, felt altered. No longer spectral and eerie, but *focused*. She still had moonbeam eyes, but sharp as a crescent shaped by the dark.

"Rosia?" Brevity crouched at the side of the basin. There was a tension in her shoulders that said she was trying. She was trying to be librarian, do her duty, hold it together by her fingernails. Claire's shoulder shivered beneath his hand. They were all exhausted, all wounded and changed, one way or another. Hero recognized with a sudden certainty that if pressed to a fight one more time, it'd be too easy to break.

The smooth skin of Rosia's brow furrowed for a moment, perplexed, before she appeared to recognize Brevity. "Hello there."

Hero's alarm stalled—not decreasing, but freezing in place. Rosia's voice had been high and soft, a whisper from a ghost girl. The voice she wore now was warm and solid, like a well-made violin.

Brevity's face knit into concern. "Rosia? Is that really you?"

The damsel appeared to take that question seriously, pursing her lips for a silent second before nodding. "Quite. I am the most me that I have ever been, in fact."

"You're not Rosia." Claire's own voice was full of cobwebs. Hero felt her shiver before she cleared her throat and tensed again. "Rosia was a specter. A ghost girl from a ghost story."

"Rosia was that, for a long time." She didn't look upset by the accusation, just thoughtful. "She wanted to be more. Knew there was more. Tried to be more. But the story kept coming through. It was like drowning." Her pale eyes diverted down to the empty basin at her feet again. Toes scuffed against dry stone. "Easier to drown in ink."

Hero made a scoffing noise in his throat, if only to make sure the roil of emotion that clotted his mouth didn't come out as a sob. "Yet you don't look drowned. It destroyed me."

"It didn't mean to." Rosia looked serious and folded her hands in front of her chest. "You asked for a story and it tried to give you one."

"I wanted *my* story," Hero hissed.

"That was a mistake. Ink can't write what's not in you." Rosia took a step forward, hesitating when Claire flinched back. She stopped near Brevity, who appeared to be staring openly at Rosia with something approaching wonder, not suspicion. "I listened—read? Yes, I read. I read and I read all the stories, until I found myself again." A smile cut through Rosia's somber affect. She grinned down at her hands, wiggling them before turning that delighted glance on Brevity. "It took a while, but I found myself in stories. I don't have to be a ghost. I'm *not* a ghost."

"You're not a ghost," Brevity repeated with a little awe. "Everyone looks for themselves in story."

"It worked the same for you, didn't it? Once you started listening." Rosia turned her attention, sharp and bright, on Hero, and it felt like a dissection. "You put yourself together with stories too."

Hero had nothing to answer that. Rosia had touched the ink and found certainty; he had only survived with more questions.

Claire's head had been bowed, but it came up slow as a rising thought. "Rosia, where's your book?"

The girl looked down at her hands. They smoothed down her ivory skirt and came away clean. There was no lump in her pocket, no place to stash a small rectangle of paper. She let out a low breath and smiled at Brevity. "Librarian, can I go home now? I'm hungry and this place is too quiet."

"Rosia, your book—" Claire began sharply.

"I am my own story now." A first thorn of defiance pricked through Rosia's voice. She paused, considering. "Or I am many. I haven't decided yet. But I am enough."

The minute twitch Claire made traveled up Hero's arm like a quake. She opened her mouth, then closed it with a shiver.

"Librarian." Rosia had focused on Brevity again, and a kind of delight softened her face. "I am glad you're still here. Don't worry; I'll help with what's next. You won't do it alone."

Rosia moved swift as a breeze. She scrambled up the side of the basin, pecked a kiss on Brevity's cheek, and walked down an aisle.

"We should . . . go after her?" Rami asked more than made a statement.

Brevity, eyes still wide, with a hand to her cheek, shook her head. "Ah . . . no, I think she's going back . . ." She blinked at the spot where Rosia had been. "I think she's okay."

*Okay.* It was such a simple word. No reason for it to roil an inexplicable rise of bile and envy in Hero's mouth like it did. He swallowed hard.

"At least someone is," Rami said quietly, with his eyes on Hero's face. Whatever he could read there had softened his frown. "But what remains . . ."

Claire shivered, suddenly shaking off Hero's hand with a flick of irritation. He was almost glad after how strangely subdued she'd been. She extended a finger and brushed the tip over the dry, uneven rock bottom. "It's gone."

Claire had a complete lack of patience for stating the obvious. Hero felt obliged to remind her of this fact. "Stunning deduction."

The glare Claire rewarded him with was familiar and reassuring, even if her next question made it sound as if the entire incident were his fault. "*How?* Ink does not simply *disappear*, no matter what it's made of! Rosia obviously wasn't stained. So who took it?"

"Oh." Brevity made a surprised sound as she approached the other side of the well. She dropped into the empty basin before anyone could stop her. She stared at Claire with wide eyes. "You did. I think?"

Judging by the way Claire rubbed her face, Hero wasn't sure just how many more revelations even a human mind as stout as hers was up to today. "Explain."

"Ink acts on the same wavelength as inspiration gilt, right? That's what Probity said when she . . . stopped your arm." Even now, Brevity couldn't keep from running nervous fingers up her scarred forearm. "When muses carry inspiration, we don't get the entire story. Just the . . . the seeds. The sparky bits that get them going. The rest of the story comes along later." She gestured expansively to the empty rock where a pool of ink—souls?—had been.

Claire had been stubbornly crouching but let herself down to the ground abruptly. "It was me. I carried the stain. And when it was loosed in the Dust Wing, when I . . ." She stopped, frowned, corrected herself. "When *it* pulled the ink from that muse, all the rest of the ink could follow."

Brevity nodded slowly. "Maybe that's where they wanted to be the whole time. With other dusted books."

"To be with other ghosts . . . Rosia was the only one who could hear it. So it was a haunting," Claire murmured to herself. Her toes crept over the edge of the basin and she suddenly looked very small.

"Claire?"

Hero knew the way that one blinked to keep poison out of one's brain and tears out of one's eyes. Claire's shoulders swayed. "All those years, everything I did to them because I thought books were merely . . . like magic. Or memory."

Hero felt locked in place. His own feelings were a strangling vine—to be spiteful, to be right, was at the tip of his tongue. She had been cruel, cruel to him and to individuals like him, and she'd been biased, and she'd been *wrong*, and saying so wouldn't wipe away the wrongness of what she had done. He shouldn't be asked to forgive her; he shouldn't have to comfort her.

But he wanted to. The want to shore her up, wrap up the hurt, was so strong it ached, but Hero still couldn't do it.

Rami brushed past his shoulder. Gratitude, and a feeling warmer than that, muted all Hero's other thoughts as he watched the angel approach and silently sit next to Claire at the rim of the empty basin. Rami didn't say anything. He never had to. Claire met his eyes, and her chin wavered before she made a cracking sound and buried her face in her hands. Her shoulders twitched and jerked in a painful kind of silence.

"Boss . . ." Brevity said softly, and that appeared to make the shuddering worse.

Claire didn't cry. Claire didn't cry, and Hero didn't forgive. It was their natures, and natures were all they had left in the afterlife, but ferocious resentment burned a hole in Hero's chest. His nature had been written in his book, and that was gone and unlikely to do him any good ever again. He didn't know who he was now. But that meant he also didn't *have* to know.

His toes scuffed over the floorboards as his feet finally decided to move. The small sounds echoed like a gunshot that made Claire's shoulders flinch even as he dropped down to her other side. She didn't lower her hands from her face. It was so easy to touch her when he was prodding, or holding her back. But this was comfort, and an entirely alien action between them. His shoulders wouldn't unclench, wouldn't lean in to lend that solid presence that Rami was capable of. His silence stewed instead of supported. This wasn't him. Or perhaps it was. Did he have to decide that now too?

"Only you would set up such a difficult impasse. You and Hell," Hero said to the empty curve of stone beneath his toes. Everything ached. "Either you have been the worst kind of demon, or I'm a soulless abomination without a book. Either you're a monster, or I am."

The breath Claire took was loud and jagged between her clenched fingers. Her hands fell to her lap by fractions. She didn't lift her head. "I thought I knew, once. I thought I understood how things worked. I just . . ."

"It's okay," Hero said. He saw the way Rami's dark eyes watched him over Claire's head. Their angel, their shepherd of souls. What a sad flock they made for him. Hero dropped his gaze. "It's okay. I'm well versed at being the monster. Comfortable, even."

Claire snatched his hand. Her palm was still damp with hot tears. She gripped it and—hell, her strength must have returned to her, the way his knuckles stung in protest.

"No." Claire's voice had steadied. Her chin was locked against her chest, but her gaze was slanted sideways, fierce and searching. "You are not an abomination. You are not soulless. You are not a monster. I won't tolerate it."

The air had left his lungs at skin contact, and Hero's face felt hot. It was unacceptable, so he made sure his grimace was especially dramatic. "Fine, fine. If I call you a monster, will you stop crushing my hand? I need it. For things and reasons."

In her typical contrary manner, instead of letting go Claire gulped a surprised sound and yanked his arm into her lap. Hero fell against her shoulders and found he didn't fight too hard when Claire locked her hands around his elbow. She was warm. Her hair smelled like smoky tea leaves. Her voice was small and soft near his ear. "I don't know what happens now."

"It seems obvious to me." Rami's voice was gravel, like earth, and rocks that you could hold on to. His arm shifted, bracing both of them so they didn't fall over. "We'll be monsters together."

Hero's laugh sounded like a bark to his ears, jagged and out of use. He shook his head and glanced across the well. Brevity had hunkered down in the curve of stone, drawn-looking and hesitant.

"What's the matter with you?" Hero asked.

Brevity's eyes were big and threatening yet more tears. "I wasn't sure—I don't know if—"

"Oh, get over here already," Claire grumbled. She threw open the arm that wasn't trapping Hero in place, catching Brevity as she stumbled over. She fell into the rest of them, and Hero caught a particularly bony elbow to the stomach.

Brevity let out a wet warble that was muffled by Claire's hair. Hero couldn't make out what she said, but Claire shook her head. Some warmth had returned to her brown skin, and her eyes sharpened as she comforted the muse sobbing into her chest. "We'll be quite all right. Really, Brev, you're dampening my blouse."

The corner of Claire's mouth quirked up when laughter interrupted the muse's tears and then subsided into sniffles. It stayed soft as it caught Hero's eye and she nodded. The way her eyes drifted back to the stone told him enough. She hadn't known, still didn't have the answers, but this—this they had.

They sat there for a time, tangled and scarred and lost with each other, at the edge of a vast, quiet emptiness where certainty had been.

# 38

# BREVITY

What is a library? What is its real purpose? Is it just a room full of books? Any storehouse could qualify, in that case.

What makes a library, then? What is this grander institution that crosses realms, gods, beliefs? How can a good solid Norseman end up in a wing located in the Christian ideal of damnation? It doesn't seem to matter what the librarians believed when they were alive—here we are.

Maybe what makes a librarian is not what they believe. Maybe what makes a library isn't what it has, but what it does.

*Bjorn the Bard, 1433 CE*

IN PEACEFUL MOMENTS, THE Library played. Books didn't wake into characters. No one stirred off their shelves, but the Library had its own kind of ecosystem and sense of balance. When it felt all was well, it bloomed in ways only Brevity could see.

Brevity had checked on the damsels—Rosia, especially, who still stared at her in ways that made Brevity's stomach flutter. Brevity had done her duties, and then she had promptly decided to hide. She'd made a blanket fort of her desk and chair. From her nest, she could see the colors stretch and yawn out of the stacks like seeking tendrils.

Aquamarine pooled out of the topmost rows like a mist, gently eddying around an energetic, spiky carmine that was probing the air. Lower to the floor, a book had industriously stretched a vine of butter yellow, almost mimicking a pat of sunshine on the rug as it reached for the other side. The books on the other side must not have felt sociable, because they held their muddled rainbows close to their covers.

It was almost peaceful, if you didn't know what you were looking at.

She'd been reading a book, pretending to read a book. There was a reason people read in corners. It was a room made of one. Spine curved, arms bracketed, and the remaining walls made of the reassuring weight of a book. A self-constructed universe, for as long as you needed it. Or as long as the story lasted.

Brevity isolated that thought with a meditative mood, which meant she noticed the troubled storm-cloud presence at the door before seeing him. "Rami?" Brevity unburied herself a little from the blanket. "What are you doing up here?"

"Claire and Hero are fine," Rami reassured her, answering the unspoken question. He crossed the carpeted expanse of the lobby with that plodding kind of silence he used to mask his nature. Brevity couldn't help but notice the books didn't reach toward him. In fact, they withdrew a little, as if sensing the former angel's purpose. "I left them asleep on the couch, though I'm fairly certain Hero was faking exhaustion merely to pin Claire in place. I came to see how you're doing."

There was reproach in his gentle tone. He was a natural sheepdog, with his need to keep them together. There were differences—Brevity knew something unique had knit between those three—but still, Brevity was firmly part of his flock. He didn't approve of her coming back up to the Unwritten Wing alone instead of recuperating with the others.

She didn't know quite how to explain that she needed it. Needed to be here. Needed to see, knowing what she knew now. She tilted her head back to eye the ceiling. It was about the only place not loaded with books and colors. "I feel like a three-day-old turd."

The honesty was precisely calibrated for the grimace that appeared on Rami's face. "All the more reason you should rest. There's no lingering . . . ?"

His voice trailed off to an effective arrow that drew Brevity's gaze back down to her lap. Her left arm had emerged out of the blankets enough to see it. She could almost still make out where the inspiration gilt had rested for years, leaving a paler cornflower line against her blue skin. But scrawled over the top was a new jagged line of pure black, rimmed by bone white skin. Brevity resisted the urge to touch it. It was faintly raised, like a scar. If Brevity paid too much attention to it, she could almost swear she felt it run with a pulse that was just slightly out of sync with her own.

She tucked her arm under the blanket again. "Whatever ink is left in that seems happy where it is."

"The ink needed something to anchor to. It was the only solution I could think of," Rami said apologetically.

"It was the best of our crappy options." Brevity turned her attention back to the ceiling again. Had there always been a parquet inlay behind the arching beams? She could swear that was new. "It's not like I hadn't stolen it to begin with."

"You cherished it, though. And you gave it up to save Claire." He paused. "You gave up a lot."

There were no cobwebs in the dark corners of the ceiling. That disappointed Brevity for some reason. Didn't seem right to have a place this big and old without some spiders. Maybe if she thought about it hard enough the Library would let her have a spider or two.

"The muses were never going to take me back," she said after a pause.

"But Probity would have."

In anyone else, it would have been a cruel statement. But Rami had a way of lobbing the truth around without malice. He didn't dance; he wasn't discreet. Gifts of silence were for Claire; glib words were for Hero. Rami was for ripping the bandage off clean and acknowledging the wound with air and sunlight.

That didn't mean it didn't sting. Brevity chewed on her lip. "I wanted it. I wanted her to be right. I wanted . . ."

Rami let the sentence lie, unfinished, for a moment. A steadying weight came down as he touched her shoulder. "I know a little something of what it means to give up the idea of one home for the sake of another. I know what you did. And if you ever need to talk, I will listen."

"I . . ." Brevity finally dragged her gaze away from the ceiling. There was no expectation in Rami's serious face, just presence. Sometimes, simply being here was all the truth needed. Brevity nodded. "I'll remember that. Not now, but . . . All the sacrifices, I'm not sure it mattered. What did it do but prolong things? Even the inspiration I had." She made a vague gesture without looking at her arm again. "I gave it up, and now it's back, and something else."

Saying it almost made it worse. It was easier to imagine the black slivers racing up her forearm as something new, foreign. A bezoar to absorb the poison of the ink. Thinking of it too much made Brevity queasy, but of course, that was why Rami was there.

"Just as well. Muses can't absorb humanity. That's why the ink overwrote your companions instead."

There was compassion in Rami's voice, but an unflinching kind. Determined to see this through. Brevity rubbed her eyes and tried not to imagine she could see contorted black figures on the insides of her eyelids. "At least Claire was able to reverse Verve in the end."

"I wish I could have done more." Rami shook his head. "I have no idea how Claire survived that. There were too many, even for me. I could only release the bits of souls that were ready to let go."

"Where do they go when they 'let go'?" Brevity was fighting the urge to look back at the stacks, see if the books were listening. "If books and humans are made of the same soul stuff, where does a released book go? Did they all really just stay in the Dust Wing? Or go to Heaven? To their authors? Not all of them were dead yet."

"I'm not wise enough to say. Perhaps where all stories go when they end. Claire might know."

"Claire doesn't know." Saying it aloud felt like a betrayal, but it was true. She saw it the moment guilt crashed down across Claire's face at the realization. She'd been making amends for her harsh treatment of characters like Hero, but realizing she'd been the jailer of unwilling souls . . .

But she hadn't known, and as a result Brevity hadn't known. Claire could be forgiven because of her lack of education—her mentor hadn't shared everything in time—but Brevity? Brevity was a muse. She had ferried story stuff to and from humanity for decades. How could she not have realized what she was carrying?

Stories were made of soul stuff, fragmented and spurred from their human authors. Humans could create because they could birth little pieces of their souls to do it. Books existed in the afterlife, because the afterlife was a place of immutable things, including souls.

"This story's not over, is it?" She hadn't intended it to come out as a whisper, but the Library seemed to swallow up her words like a hollow prophecy. She cringed and finally risked a glance at Rami.

The Watcher angel always looked tired, shabby and rubbed thin around the edges, like an old worry stone. His brow knit, then smoothed. Little quakes of thought. "There's got to be a reason the Library has kept the nature of stories secret for so long. If the Library contains fragments of souls, it is always going to be at risk of being used by its host realm."

"Andras knew." The realization hit Brevity hard, making her pulse race. His sharp teeth and mocking mask of a gentleman's face. The smothering smell of burning books. "Andras knew; he knew the Library could be used. That's why he wanted it."

"He might have suspected, putting the pieces together like we did." Rami considered for a brief moment before appearing to shrug off the memory of the demon as violently as he deserved. "No secret lasts forever, not in the afterlife. We should prepare for what will come when the nature of books is a known fact."

"Great. More demons."

"Not just demons," Rami said. "Souls are the weave of all the realms. I don't think any host realm could withstand the temptation of a library right at their doorstep."

Not just the Unwritten Wing, the *Library*. Brevity thought of Bjorn, his cozy clutter of scrolls and sagas in Valhalla. Of the stately poems of Duat. The longing letters of Elysium. The mad dead of the Dust Wing. The dull ache of Brevity's self-pity burned abruptly away to make room for the holy terror of it all. "The entire Library's in danger."

Her breath was already coming fast, but Rami's hand was on her shoulder like an anchor. He handed her the teacup she'd forgotten. The strawberry tea had long gone cold, but a gulp of it was astringent enough to force her thoughts in line. "Not if we make our own plans."

"Everything's changed." Brevity was already shaking her head. "We've all changed. Look at us! I'm infected, Claire's haunted, Hero . . .

Who knows what Hero is!" She'd bitten her nails; when had she bitten her nails? Brevity dug her hands into her hair instead. "Verve is out there, and now Probity has got to know too. What are we doing?"

The silence rattled around Brevity's head, chasing her already racing thoughts. Rami's hand came away from her shoulder. When she looked up, he had his arms crossed. It made the feathers on his coat fluff up in a vaguely intimidating gesture. "You're changing. That's what happens."

"In stories?" Brevity finished weakly.

"In life." Rami looked flummoxed for a moment. "Almighty heavens. I'm not a book, or a writer, or a muse. I've lived too long to see everything as a metaphor for a story, like the rest of you do. I don't think in plot arcs or theatrical roles. Life—it goes on. Change happens. Secrets get out. Challenges appear. Decisions are forced. Whether we're ready for them or not."

"I vote *not*," Brevity said into her lap.

"Then you will get ready. You are the librarian, after all," Rami said firmly. He swept a hand out, gesturing, and Brevity forced herself to look again at the stacks. A spectrum streamed from the books, weaving a stained glass of light in the air above each aisle. Every color, individual, intermingled, alive. "You have an entire library of souls depending on you."

# ACKNOWLEDGMENTS

As much as Hell's Library is a series about stories, it's also a series about finding your family in unlikely places. Family, I think, is one of the most powerful stories we tell ourselves. Necessary in Hell, and more necessary on earth. I think of acknowledgments as a story about the family I've found and made while writing these books. The story of us.

As ever, I need to start with gratitude for my agent, Caitlin McDonald, for being the best advocate a series could hope for. Also thank you to my editor, Miranda Hill, whose endless enthusiasm for Claire and the gang has made the publishing process go smoothly. I also want to thank editor Rebecca Brewer for her unflagging support and smart feedback on very early versions of this book. I'm grateful to the entire Ace team that I've had the honor to work with, including Alexis Nixon, Jessica Plummer, and Lauren Horvath.

Thank you to Jennifer Mace, who graciously allowed me to borrow her characters for a cameo appearance in the damsel suite. Mace books are particularly unruly, according to Claire. Please come and retrieve your murder children.

One of the fun things about this series is the ability to slide in sly or not-so-sly references to books and writers I personally adore. Sharp eyes might have caught jars in Walter's office referencing the works of

Seanan McGuire, Neil Gaiman, Valerie Valdes, C. L. Polk, Rachel Caine, Tyler Hayes, and more. Thank you, all, for the wonderful things you create. This book might not exist as it is in its current form if I hadn't encountered your work.

Every step of the way was helped by the center of my chosen family. My partner, Levi, who is my favorite story. My sister, Kate, who I'd choose even without random chance. This book benefited greatly from early feedback from a really stellar crew; thank you to Tyler Hayes, Chris Wolfgang, and Rebecca Littlefield for your insights and support. I am also incredibly grateful to the various groups of word friends who lent moral support during this book's creation: my Viable Paradise class, the Isle, and the friends at the Pub.

I had the privilege of starting a small Patreon during the editing stage of this book. I can't express enough my gratitude to those who have chosen to support me there, month after month. Words and worlds don't happen without you. Thank you, all of you, for making stories with me.

**A. J. Hackwith** is almost certainly not an ink witch in a hoodie. She's a queer writer of fantasy and science fiction living in Seattle with her partner, her dog, and her ghosts. *The Archive of the Forgotten* is a sequel to A. J.'s first fantasy, *The Library of the Unwritten*. She is a graduate of the Viable Paradise writers' workshop and her work appears in *Uncanny* magazine and assorted anthologies. She has also written sci-fi romance as Ada Harper. You can find her on Twitter and in other dark corners of the internet.

### CONNECT ONLINE

AmandaHackwith.com

🅵 AJHackwith

🆈 AJHackwith